CHILDREN
OF THE
RUINS

CHILDREN
OF THE
RUINS

THOMAS
WISEMAN

JONATHAN CAPE
THIRTY-TWO BEDFORD SQUARE LONDON

First published in Great Britain 1986
Copyright © 1986 by Thomas Wiseman

Jonathan Cape Ltd, 32 Bedford Square, London WC1B 3EL

British Library Cataloguing in Publication Data

Wiseman, Thomas
Children of the ruins
I. Title
823'.914[F]   PR6073.I77

ISBN 0 224 02398 5

The poetry on pages 127 and 128 was translated by the author from
Baldur von Schirach Hitlers Jugendführer *by Michael Wortman*
(Bohlau Verlag GmbH & Cie., Cologne).

Printed in Great Britain by
Butler & Tanner Ltd, Frome and London

FOR MY SON
B O R I S

AUTHOR'S NOTE

*This book is a work of fiction and the characters
and their relationships are of my invention. However,
the principal events I have depicted did occur, and
what happens to my characters in these pages corresponds
in the main with what actually happened to the real
people who inspired this novel.*

PART ONE
Cologne
March–October
1939

UNRULY ELEMENTS

ONE

Between Lenau Platz and Subbelratherstrasse was Navajo territory, while in the triangle which that long thoroughfare made with the railway tracks the Mobsters ruled: an area of small, mean streets for the most part.

Rolf Hacker, known as Louse Boy, and Otto Osche, who went by the nickname of Robber, lived in Schluttergasse, which came to a dead end at the railway arches.

Though they'd been living within a stone's throw of each other for some time, it was only recently that they had become best friends — when Rolf was trying to get into the Mob. Normally, you had to be at least twelve to join, and Rolf wasn't eleven yet. Someone his age was considered a possible liability in street battles — might run off crying to his Mama. But Otto had vouched for him, saying he was a tough little blighter, very unruly, and so they'd taken him. Otto being the biggest and toughest boy in the whole area, his word was heeded.

It was a poor area, at the heart of the predominantly working-class suburb of Ehrenfeld, just beyond the periphery of the old inner city of Cologne; their district had its "better sections" and its "worse," and around where Rolf and Otto lived was definitely "worse." Many of the old houses were crumbling, damp places, dingy workers' dwellings of the previous century that had been modernized only up to a point; and the new flats, built in the early thirties, while they had proper bathrooms and kitchens and rubbish chutes, and even window boxes (used for hanging out laundry, mostly), were soulless and cramped. To the west there was the gasworks and to the east the municipal slaughterhouse; their triangle contained a junkyard, a sawmill, a metal workshop, motorcycle repair places and bicycle shops, several small factories, warehouses, a furniture repository, and lots of small family retail businesses. It couldn't boast any fine old turn-of-the-century houses like the area around Lenau Platz, which was more residential in character, and where successful local merchants and people like doctors tended to live, but Rolf and Otto preferred it where they were. They liked being close to Subbelratherstrasse, a long, bustling commercial artery where there was always something going on. With its many restaurants and snack bars and beerhalls and cinemas and amusement arcades, it was lit up until late at night and lively with activities. It wasn't dead. They hated places that were dead.

From their street they could walk easily to Blücher Park, which was where the Mobsters met, in the "witch's hut," an open-sided park shelter. There they swopped American swing records, and if they saw any Hitler Youths rowing on the lake, threw stones at them to try and sink them.

It wasn't quite spring yet, but the weather had turned unexpectedly mild, and the clear, open skies and the soft air and the trains rattling by had given them a touch of wanderlust. On a day like this they couldn't sit still in a classroom, staring at a blank wall. In their school, the windows were all above eye level, so that pupils would not be distracted by things going on outside. All there was outside was a concrete playground with bicycle racks and a single tree inside a kind of iron cage. Not much to distract anyone — Rolf could think up a lot better distractions inside his own head. Though not good at schoolwork, he did not lack imagination, and his flights of fancy readily put him in exotic situations of peril and adventure.

Ambling along, socks sagging, one shoelace untied, he was playing his guitar and singing rude limericks that made his friend Otto explode in guffaws of wild laughter. The guitar was the best thing Rolf possessed. Otto had swiped it for him from a pawnshop in Venloerstrasse, thereby cementing their newborn friendship. Otto was good at swiping things. That was why he was called Robber, with respect. Before he got this one, which was a proper musical instrument, made of the finest and most resonant rosewood, with ebony fingerboard and inlaid pearl position dots, the guitars Rolf had played were just toys, really.

There was a public lavatory past the corner, and Otto said he'd got to pee. They both went down and whilst Otto was peeing, Rolf sang a song to annoy "Fat" Schlammer, the attendant.

> When guitars go ping,
> And girls fall in,
> What has the Hitler life to bring?
> We want to be free.
> We want to be free.

Schlammer had come out of his cubicle and was regarding them balefully from behind all his fat, carefully noting the subversive lyrics in his mind. Chortling, they let him chase them up the steps to street level and ran all the way to Venloerstrasse.

5

This was where all the best shops were. The Steiner Kosmetik Studio had closed down months ago and its roller shutters were plastered over with beer advertisements and official proclamations; along the length of the shopfront someone had scrawled, "Perish Judah!" Next door, Hirsch's button shop was open still, though his name had been removed from the sign and replaced by that of the newly appointed "trustee." Peering inside with foreheads pressed against the glass, and making tunnels of their hands in order to see in, the two boys observed Hirsch up on his railed ladder, handing down dusty boxes of buttons from the high shelves to his eldest daughter, the lovely Malshi.

"Don't turn round," Rolf hissed to Otto. He had seen Herr Gast, their street leader, cycling towards them. They kept their faces covered with their hands. Instead of cycling past, Gast stopped at the button shop, got off his bike, and went inside. They watched him. He wasn't buying buttons, though he was engaged in some transaction, it seemed: they saw Hirsch give him an envelope, which Gast put in his breast pocket before coming out. As he emerged, they turned away to hide themselves, but he'd seen them.

"What are you young hooligans doing here? Why aren't you at school?" he demanded roughly.

"Sprained my ankle," Otto said, and hobbled about, pulling a face.

"Is that so?" Gast scoffed. "And your little gangster friend?"

"Inflammation of the eye," Rolf said, screwing up his eye and twitching.

"Go on, get off! Good-for-nothings!" Gast gave each a smack on the back of the head.

"Yes, Herr Gast."

"Yes, Herr Gast."

"You better be in school tomorrow, or else . . ."

"Oh, we will be, Herr Gast. My eye's almost better."

6

They scampered off, speculating what was in the envelope that Herr Gast had put in his breast pocket.

"Bet it was money," Rolf said. "That's what I bet it was. He's got his fat fingers in every pie, Herr Gast."

They decided to head for Lenau Platz. On their way they picked up a couple of bottles of milk left on a doorstep. The tenants were probably away. No point leaving good milk to go sour. They were thirsty from walking in the dusty streets.

Reaching the square with the little green in the centre where elderly people sat on park benches taking the air, they first of all tried the return-money button in the telephone kiosks, but had no luck with that. Then they shared their last ciggy, smoking it alternately, down to the burning embers. A dog came and pissed against the *Litfass* pillar where they were lounging.

Didn't seem to be a lot happening in Lenau Platz, so they decided to go down to the Agrippa milk bar where there were a couple of pin-tables, and a slot-machine with a grab-claw. They might run into some of their friends, and Rolf was good at manipulating the grab-claw. That was one way to get cigarettes. They were chain-smokers, and not having cigarettes was hard on them.

The Agrippa was the other side of their territory, bordering on Navajo lands. They cut down through little streets, past an electrical spare-parts shop, past several *Lebensmittel* stores, their shelves packed with bottles of vinegar and tinned sauerkraut and sausages in brine, past a hole-in-the-wall place selling tins of shoe polish and shoe brushes, which was not doing much business, since nobody around here polished his shoes. They slouched across the street, round the corner, past a Lutheran church, past a low block of workers' flats, its walls covered in grey pebble-dash finish, its windows small and square, like in factories. Tiny kids, too young for school, played in the street, tearing about on scooters, or making mud balls with spit and dirt. One or two pollarded trees were in blossom. The softness of the air made the whole city seem open to them; it wasn't like winter when you had to stay huddled in doorways: you could go out and about anywhere on a day like this. They felt so full of life they would have liked to break some windows, if there'd been some good ones to break around here. Those of a police station, for instance. Instead, they kicked stones and tried to get them down drains from a distance of ten metres.

In one of the streets that they went along, there was a shop selling wheelchairs and crutches and trusses for hernias and elasticated stockings and surgical boots, and they were inspired to give imitations of cripples staggering about grotesquely, of blind men feeling with flailing arms in the dark, epileptics choking and spitting. Passers-by glared at them disapprovingly.

"You ought to be ashamed of yourselves," an elderly well-dressed woman carrying a white poodle in her arms told them.

"It's against our religion, mother," Rolf shouted back.

He and Otto began a maniacal sword fight that ended with Rolf being run through the heart and sinking slowly to the ground, where he lay prostrate and dead for at least a minute. Brushing him down, Otto began to punch him in play, and Rolf punched back. Soon they were fighting. Which was a foolish thing to do with Otto, Rolf knew, since Otto was about twice as big as anyone else, and three times as strong, and you couldn't actually hit him so that he'd feel it. After a few minutes, Rolf stopped fighting him.

"It's no use hitting you," he complained. "You don't feel it."

"But you feel it when I hit you," Otto gloated. "Hah-hah-hah!"

Rolf agreed. "That's why it isn't fair."

Fighting, they had got to the Agrippa; they went inside and started playing the machines. Rolf tried for the cigarettes, but lost them, and had to make do with a lipstick. The lipstick was easier to get out. He could give it to Franzi, his big sister. She already had dozens of lipsticks, but she could use another one, because she was always changing the colours. This one was cerise. She had cupid-bow lips, which people thought were pretty.

All of a sudden there was a chill in the air: cloud covered the sun and the day became dull. In a second their high spirits evaporated and they slunk by houses of crumbling beige and brown stucco, feeling thoroughly disgruntled. They had nothing to do: the rest of the day stretched emptily before them; they saw it getting duller and duller, until finally this dullness would turn to dusk, and then night, without anything having happened. Once more! There was a moment when it looked as though something might happen, and then it didn't. That was just life.

Rolf would have liked to smash the window of the local Nazi Party office. That would have been a good window to smash.

There was a strong smell of benzine coming from a dry-cleaner's. A tram clattered by, passengers clinging to the footplates, its bell ringing. They raced after it, caught it up at its next stop, and as it was starting off again, leapt onto the connecting rods between the front and rear carriage and rode free for one or two stops before the conductor spotted them and made them get off.

"Let's go and see Kurt," Rolf proposed. "He'll give us a ciggy."

Kurt worked at Schleidhuber's motorcycle repair shop under the railway arches at the end of their street.

They started to retrace their steps.

Kurt wasn't "local": he was a Northerner, from Kiel, with red hair and pale, almost colourless eyes and a violent stare that had earned him the nickname "Mad Kurt." They also called him that because of the crazy way he rode around on his motorbike. He'd make it rear up on its back wheel like a wild stallion, and then ride on one wheel along the edge of the river embankment. Or he'd drive on top of a wide parapet — or cross-country: roaring up and down hillsides, through shallow ponds, weaving between trees in thick woods. Once, he'd ridden out to a site where a whole lot of Faith and Beauty girls were camping, and while they sat in the high grass playing their flutes, he'd gone tearing around them, round and round to make them dizzy, getting their white blouses splashed with mud. Rolf and Otto were sometimes given rides on the back of his motorbike, and Rolf would never forget the terror and excitement. Then they'd hang around the docks with Kurt. You could pick up stuff that sort of fell off the backs of lorries. Cartons of cigarettes, for instance. They flogged them to tobacconists for a good price, and split the takings three ways.

Reaching the end of their street and ambling up to Kurt working on an overturned motorcycle, Otto proposed casually, "Feel like going down to the docks, later?"

"No. I've got no time."

They hadn't done much with Kurt lately, because he never seemed to have time.

"Got a fag for us?" Rolf cadged.

"No, I haven't." He looked up. "You shouldn't be smoking at your age. It stunts your growth. Didn't you know that?"

"We don't care," Rolf said. "We don't want to grow any more anyway. We're fine as we are." He lowered his voice. "They're unloading a big cargo boat from Rotterdam down at the Mullheimer docks."

"I got things to do."

"What things is that, then?"

"Never you mind."

A train went by on the railway track above their heads and the whole workshop shook. Rolf and Otto pretended they were in an earthquake in China, and then, changing the story, Rolf put out his arms and made himself undergo the convulsions of someone being electrocuted in the electric chair. Then, in flashback, he was mowing down cops. Otto joined in. *Rat-at-at-a-tat!* They hated all cops. Especially those Secret Police arseholes with their badges behind their lapels. They were the worst: the Gestapo.

When the train had passed overhead, they adopted casual positions, slouched up against the wall.

"Give us a drag of your ciggy, then!" Rolf proposed, with an air of that being the least Kurt could do.

"It's against the law for minors to smoke in public," Kurt reminded them, not looking up from his work.

"Since when you been so keen on the law?" Rolf demanded with a sneer. "You'll be joining the Hitler Youth next."

"You guessed it," Kurt said, not looking up.

"What! You joined?"

"I'm training to be a youth leader."

He was looking sheepish, Rolf thought. God, what turncoats people were!

"Why'd they take *you?*" Otto demanded with scorn.

"I expect they think that somebody like me might be able to handle roughnecks like you."

"Handle us!" Rolf cried, horrified. "Catch us being in the *Hitlerjugend.* We hate their guts."

"Membership's compulsory, as you well know," Kurt pointed out.

"Not for us, it isn't. We're a disgrace to our neighbourhood. We're *delinquents.* They don't want the likes of us in the HJs. We'd let them down."

Kurt shook his head.

"A lost cause, you two are. . . . You don't want to better yourselves, you *glory* in what you are."

"That's right," Otto said.

Kurt grinned and threw them each a cigarette.

"Don't smoke them round here. I could get into trouble providing minors with illicit goods."

"We won't. Thanks, Kurt," Rolf said."

"Yes, thanks, Kurt," Otto echoed grudgingly.

11

"Seen Franzi?" Rolf asked, slouching off.

"No."

"Somebody said they seen her come by here on her bike."

"If she did, I didn't notice," Kurt said.

Rolf considered that unlikely. Though his sister Franzi was only fifteen, and hardly even grown up yet, when she rode by on her bicycle Kurt would have noticed. *And how!*

"Thought you were sweet on her," Rolf teased.

"Go on, get out of here, Louse Boy."

"What'd I say?" Rolf demanded innocently.

"I've got work to do. Piss off!"

"You don't have to bite my head off. All I said was that I thought you were sweet on her. Is that such a crime?"

"Yes, it is," Kurt snapped back at him. He looked up at Rolf. "Your sister's still a minor. If she carries on like this, you know how she's going to end up? Walking the streets. That's what's going to happen to her."

Rolf had heard it said that Ilonka of the Gutenberger-strasse, who was about Franzi's age, had "done everything" and he wouldn't have been surprised if Franzi had "done everything" too. But probably not with Kurt, seeing how he got all hot under the collar about her. Had he changed! This training course he was doing to be a youth leader was probably where he was getting all that stuff about girls who were under-age, and about kids not being allowed to smoke.

Better leave Kurt be, Rolf decided. Since he was so touchy.

"Let's go," he said to Otto.

They made their way along the Ehrenfeldgürtel, smoking their cigarettes and looking in shop windows. As they reached the corner with Huttenstrasse, they saw a platoon of *Hitlerjugend* approaching, marching and singing. They were ten- to twelve-year-olds. The leading one carried a drum almost as big as he was, and the others bore heavy packs on their shoulders. They wore belts and crossbelts, and the sleeves of their brown shirts were rolled up and their long knee-socks rolled down over the ankles. As they marched, their lean, open faces shone with fervour and locks of blond hair bobbed across their foreheads. The drummer boy was in the lead, alone; behind him, in the centre of the first row, a boy carried a wide swastika flag attached to a long pole. They seemed to be very small boys, with their big flag and their large shoulder packs weighing them down, but they sang spiritedly, warding off weariness with a kind of drummed-up energy, and their voices were high and unbroken:

> *You gave us your hand and a glance*
> *From which our young hearts tremble still:*
> *It will make us live mightily this hour,*
> *And be with us everywhere, our good fortune.*

"Howdedoda! Swing Heil! Swing Heil!" Rolf shouted as the HJs passed. It was difficult to make himself heard against all those high-pitched boyish voices. "Heil Benny Goodman!" he cried defiantly, and one or two heads turned towards the ruffian, giving him the contemptuous glances that his lowdown appearance, his sagging socks, filthy shirt, and mass of hair, earned him. They carried on singing in their sweet, intense, melodious voices:

> *One thing they cannot steal from us,*
> *That we believe in you with all our soul,*
> *Because you are Germany's future. You alone!*

"We better go to school tomorrow," Rolf said when the *Hitlerjugend* had passed. There didn't seem to be much else to do. They were bored.

"Let's take a look in the park, see if anything's doing," Otto suggested, and Rolf shrugged and said, why not?

It had become windy. In Blücher Park they stood by the edge of the lake and watched the wind make the water ripple — it reminded Rolf of a cat having its fur stroked. He picked up stones and threw them as far as he could, and saw circles spread outwards from the point of impact. Otto threw stones too, each boy trying to throw farther than the other.

"What'd he do, your old man?" Rolf asked between throws.

Though they'd become "best friends," they hadn't as yet asked each other such personal questions.

"Robbery with violence," Otto said, throwing hard. "Laid out a couple of cops when they come for him. Did he bash them up! He's very violent, my old man. He got five years."

"Mine got six," Rolf said, a touch boastfully.

"What'd he do?"

"Theft."

"He got six — just for theft?"

"Oh, he's a big thief. He steals as he breathes. He'll steal anything, he will. Light bulbs. Alarm clocks. Paraffin stoves. Hairbrushes. Shoelaces. He once stole some skis! Couldn't even get rid of them."

"Mine's done *proper* robberies," Otto said. "Hold-ups."

"Like in films? Has he got a gun?"

"Of course, stupid! Hasn't yours?"

"No, I don't think so. Anyway, I never seen one. Not where we live."

Rolf threw as hard as he could, but his stone fell far short of Otto's. Otto had powerful arms — he could throw a long way.

"You live with your mother, do you?"

"Yes. And Franzi."

"I like Franzi," Otto said.

"What about you," Rolf asked. "Who's it you live with?"

They'd always met in the street, never gone to each other's flats.

"My stepmother," Otto said disgustedly. "I always had stepmothers. Far as I can remember. That's because my real mother went off with somebody. So my old man got all these stepmothers in to look after me. I hated them all. This one's the worst. A real cow. But," he said, brightening, "I like Franzi. Wouldn't mind getting to know *her*. Know what I mean?"

"You're going to have a lot of competition there, Robber."

14

They had both reached the point of throwing as far as they could, and decided it was time to go home. School would be over pretty soon, and they might see some of their pals.

Sure enough, when they got back to their street Charlie-Blow and Black Hand were there. They wore coloured-glass collar studs in their buttonholes, and shoes with thick crepe soles for creeping up on people without being heard. At dusk they crept up on HJs to rough them up and teach them a lesson.

Black Hand and Charlie-Blow exchanged greetings with Louse Boy and Robber.

"Ship ahoi!"

"Hummel, hummel!"

"Howdedoda!"

Franzi was there, with another girl, and they giggled at these exchanges. They thought the catchwords and the secret signs and code signals childish. Girls didn't understand. They thought it was silly for Charlie-Blow and Black Hand to wear collar studs in their lapels, and to hang Death's Head key rings onto the clips of their belts, and to have scarves that they could pull up over the lower parts of their faces as masks.

Franzi's bike was leaning against a wall. She was playing hopscotch with her friend, and Otto stood staring at her. From time to time she looked up at him with her flashing eyes. Could she make her eyes flash! She didn't even know she was doing it. It was giving Otto ideas, they way her legs kept showing as she played. Then she stopped playing and got on her bike and started pushing herself back and forth, back and forth, letting her feet drag along the pavement, and sometimes slumping forward over the handlebars and acting dead.

Rolf was having a conversation with Charlie-Blow. Charlie was a bugler. He could play taps and reveille and swing on his bugle. Charlie could really blow.

Just then a bunch of about seven HJs turned up at the end of the street, led by Rolf's former best friend Addi. They were marching in tight formation: a *Strafendienst* patrol, part of the HJs' self-policing system. In the HJs they had a motto, "youth leads youth," and these patrols were supposed to enforce discipline and good behaviour.

Rolf and Otto exchanged looks with Charlie-Blow and Black Hand. They were four against seven. Rolf grinned. He wasn't bothered by the disparity in numbers.

"Heil Hitler!" Addi said, stretching out his right arm to eye level.

"Howdedoda!" responded Rolf, raising one finger of his left hand to his dirty mop of hair in a mock salute.

"Hummel, hummel!" chorused Otto, Charlie-Blow, and Black Hand.

Addi looked severe. He stepped forward slowly, and deliberately unbuttoned the pleated pocket of his brown shirt and withdrew a small notebook with pencil attached. Looking meaningfully from one offender to the other, he made a formal note, then closed the notebook and looked straight at Rolf.

Relenting in sternness a little, he said in a low voice:

"What happened to you, Rolfie?"

"What you mean, what happened?"

"You haven't showed up for a week," Addi said. "A whole week."

"Didn't feel like it," Rolf said.

"It doesn't matter what you *feel* like," Addi rebuked. "It's your duty to attend meetings."

Rolf had taken out of his pocket a Dom Hotel bookmatch and he was tearing off matches and striking them one after the other, defiantly. He said nothing.

"Look," Addi pleaded with him. "You know the rules. You got to follow your führer unquestion'gly. That's the *law*. You know that, Rolfie. And I'm your group führer. So you got to do what I say." He drew himself up, looked over his shoulder at the rest of his troop for moral support. "I'm giving you an order, R. Hacker. You got to be at group HQ at the next meeting, Friday."

"I won't be there," Rolf said. "I've quit, see."

"You're not allowed to quit."

"I don't care what's allowed." He shot Otto a grinning glance.

"What your problem is, is you can't accept authority," Addi said in the tone of the training manual. "That's your problem, Rolf Hacker. Why don't you grow up?"

"Don't see the profit in it."

Addi looked over his shoulder and gave a signal to his troop to come close for support. They were looking a bit awkward and uneasy at the way the exchange was developing. One fat little boy with steel-rimmed spectacles couldn't stop himself tittering, even when his group führer told him sternly to shut up.

"Call yourself a soldier," Addi told him with scorn. Once more he took out the little notebook, opened it, and stood with pencil poised threateningly.

"If you don't promise me, cross your heart, to come to the group meeting Friday, I'll have to report you to the higher branch führer. You know what that could mean. They could kick you out, Rolfie. Expel you. For indiscipline and insubordination to a superior, and refusal to obey the command of your group führer."

"They can't expel me," Rolf said.

"Oh, can't they—"

"—because I quit, and you know where you can stuff your notebook, Adolf."

The gang members tittered at the mention of his full name, and Addi flushed red. He looked again over his shoulder as if to make sure that his troop was still there, giving him support, that he hadn't been left to face these roughnecks alone. From their wan expressions he gathered that some of his men were not exactly spoiling for a fight; the fat boy was pulling at

17

his führer's sleeve and advising a tactical withdrawal, but Addi had been taught that leaders were required to lead and he was going to do so willy-nilly, whatever his reluctant troop felt about it.

"Nobody asked your opinion," he snapped back.

"I was only making a suggestion," the fat boy grumbled.

"Well," Addi said a little breathlessly, facing up to Rolf and these other unruly elements. "This is your last chance. Do I get your true promise to obey orders in future?"

"You know," Rolf told him, "if my arse looked like your face I'd be ashamed to shit."

Addi went redder still, and wrote in his notebook. His eyes noted the offenders one by one, and they responded with a mock bow, followed by a hand-on-nose sign.

"You heard what I called you," Rolf said challengingly. "What you got to say to that?"

"Everything I've got to say about you," Addi replied smugly, "I will put in my report to the higher branch führer."

"Why — you scared to say it to my face?" Rolf taunted.

Addi couldn't take this without replying in kind. It was a question of honour. He had to show his troop he wasn't scared.

Mouth twitching, he searched through his repertoire of insults for one sufficiently ripe and foul. Then he said:

"I tell you what *your* face looks like. Your face looks like a pigsty covered this deep in pig shit."

"You should know," Rolf retorted, "seeing pig shit was what you crawled out of in your Mama's belly when you was born."

This insult turned Addi's cheeks from deep red to white. He was a tall boy, as tall as Otto, and he wasn't going to take any more from a little squirt like Rolf Hacker.

"I'm going to ride you like a sled," he said, grabbing Rolf by the throat.

"You and whose army?" Rolf said, violently knocking away Addi's hand.

18

Addi responded knock for knock, giving Rolf a push in the chest, and Rolf retaliated by pushing Addi in the chest. Each push by one boy produced a retaliatory push from the other, and this went on for a while. Addi's arms being longer, Rolf was soon beginning to get the worst of the exchange, so he decided to change the basis of their encounter and spat in Addi's eye.

Incensed, Addi came rushing at Rolf, punching wildly. Rolf warded off the hail of blows by crossing his arms protectively before his face, and at the same time jerked up his knee into Addi's crotch. Addi let out a yell of pain and smashed his fist through Rolf's defences, striking him a glancing blow on the side of the mouth. At this point, seeing that he was being left to do all the fighting while his troop were standing idly by, he called to them, "Come on. I want him placed under detention. Get him." Somewhat uncertainly, the other members of 'the *Strafendienst* patrol encircled Rolf and closed in on him, while he moved back, lashing out with fist and boot at anyone who came too close.

Up to this stage, Rolf's friends hadn't interfered. But now that Addi had brought in his troop, Otto, Charlie-Blow, and Black Hand were entitled to join in, and did.

Otto waded in first, grabbing a couple of little HJs by the scruff of the neck and pulling them out squealing and kicking. Then he went for a bigger boy. Fists flew, Otto ducked and dodged and lashed out, and there was the sound of hard knuckle cracking into bone and flesh. Charlie-Blow and Black Hand were using their Mobster techniques, getting HJs in holds that were designed to break necks and arms. For all their sporting accomplishments and their knot-tying proficiency — and their superiority of numbers — these HJs were no match for boys blooded in earlier street battles. Especially, they were no match for Otto. Addi and two of his biggest patrolmen tried to tackle him, one boy jumping on his back and seeking to pin his arms back while the other two bashed their fists into him. But the boy on his back was thrown off and sent flying, and the blows that landed on Otto's body served merely to goad him, and he swung at his attackers with a vengeance. Addi got a fist in his face and another in his stomach, and blood began to spurt from his nose. It ran down his black neckscarf and brown shirt. Having dealt with his first two attackers, Otto dealt with the third by reflex action, jabbing the elbow of the arm that had just struck Addi into this other boy's teeth, knocking out two and loosening several others permanently. Otto was following through, hitting Addi and this other boy in swift alternation, delivering bone-cracking punches to eyes, noses, jaws, and ears. He was going at these boys like a steam hammer, and Rolf, fighting off his own attacker, saw what was happening and thought, God! the Robber's going to kill the sods, he's going to smash their faces to bits. It was a bloodbath. The HJs were getting murdered.

Herr Gast had seen the scuffle from the end of the street, and at first it had not seemed anything more than the usual rough-house stuff. The street gangs and the HJs were always at each other like cats and dogs. This time the HJs were definitely getting the worst of it. They were being slaughtered. He'd have to intercede, break it up. He turned in the street, cycling as fast as he could towards the fray. He didn't mind a bit of a scrap: years ago he'd been a boxer in the army, and though he was no longer in as trim shape as he might have been (too much beer, too much food), he still had the build and the skill to look after himself. As he came pedalling hard into the thick of the fight, what first caught his attention—for an instant, but it was a powerful instant— was one of the onlookers, a little blonde girl standing astride her bike, on tiptoes, and jumping up and down with excitement. She could only have been fourteen or fifteen, but she was a pretty thing, and to Gast's mind (coarsened by the business of making his way in life—life was a coarse business), the way she was bouncing about on her saddle caused a strong sexual current to go through him. He didn't have time

20

to dwell on this, since blood was being shed and the *Hitlerju-gend* were on the verge of being vanquished by the riffraff of the streets. He could see one brawny boy battering another boy relentlessly, and Gast having encountered the killer spirit in fighters, having it himself, to some extent, recognised it at once in Otto. He would have to stop him. Even as he jumped off his bike and rushed in to prevent further mayhem, his mind, which was calculating as well as coarse, registered opportunity. It was confirmed by the difficulty he had (him, an ex – heavyweight champion!) in grabbing Otto and pulling him off the boy he was on the verge of killing. This was what truancy led to. Blatant hooliganism. Murder in the streets — it could come to that. At the same time, he couldn't help thinking, as he succeeded finally in restraining Otto, that in this roughneck there was the makings of a youth champion who would bring glory to his street and the street leader Herr Gast.

TWO

Next day, after completing his rounds (it was his duty as street leader to collect information from the various block leaders under him, and to hand out Party literature for them to distribute or pin up on notice boards), Gast made his way to the Schluttergasse, to the spot near the railway arches where he had broken up the fight. Vaguely, he thought he'd go along and see: he did not ask himself, *what?* He was not a man given to asking himself too many questions. We shall see what we shall see, was his attitude.

It was a shabby street of workers' tenements, with kids tearing around on scooters rain or shine, and the bigger ones playing a makeshift form of football, with the goals drawn out in chalk on grimy brick walls. Small and not-so-small girls hung about, talking among themselves, watching the boys, and sometimes engaging in loose talk with them. There was much rude banter, a lot of messing around before coming to the point, which finally they did come to — as he'd found out: at night shining his torch under the railway arches.

The little blonde girl was nowhere to be seen, and he was disappointed. Had he come to find her? That was the sort of question he did not ask himself. She was just a child. Then why was he looking for her? Don't ask me, he told himself. *Don't ask me.*

He saw the big lout who'd been beating up the HJs, and thought again that if he could be controlled he was the stuff of which youth champions were made, and went to have a word with him.

"You ever done any boxing, Otto?"

"You mean in a ring?"

"Yes."

"No, I never done that."

"You could be good, if you trained."

"What for?"

"Keep you out of mischief."

"Maybe I don't want to keep out of mischief."

"There could be other rewards."

"What sort of other rewards?"

"Girls love a champion, Otto. Haven't you found that out yet?"

"*Yes . . .*"

It was a noisy street, with gruff bellowing shouts from the boys and periodic screams from the girls, the regular thump of a football being kicked up against a wall, the sudden tinkle of a bottle shattering, and from time to time the raised voices of domestic strife.

A window above them was flung open and a woman leaned out and shouted down: "Be quiet! Be quiet! *Rotzbuben!* 'The Lord God saith — It shall come to pass. . . . The city shall be as dust. . . .'"

Otto grinned and made a little circle against his head.

Gast looked up at the madwoman. She wasn't old, but her hair was white, dirty white and dishevelled, and her features

23

were in disarray, as if not yet composed for the business of the day. He saw the little blonde girl drawing the woman from the window and closing it.

"Who is she?" Gast asked.

"That's Rolf's Mama. It's the Louse Boy's Mama—she's got a couple o' screws loose."

"And the girl?"

"Rolfie's big sister." Otto grinned meaningfully. "She's a bit of all right, Franzi."

"There you are," Gast said, proving his point. "Bet you Franzi likes a champion. What women go for," he confided, "is a man that's on top."

"*Yes . . . ,*" Otto said with a snigger.

"I could give you some coaching," Gast offered, a little later, seeing Franzi come out of the house and look up and down the street. "In the army I was heavyweight champion of my battalion. Oh, I could teach you a thing or two! Come on, try and hit me, Otto-boy." He gave Otto a light playful punch on the chin to get him started, and was gratified to see that Franzi's wandering attention had been caught. "Come on, Otto. See if you can hit me." He offered his broad chest, his fleshy abdomen for a punching bag. "Hit me as hard as you like. Go on! Try!"

Otto, having caught sight of Franzi watching them, swung with relish at the tempting target and was amazed to find it no longer there, that instead his wide punch was locked under the big man's right arm, while the left hand slapped Otto about—to the amusement of Franzi.

"That's it, that's it," Gast encouraged. "A good try. Let me show you something."

He proceeded to demonstrate to Otto how to dance clear of punches, and other tricks. All the time out of the corner of his eye he watched Franzi. She had got on her bike, but instead of riding off was pushing herself back and forth, back and forth. She appeared to be far away in her thoughts, and Gast found the regular to-and-fro movements inflammatory, and kept

24

taking his eyes off Otto to glance at her, putting himself in some danger, quick as his reflexes were, of being felled by a stray punch. If one actually landed, it would knock him flat. Gast used every trick he knew, feinting and dancing and ducking, while the little girl on her bike went back and forth, plump little behind squeezing down on the bicycle saddle, eyes dreamy. Was she deliberately giving herself pleasure — conscious that he was watching her? Oh, what a little co-quette! Dodging and ducking the increasingly fierce swings of his pupil, Gast was again and again drawn to look at Franzi: to watch the play of expressions on her face — how heavy her eyelids were, how she bit on her lip, and how suggestively she fidgeted about on the bike saddle! From time to time her eyes went to the pair of them sparring, and then she returned to her own preoccupation, whatever that might be. Her face indicates rapture, Gast told himself — no doubt, no doubt! She seemed to undergo a brief trembling, starting at the neck, and Gast, more and more in danger of being knocked down at any moment, thought: I don't believe it — in public! What coarseness! What sensuality!

He manoeuvred to get closer to her, moving around Otto and then dancing away from him so as to bring himself near enough to see her eyes. They were hazy blue, he presently saw, with greatly enlarged pupils, the irises no more than rings: smoky rings of Saturn! Oh, he was sure those enlarged pupils told of other enlargements, of the engorged condition of humid private parts pressing down so blatantly on a bicycle saddle in a public street! If she knew that he had seen, and went on nonetheless, it was a secret between them, a kind of pact.

And then, suddenly, she changed and was a child again — and the hot secrets were blown away and she was sticking out her tongue at a youth who was teasing her about something or other. And Gast, noting the immature face, rounded out by puppy fat, the large naïve eyes (naïve and bold at the same time), thought: perhaps I imagined it. It's just a little girl on her bike. Again, her eyes flashed and he could feel their hot, secret grip, and thought: no, I didn't imagine it.

Now she was dismounting from her bike and going to play hopscotch with another girl.

Fascinated, he watched them; to avoid getting himself knocked down, he instructed Otto to practise punching by himself for a minute, and Gast corrected his posture, the slant of his shoulders, saying, "Good, good," while watching Franzi stoop to pick up the coin from the chalked square and wobble about on one foot: he could see her fully developed form under her dress, the damp thighs, the underneath part of her like an overstuffed cushion, the underwear material crinkled together on one side, exposing a plump little bottom cheek, enticing little strands of blond hair.

Willi Gast, one-time bartender, had been coming up in the world lately. At one time men would snap their fingers to summon him and demand who was that pretty young girl sitting by herself, and he would be instrumental in arranging matters, and so earn himself some extra money. But now Gast was no longer at the beck and call of every barfly, no longer dependent on those sorts of "introductions" to supplement his otherwise meagre income. He had stumbled upon the advantages of being a Party official. It was unpaid work, and Gast had never been one to do something for nothing, which was why it had not dawned on him sooner what pickings there were to be had in this line of activity. It was through his old drinking buddy Schlink that he had found out, and it was a moment of revelation to him. Schlink worked in the Gauleiter's office and had told Gast of the benefits to be gained by those in a position to expedite applications, take someone off one list and put him on another, forward recommendations or not, as the case might be, grant or withhold special dispensations, trace and verify and certify Gentile ancestry, and etcetera. A world of opportunity had opened up before Gast as a result of this conversation with his drinking pal. No longer would lack of education or other forms of qualification stand in the way of advancement: the Party was not prejudiced in this way. It gave a chance to anyone of the right mettle, and Gast was the right mettle. He was a man with connections with men who came to his bar and asked for a certain girl to be brought to their alcove, and if she was not suitable, for another to be found. These girls were not prostitutes necessarily, or at any rate not full-time ones; rather, they were working girls who had fallen behind with the rent, or had to pay for a sick mother's operation, or had become highly strung and needed a holiday in the sun. For whatever reason, they were in need of money; and Gast, with his connections, was in a position to help them. That was why they came to his bar, and that was why his connections came to his bar.

Once his eyes had been opened to the possibilities, Gast was in a position to offer his connections something special in return for favours granted to him. One introduction deserved another, did it not? In this way he had entered the movement, late in the day, and yet in a short while had a foot on the ladder. It was the lowest rung, block leader, but it was a start. And pretty soon, with the favours he was able to do, he was on the next rung: street leader. While this position enlarged his domain only by the extent of one street, and not a very salubrious street at that, it had given him authority over four block leaders and, more important, half a dozen burly Storm Troopers, men with strong fists and knees. Having them behind him gave Gast undoubted authority. This was when he started to insist on being addressed as "Herr Gast" —no longer "Willi this" and "Willi that." He was now a man to be respected, and anyone failing to show him respect was liable to wake up with his arm in a plaster cast and discover his business premises had burnt down.

It was quickly seen that since his office was unpaid, some form of remuneration must be provided for the street leader to be able to fulfil his duties. These were many, if he so wished, which he did, and vague. Vague enough to enable

27

him to develop those that might prove remunerative and ignore the others. For protecting them against the insidious machinations of international Jewry and its agents, and against Communism too, he asked for contributions. The people of his street were at best making a scant living from their little shops and businesses, and these contributions made their living even scantier. Beyond a certain amount, he could not wring them any drier. Somewhat more profitable was the taking over of Jewish properties, one of those little sidelines that he had found could be channelled his way. Since Jews were no longer permitted to own businesses, were obliged to give them up for derisory compensation to a Gentile "trustee," who better to act as trustee than a local Party leader? Who else could give such an assurance of safety and protection? In return for having the profits made over to him, or his nominee, Gast was willing to employ the Jews in their own businesses, at a living wage. The problem was that there was so little profit in these businesses, the living wage had to be cut to the bone in order for Gast to get anything at all. But it was better than nothing, and Gast took the view that he was building up. If only he'd had a larger area to exploit, and a better class of Jews! There were four with businesses in his catchment area, and what miserable businesses! He was sure he had got the most miserable and the poorest four Jews in the whole of Cologne. Three were tailors — one a little shitter of an invisible mender, with no profits at all and not even a living wage for himself. The fourth was Hirsch the button dealer, who was not much better off. What could you get selling a few buttons? What a stupid business to be in, raged Gast.

He told Hirsch, "You may not be Rothschilds exactly, but you're the best I've got, so I've got to make the most of you."

He, personally, had nothing against Jews, he explained; he was broad-minded, tolerant; "live and let live" was his motto. Unlike some. Hirsch should consider himself a fortunate man to have Herr Gast as his protector. Who better?

But there was one thing he insisted on and that was honesty. Hirsch must not think he could get away with any cheating, any concealing of profits. Gast had a nose for such things and would find out, and then Hirsch's goose would be cooked. "All my influence and goodwill won't save you if you cheat."

How could Herr Gast think that of him, Hirsch protested. He was a man with a family, with five young daughters and a wife. Would he cheat Herr Gast and put them all in peril?

He was a tall, handsome man with a wide jet-black beard and fiery eyes, this Hirsch.

The business did not make much money.

"What can I do?" Hirsch said. "You can see for yourself. I am not very busy. Buttons you don't sell in the thousands, in the hundreds: you sell one or two. How often does somebody lose a button? It's rare."

"Why are you in such a 'rare' business?"

"Ah, what do you want? That I explain my life to you? A man makes choices, a man makes mistakes. That's how life is."

But Gast was not satisfied with this excuse. Did not Frau Hirsch have a silver fox? Could she not sell it? What about the silver, the candlesticks? Jewellery. He could pawn his wife's jewels. Postpone his daughter's wedding. This was no time for weddings. Hirsch could not see his daughter married at Herr Gast's expense. Herr Gast could not provide protection — peace of mind — for nothing, for the pittance that he got out of the button shop's takings.

How was it that Hirsch had such a fine apartment, that this wife and daughters dressed so well, that he could even have *thought* of letting his daughter marry with all that that entailed in the way of costs, the cost of the reception, the dowry, the honeymoon? If his shop was doing so badly.

"It used to do better. Business is not good at present," Hirsch explained. "You people urged your fellow citizens to boycott Jewish shops. So what do you expect? Business is

29

rotten. Naturally. I live on my savings, and they are now practically all gone. The wedding was already postponed before you mentioned it. I have no dowry to give her. Honeymoon? In these times? Who thinks of honeymoons? My wife's jewels? They were pawned long ago. There is nothing left, Herr Gast.''

''The apartment?''

''I rent it, and soon I won't be able to pay the rent. What do you want, Herr Gast? That I give you more? And what do I live on? You want to kill the goose that lays the golden egg?''

''Some goose, some golden egg,'' Gast observed.

For the moment he had to accept the situation, but he kept his eye on Hirsch's shop, checked the customers going in and out, calculated the business turnover, made unexpected appearances to see how much was in the till.

He still thought that Hirsch must be cheating him.

Wham! Shadow-boxing, Otto had got carried away and lashed out wildly, and seemingly by accident landed a punch in Gast's lower belly that knocked all the breath out of him. What a lowdown trick—to hit him whilst he wasn't looking. While his eyes were elsewhere: on a little girl's plump arse. At the same time, Gast, gasping though he was, concluded that it was a good sign. This boy did indeed have the makings of a champion—champions had to be tricky. And Gast could do with such a boy to further his own career: if he could obtain the position of local *district* leader for himself, his catchment area would be enlarged to include one or two better-heeled Hebrews.

Franzi had tired of hopscotch and was getting on her bike, and riding off down the road. Gast got on his bicycle too, and followed her; at the end of her street she turned around and started cycling back.

Gast carried on, with a little disappointed sigh at losing sight of her. He had notices and proclamations to distribute. There were some minimal aspects of his position that it was best not to neglect, and in the course of making his rounds he was able to keep his eyes open for opportunities.

Outside the public lavatory in the Giesingerstrasse he came upon the attendant, Fat Schlammer, sitting on a folding stool eating his lunch of black bread thickly spread with goose dripping, and gave him his notices to put up. Where information could be laid against various categories of offenders. About a blackout exercise announced for the following Tuesday. Citizens were urged to volunteer for civil defence training. A poster headed IN THE EVENT OF ENEMY AIR ATTACK showed how incendiary bombs should be picked up with iron tongs, placed in a bucket, and covered with sand.

"These will be prominently displayed to have maximum effectiveness," the lavatory attendant promised, wiping his greasy hands on his trousers before accepting the notices. "Rest assured, Herr Street Leader, every precaution will be taken to prevent defacement by hooligans. I keep a sharp lookout from my bureau. Even if I appear to be asleep, I am actually watching through lowered eyes. That's the way I catch 'em red-handed. In a second I am out and have got the little louts by the ear."

Gast raised an eyebrow at the notion of Fat Schlammer being out in a second, but let the remark pass. Schlammer was anxious to please, and he was conscientious. His lavatory shone. Whenever Gast passed by, Schlammer wanted to show him how spick-and-span his toilet bowls were; you could drink your soup from them, he liked to say. The lavatory attendant waged a continuous battle against dirt in every form, and against those youths who defiled and defaced public notices, or wrote obscenities on walls. He fought them with scrubbing brush and disinfectant and carbolic soda (the lavatory reeked of these powerful cleansing agents), and if the youths had recourse to penknives to carve their filth into the woodwork, Schlammer fought them with paintbrush and lime.

31

"Let me show you, Herr Gast."

"I'm pressed for time, Schlammer."

"Won't take a second."

Schlammer had funny ideas of the duration of a second.

"I can't now, I've other calls to make."

"It's a matter of grave public concern."

"What is?"

"You see for yourself. Come!"

Wearily, Gast followed Schlammer down the tiled steps, through the lower-ground entrance where the brasswork all gleamed and the floor was spotless. Here the attendant drew Gast into the small cubicle in which he sat all day with his cleaning materials, his sandwiches in a metal tin, and his register.

"Look at this."

Grave-faced, he partially unfurled a poster as if it were a secret State document. The poster was headed:

THE FÜHRER-PRINZIP

The text read:

EVERY LEADER, NO MATTER ON WHAT LEVEL,
FROM THE HIGHEST IN THE LAND TO
YOUNGSTERS IN THE *JUNGVOLK*, HAS THE
UNQUALIFIED RIGHT TO EXPECT TOTAL
OBEDIENCE FROM THOSE UNDER HIM. THAT
IS THE FÜHRER-PRINZIP.

With an air of manliness, Schlammer unfolded the rest of the poster to show Gast the filthy thing. It was crude and executed without much skill, in the manner of such drawings. It showed spread buttocks, with the anus being penetrated by a spike-like male organ, and below, in a childish hand, the message: THE FÜHRER-PRINZIP!!!

Gast could not resist a faint smile.

"I know who did it," Schlammer said. "I saw them. Unfortunately I was not fast enough. It was that little *Lausbub* Rolf

Hacker, and his pal Otto. The one they call 'the Robber.' I entered their names in my register. You see . . . *look! There.* I keep a register, noting down all offences that come to my notice. I have sent their names to the public prosecutor's office. I removed the poster; naturally I haven't erased the drawing in order not to destroy evidence. I keep it locked up, of course."

"Good, Schlammer. Very good," Gast said. "Your vigilance does you credit. You're lesson to us all. If only everybody took their public duties so seriously we should have routed out these unruly elements long ago. Good work, good work. I'll put it in my report, Schlammer."

"Thank you, Herr Street Leader. I am gratified that my work is appreciated. As you know, I was not always in such a position as I am now. Before — before my misfortune — I was gatekeeper at Eau de Cologne. For eight years. My record was spotless. I had important responsibilities. My duties included that of fire officer and watchman. I was required to search workers suspected of pilfering. I was given several commendations for thoroughness. It was the Jews who wished to get rid of me, it was due to them I was dismissed."

Gast, having heard the story before, had taken this opportunity to have a pee. The attendant continued: "Herr Gast, I'd like to ask a personal favour, I'd like your opinion. Relating to my chances. You know I've been doing volunteer work, in regard to the registration and transportation of Jews. I have been a Party member for five years. Never missed a meeting! I have a small room, modest but sufficient for my needs, in the basement at Schluttergasse 15. The position of block warden is becoming vacant there, due to the fact that Frau Bier is retiring. You consider I have a chance? Put another way, Herr Gast: will you support my application?"

"I'll bear it in mind," Gast said, having finished. He buttoned up. "I'll certainly bear it in mind."

"I'm grateful, Herr Gast. Can't tell you how grateful I am."

Cycling back to his poky little office in a seedy backstreet off Subbelratherstrasse, Gast wondered if he should recommend Schlammer for the position. He was well suited to it, since what it mainly required was a snooper, which the lavatory attendant undoubtedly was. A prying, nosey, self-important snooper and sneak. Schlammer was perfect.

I'll recommend him, Gast thought. He'll be grateful to me, and that may be useful one of these days.

* * *

In the Schluttergasse a few days later, Detective Nold was hiding in a doorway, watching the rain. This black rain. Black from all the soot in the air, belch'ed out by all the locomotives that went by. Over the years this soot had impregnated the walls of houses, and left stains on everything. Net curtains were black as soon as they were put up, windows thick with coal dust. Nobody bothered to clean them anymore, they just became grimier and darker and let in less and less light. What was there to see outside anyway? People opposite the railway line lived behind permanently drawn curtains.

It was raining hard, and the water rushing along the gutters was black too. Everything was black in this street, including Detective Nold's mood, which was soured now, as it often was, by indigestion, from which he suffered continually. Detective Nold was cursed with a body metabolism that produced excessive quantities of acids. These acids fomented in his stomach, giving him heartburn and dyspepsia, and they entered his bloodstream to give him periodic attacks of gout. The acids also soured his brain and gave him a melancholic disposition.

He watched the two *Rotzbuben* marching in the gutter, shouting and splashing each other. When they were level with him he leapt out of the doorway and grabbed them.

"Empty your pockets. Come on."

"What for?"

"You'll see what for, lout!" He gave Rolf a smack on the back of the head. Rolf, with an air of exasperation, turned out his pockets, in doing so producing five packets of Orients.

34

"How'd you get five packets?"

"I'm a heavy smoker."

"Where'd you get them?"

"I found them in the street."

"All right. You — Robber."

Otto turned out his pockets and produced three more packets of Orients.

"What d'you know about Herr Dornebusch's newsstand in Lenau Platz?"

"Nothing."

"You — Louse Boy."

"Nothing, Herr Nold."

"Liars!"

"We don't read the news," Rolf explained. "We don't think it's worth reading, see. Not the class of news you get nowadays."

"But you smoke cigarettes?"

"That's right."

"And Herr Dornebusch also sells cigarettes. Orients."

"Oh, does he? We didn't know."

Nold raised the packets of cigarettes he had taken from Rolf and Otto.

"Did you know these packets have stock numbers on them? We can trace where they came from."

"Are you saying, Herr Nold, that the robbers who broke into Herr Dornebusch's newsstand dropped the cigarettes in the street? Where we found them?"

"I know who the robbers are."

"Did somebody see 'em do it?"

"You were seen there this morning, both of you."

"We just come to look. We heard about it and we come to look. It was a funny thing to see — Herr Dornebusch's newsstand all over the Platz. And with all the flags too. Like a wind had blew it down."

"It wasn't a wind," Nold said. "Somebody put a chain around Herr Dornebusch's newsstand and attached the other

35

end of the chain to a tram, so that when the tram moved off—"

"Oh, *Mensch!*" Rolf cried. "Is that what somebody did?"

"And then when it was pulled down they robbed it."

"He's a Party bigshot too, Herr Dornebusch. Bet he was mad . . . getting all his flags muddy. He must have been good and mad."

"I'm going to get to the bottom of this crime, and the culprits are going to pay. Don't think you've got away with it," Nold warned them, starting to walk off.

"Can I have my ciggies back?" Rolf asked cheekily.

"You think I'm going to return stolen property to you?"

"Why—d'you smoke Orients, too, Herr Nold?"

Nold aimed a clout at the boy's head, and Rolf, skilled at ducking clouts, ducked smartly out of the way.

The two boys dashed off into the black rain, and Detective Nold put the eight packets of Orients in his deep raincoat pocket.

*　　*　　*

Now there was hardly a day when Gast did not stop in the Schluttergasse, near the railway arches, to give Otto a lesson in boxing while a group of kids that often included Rolf and Franzi watched.

When Franzi's eyes were on him, Gast couldn't help showing off: he danced around Otto, invited punches in order to dodge them, offered his belly with stomach muscles tight to demonstrate his hardiness. Who would have thought that he was forty-four? He had hardly a grey hair, and though he had fleshed out around the neck and waist, he considered himself a fine figure of a man, and when he studied his smile in the mirror he told himself, "You've got charm, Herr Gast. You have a lot of charm for women. No doubt about it. What you've got is presence. Personality. A touch ruthless, a bit rough at times, but women like that. Women don't like men who are too delicate with them. They like a bit of roughness.

36

They like a man who's a man. Who's got something worth showing down below.''

From time to time in the course of the boxing, Gast would turn and fix his eyes on Franzi and give her a wink while he held Otto at bay with his outstretched arm, courting a punch on the jaw: Otto could move swiftly and was becoming more dangerous with every lesson.

At the end of the sparring, Gast gave the kids sweets or cigarettes, including Franzi. He would offer her chocolate or a cigarette. Sometimes she accepted, sometimes she didn't. She was capricious. There were times when he came and boxed with Otto and she took no notice at all, just carried on skipping or roller-skating, and Gast seethed to be ignored. At such times he would really go for Otto. Seeing an aghast expression on her face — women's response to a little blood! — he was gratified.

Apart from giving him a pretext to see Franzi, sparring regularly with Otto confirmed in Gast's mind that the boy had potential. He had a streak of pure savagery in him. You could see it in his face — the relish for getting the better of the other person. Good, good, Gast thought. He did what he could to provoke Otto by inflicting humiliations on him and hurting him enough physically to make him want to get his revenge. The killer spirit was something that had to be carefully nurtured in a boy like Otto.

Pushing him around, slapping his face with an open hand, making the boy pant and gasp in his effort to break through Gast's guard, Gast said in Franzi's hearing, giving her a broad wink:

"If you'd stop wanking so much, Otto-boy, you'd have more wind.''

Franzi giggled and Otto went scarlet and his teeth bared into a wolf snarl as he threw himself at Gast with wild fists. Gast easily evaded the blows and continued the provocation.

"Come on, Otto, get your hand out of your pocket, hit me,

hit me! Try and hit me! Come on! Come on! You want to cut down on that, Otto-boy, or your hair'll fall out. Won't it, Franzi?"

Gast saw naked murder in Otto's eyes, and was well pleased. That was the way to make champions. And also he was raising himself in Franzi's eyes, he was sure. He must play his cards right, present himself in the most favourable light, while belittling Otto. He had not failed to notice that Otto was by way of being in the running for Franzi's favours; his interest in her was obvious, and she, for her part, had shown signs of being impressed by him, her brother's big friend, this tough boy who beat up HJs. Gast had put him in his place: demonstrated that he could whip him if he wished. All that, he judged, would help him in his plans. Which were increasingly concerned now with finding a way of winning Franzi. It was not going to be easy, because of her being under-age. The street leader might lay himself open to charges of corrupting the young and this could put an end to his career. He would have to make sure Franzi did not give him away. He would have to bide his time, and then when she was ready for him . . . meanwhile fend off anyone who might come on the scene and queer his pitch. He believed he had already eliminated Otto, but he'd have to watch out for others. There were many after her who might not be ready to wait as he was.

One day, failing to see her in the street, Gast asked Rolf where she was.

"How should I know?"

"Does she go out?"

"What d'you mean?"

"With men — boys?"

"'Xpect so."

"What d'you mean? Does she . . . ?"

"What d'you think!"

Gast did not know how far to press Rolf. Did Rolf understand what the questions meant? He was only ten, but a very knowing ten, very knowing about the world's ways. Still, Gast could not be certain to what extent this knowingness was real or just kids' bravado.

"Look here," Gast said, "she wants to be careful who she goes around with. Doesn't want to go getting herself a bad name. You're her brother, you should protect her. If a girl's not decent, no man'll want to marry her. All she can be then is a prostitute. You understand?"

"Sure."

Gast cycled off, and returned an hour later to see if she was back. He stood around looking for her, and after a few minutes saw her at her window, chin propped on chubby arms, face twisted into a schoolgirl scowl; she had the frown of someone not too good at her lessons, racking her brains. She was sucking and biting at the end of her pencil; having got stuck, she had come to the window to find distraction, and saw him looking at her from below, and for a moment their eyes held.

Ambiguous in import though the look was, Gast was inflamed. Oh, he would have to have her. Damn the risk!

At that moment, as if his lustful thoughts had been proclaimed to the whole street, the white-haired mother appeared at the window, pulled her daughter away, and pushed her inside.

Then she leaned out, her face filled with the secret knowledge possessed by madwomen, and shook her finger at him, crying:

"The Lord God destroyed Sodom and Gomorrah for its sins. Filth! Filth! What d'you want with my daughter, you filthy man? The Lord God said, 'I will cause the sun to go down at noon, and I will darken the earth in the clear day.' You're an evil man. Evil. Evil. Go away. Go away. She's a child. She's only fifteen. Go away, you evil man. Transgressor of God's commandments. I know there's evil in your heart. . . . I read your heart. 'And the Babylonians came to her into the bed of love, and they defiled her with their whoredom; and she was polluted with them, and her mind was alienated from them. . . .' "

Franzi was at the window again, trying to pull her mother away.

Gast thought: how does the old madwoman know what's in my mind? She reads me, she reads me, the old bitch, the old cow. How will I get past her to the daughter if she can read my thoughts, when I haven't even made a move yet?

The mad mother is going to be my stumbling block, Gast warned himself. She stands in my way, the old harridan. The witch.

A few days later, from a doorway opposite Hirsch's button shop, Gast watched the shopkeeper roll down his metal shutters three-quarters of the way with the long hooked pole, stoop underneath to lock the shop door, come out, push the shutters to the ground, and fix the heavy padlock at the bottom. Then he went off along the road to the tram stop.

Gast followed close behind.

Hirsch went into the first carriage of the tram, Gast into the second.

When Hirsch got off at a stop in the Aachenerstrasse, Gast got off too.

The light was fading but it was not difficult to keep the button dealer in sight. He was walking like a man with an urgent appointment to keep. Gast followed him to the entrance of a small block of apartments in the Grünergasse. It was an old building, the date of its construction, 1908, inscribed in swirling lettering above the entrance door, the windows surrounded in sculpted designs of leafy foliage: a place of some standing, Gast could see.

Hirsch let himself in with his own key, and the glass and wrought-iron entrance door had closed on the pneumatic door closer before Gast could follow. Shut out, he studied the names on the brass plates beside the doorbells: Hirsch's was not among them.

So! So! Something fishy going on, as he'd suspected.

He decided to wait awhile and see what happened.

Was Hirsch coming here to conduct some secret business in buttons, thereby depriving Gast of his profits? If so, when he reemerged from his illicit trading Gast would be waiting for him.

After half an hour, he was not out. Tired of waiting, Gast rang the concierge's bell. She was, as he had anticipated, also the building's block warden, and although in a different district to his and so not under his jurisdiction, she was used to doing what she was told by her Party superiors, and from his credentials she saw that Gast was a *Zellenleiter*, in charge of a whole street.

No, there was nobody called Hirsch in the building, but when Gast described him — a tall Jew with a large black beard — the concierge had no difficulty in identifying him as the uncle of Fräulein Bott, who lived on the second floor.

Fräulein Bott was a very fine young lady, a chiropodist in a high-class establishment in the Neumarkt. A charming and generous person, and her uncle too, despite his race, was a decent sort, said the concierge. A businessman, she had gathered, a man of means. At any rate, he was not stingy, she intimated, expressively rubbing her thumb across her fingers. Fräulein Bott was a thoroughly respectable person, thoroughly. There was never any noise or drunkenness; Herr Gast could rest assured she would be the first to sniff out any impropriety, immoral usage of the apartment, et cetera. Bills were promptly paid by the uncle.

Ah! said Gast. *Ah!* Now he understood everything. Did she have a passkey to Fräulein Bott's flat? No, she didn't, she said.

"Then you must go up, bang on the door, and ask them to open up — say there's a gas leak."

Together they went up in the lift, and outside apartment seven she banged on the door, and called through:

"This is the concierge here, fräulein. So sorry to disturb you. Beg your pardon, fräulein. A question of a leak. Yes — a

41

gas leak. It's necessary to have immediate admission, if you wouldn't mind opening the door."

There was a muffled response from inside, but the door was not opened straight away and at Gast's insistence the concierge banged again and again.

"Coming, coming. A minute. Just one minute, Frau Dussendorfer . . ."

A little while later the door was opened very slightly and a young woman's tousled head appeared in the crack while the rest of her remained concealed behind the door.

"Yes, Frau Dussendorfer, what is it?"

"There is this gentleman . . . ," began the concierge, and by way of presenting himself, Gast put all of his considerable weight against the door and pushed hard.

The door flew open.

The young woman, who was wearing a pink corset, screamed as Herr Gast entered the apartment precipitately, in the manner of a circus tumbler.

Hirsch appeared at the bedroom door, agitatedly tying the belt of a scarlet silk dressing gown lavishly decorated with Japanese motifs.

"What is this?" he began dazedly, and then seeing Gast, froze. "You better go," he told the concierge and automatically slipped money into her palm, as if she had done a service for him.

The concierge looked to Gast for her instructions.

"Go," he said, and she went.

When she'd gone, Gast leaned against the door. "Well, well, well," he mused. He was taking his time now, savouring the situation: his eyes went to the young woman in the corset and then to the bearded patriarch in the Japanese dressing gown.

"So this is where my profits go — on keeping whores."

Hirsch gave an apologetic shrug. "You and I," he began, "we are businessmen, we are men of the world." To the girl

42

he said, "Go in the bedroom, let me talk to Herr Gast. Don't be afraid, Herr Gast is our friend. He's my protector. I owe everything to him."

"I'm glad you realize it," Gast said. "Yet you cheat me. After all I have done for you!"

"I will make it up to you," Hirsch promised, "I will recompense you."

"Oh, you will, you undoubtedly will."

"I wish to make you a gift," Hirsch said. "As a token of my appreciation. Of my deep gratitude, Herr Gast, for all you've done for me. A solid silver cigarette case, engraved with your initials." He watched Gast's face. "What am I saying, Herr Gast? What I meant to say was — a gold cigarette case. As a little *preliminary* token," he added quickly.

"Yes?" Gast asked.

"I would like, in addition, if that is acceptable, to make you a small gift of one or two cases of champagne . . . and, furthermore, in addition . . . two — or three — cases of cognac. To express my gratitude."

"You call that gratitude?" Suddenly Gast's patience evaporated, and rage built up in cheeks and mouth, exploding into violent words.

"You pig's bladder, Hirsch! You mingy mealy fart! What a diseased arsehole you are! What a suppurating flea-eaten venereal sore on the testicles of a donkey! You think a gold cigarette case expresses gratitude? You know what you owe me, you frozen piece of piss?"

"I am very grateful, Herr Gast."

"Up to now, Hirsch, I have kept you and your daughters off the list. I have let you live in peace, and you cheat me! You can't afford for your daughter to get married, but you can keep young women in secret apartments with luxury furniture, while to me you say your business makes no money."

"Herr Gast, the simple explanation is I am also a *wholesaler*

43

in buttons and costume jewellery. The wholesale business was not as badly hit as the retail, you understand. That has enabled me to have some small comforts—"

"Small comforts!" Gast shook his head in the direction of the door behind which the chiropodist Lena Bott had retired. "You deceive me. You deceive your wife, you deceive your daughters for your small comforts."

"It is not what it appears to be," Hirsch tried to explain. "She is someone I am deeply fond of, Herr Gast. A fine young woman. Were my situation different I would marry her."

Gast looked about the place. It was to his taste. Here was luxury! Thick carpets, fine soft wallpapers, venetian blinds, white porcelain lamps in silk shades. Paintings on the walls of nude women, of sunsets: mountain tops, harbours, boats. There was a mirrored ebony cabinet, he saw, with many bottles of liqueurs and brandies, and the shiny chrome implements for making and pouring cocktails.

The button dealer was wallowing in luxury, while he, Gast, his protector, lived in a one-room apartment with damp coming through the walls and rotting linoleum on the floor.

In the bedroom there was the chiropodist Lena Bott, who had begun by cutting his corns, holding his smelly feet in her soft hands, but soon was holding other parts less softly.

"We love each other, Herr Gast," Hirsch explained. "She means everything to me."

"Love?" Gast scoffed. "She is a Gentile?"

Hirsch hesitated. "Yes."

"So—an offence against the race laws!" Gast shook his head, a man much put upon. "You expect me to protect you from the consequences of your lewd sensual appetites for Christian girls? You expect all that, and yet you don't want to pay."

"Herr Gast, I will pay you. I will pay you what I can."

Gast walked about the flat. He went to the window and adjusted the slats of the venetian blinds to look out: it was a discreet apartment in a discreet street. The building opposite also had venetian blinds. You could not look into other people's lives here. He turned around: long, low sofa, covered in red velvet; small tables with heavy glass ashtrays; many cushions. Pleasant, very pleasant.

"I like this flat," Gast said, opening the doors of cabinets and looking inside, pulling out drawers. "A very nice flat. And convenient. Close to public transport in the Aachenerstrasse, and at the same time, quiet and out of the way. It's what you'd call . . . discreet. I like it. I like the furnishings, too. I congratulate you, Hirsch, on your taste in furniture. And paintings. I can see you're a man of taste, Hirsch." He opened a cigarette box, weighed it in his hands. "Solid silver? Must cost a pretty penny, stuff like this. You know, Hirsch, this is exactly the sort of apartment that I always wanted to live in myself. You and I, we have the same sort of taste." He threw himself down onto the sofa. "Soft, very soft indeed. A pleasure to lie on." He put his feet up. "Delightful, Hirsch. I must tell you, I find your flat agreeable."

Hirsch offered him a cigarette from the silver cigarette box, and lit it for him.

"This flat, Hirsch," Gast explained, "would be quite convenient for me, and since you can't use it anymore, considering present circumstances — the race laws — the property laws — since you can have no further use for such a place — for the seduction of Christian girls — a capital offence — I'll take it over from you and save your neck. What d'you say to that? You can't expect to go around seducing Christian girls and not have to pay for it."

"You misunderstand! She is the only one."

"What difference does it make? One? Ten? The offence is the same. Still, I will do my best for my old friend Hirsch. I shall try to push the offence under the carpet. But it's best you don't ever come here again. You understand? I'll take over the apartment and that way anything which has occurred here cannot be laid at your door. That is the best. Yes. Yes." He mused for a moment. "Get dressed, Hirsch! I want you out of here in fifteen minutes. And you must leave me your keys. All of them."

Hirsch stood rigid, dazed. "I can't——" he began.

"I don't think you realize, Hirsch, what a service I am doing you by taking over this apartment. Anyone else would report you to the *Geheime Staatspolizei*, and you and your family would be on the next truck to one of those places— Dachau?—for resettlement. Instead of which I enable you to return to the bosom of your family, your daughters, your wife. You're a fortunate man. You've had a close shave, Hirsch. Like this, all you lose is . . . the gratification of your sensual appetites for Christian girls."

Hirsch started to leave the room.

"Where are you going?"

"To the bedroom, to get my clothes."

"Stay here."

In the bedroom, Lena Bott was sitting on the bed in a loose wrap, smoking a cigarette nervously. She watched Gast pick up Hirsch's clothes and throw them out to him in the corridor.

"I am taking over this flat," Gast said, examining her from the door. She was in her thirties, with long straight blond hair almost to the shoulders. The neck and cheeks were showing the first signs of a developing chubbiness, but on the whole she was not bad.

"I have to move out?" she asked.

He considered the question. No need to throw out the baby with the bathwater, he told himself.

"Not necessarily," he replied, "as long as it's understood . . . that I will be using the flat."

"You'll be sleeping here?"

"From time to time," he said.

"There is only one bed," she pointed out.

"Well, that can't be helped." He shrugged. "If it doesn't suit you to stay, please yourself. . . ." When she said nothing, he told her, "You better get dressed and pack your things."

46

She waited for him to go out of the room, but he lacked the graciousness to do so, and since he had already seen her in her corset, she began to get dressed in front of him, starting by putting on her stockings. He watched her from the open door, unabashedly. As she sat on the bed fastening suspender clips, it was awkward keeping her thighs pressed together the whole time and she did not bother. He inclined his head to one side, regarding her coarsely, without a trace of shame: the bright ginger bush, the humid underfur, as she raised her thigh to clip the stocking in place — thick plump parts glistening damply. This dampness stirred his loins as he continued to stare. Was she perspiring in the overheated flat? Or . . . ?

When she was dressed, he said, "You've decided not to avail yourself of my offer?"

"I've decided to stay until I find somewhere else," she said.

"In that case," he said, "you did not need to get dressed."

"True, that is true." She stood nodding her head.

He came towards her and she looked up and did not flinch when he roughly put his hands on her: indeed, she opened her mouth. He did not kiss her, though; instead spun her around so that she was facing the wall. He felt her buttocks while she stood still: then he pushed her forward and she put out her arms to support herself against the wall. She let out a long gasp, as if she had been doused with ice-cold water, as he yanked up the dress from behind, and pushed her underwear down to her knees. He undid the hooks and eyes of her corset and peeled it open.

Looking over her shoulder in her bent-over position, she saw that he had unbuttoned himself and was sticking up like a ram's horn.

A bright girl, Gast decided. Knew which side her bread was buttered. Probably thought she could get around her new landlord as she had done with the old. No harm in letting her believe it; in fact, some profit. She was lively in her responses, which was always preferable to the sort who acted like a dead fish. She had a lively arse, this one, and a moist pouting little hole at the back, much to his taste, like everything else in this luxurious apartment. She didn't demur, clever girl, oh, a girl who certainly knew which side her bread was buttered and who her new landlord was, for she facilitated it all with her own delicate fingers, but even so, it was a job and there was no room for gentleness. He did not know if her scream indicated hurt or pleasure, but she began to shake at once.

He, however, took his time: wallowed in the lap of luxury. Her new landlord was not going to let himself be so easily got round as the old one, now waiting in the corridor to leave his keys.

"Leave them on the table," Gast called to him. "I'm busy right now."

Behind his back Hirsch held the long bone-handled knife from the kitchen drawer.

"What are you standing there for, Hirsch?"

A bloody vision filled Hirsch's mind like a Biblical prophecy. His moist palms tightened on the carving knife.

"The keys," Hirsch stammered, moving the knife to the side of his body in readiness. He prayed to God to forgive him.

"I told you — leave the keys on the table, and get out."

Hirsch put them on the table in the corridor and then he put the knife back in the kitchen drawer, and left.

What else could he do? Risk his daughters?

From outside the apartment door, he heard his protector utter a roar like a bull, and thought: it all passes, the agony as well as the pleasure; it is all a passing thing.

His lust satisfied, Gast felt disillusionment with all of womankind. Oh, they were all the same — whores at heart.

"Find yourself somewhere else as soon as you can," he told the chiropodist. He was not planning on it being a long relationship. He had other uses for this *de luxe* apartment.

He could picture Franzi there, amid all the finery.

THREE

At the beginning of April, Fat Schlammer, on Gast's recommendation, succeeded Frau Bier as block warden of the building where Rolf lived.

In his Brownshirts' uniform, his massive flesh straining against belt and crossbelt, keys jangling at his waist (for he had also been given the job of janitor in the building), he pinned up blacklists of proscribed books, ordinances about the registration of Jews, and the activities and professions in which they must not engage. There were edicts headed, FOR THE PROTECTION OF THE PEOPLE, issued by the Gauleiter. There were editorials, with passages underlined, from the *Schwarzes Korps* and from the *Völkischer Beobachter*. Announcements of meetings and rallies, sporting events and fire exercises.

This morning as he approached the board he saw that hooligans had been at work again. The edict headed, FOR THE PROTECTION OF THE PEOPLE had been altered to read, FOR

THE ENRICHMENT OF THE GAULEITER. An editorial that spoke of "every leader having the unquestionable right to lead" had had a few scrawled words added to it, so that now it read: ". . . unquestionable right to lead us into the shit."

Schlammer was sure he knew who had done this. It was that little lout Rolf, and his friend Otto.

Sweating and cursing, Schlammer worked quickly to remove the defaced notices and to pin up others in their place. As he was doing this Rolf and Otto sauntered by, cigarettes dangling from their lips, and called out to him:

"Writing on walls again, Schlammer? You dirty old devil! You should be ashamed of yourself. At your age! Disgusting!"

They went off chortling and he called after them, "You'll be laughing on the wrong side of your faces one of these days, just you wait and see. *Lausbuben!* Juvenile delinquents! I catch you and you'll be in hot water. Very hot water, my lads."

"You won't catch us, you won't catch us," they called back, and putting their hands to their noses chanted, "You won't catch us, you won't catch us — uh-uh-uh! Old Schlammer is too fat, old Schlammer is too old, can't even catch a cold . . ."

"You just wait, you little buggers!"

Otto had got a new belt: it was handsome, black and broad, fastened with a heavy porcelain buckle. It had nickel rings to which a variety of desirable objects were attached: a water canteen; a jangling loop of rifle cartridges; an all-purpose army knife, embodying instruments for opening tins and bottles; and at the front he wore a watch chain to which was attached the skull-and-crossbones emblem of a Hussars unit.

"It's *classy*," Rolf said. "Where you get it from?"

"Picked it up," Otto said. He had a self-satisfied smirk on his face.

"Come on, tell! Tell where you got it, Robber."

"Picked it up in the street."

50

"Yaaaaah?" Rolf scoffed admiringly.

They ambled along down the street, going nowhere in particular.

All of a sudden Otto pinched Rolf's arm with pincer-like fingers. It hurt.

"What you do that for?"

"I seen a brown dog."

A while later he did it again.

"Lay off, Robber."

"I can't help it. I seen another brown dog."

Five minutes later he did it for the third time.

"Ouch!" Rolf yelled, and protested, "You didn't even see a brown dog that time."

"No, but I seen a black cat."

"Why've you got to do it when you see a black cat? I thought it was brown dogs."

"It's black cats as well."

Some distance further on, Rolf suddenly kicked Otto hard in the shin and ran. Otto came after him, but Rolf could outrun him easily. He could run around him and dodge him.

When Otto eventually tired of trying to catch Rolf, he demanded peevishly, "What you kick me for?"

"I seen a pile of horse dung."

Otto considered this for about a minute. His mind did not work fast.

"Have you got to kick me every time you see a pile of horse dung, then?"

"Not if you don't have to pinch me every time you see a brown dog or a black cat."

Otto deliberated for the next three minutes as they walked in silence.

"I don't *have* to pinch you," he conceded. "Shake?"

They shook on it, and Otto, in a flash, twisted Rolf's arm behind his back and forced it up.

"Lay off, Robber! Lay off, you sod!"

"I could break your rotten arm, Louse Boy."

51

"Get off, get off, Robber. If you don't leave go, I won't trust you ever again."

"I was only fooling around," Otto said, letting go of Rolf's arm.

You had to watch out with Otto. Something got into him, and then he just had to do rotten nasty things to you, like twist your arm up behind your back, or grab your balls and squeeze hard.

He just had this nasty, lowdown streak in him. You had to defend yourself. Rolf's defence was that he was quicker and smarter than Otto and could outrun him and outwit him.

Although the Robber was Rolf's best friend, Rolf never trusted him entirely. You couldn't trust anybody. Not even your best friend. That was the way life was.

Coming in late after a gang get-together at Blücher Park, Rolf found that the stairs were dark. *Again.* There being no windows in the hall or upper landings, without electric light it was pitch-black inside the building.

It happened from time to time that there was no light, and Rolf had discovered why. Somebody took the light bulbs out. Not to steal them, as he'd at first supposed, but in order to be in the dark.

Rolf crept in silent as a mouse and stopped to listen.

He could hear them. That sort of gasping sound. Somebody catching their breath.

Well, so what? No skin off his nose.

He could hear them in the back where stairs went down to the coal cellar.

They were trying not to make any sound, but he could hear them because he had good hearing, and he knew what it was.

It wasn't anything to do with him what anybody did. So what! He crept up close to them, to hear better, and he heard the girl draw in her breath sharply, repeatedly. He could hear everything, even though they were trying to keep quiet, and the man kept saying, "Shhhh! Shhhhh!"

52

He could hear everything.

The girl kept saying over and over, "Oh, it's good, oh, it's good," and the man kept shushing her.

Rolf wanted to see what they were doing that was so good, and he lit a match and held it up and saw a soldier sort of half-seated on the iron pipes that ran along the wall there, and the girl wriggling about in his lap, wriggling like a hooked fish, and there was that fishy smell.

He raised the match and saw the hooked fish was Franzi.

When he got in, his mother wasn't well; she was often like in a daze, staring, as if she was watching a film, but not looking at anything, really.

He said, "How are you, Mutti? You all right?" but she didn't answer.

She was breathing strangely, a gurgling sound coming from her throat, and he got scared and didn't know what to do. There was a pool of wet on the floor near where she sat. She'd made a mess again.

"Mutti," he said, "Mutti. Please, Mutti."

Franzi should have been there to do something, instead of wriggling about on people's laps.

He wetted a cloth with cold water and pressed it to his mother's forehead to try and revive her. Her skin was cold and clammy. And she gave sudden big gulps, her throat rattling.

He tried to take her pulse but it was so fast he couldn't count the beats. He could see the vein in her neck jumping all the time.

"Oh, Mutti," he kept saying, "oh, Mutti." He thought he was going to cry, but he bit his lip hard enough to make it bleed and that way prevented himself.

I better go and fetch Franzi, he thought.

When he got to the bottom of the stairs and called, "Franzi, Mutti's not well," he heard shuffling and movements. He had to repeat it.

"What?" Franzi asked, trying to put on a normal voice. She

53

coughed, and said, in a very annoyed tone, "Rolfie? What's wrong?"

"I don't know, it's Mutti. You better come."

He heard some low whispered exchanges, and then Franzi started coming up the stairs, straightening her clothes. She ran in, went to their mother, and flicked water over her until she came out of the spell.

"You've had one of your queer turns, Mama. How're you feeling?"

"What's that smell?"

"What smell?"

She wagged her finger at Franzi. "I wasn't born yesterday, you know. You may think I'm an old madwoman, but I know what's what. I know when a young girl's decent and when she isn't."

"I don't know what you're talking about, Mama. Calm yourself, Mama. You're not well. Look — naughty! *Naughty.* You've made a mess again. Come on, let me take you to your bed. Help me, Rolf."

Together they took their mother to her bed and made her lie down, and Franzi took off her shoes and stockings, and then she sent Rolf out of the room to make a cup of cocoa.

When he came back with it, his mother was still going on about the smell.

"It's woman's smell, that's what it is. Think I don't know?"

Franzi got some Eau de Cologne and wetted a handkerchief and put it under her mother's nose.

"Trying to disguise it, are you? *Schlampe!* Little whore! I know what your father did with you. I know what happened when you sat on his lap, wriggling about. Think I'm stupid? You were always wriggling about. Men couldn't help lay their hands on you." Her head twisted round and she stared fixedly at nothing.

"Don't work yourself up, Mama. If you work yourself up I'll have to call the doctor and he'll have to give you another injection."

54

At this she became afraid, and the focus of her eyes changed; she was looking at them quietly.

They propped her up, and Rolf held the hot cocoa to her mouth and she drank.

Her mind made one of its sudden jumps.

"Oh, he got good tips on the pleasure steamers, and in the beerhalls. Say anything you like against him, he could play the accordion. Know how he presented himself to me?" She gave a little bow, imitating him. " 'Ernst Hacker, musician!' " She gave a laugh. "I was just a young girl, what did I know? I didn't know anything about men, I was that innocent. A musician! Of course I was impressed. Who wouldn't be? He was a handsome man, your father. He could get any girl around his little finger, why'd he be interested in me? How did I know he was a thief? I thought he was a musician, that's how innocent I was. It was difficult times. You couldn't get work as a musician. Even on the pleasure boats and in the beerhalls, even without any wages you couldn't — just playing for tips. So he had to play in the streets, with a hat. Ernst Hacker, musician. I had to go out to work scrubbing floors so he could put money on horses. He was going to make a fortune but the horses let him down." She shook her head bitterly. "If he did have a win, once in a while, you think *we* ever saw one pfennig? It all went on his women, his little whores. That's where. Never his own family. We didn't count. We only existed when he needed somewhere to sleep and eat. But when he had a few marks in his pocket, he was off. He liked Franzi though," she said darkly. "He likes *her*. 'What a heartbreaker you're going to be,' he says to *her*."

Rolf could see she was working herself up again.

"Don't, Mutti . . ."

"I'm cold. It's cold in here. It's like winter."

She started to cry. Both Franzi and Rolf put their arms round her to comfort her.

Franzi said, "It's going to get warm soon, it's spring."

55

"No, it's winter," their mother insisted. "Don't try to make a fool out of me. Don't think I don't know what that smell is. I know a lot more than you think."

A few days later, seeing Franzi by the window with nothing on, she started hitting her, and shook her fist at Gast and his Brownshirts below, and shouted at them in her high, strident voice which quivered with her madness:

" 'God called him from the fields so that he would spread His word to the people. And he called the people and the church and the king back to him because they, all of them, had abandoned God. They were intoxicated with arrogant pride, they prayed to strange gods, and lying and cheating and feasting and luxuriating had spread through the life of the people. And the Lord God said, Lo! And the city shall be as dust. . . .' "

One day in the middle of April Rolf, Otto, and Franzi were on their way to school when they saw something going on in the vicinity of Lenau Platz and stopped to see what was happening.

Police vehicles were blocking off a section of one of the better streets, where shop owners and doctors and dentists lived in stylish houses, with dates over their entrances: 1899, 1900, 1908. A knot of spectators had gathered, among them local tradesmen, passers-by, a postman, a delivery boy, schoolchildren, neighbours in dressing gowns. They stood solemnly waiting and watching. The men in trilby hats and long overcoats had got out of their vehicles, leaving the car doors open.

Rolf pushed his way to the forefront, expecting to see a fight or a dead body. But there was nothing — for the moment. He asked the person next to him, "What's happening?" The man didn't even answer. Rolf called to Franzi and Otto to come nearer, so they'd be able to see better. *Something* must be happening, or all these people wouldn't be standing about. The cars were police cars, and there was also a lorry there, tail flap down, wooden planks making a ramp up to the back of it.

Presently a woman, a man, and two children came out of a fine house, each carrying one suitcase and some bundles. They looked as though they had dressed in a hurry. The man had not had time to put on his shirt collar and was pulling on his jacket as they were all marched to the lorry. The little girl was crying. The boy, Rolf's age, was making a brave face, and the father was trying to keep everybody's spirits up; he appeared to have made an attempt at a joke, but it fell flat. Nobody laughed. Men in trilby hats hurried the group along, prodded them up the wooden planks onto the back of the lorry.

Now people were coming out of other houses as well, and the men in trilby hats were ticking off names on their lists and getting everybody up onto the lorry. Those already on were being squashed together to leave room for others to come.

Many of the women were weeping — one very old woman was giving vent to loud, ringing lamentations, embarrassing the spectators by her lack of self-control. The majority of those being led away were silent, white, looking neither to left nor right.

Rolf saw Gast ride up on his bicycle, dismount, and push his way through the spectators into the clear space in the centre where the policemen were standing. He found the one who was in charge of the operation and started speaking to him. Gast was talking a lot, and finally the policeman in charge produced some typewritten sheets of paper and the two men cast their eyes over the lists.

Gast pointed, spoke persuasively, and the policeman listened, but, finally, shook his head. Gast gave him a cigar, and said something into his ear. The policeman laughed and shook his head again, though less certainly. Finally, he shrugged. Again the two men studied the lists, and Gast was seen to point to various names. The policeman kept shaking his head. Gast gripped his arm, raised a forefinger in a questioning sign — one? The policeman shrugged. The two men studied the typewritten pages again. Gast pointed to a name, and the policeman shook his head. Gast pointed to another name and said something low and insistent, and this time the policeman, with an air of impatience and not wanting to be bothered anymore, shrugged consentingly. He took out a pencil and made a line through some name, and then handed the lists to one of his subordinates, and Gast went back among the growing crowd of onlookers.

Among them was Kurt Springer. He had been riding through Lenau Platz on his motorbike on his way to work when he saw all the commotion down the road. Now, engine off, he was pushing himself forward bit by bit, towards the spot where he'd caught sight of Franzi a moment ago. Franzi, looking round at the time, had seem him too but pretended she hadn't.

"What d'you think's happening?" she asked Rolf nervously.

Kurt had rolled forward far enough by now to be able to answer for Rolf.

"They're taking away Jews."

"What for?" Rolf asked.

"To resettle them among their own kind, in Poland," Kurt explained. "Jews like to stick together, they're very clannish. They'll be better off there."

"They don't look as though they'll be better off there," Rolf remarked.

Kurt was turning the handlebars of his motorbike this way and that, as if about to set off on one of his crazy rides somewhere. He seemed very restless and jumpy.

"Want a ride?" he offered generally, addressing the invitation to whichever one of them wished to accept it.

"No thanks, don't feel like it," Rolf said. "We've got to go to school."

"I'll take you to school," he offered, looking at Franzi.

"No, we'll walk," Rolf said. "Thanks all the same, Kurt."

Rolf caught his breath. He'd seen bearded Hirsch the button dealer being brought out of his house. From his bedraggled appearance it looked as though he had been in a scuffle. Behind him came a dark-haired woman who must have been Frau Hirsch, and then came his five daughters, the eldest, Malshi, nineteen, the youngest, Ruthie, eleven. Rolf bit his lip. He knew Ruthie; she went to his school.

"That's Ruthie," he said to Otto. "She's in my school. I know her."

"Didn't know you know Yids," Otto said.

"I didn't even know she was one," Rolf said, and added, "She's all right."

Hirsch was making a scene with the men in trilby hats. He was arguing with them, refusing to be led away. They dragged off his wife and daughters, while he stood his ground, protesting volubly.

All around there were faces at windows.

Hirsch was explaining to one of the policemen that a mistake was being made, that he and his wife and daughters were not supposed to be deported; that this was something agreed and settled on an official or semi-official basis, and to please check on the matter with his superiors. He was trying to get to the policeman in charge, so as to explain to him, but was being stopped by the men in trilby hats, who would not let him by, who were becoming increasingly belligerent in the face of his intransigence. Hirsch was being punched and forcibly dragged towards the lorry, and as this was happening he spotted Gast and cried out to him at the top of his voice, "Herr Gast! It's *Hirsch*. They're taking me away! Explain to them, Herr Gast! Look! Look! They've already put my daughters on the lorry. Herr Gast! Herr Gast!" His shouts were becoming increasingly desperate as he received no answer, and the men pushed and dragged him and punched him in the mouth to shut him up. His daughters on the lorry wept and hung their heads, seeing the blood on their father's face.

At the foot of the ramp, Hirsch succeeded in momentarily freeing himself from the men in trilby hats, and he shouted into that part of the crowd where he had seen Gast disappear: "Herr Gast! Are you not my protector? Answer me, Herr Gast! Do we not have an agreement?" His voice filled with a deep, ringing bitterness. "Don't hide your face in the crowd, Herr Gast. You and I, we have an understanding. Haven't I given you everything I possess? We're being taken away, Herr Gast. You promised me. You said you'd protect us. Are you going to abandon us now, after everything you promised, after all I gave you?"

But there was no answer from the crowd, and by now three men in trilby hats had got hold of Hirsch and hoisted him bodily onto the back of the lorry, since he was refusing the ramp.

The lorry full, the planks were removed, the tailgate was raised, and metal toggles were inserted into their housing, closing up the back.

A few moments later the transport moved off, and as soon as the Jews were all gone, Gast emerged from the crowd to talk to his friend, the policeman in charge. Further bargaining ensued. Everybody was more relaxed now that this part of the operation was concluded. Gast offered cigarettes all around.

The men in trilby hats were going inside the houses where the Jews had lived, and came out, after a while, carrying cardboard boxes filled with objects of various kinds: bric-a-brac, silver-plated cutlery, silver candlesticks, cultured pearls, hats, gloves, leatherware, cameras, clocks, ice skates, bottles of liqueurs, shoes, dresses, silk robes, dress suits, shawls, fur muffs. These boxes were being carried to the police cars, where Gast and the policeman in charge examined the various items, and entered into a discussion of some intricacy. It was several minutes before the ticklish question that occupied them was settled to their mutual satisfaction, whereupon Gast came forward and addressed the remaining onlookers, among whom he'd spotted Franzi and her brother Rolf and his friend Otto.

"I wish to announce," he told them, "that as acting local district leader, in consultation with the police department, we decided that some of these goods formerly the property of Jews should be distributed among those who long suffered exploitation at their hands. Who wants this vase?" He raised the item in question like an auctioneer calling for bids. Nobody seemed to want the vase, and he dropped it to the ground, letting it smash. He gave a contemptuous snort. "Hideous, isn't it? Some people got no taste. Here are some long white gloves. Anyone want long white gloves? For the opera? Nobody goes to the opera here? Good for gardening. No?" He discarded the unwanted opera gloves. His jocularity served as a transition from the disagreeable scenes they had been witnessing. "Never mind about the damned gloves. Here's a box of silver soup spoons. Quite nice. Who wants them?" Several people wanted the silver spoons, and Gast gave them to a woman who sold bundles of firewood and coal on the other side of Lenau Platz. A small girl spoke up and said, "I'd like a pair of ice skates, please, sir."

"I don't know if we have ice skates. We have? Then you shall have them, my angel." He gave her the ice skates, which were about twice the size of her feet, and a kiss on the cheek.

"I know what you want," he said to Franzi. "You want the leather toiletry box. It's real crocodile." He went to get it, and opened it for her. The interior was lined with suede. There was a mirror on the inside of the lid, silver-back hairbrushes under loops, a tortoise-shell comb, a silver powder compact, phials and jars of make-up, with brushes and tweezers, and a complete manicure set.

"This has got to be for the prettiest girl here," he said, holding it out to her.

She reached to take it, without thinking, giving him a

61

warm, intimate smile that inflamed him — it was the sort of smile that she couldn't help giving to any man who was being nice to her, or at any rate taking notice of her.

"Don't take it!"

The words were spat out by Kurt sitting astride his motorbike. "It's stolen goods," he said. "You can get into trouble. He doesn't have the right to give these things away. They're not his to give."

Outrage spread across Gast's face.

"What d'you know about it?" he demanded. "There're policemen here."

"I know the law," Kurt said. "I've gone into it. Property confiscated from Jews has all got to be officially accounted for. It's got to be entered on a register."

"Who d'you think keeps the register, know-it-all? Me. I'm the acting local district leader. It's for me to decide."

Kurt shook his head. "It's illegal."

"Have I taken anything for myself? Do I stand to gain?" Gast threw at Kurt. "So where's the misdemeanour? Show me the crime I'm committing. You can't."

Kurt didn't answer. He looked at Franzi meaningfully, but could not speak the thought in his mind.

Although Gast seemed to have wriggled out of the charge so intemperately hurled at him, it was obvious that the mood had been soured and that Franzi would not now take the toiletry box, and even if she took it he would be in no position to exact any advantage from having made the gift, not after what had been said.

"The share-out is suspended for the time being," he announced. "All these items will be held at the local Party office and entered on a register and anyone with any claims should come there and see me." He looked at Franzi directly, and said in a lower voice, "I'll keep this for you. Come by after school."

Kurt heard, and said angrily, "What's a schoolgirl want

make-up for? She's a child. Or maybe you don't realize that, Gast."

"What I do or do not realize is none of your damned business," Gast told him, getting on his bicycle and riding off.

Now that all the excitement was over, the crowd was breaking up, tradesmen going back to their shops, neighbours inside their houses.

Rolf, climbing over the fenders of the police vehicles which had been tightly grouped together to block the road, discovered a boy on his hands and knees between two cars, a dripping paintbrush in his hand. Written all over the side of a van, in red, were the words: NAZI THIEVES AND MURDERERS. Rolf grinned at the boy, who was about fourteen, very thin and very serious-looking. Policemen were approaching, and a younger boy was standing blocking them and making frantic signs behind his back.

"Run!" Rolf hoarsely advised. "Run!" But the serious youth, calculating the rate at which the police were approaching, decided he had time to finish what he was writing across the back doors of the van, through which arrested men entered, and completed the exhortation — WORKERS OF THE WORLD UNITE!

Then he ran, and Rolf, much impressed by such coolness vis à vis the cops, ran after him, gesturing to Otto to follow.

After they'd gone around corners and put several streets between themselves and any pursuers, they stopped in a doorway and pantingly introduced themselves.

"I'm Klug, Theo Klug," said the boy who'd written over the cars, "and this here is my little brother Benno. He's a bit of a mess, but he's all right," he explained, pointing to the smaller boy who'd been acting as lookout for him.

"I'm Rolf, I'm called Louse Boy. And this is Otto the Robber."

"Is he really a robber?" Benno asked.

"'Course he is, why shouldn't he be?" his brother Theo

said. "Since society's robbed *him* of his birthright, he's got every right to rob society. It's what's called poetic justice."

"We'll call you 'the Brains,'" Rolf told their new friend, "because anybody can see you're brainy."

Theo accepted his nickname without demur.

"You one of us?" he demanded of Rolf.

"What d'you mean?"

"Part of the struggle for freedom."

"Oh yes, definitely. And so is Otto," Rolf quickly said, since he liked this serious boy a great deal and did not want to lose his friendship. He had never seen anyone quite as white-looking as Theo, and now he realized this was not solely due to his natural pallor but also to the white chalk that filled his pockets and got over his hands and face. Rolf discovered this explanation, seeing Theo suddenly reach in his trousers, pull out a bit of chalk, and draw a hammer and sickle on the door against which they were leaning. He wrote the words, FIGHT WITH US FOR FREEDOM, and then with a jerk of his head signalled to the others to follow him.

Next time they stopped it was by a *Litfass* pillar plastered with cinema and theatre posters. There was a picture of the film star Christina Söderbaum, looking childlike and rape-prone, and of a Jew with hooked nose and black long hair, seemingly bent on ravishing her. Each boy looking in a different direction, when the coast was clear Theo fished inside the lining of his jacket, going in by way of a hole in the pocket, and produced a small bottle of black Indian ink and a broad-nibbed steel pen and with it wrote neatly across the prone body of Christina Söderbaum: HITLER RAPES GERMAN YOUTH.

Running again, Rolf pantingly asked: "You do this all the time, Brains?"

"Whenever I get a chance," Theo replied. "You going to come in with us?"

"I'm not much good at writing," Rolf said, out of breath.

"You can hand out leaflets."

"I'll see," Rolf promised.

"What about your friend?"

"He'll see too," Rolf said on behalf of Otto.

They continued together down the road, Benno stumbling over his untied shoelaces every so often.

"Why doesn't he tie them up?" Rolf asked Theo.

"Because he's all over the place," Theo said, "he's sloppy. I have to look after him. If I didn't he'd break his neck, he's so sloppy."

When they got to Blücher Park they sat down by the edge of the lake and threw stones at the swans, making the elegant creatures glide smartly away. There was never any danger of hitting the swift swans, they were always too quick. You could throw stones at them for the sheer pleasure of seeing them glide away beautifully. Rolf thought, if they had to, they could fly off, though he'd never seen them do that. He would have liked to be able to glide and fly like a swan.

They went to the "witch's hut" and sat on the ground and Benno shared his chocolate bar with them. While they were eating it, Theo told them, "Hitler's going to start a new war and it'll be bigger and more terrible than the last one. See, Hitler wants to destroy the Soviet Union, he wants to bring the workers of the world under the heel of his tyranny, and also war is the only way out for the bourgeoisie. See? It's the only way capitalism can continue to exist. National Socialism is the tool of the capitalist imperialists, see. Only by building an anti-Fascist popular front with reformist groups and the youth of Germany can we mobilize the masses against Hitler's war, which is also the imperialists' war."

"Wheww!" Rolf said. "I was right to call you Brains."

On the wood plank floor of the "witch's hut," Benno was writing something in chalk. They all stood around trying to make out what it said.

Rolf read it aloud:

"DOWN WITH THE NAZZI BEESTEE."
"He can't spell for toffee," Theo said, and Benno giggled.

Theo and Benno lived over towards Severins, not far from the Rheinau docks, in a stunted grey tenement building with the commonplace pebble-dash finish. Their flat was on the top floor, directly under the roof space where the water tanks were. From their windy little iron balcony (boiling hot in summer, like the whole flat, when it got the full blast of the sun) they could see the quay on the eastern bank of the Rhine where their father, Albert Klug, worked as a derrick operator unloading the long chains of motorbarges bringing coal and other industrial goods from the Ruhr. Mornings and evenings they could see the dense streams of workmen cycling to and from work over the Südbrücke.

Rolf thought he'd rather be a sailor plying the Rhine ports than a dockworker; a sailor got to see more. You could go as far as Rotterdam or Amsterdam or Antwerp, or down to France and Switzerland on the coal barges.

Rolf's mother had told him that his father, before he went to jail, years and years ago, when he was young and not married, had played the accordion on pleasure steamers that went up and down the Rhine. There was a photograph of him in a short loden jacket with horn buttons, and he had on a green felt hat with badger's tail, playing his music while people danced on the boat deck strung with faery lights.

Rolf thought perhaps he could play his guitar on the Rhine steamers and sing American swing music. That would be better than working in the docks or in the timber yards or the synthetic-rubber plant.

Since he and Otto had become friends with Theo and Benno, they'd been going down to the river a lot, mostly messing about, though Theo didn't really mess about — he always had his pockets full of chalk or other writing materials, and whenever he saw a good space anywhere he'd want to fill it with some message like YOUTH AWAKEN or WORKERS

ARISE. While Rolf and Otto kicked stones in the river, Theo told about his plans for overthrowing the Nazis.

"Who else is there coming in with you?" Rolf wanted to know.

Theo said, "There's Charlie-Blow, Black Hand, Mac the Knife, Jumbo, Sonny Boy . . . and . . . and you and the Robber."

"We going to be enough?" Rolf asked slyly. "And Otto and me aren't even all that sure."

"There's lots more are thinking about it, like you and Robber. If you two came in, I bet three or four others would too."

"I expect you're right," Rolf conceded.

Early in May, returning with Theo and Benno to their flat, they all saw a big open car outside, which was unusual because nobody in the building had a car or knew anyone who had a car.

They walked around it, suspicious and fascinated, examining the packed instrument panel, the spacious rear compartment that could seat six or seven.

"Come on," Theo said. He had suddenly become very white-faced, and was making a sign for them to follow him. They rushed inside and started up the stone steps, sticking their heads into the narrow shaft of the stairwell and looking up. They couldn't see anything, but they heard crashes and smashing sounds coming from the top floor, and running up the stairs saw neighbours standing just inside their slightly open doors, listening.

On the third floor, panting hard, they stopped momentarily to catch their breath. Screams rang out to make the blood stand still.

"That's my Mutti," Benno said, starting to cry.

Theo said, "Shut up, stupid! Shut up!"

Frau Schäfer, on the third floor, shook her finger cautioningly and made signs to them to wait in her flat, but Theo wouldn't. Making a snake of himself, he crawled up the stairs, with Benno, Rolf, and Otto following in a like manner.

All the time the smashing sounds were getting louder, and also the cries. Theo was level with the top landing when the front door of the flat flew open and he saw his father being dragged out by the hair. His face had been smashed into a pulp; one eye seemed displaced, but was open like the eye of a dead fish, while the other was covered over with swollen flesh and blood, and as he was dragged along by the hair, Brownshirts carrying firemen's axes kicked him casually in the face, the chest, the loins.

Theo could hear his mother screaming inside the flat. He made a sign to the others to slide back down to the landing below, and slithered after them, just a second or so in advance of his father being dragged down like a sack of potatoes. The door of Frau Schäfer's flat was slightly ajar and this time they accepted her urgent beckoning and went inside. Eye to spy hole, Theo watched the bloody procession go by.

When it was past, they opened the door a fraction and Theo and Benno crept out on their knees; they saw their mother at the top of the stairs, Storm Troopers pulling her by the arms.

"You stupid old sow! This is your last chance, Communist shitbag. You going to tell us where the leaflets are?"

"I don't know," she said.

One of the Brownshirts struck her across the face with the wooden handle of his fireman's axe, raising a thick blue welt in a dark stripe, which rapidly turned mauve with the pressure of blood. Her legs gave way and she fell into a muddled heap of tawdry underclothing and thick, brown, tattered stockings, and the Brownshirts began to push this heap along with their boots as if it were some kind of disgusting mess they did not wish to touch with bare hands. They pushed it to the end of the landing, this inert bundle of soiled linen, and then they pushed it over and gave it a kick, making it roll down, and when it stopped rolling they gave it another push with the toe caps of their shiny boots to make it roll another few steps.

Theo and the others had gone back inside Frau Schäfer's

flat, and through the spy hole Theo saw his mother lying on the landing like a ripped-open parcel with all its contents spilling out. Lacking the assistance of gravity, the Brownshirts worried at the unbudging pile with impatient kicks, moving it along to the edge of the next flight of stairs, where gravity once more took over, rolling her helter-skelter, bones breaking, down to the landing below, and then to the next, and finally to the street. Semiconscious, the Klugs were thrown onto the floor of the large car, and the Storm Troopers got in after them and sat with their boots on the faces of the prostrate pair.

Theo saw it from a landing window; he didn't let Benno look.

They allowed about a quarter of an hour to go by to make sure that the Brownshirts were not coming back for any reason, and then leaving Otto as a lookout on the third floor, the others went up.

The flat was a shambles. Cupboards and wardrobes that were not even locked had been axed open, floorboards ripped up, gaping holes torn out of walls. The settee was cut to shreds, the upholstery and cushions slit open. In the bedrooms the eiderdowns had been chopped to rags in a frenzy of hacking axe men; little white feathers floated about still.

In the kitchen every item of crockery had been smashed. Glass lay all over the floor. The kitchen cupboards were reduced to firewood.

Theo noted everything in this wrecked flat, like someone making an inventory. Then he told Benno to go outside the door, close it, and watch Otto, and at the first sign from him to rap three times as a warning of danger.

Now Theo got on a chair and pulled himself up through an open hatch into the roof space. The Brownshirts had been up here too, looking around among the lagged water pipes and the water tanks. Theo felt his way in the dark, dusty space beneath the flat asphalt roof: central-heating flues, ventilation shafts, bunched pipes, electrical cables, bags of cement, piles of bricks. He shifted the wooden coverings of the water tanks and put his hand inside until he touched water, and then went to the next one and the next. When he put his hand inside and did not touch water, he removed the covering, reached down into the tank, and pulled out a bundle wrapped in newspaper, and another, and another. He took these bundles to the hatch and handed them to Rolf below, climbed down, and replaced the trapdoor.

With Rolf watching him, he undid the bundles, peeling away the various protective outer layers of old dusty and yellowing newspaper, until he came, eyes glittering, to the precious contents: batches of freshly printed leaflets.

He handed one to Rolf, who read out the bold black print:

WORKERS! JOIN THE POPULAR FRONT AGAINST THE
FASCIST-IMPERIALIST WARMONGERS.

Theo opened another bundle and took out a stack of underground newssheets. The title of the paper was *Freedom*. Rolf read the quotation beneath the masthead:

FELLOW COMRADES! IT IS BETTER TO DIE ON YOUR FEET
THAN TO LIVE ON YOUR KNEES — Rosa Luxemburg.

Rolf reflected on this. He said nothing. He felt choked up by what they had witnessed and in no mood to argue. There were some things even he couldn't argue about.

Next day, after school, all four went to the Franz Clouth rubber plant in Nippes, and as the workers left to go home they had leaflets and newssheets stuffed into their hands, or into the saddlebags of their bicycles.

The boys kept their heads down and wore scarves around the lower parts of their faces.

The following morning, instead of going to school, they worked the bus terminals and railway stations, and as their stocks were beginning to diminish rapidly, they took the afternoon off to sit in the "witch's hut" in Blücher Park and learn the texts off by heart, and were able to memorize them — they tested each other — better than the poems of Schiller and Goethe that they were supposed to have learned ages ago.

The subject the class had been set was, How Everyday Life Has Changed Under National Socialism.

In the classroom absolute silence reigned, broken only by the regular squeak of pen nibs on paper and occasional clearing of throats.

After he'd written one or two sentences, Rolf stopped and looked in the direction of the high windows that offered pupils the least possible distraction: he could see the top of the caged lime tree in the playground, and a blackening sky, and that was all. There was a storm coming. The clouds were massed and sombre, and Herr Tigges had switched on the electric lights.

Rolf gave an involuntary yawn, scratched his head, and fell into a staring daze. He could put a secret spell on himself by staring at something like a spot on the ceiling or the gleam of Herr Tigges's spectacles or a bird sitting on top of the branches of the lime tree. By getting himself in such a daze, the boredom of lessons could be avoided.

"Hacker! Hacker! Since you appear to have finished ahead of everybody else, perhaps you would give the rest of the class the benefit of your quickness of mind and read them what you have written. On your feet, Hacker."

While speaking, Herr Tigges had come up close to Rolf and was now facing him, eyeball to eyeball, flecks of white spittle around his tight, small mouth.

Rolf stood up reluctantly.

"Read!" Herr Tigges ordered.

Rolf swallowed and began to read:

"The man laid in a pool of blood. He was beat to death. It was Brownshirts who'd done it kicking him in the face and

71

everywhere and they dragged him out by the hair and down the stairs and they threw his wife downstairs after him and broke all her bones . . .''

There were titters from the class as Rolf read.

"Yes?" Herr Tigges demanded.

"That's as far as I got."

"I had the impression, from the fact that you had stopped working and were looking out of the window, that you had finished your essay."

"I couldn't think what else to write."

"Couldn't think! Very well — let us take what you have written so far. 'He was beat to death'? What's wrong with that?"

Rolf scratched his head, clowning.

"It's ungrammatical. It should be . . . yes? . . . yes? Anyone?"

"Beaten," a bright pupil offered.

"Beaten to death, Hacker. The past participle of the verb to beat is 'beaten.' " He paused and his face assumed its accustomed sarcastic expression. "And what film, American, no doubt, inspired you to such bloodthirsty inventions?"

"It wasn't a film, sir. It happened before my eyes. I seen it happen."

"You saw a man beaten to death, and his wife thrown downstairs?"

"Yes, sir."

"How d'you know he was beaten to death? Are you a doctor, Hacker? Did you take his pulse? Did you listen to his heart?"

"No, sir."

"Then how can you know?"

"They kept beating him."

"He was probably a criminal, a gangster of the kind you and your friends admire so much."

Rolf said nothing; he could feel the entire class's hostility towards him. He didn't have any friends here.

72

"You're a little gangster yourself, from what I hear, Hacker. Isn't that so? A thief and a hooligan and a louse boy. Isn't that your nickname?"

"Yes, sir."

"And so, naturally, you side with one of your own sort. I think we may take it that if this man you speak of was subjected to some strong treatment at the hands of the authorities, it was because he had amply earned such treatment." Herr Tigges paused, allowing himself to wax philosophical for a moment. "The maintenance of a state of order in society does sometimes require taking firm, even harsh action. A great nation cannot be ruled by a bunch of milksops. I commend to you all a quotation from Goethe: 'I would rather put up with an injustice than tolerate a state of disorder.' Disorder is something the German spirit does not tolerate readily. And speaking of disorder, Hacker . . ." He picked up Rolf's exercise book and held it up for everybody to see: this offensive, disgusting article. "Look at it, Hacker! Ink blots everywhere. Every page full of grubby finger marks, every page dog-eared. Your handwriting! Your spelling! Beyond belief—beyond . . ." He became speechless. "Like the scratchings of ape-men. You are disorder incarnate, Hacker."

"I didn't think I was as good as all that, sir," Rolf piped up.

"Shut your filthy mouth, refuse of the streets!"

"Are you talking to me, sir?" Rolf innocently asked. "Because, I remind you, sir, I'm Rolf, not Refuse."

"Shut your mouth, you insolent boy!"

Going home it was raining and cold, with the wind blowing the rain right into his face. It stung. He tried walking backwards: that didn't help a lot, the rain just went in his collar. He didn't have a raincoat. He put his school satchel on his head when it started really pelting down, but even so was soaked by the time he got home, and sneezing and shivering.

His mother was very cross with him that he had got so wet. As if it was his fault! He couldn't help the rain, could he? She kept wanting to put her red wool scarves around him. When

73

Franzi came home she got him to take off his wet clothes and wrap himself in a blanket, and made him hot cocoa.

It was cold in the flat. He wanted to make a fire but Franzi said there wasn't any coal, she'd already looked. They hadn't expected a cold day like this in May.

She pressed her mouth on his bare back and blew her warm breath all over him, giving him warm shivers.

"Promise me something, Rolfiele," his mother said. "Promise me you'll be a good boy. Don't take after your Papa. Promise me that."

"I promise, Mutti."

There were times when Rolf's mother was fairly normal in her behaviour and speech, if nothing had upset her to trigger off one of her spells. She just sat there all day knitting scarves. But she never cleaned her room or changed her sheets, and she didn't do any cooking and wouldn't have eaten if Franzi hadn't shopped and cooked. Franzi had to do all that when she came home from school. They lived on welfare payments and sickness benefits. Mutti was "not all there" at times, but you wouldn't have thought that she was out of her mind, really. Old Dr. Leventhal said it was "the change"—"the change of life," he sometimes called it—and that a lot of women who'd had a difficult life and suffered with their nerves had these "funny spells." Once they'd adjusted to "the change," they often got completely better. Rolf and Franzi would have to look after their mother and not mind that she was peculiar occasionally.

FOUR

After his cocoa, Rolf met Otto down the road and they walked in the rain, getting themselves soaked. But they preferred to be out. What could you do at home?

They had been going from one haunt to another; now they were sheltering in the doorway of a little corner tobacconist's in a dreary narrow street that ran diagonally between Subbelratherstrasse and Venloerstrasse, sharing their last cigarette. Rolf took a long puff, inhaled, and passed the butt to Otto.

"About time you did another robbery, Robber," Rolf said. "It's ages since you did one."

"You don't want to rob just anything," Otto said. "Just for the sake of it. You got to rob something worth robbing, or there's no point. See?"

"I think you're losing your touch, Robber," Rolf said provokingly.

"Just keep your filthy trap shut, little squirt," Otto said.

"Call yourself a robber!" Rolf mocked. He couldn't help it. Sometimes he just had to mock. He thought Otto was going to hit him and was ready to run for it. But just then old man Rumpf the coalman came by on his open cart, yelling at the steaming horses, and Rolf dug Otto in the ribs.

"Yes," Otto said, eyes gleaming, "y-e-e-e-s."

A few houses along, Rumpf reined the horses to a stop and got down from his high cab to make a delivery. He wore a big oilskin hood over his head and shoulders, and was bent low from the bag of coal on his back; he wasn't looking anywhere except at his feet.

"We can do it easy," Rolf said. "He'll never see us."

The coalman was returning to his cart; he threw the empty bag in the back, and laboriously hoisted himself up by the metal footholds to his driving post. He cracked his whip and shouted, *"Jeeyyupp!"* The cart creaked forward slowly, bits of coal falling off the back, but Rolf and Otto were not satisfied with such droppings today. They followed at a distance of ten paces, hearts pounding, and watched how Rumpf called *"WHOOOAaaaa"* to his horses, pulled on the reins, and then put on his handbrake; he climbed down from his perch and went to the back of the cart, dropped the tailboard, and reached in to pull a bag of coal forward. Bent low and reaching behind him, he eased the load onto his back, and then walked with slow deliberation to the coal hole. With his copious headgear and the rain coming down thickly, he was inside a curtain. Even if he saw Rolf and Otto as they followed his cart he paid no attention to them, being used to kids following him and picking up bits of coal that he left in the streets. He just wanted to be finished and home on this chilly wet day, with the light fading rapidly; but he still had one or two deliveries to make, due to the unseasonal cold spell.

"Let's do it now, Robber," Rolf said. He couldn't stand his heart beating so hard much longer.

They worked it out between them.

When old man Rumpf made his next stop and was once more staggering away, weighed down, Rolf jumped quickly onto the back of the cart and dragged a sack of coal to the tailboard, where Otto stood ready. Rolf gave a push—and looked nervously to see where the coalman was. He wasn't looking around, he was setting down his bag, prising up the grating. Rolf said, "Go on, Robber, go," and with a little shove gave him the bag on his back. Otto nearly collapsed under the weight, but he was a strong boy and recovered. Staggering, he moved slowly down the street.

Rolf watched nervously as the coalman finished his delivery, folded up his bag, and returned towards his cart, stooping low the whole time. This had become his normal gait. He saw only the rain dripping down from his hood.

Rolf, hiding by the side of the cart, watched him throw his empty bag in the back, put up the tailboard, and insert the toggles, and that was when he straightened up, as much as he could after all these years, and saw Otto staggering off through the rain.

Rage made him stand up straight and shake his fist, and he started after the thief; Otto, weighed down, was rapidly overtaken, and seeing he was about to be grabbed, he let go of the bag of coal and took off at full speed. Unladen, he was able to get away easily and Rumpf stopped the futile pursuit. Glaring around, he saw Rolf running in the other direction, and began to shout, "Stop, thieves! Stop, thieves!"

Rolf ran with all his might: he'd be safe once he was round the corner in Subbelratherstrasse, he could disappear there. There was a beerhall ahead. Workmen had come out, alerted by the shouts. If they tried to stop him, he'd dodge them. He was good at running rings round people. There was someone standing in his way now, arms outspread. Rolf ran straight at him and at the last second threw himself sideways, like a footballer dashing for a goal, and he was round him, and around the next man who tried to block him, and the next

77

one as well. He was weaving his way around all these men — only to rush straight into a massive form, like a fall of rocks, sheer, unbudging fat, against which he struggled in vain. His ear had been caught in a steel clamp, and though he was kicking and biting and scratching and punching, he couldn't free himself, not without leaving his ear behind.

It was Fat Schlammer who'd got him by the ear, and now was dragging him along by it, as if pulling a mule along.

"It's the cops for you this time, Louse Boy," Schlammer said.

*   *   *

Much occupied with making the best possible use of opportunities that presented themselves, or might present themselves, Gast had been mulling over the fact that Detective Nold had recently transferred from the Police Presidium to the *Staatspolizeistelle* in the EL-DE-Haus.

At times in the past the policeman had been obliged to warn Gast about some of his activities — introducing girls to men, that kind of thing — and Gast had taken these warnings to heart and introduced the policeman to one or two suitable girls, and after that had had no further trouble from Nold, had indeed come to consider him a good connection.

How to make the best use of his good connection now that he was working for the Gestapo? To have a policeman in his pocket (more or less) was useful, but Gast felt sure that a man of the Gestapo, with a weakness for women, must be even more useful, if not now then *one of these days*. Gast being a man to cultivate his connections, he decided to pay Nold a visit: he would discuss with him the problem of youth offences, and get a foot in the door.

A foot in the door of the EL-DE-Haus! The thought of that had a macabre appeal. The screams of the Gestapo's victims were said to rise up out of the pavements of the Appellhofplatz, from the cellars and dungeons below. No doubt that was exaggerated. He had often crossed the Appellhofplatz without hearing any screams.

From the way people talked, you would have expected a Gothic castle of infamy, with torture chambers and the rest of it, instead of which it was a modern corner house, in the plain post-war style, with wrought-iron window boxes. There were no flowers in the window boxes. You could not expect flowers. It was like a modern block of flats, with a quite ordinary glass entrance door, and iron lanterns each side. The only rather sinister aspect of the place was that when the lights of all the other offices in the street had been extinguished, those in the EL-DE-Haus blazed still — the whole night long, often. The *Geheime Staatspolizei* were known to work late hours. Arrests were usually made in the middle of the night, necessitating the presence of a permanent night staff at the office.

Arriving to see Nold, Gast found a cramped little entrance hall on the ground floor, like a tramways terminal where people sit around for many hours. It was sometimes a long wait to see the Gestapo. Either the Gestapo wished to see you, in which case there was no waiting at all, at least not in a public waiting room, or, if you wished to see them, for any reason, you might have to wait a very long time. The Gestapo were very busy.

Gast, however, had an appointment, since he had a position in the Party and was also known personally to Nold.

There was a big board in the hall, showing all the departments on the different floors. He found Nold's name above Oppositional Youth Groups, Unruliness and Unrest, Youth Offences, Enemies of the People, Corruption of Minors, Street Gangs. Sub-section C6, Room 77b, Third Floor.

Gast took the lift up, walked along a corridor of parquet-patterned linoleum, at the end turned right and Room 77b was in front of him. He knocked and was told to come in.

Nold sat behind a green metal desk. Sunlight came in through the venetian blinds, slicing through the pall of cigarette smoke in the small, full office.

From his briefcase Gast produced a bottle of champagne

wrapped in pink crepe paper and garnished with a satin ribbon tied in a bow.

"For your mother," he said. "I hear she's been in hospital. To wish her better."

"Good of you, Herr Gast. But I'm sorry to say she died some weeks ago."

"What a shame! She was a fine old lady. Well — the champagne won't get wasted, I'm sure."

Nold put the champagne away in a drawer of the green metal desk and gave a lopsided smile in which one half of his face did not participate at all.

"Drink a toast to the memory of the old lady for me," Gast requested.

"Did you know her, then?"

"Not personally, no, I didn't have that honour."

"Ah! *Ah!*" There was a pause. "What can I do for you, Herr Gast?"

Gast spread his hands. "Nothing in particular. I like to keep in touch. Cigarette?" He offered his silver cigarette case, clicked open, one side displaying cork tips, the other Schwarz-Weiss filtreless. Taking the proferred case to help himself, Nold admired the gold script embossment, *"Herr Gast."* He took a Schwarz-Weiss and returned the case.

"Present from a satisfied customer?"

"You've guessed it."

"What line of business are you in these days?"

"This and that."

"It seems to be profitable. You look more prosperous than the last time I saw you. Those waiters' suits can get very shiny after a while."

"I was lucky in certain of my investments."

Nold drew cigarette smoke deeply into his lungs and was racked by a violent bout of coughing.

"On the phone you said you wanted to talk to me about the problem of the young," Nold reminded him, still gasping a little.

80

"Yes, they are a problem. Wild youth! Swing youth! A problem. There is a tremendous lot of hooliganism in the streets these days. It seems to be on the rise."

Nold nodded.

"What can be done about it, in your view?"

"Not a lot." Nold gave his lopsided smile, half his face grim.

"Why is that?"

"Boys will be boys. No?"

"True, absolutely true," Gast conceded. "But some of this goes too far. Have you seen the stuff they write on walls? Not merely obscene, you understand me. *Subversive.*"

"What d'you want me to do about it?"

"Catch some of them, teach them a lesson."

"The little buggers are difficult to catch, they have lookouts, and young legs. They can run fast." He coughed violently again. "Faster'n me."

"You people have weapons."

Nold blinked several times. He wiped smoke from the corners of his eyes.

"They're children," he pointed out. "Ten-, twelve-, thirteen-year-olds, some of them."

"Some are older. Look — I don't suggest you fire to kill. Your men could fire in the air. Call on the louts to stop or else. Give them a good scare."

"They don't scare so easy, Herr Gast, that sort."

"*Something* has got to be done. It's a state of affairs that can't be allowed to continue. Young boys of the *Hitlerjugend* are beat up all the time. I had to intervene recently, I just saved two boys from being almost killed. Young girls — girls of the German Girls League — are subjected to lewd propositions. I didn't think young children knew what such words meant."

"They know a lot more than we think, these days," Nold said.

"There I agree with you." He paused, looked around, smiling. "Well — of course — it's your department. I'm merely

81

an outsider in this, an amateur. The man in the street, so to speak. Though as street leader I do have certain duties. But I'm sure you do what you can. However, if you want to call upon me for assistance in any way . . . I came by so that we would be in touch with each other, it's always useful to know somebody in your position. And for my part, I also can be of help sometimes." He paused, having thought of something suddenly.

"D'you know The Rio?"

"I've heard about it," Nold said.

"I'm often there," Gast said. "A congenial place." He laughed. "The atmosphere is congenial. Lovely girls. If you ever feel like dropping in, we can have a drink together. If I'm not there, just tell them you're my guest." He took a plain business card out of his pocket, wrote something on it, and passed it across to Nold.

He stood up.

"Let us keep in touch. Hmm? Heil Hitler!"

Nold replied, "Heil Hitler!," raising one hand at shoulder level in a somewhat slovenly rendering of the salute.

When Gast had left, the detective took an indigestion mixture from his drawer and swallowed a spoonful.

He was going to have to do something about these street kids. Hardened thieves, some of them, at ten or eleven — like this louse boy Rolf, caught stealing coal off a cart. Now Gast had brought up the matter, this sort of offence couldn't be dismissed lightly. You never knew how much power these Party men wielded.

He picked up Gast's card and put it away inside his wallet. He made a sour grimace. The Rio. Yes, he'd heard about The Rio.

It worried Gast what Franzi got up to when she went off on her own.

Now he was following her on his bike as she cycled up Subbelratherstrasse slowly. Periodically she dismounted and

82

wheeled her bike past the shops, looking in windows
. . . imagining herself in some outfit or other. She stayed so
long outside one dress shop that the shopkeeper came out
and tried to encourage her to enter, but she shook her head
and went away. She obviously had no money.

Following her from shop to shop, he thought of offering to
buy her some of the things she wanted. She was enraptured
by sheer stockings, by lacy underthings, by blouses, by hats
with nose veils that were much too grown-up for her, by
delicate high-heeled shoes with exquisitely tapering heels.
Even from a distance he could see, or sense, how her eyes
shone as she peered at the tempting displays.

Gast would have bought these things for her gladly (or
obtained them by one means or another) had he judged the
moment ripe. But it was not. One false move — buying her
clothes! — and the ever-suspicious mother would denounce
him as a corrupter of little children. That was all he needed!
Such a denunciation could wreck his chances of further advancement in the Party. The Party could be quite sticky about
sexual offences. (Monks who in the course of their nursing
duties were obliged to hold the penises of their sclerotic pa-
tients had been arraigned for homosexuality.) One could not
be too careful — especially in the case of a girl who was
under-age.

It was getting late and shops were shutting. But she continued along Subbelratherstrasse, the upper end of which was
much less lively, with shops further apart and smaller, and
offering less expensive goods. She wasn't so interested now,
judging from her expressions. What would she do? Go home?

One more shoe shop to look at. She stopped in front of it.
How could anyone look so long at shoes? Gast was becoming
very impatient as he waited two or three doorways along,
peeping out every so often to see what she was doing.

He had decided long ago never to run after a bus or a
woman, there was always another one along in a few minutes: that was his attitude. But his passion for Franzi overrode

83

his former philosophies of life. He was prepared to devote more time and effort to her. Even so, this was getting to be too much — he was a busy man, and Lena Bott, of lesser interest but paying a more immediate dividend, was at the apartment, her continuing tenancy dependent on receiving him in her bed at whatever time of day or night he chose.

He noticed that the shoemaker had come out of his shop and was talking to Franzi, smilingly indicating shoes in his window that he thought would suit her. She was shaking her head, probably telling him she had no money. He appeared to make light of this, urged her to come in· take a look round, no obligation. He had a persuasive manner. Avuncular. An older man. In his fifties. Wore a cobbler's leather apron. More of a shoe mender than a retailer of shoes, but he did have some to sell as well. Judging from his shabby little shop, and his shabby appearance, they would not be particularly smart shoes, and yet Franzi was allowing herself to be persuaded to go in.

Gast waited. He could not leave now, while she was in the shop. Once the shopkeeper discovered she really had no money, he would soon send her on her way. But after ten minutes she was still not out and Gast decided to see what was going on; he strolled by the window and saw that, despite having no money, she was trying on shoes. There were half a dozen boxes open on the floor and the cobbler was climbing his high ladder and bringing down more. Gast watched him unwrap shoes and hold them up for Franzi's inspection and approval. These would suit her, they were very pretty, very smart. They would look lovely on her, he insisted. Squatting in a rather wobbly fashion, he took off the shoes she was wearing and slipped on the ones he had just brought down. They were a little tight. He found talcum powder, sprinkled it on his hands, and powdered her stockinged feet. Still a bit tight? It was necessary to make her push, push hard, while he held the shoe against himself — push, push, he insisted, and she laughingly pushed and was in. Ouch! they're tight, her expression said. He said they'd stretch with wear, and to try wriggling her toes. Which she did. And then he wanted her to rotate her ankle and she did that, too, laughing. No, they really were too tight. He took off the shoes again and rested her foot in his lap, having seated himself on the floor, and tried more talcum powder. Then, as if remembering suddenly, he got up and pulled the shutter down three-quarters of the way.

"I'm closed," he told the man standing at the door.

On his knees, pushing his head to the ground, Gast could see Franzi raising first one and then the other foot to enable the cobbler to try more shoes on her. She was becoming very careless about keeping her skirt drawn down over her knees, or keeping her legs together, and only the uncomfortableness of his position, with the blood pounding to his head, forced Gast to stand up without seeing the outcome. But he feared the worst.

These fears were reinforced when, five minutes later, just as he was about to start banging on the door of the shop, Franzi came out, wearing a pair of new high-heeled shoes of midnight-blue patent leather. She wobbled in them to her bike, and only when it was clear she would not be able to cycle in them did she take them off and put on her old strap shoes.

*   *   *

Most days Dr. Leupold arrived at his office in the *Generalstaatsanwaltschaft* by the side entrance of the district court building and then took the lift up to the fourth floor. But sometimes, as today, he chose to enter by the pillared main entrance in the Reichensperger Platz and climb the great sweep of curving marble stairs under their echoing glass dome, finding in this more ceremonious arrival a fitting reaffirmation of the gravity of his function as public prosecutor.

Since the advent of the New Order, his office had acquired additional responsibilities, with a progressive blurring of the distinctive roles of judge and prosecutor. With the new powers and initiatives granted to someone in his position, Dr. Leupold had to bear the burden of knowing that in many instances it was mandatory upon the court to accept his demands, and there were now almost forty categories of crime for which he was able to demand the death penalty.

Dr. Leupold was a "true Roman," with the patrician nose of the Caesars, and like his distinguished forebears was accustomed to administering the law in the name of the king; authoritarianism was part of his family tradition and he did not shrink from the additional powers given him. Unlike some other occupiers of his office, he did not dispose of these powers callously or recklessly. Dr. Leupold belonged to a class of men who considered that part of serving their king was to instruct and educate him, and even though Dr. Leupold was not optimistic about the possibility of being able to educate Hitler, he liked to think of himself as a moderating influence in a time of extremism. He was a man of God, a Catholic — his brother was Cardinal Leupold — and a person of great scrupulousness. He tried to administer the law with justice and compassion, even in these difficult times, when seemingly intelligent and rational people were maintaining that since National Socialism and justice were inseparable, there should be no distinction at all between judge and State prosecutor.

When he argued against such revolutionary concepts, it was attributed to his conservatism and to his attachment to legal niceties, and not to any fundamental opposition to the regime; and Dr. Leupold, aware of his Christian duty not to get himself killed if he could help it, exercised discretion in his espousal of "older values," as also did his brother the Cardinal. Both considered that they could be of greater service to their cause alive rather than dead, and from within the New Order rather than from without, and so sought to reconcile their personal beliefs with service to the State.

At their first meeting, in 1935, Hitler had said to Dr. Leupold, "Leupold, I need your help," and the prosecutor had promised to give it, without, be believed, compromising his honour. Whatever he might think of Hitler, he was the legally appointed Chancellor and Head of State. It was a fraught and difficult period for the Church and the judiciary; the Pope having no divisions, the Leupolds had to rely on their education at the hands of the Jesuits to hold their own against the new pagans. When a man lacked other means of defending himself and his values, God did not forbid secrecy and cunning as means to an end.

In appearance, Dr. Leupold was a gravely handsome man, tall, thin, with a domed forehead and a monocled eye, given to wearing dark suits of good, plain materials, white shirts, black shoes. A widower with two sons, one of eighteen, the other of twenty, he lived with them in a large apartment in the *Altstadt*, where his unmarried sister, Marthe, kept house for them.

Now as he made his contemplative and stately ascent by the balustered stairs, he was in a sombre mood, sensing that for all the efforts of honourable men, the country was marching inexorably towards catastrophe. The people in Berlin were becoming intoxicated with their "total power"; it was madness, madness — a frenzy of self-exaltation; all restraints were being abandoned, reason, logic, and legality sacrificed to "the sound feeling of the people," a very dubious criterion, on the basis of which much law now had to be practised, in a spirit of vendetta and vengeance.

Dr. Leupold sought to mitigate the worst excesses, clinging to "the rule of law" in the face of prejudice and vindictiveness. But legal arguments were becoming increasingly academic and parochial, considering that the country was bent upon war, no longer possessing a mind of its own, following slavishly its hypnotic Führer. Dreadful, dreadful! Who could stop the calamity? Dr. Leupold was appalled by how many of his friends and associates were infected by the madness. He could not express his fears for the future in case they would consider him to be of a "deviant nature." Doubters were guilty of self-subversion. Therefore he had to keep his apprehensions largely to himself, sharing them only with his brother the Cardinal to whom he was able to talk in their private language, quoting chapter and verse: "the Beast that riseth from the sea," he would remark, and the Cardinal understood exactly.

As far as others were concerned, he hid his feelings behind a grave demeanour, a formal manner: his attitude was correct, his language carefully chosen, and his monocle always firmly in place. People could not recall seeing him without it, and the humorous journals and the cabarets had in laxer times chosen to speculate as to whether he even removed the eyeglass in his most private moments, so much was it part of his *imago*.

The truth was that he did not wear the monocle for optical reasons but because he suffered from a tic of the left eye that degenerated into a wild spasm of nervous winking at times and was arrested only by the solid wedge of glass. When he was alone, he did remove the monocle and let his eye twitch and grimace and the cold tears run down his cheek. He was not willing to make a public spectacle of himself, however.

Arriving at the top of the marble stairs and pausing for a moment to regain his breath, Dr. Leupold was approached by one of his law clerks.

"Herr Generalstaatsanwalt, there are two individuals here, claiming to have an appointment."

"Who are they, Bendler?"

"One is a policeman called Nold, or rather a member of the Gestapo, it seems. And with him there is a . . . well, a *Rotzbub*."

"Ah yes," Dr. Leupold said. "It's quite true, they do have an appointment. I will see them. Send them in to me at . . ." He looked at the time on his pocket watch. ". . . at quarter to ten, Bendler."

Rolf couldn't understand what was going on. This was the third place he'd been taken to. First, the police station. The usual. A few kicks and slaps. But instead of letting him off with a warning, as in the past, this time they'd taken him to the EL-DE-Haus. To see somebody in the Gestapo. Well, it was only old Nold. He'd asked all sorts of stupid questions about "Edelweiss Pirates," and about some of the songs. It was just a bag of coal, Rolf kept saying, that's all it was. Now they'd brought him to the *Oberlandesgericht,* this huge great building where they sentenced people to death. Come in by the main entrance too. Up hundreds of marble stairs, and then along endless corridors, and he'd heard Nold ask for the Generalstaatsanwalt, Dr. Leupold.

The public prosecutor himself wanted to see Rolf. Crikey! Jesus Christ, what did I do?

At quarter to ten sharp they were shown into the prosecutor's office. Rolf stood slouched, hands in pockets, before the big desk while Dr. Leupold examined him closely, saying nothing at first.

"This is the little robber," he said to Nold.

"Yes, Herr Generalstaatsanwalt."

"A coal thief! They start young nowadays. How old are you, Rolf?"

"Ten and a half."

"Has nobody ever taught you how to behave, Rolf? How do you address your superiors. Hmm? And how do you stand? Come on, take your hands out of your pockets."

"It's long to say Herr General-staats-anwalt all the time." He drew out the title to make it even longer than it was.

"You could say it sometimes, as a sign of respect," Dr. Leupold observed mildly, adding, "I can see you're a comedian."

"What, me?"

"Yes, you. A cheeky little devil, hmm? You think it's clever. You think it's clever to steal coal and hang around with other good-for-nothings."

Rolf said nothing. He looked down.

"Well, answer me. Don't be afraid."

"I'm not afraid."

"I can see you aren't. Usually people *are,* when brought to this office. Do you know who I am, Rolf?"

"The big bad wolf?"

"Of whom you're not afraid? Hmm? Hmmm?" he mused. He rose and slowly came round to Rolf's side of the desk, pulled up a chair, and sat down. He indicated for Rolf and Nold to sit down too.

"I'm the prosecutor, Rolf. It is for me to bring criminals to justice and to ask the court to impose the sentences their crimes deserve."

"Like the death sentence, Herr General . . . ?"

"Sometimes. You're still not afraid, Rolf?" Dr. Leupold smiled at the boy.

"Nahhh. You don't scare me, Herr General," Rolf said with a show of defiance.

"Courage is a virtue, Rolf. But bravado is not. Your kind of showing off can get you in a lot of trouble." Dr. Leupold noticed the blood clot around the top of Rolf's ear, and turned the boy's head to examine the lesion.

"What happened to your ear?"

"Fat Schlammer tore it. He practically tore it off. Pulling me by the ear."

"How did that happen?" Dr. Leupold looked at Nold.

"He was trying to run away and had to be detained."

"By the ear?"

Dr. Leupold examined the stitches, not yet removed, where the ear had been partially torn from the side of the head.

"He struggled very hard. They can be like wild animals. . . ."

90

"And Schlammer hung on to him by the ear?"

"So it would appear, Herr Generalstaatsanwalt."

"That's not true," Rolf chimed in. "He dragged me along by it. He dragged me all the way by the ear with all his strength, all the way to the cops. Fat sodding pig's arsehole!"

"Who is this Schlammer?"

"He's the one who apprehended the boy."

"Has he been charged — has he been charged with causing grievous bodily harm to a minor? If not, he should be."

"As far as I know, Herr Generalstaatsanwalt, no, he has not been charged. He was acting in a quasi-official capacity. He holds the position of *Blockleiter*."

"Ah yes, one of those." Dr. Leupold appeared to accept this explanation as being sufficient. "The wound has been sewn up professionally," he observed, and dismissed the matter. "You must be asking yourself, Rolf, why the public prosecutor should concern himself with the theft of a bag of coal, hmm?"

Rolf shrugged and Dr. Leupold reached behind him and took a substantial file from his desk.

"All that about me?"

"Not all about you, personally. It's about you and children like you. The unruliness that gets into you." He turned the pages of the report. "There appears to be quite a movement of . . . of mass disobedience among a certain class of children of your background. Their parents are at their wit's end to cope with you. While the vast majority of the young people of today are imbued with a new spirit of idealism and the desire for 'self-overcoming,' a small minority appear to have taken the opposing path, wishing only to wallow in the gutter, to engage in unruliness of every kind, to spit in the faces of their elders and betters. To defy authority. I think it behooves us to ask ourselves what our children are trying to say to us by means of such antisocial behaviour. I was wondering if you could, perhaps, help me there, Rolf."

"Me? Help *you* . . . Herr General?"

"Yes. Why d'you do it?"

"What?"

"Steal coal, for example."

"We were cold. It was a wet, cold day."

"And why do you beat up *Hitlerjugend?*"

"They're our enemy, aren't they?"

"I don't know. Are they? Why are they your enemy? According to the regulations you should be in the *Hitlerjugend* yourself."

"We hate them."

Dr. Leupold turned the pages of the report in his lap. "Not long ago, you and your friend Otto apparently became involved in a fight with some *Hitlerjugend*, in which three or four of them received injuries of such severity that they had to go to hospital for stitches."

"They attacked us first. Addi pushed me."

"I gather he was exercising his legitimate function as your group führer and leader of the *Strafendienst* patrol, inquiring why you hadn't turned up for the activities of your unit."

"I left," Rolf said. "I'm not in it anymore."

"You're not permitted to leave. Membership is obligatory on everyone of your age."

"Me and my friends, we don't believe in it."

"I see. You don't believe in it," Dr. Leupold said in wonderment. "You think you and your friends can decide what you do and do not believe in and act accordingly. Ignore laws and regulations that apply to everyone else."

"They can't make us, can they?"

"Oh, I think they can, Rolf. Amongst your other offences, I see, is defacing public notices, writing obscenities on walls, making jokes about the government and the Führer, failure to give the German greeting, replacing it instead with mocking salutes of your own. *Howdewitza? Heil Benny Goodman?*"

"We like Benny Goodman. We like swing."

"But not German music? Only American."

"We don't like that stuff that the HJs sing."

"These songs that you sing, where d'you get them?"

"I dunno. You hear them. You sort of pick them up."

"For instance, this one—" Dr. Leupold read from the file before him:

> Hitler's rule makes us small,
> We are in chains still.
> But some day we will be free,
> Some day we will break the chains.
> Because our fists are tough,
> And our knives are loose
> To fight for the freedom of youth.
>
> Navajos!

"Where did you get that one?"

"You pick up a bit here and a bit there, and you add on a bit."

"It's subversive. You know what subversive means?"

"It means being against all the ones who run everything."

"It means you can get into a lot of trouble singing songs like that."

"I know. I *am* in a lot of trouble. Or I wouldn't be here, would I?"

"It's beginning to dawn on you, then."

"Yah, it's dawned on me, you could say."

"Has it sunk in? Since when have you been a member of the 'Mobsters'?"

"We just go around together sometimes."

"And steal together, and deface public notices together. And sing subversive songs together. You're quite a little revolutionary. Why d'you do it? To be different from all the rest? To show your contempt for those older than you, with more experience of life? Is it just for the sheer perverse desire to be against what other people are for?"

"What some others are for, it's not hard to be against, Herr General."

"It's obvious that you are a congenital lawbreaker and—"

"What's *congenital* mean?"

"From birth."

"It wasn't from birth, Herr General. I didn't start till I was about two."

"*Two?*" Dr. Leupold smiled. "Took a little while to come out, did it? There are people like you, Rolf, who seem to think that laws are made for everybody else but not them. Don't you realise, Rolf, that without laws we would all be savages? We'd be like wild animals. Each out just for his own satisfaction. There have to be principles on the basis of which we conduct our lives." He paused. "You may think there is nothing much that can be done to you, because of your age. I warn you not to count on that, Rolf. These are very dangerous pirate games you are playing, and one of these days you may find that you have got in deeper than you realise." He got up and returned to the chair behind his desk, turned through pages in a file. "I have here a recommendation from your street leader, Herr Gast. He proposes that as your mother is not a fit person to look after you, and as your sister is still at school, a place be found for you in a State youth hostel. For my part, I am ready to support his recommendation. I think such a hostel will do you a lot of good. You'll be taught discipline. You'll be given strenuous activities to keep you out of trouble. I think it's the best solution. The hostel will make a man of you — with luck!"

"I don't want to go to the hostel, Herr General."

"Consider yourself lucky, if Herr Gast is able to find you a place. Not everyone gets in, it's considered a privilege. Anyway, it won't do you any harm."

"I don't want to go . . ."

"You'll have to go, like it or not. And that's the end of it." He stood up to dismiss them both.

Being in the Gestapo had not improved Nold's disposition, or indigestion. There was a burning all the time around his heart and in his stomach, and lower down a dull kind of

94

nagging lust. He was a bachelor who frequented prostitutes. They did not satisfy his craving, but temporarily his spleenful passion was appeased.

He was a thin, taut man, with a pitted face, the result of adolescent skin inflammations that had plagued him for years but were now burnt out. His eyes were flecked with green and yellow, and cynical. He had a low opinion of humanity. Most people were contemptible, some more so than others, and the worst were those who thought highly of themselves while their hearts were the blackest of the lot. Herr Gast was in this category: a cheap little pimp and petty gangster, puffed up with self-importance because he had half a dozen Brownshirt thugs to do his dirty work and push people around. Thought he was somebody. Considered that he was going up in the world, which perhaps he was, you could never know: plenty of these bastards were making their way into the upper echelons of the Party bureaucracy. They propagated their own kind like rats infesting a sewer. Nothing surprised Nold in this world, and it didn't surprise him that such arseholes were climbing to positions of power, all frantically scratching each other's backs.

Gast had a prosperous air. They all had their rackets. The whole Party system at the local level was one big racket, with rake-offs for every jumped-up little hanger-on who happened to be in a position he could exploit. The system of mutual denunciation that the Party promoted was carte blanche for the blackmailer with access to the inflowing information. The Jews were another good racket for Party men, who always got in first at compulsory sell-offs of Jewish property and valuables. The word went around in the district where there was a fat Jew to milk—diamonds going incredibly cheap.

Somehow none of these advantages had come his way, even now that he was in the Gestapo. He had schemed to get himself in, but much good it had done him! They had put him in "Oppositional Elements," subsection Children and

Youths. No rake-offs there. Nothing but street louts. Kids who wrote on walls and robbed cigarette machines. No profit in that for him. These kids had no money to pay you off. They just spat in your face.

Walking back to his room in the Aachenerstrasse, he felt in his pocket for his keys and found the card Gast had given him: The Rio. He'd heard about it. One of the bars where Gast used to work. Nold knew what that meant; he had once or twice come close to arresting Gast for his pimping activities. Gast had passed him girls in those days, and he might do so again now. Of a better class than the sort he could afford on a policeman's pay.

Why not? He had nothing to do at home in his furnished room. Fry himself some eggs on the gas ring, a bit of sausage and bread, and to bed. He didn't read. Books bored him, and the newspapers were full of lies. He did like music — Beethoven, the symphonies. The big stuff with a lot of sound. But his landlady objected if he played the symphonies too loud. Disturbed other tenants. She didn't know he was in the Gestapo now, thought he was still an ordinary policeman. He would tell her soon, enjoy giving her a little shudder.

But not now. The prospect of going to his room, to the hissing gas fire, the brown mock-oak wallpaper, the cold bathroom with the stained bath, the smelly little toilet with the linoleum coming up, mouldering in the corners — the prospect of returning to all that sickened him. He preferred to spend his evenings off in bars, getting steadily, quietly drunk. Drink never made him noisy or obviously inebriated. After a fixed amount, he was ready for a woman, and would hang around certain street corners to look over the possibilities. Sometimes there was one who was new to it and young, but that was rare. That sort tended to work in expensive bars and clubs, instead of walking the streets.

The Rio, Nold thought. I'll try it. What have I got to lose? If that rat Gast is paying the bill.

Being in the Gestapo should be worth something!

The prospect of making Gast pay lifted his spirits, and made his mouth form a sour smile. Charge it to Gast, he thought, and chuckled.

A tram was coming and he was just able to catch it. He stayed by the pneumatic doors, smoking, and got off at Neumarkt. He remembered that The Rio was in one of the little side streets off the square, and wandered around looking for it for five minutes, until he caught sight of the neon sign. There were some stairs to go down, and then it became very dark, suddenly, pleasantly so, as far as Nold was concerned. He was more at home in the dark. It was a relief not to be seen too clearly. Alcohol helped too. He was glad to perceive, as he felt his way towards a table, that in this darkness there were gleaming areas of flesh. Expensive flesh, no doubt, but so what?

He was beginning to cheer up.

In reply to the waiter who asked what he wished, Nold handed over the card that Gast had given him. Take the gentleman's coat? No, no, Nold said, hanging on to his mackintosh; he was not going to incur cloakroom charges in a place like this if Gast's invitation turned out not to be good.

While he waited, he looked around. The two girls sitting up at the bar, chattering madly to each other, were pretty and young, as far as he could make out in the dark mirrors in which they were sometimes reflected. You would not think hat such girls were whores, but what else could they be, in a place such as this? A place to which Gast had invited him.

The waiter came back, smiling. Everything was in order. He was indeed Herr Gast's guest. What would the gentleman care for?

"A large cognac and water," he said, enjoying himself now that Gast was definitely paying. "And cigarettes. Bring me a packet of Passions. And tell me, those two girls . . ."

"Charming girls."

"How much?" Nold demanded.

"I believe the gentleman has got the wrong idea," the waiter said. "They are models."

"In a pig's arsehole, they are," Nold said.

"I believe that Herr Gast will be in shortly," the waiter said.

Nold had drunk several more cognacs and was in a much better frame of mind by the time Gast did arrive. He offered the detective a cigar, and lit it for him.

"This is all right," Nold said, savouring it.

"Jamaican," Gast said. "They've been looking after you all right?"

"Oh, fine."

"I'm glad to hear it."

The two girls were still at the bar, still chattering away. Nold nodded at them with a questioning leer.

"Tip top," Gast said confidentially.

"Models, according to the waiter," Nold said, chuckling.

"The best," Gast said.

"You know them, Willi?"

"Yes, I know them. You're . . . interested?"

"Yes and no," Nold said to make matters clear. "You know what cops are paid. Not like you lot, with your rich pickings."

"Nowadays there are opportunities for everyone," Gast said. "Believe me."

"I do, I believe you."

"It's just a matter of taking them when they present themselves."

"Never present themselves to me," Nold complained, ogling the bare backs of the two girls wistfully.

"It's a matter of *seeing* them, the opportunities," Gast said. "That's all it is. I assure you, Fritz."

Gast called for more brandy for both of them.

"I'll give you an example," he told Nold. "You know the young roughneck Otto Osche. The one they call 'the Robber.' I see in him a future youth champion. *There's* opportunity. If we can make a champion of material like that, what a feather in our caps that'd be."

"What's the advantage of it?" Nold asked, failing to comprehend such long-reaching strategy.

"Puts us on the map. Our street, our area."

"Yes?"

"A possible future Reich youth champion. That must reflect credit on his sponsors."

"He'll never train," Nold said. "He's a lout."

"Give him the incentive and he'll train."

"Not him. I know those kids. They just want to hang around in the street and do nothing."

"That's true," Gast said, reflecting. "But suppose Otto was sent to a youth hostel, like his pal Rolf. They'd make him train."

Nold was peering at Gast in the dark, trying to comprehend what he was up to. "Maybe," he conceded.

"It would be for his own good," Gast said. "And speaking of that, the Hacker woman, the one who's mad, ought to be put away. She has a harmful effect."

"She's a bit crazy," Nold conceded.

"She's a health hazard. She can't look after herself — how can you expect a young schoolgirl, all by herself now that her brother's in a hostel, to take care of such a difficult — dirty — old woman? You know she is completely round the bend. Performs her natural functions on the floor."

"Those two girls," Nold began, seeking to change this irrelevant subject.

"I'll invite them to join us for a drink," Gast said. He paused. "You know that the Hacker woman says the most outrageous things. It's plain subversive. About the godless times we live in. The people led astray by false leaders. The corruption rife in the land. She wants Amos to come from the fields and lead the people back to God. She may be a crazy old sow, but she's a troublemaker as well, and dangerous."

99

"Does anyone take any notice of her?"

"Who can say what people take notice of. It's something that should be stopped. It's a scandal."

Nold frowned. He could not understand what Gast was after, could not follow the tortuous paths of his scheming mind.

"What do you suggest?" he asked.

"In my opinion," Gast said, "it's a matter on which the Gestapo should take action. For the protection of the people and the State."

"What kind of action?" Nold asked.

"She should be committed. To an asylum. For her own and everybody else's good. That's my opinion."

"It would be for doctors to decide whether she came in the category of being committable."

"Yes and no," Gast said. "My understanding of the Troublemaking statutes suggests she is covered by them. The area of religious maniacs, hot gospellers, Bible-thumpers — there is a section for that in the Gestapo, no?"

"Yes," Nold said. "There is such a section."

"Can you speak to them? An exchange of information on an unofficial basis."

"I don't know anyone in that section."

"It's just a matter of taking the lift to the next floor and knocking on a door — surely?"

"Yes . . . yes." He could not understand this concern of Gast's. "Is it important?"

"I think it is. Let me put it to you like this. I was talking before about opportunity, and needing to see it — well, can't you see it?"

"I'm beginning to."

"Then let's leave it at that. I will say no more. Which of the two girls appeals to you most?"

"The one on the left."

"Lilli," Gast said. "Yes, I can recommend her, thoroughly. Take my word for it."

100

"Yes?"

"An excellent choice."

"The problem is — I'm broke."

"That *is* a problem," Gast admitted. He pondered the matter, keeping Nold on tenterhooks for as long as possible. "Perhaps I could see my way to helping you out since you're temporarily short of funds. Let's see now."

"If you *could* see your way to doing that," Nold said, trying not to appear too obviously eager, "I'd be indebted to you."

"You would be," Gast said with a laugh. "You sure as damnation would be. Well, I tell you what. Take the lift up to the next floor to Religious Maniacs and Bible-thumpers and have a little word with them and I will take care of any costs you might be involved in with the charming Lilli."

Nold shrugged. It seemed cheap at the price, but he still couldn't understand Gast's angle. "What's your interest?" he demanded.

"For the good of the street. The old woman is an annoyance, and very disturbing to everyone."

"I'll see what can be done," Nold promised.

Gast stood up.

"Good, good. I'll go and have a word with Lilli.

FIVE

Born on the night of February 11–12, around midnight, Franzi had a birth chart that was exceptionally "watery," according to the Gypsy she had consulted during Carnival. When she was born, this woman told her, half the planets were in Cancer, Scorpio, and Pisces, which meant she was someone "adrift on emotion and love."

"You float on an ocean of feeling," she said, "and sometimes that ocean blows up a terrible storm, tossing you about."

"It's true," Franzi had to admit, recognizing herself at once.

"You're like a boat without a rudder. You're pulled this way and that by your feelings, and men, the wicked devils, will take advantage of your giving, sensual nature when you grow up." All this was in her stars.

"Oh, they do already," Franzi admitted, since there was no

point concealing anything from a Gypsy. They knew everything anyway.

"Ah!"

"What is it? What have you seen, Madame?"

"You are a chameleon."

"What's that?"

"You change all the time, according to the person you are
with. Especially men. You change yourself to be what each
man wants you to be."

"Yes, that's true," Franzi said in amazement. This Gypsy
could see right into her.

It was true, sometimes she had no will of her own, just *had*
to do things. A certain mood got into her and forced her. This
mood made her show herself naked at the window, and in
cinemas sometimes prevented her from standing up and
leaving when a man sitting next to her pressed his knee
against hers, and she couldn't move away even when he put
his hand under her skirt. She had to let him. She would look
straight ahead, watching the film, and act as if nothing was
happening, even though she was letting the man touch her
there — she didn't look at him, kept her eyes firmly fixed on
the screen (once it was during *Dream in White* with Sonja
Henie), and lost herself completely in the story.

As the Gypsy woman said, she had a sensual, giving nature,
though most of the time she didn't let things go too far. She
had a rule that if she pulled down her underclothing, the man
had to keep his on, and vice versa: if he took his off, she kept
hers on. It was for protection, and because she wasn't like
that, not the sort who went all the way. Not intentionally.
Sometimes things got out of hand and you couldn't help it,
like the time under the stairs with the soldier. She'd been
wriggling about on his lap for hours and hours, keeping to the
rules, and then he'd cheated and taken advantage of the state
she was in, and before she'd realized it he'd got his buttons
undone. It was lovely, she had to admit, and though she'd
told him to get off, get off, and kept pushing him, it was a bit

halfhearted, and finally she gave up and enjoyed herself. She was careful, though, that he didn't do it inside her. She knew from a man's movements and from his breathing when the danger point approached, and removed herself in time. Though it was lovely, the nicest sensation, better than all the chocolate in the world, once a man had misbehaved like that she didn't go with him again, because it meant you couldn't trust him.

She had known for a long time how untrustworthy men could become when they wanted that. Something got into them and they became dirty devils. The most surprising people. One minute they were acting all superior, telling you off, treating you like a child, and then a change came over them, because of something she'd said, or done, or the way she looked, and their whole expression became sly — coaxing, almost begging. It was like making dogs get up on their hind legs and beg, by offering them a piece of sugar. You just had to say "Beg!" to them, and they did! Even Herr Flüss, her science teacher — God, was that a surprise! After all the times he'd given her lines for not doing her homework, and suddenly . . . She did it because it put him in her power: couldn't give her punishments after that. Had to treat her well or she would tell on him. He was terrified that she might. They hadn't done much, really. She'd only sat on his lap and wriggled about.

Most men were too scared even to do that, she being under-age.

She liked to give them hot looks and see the effect it had. It was tremendously satisfying to make them hang around and follow you. If they did make a move, she'd act all surprised and innocent. Or horrified. To scare them that she might tell. Once they'd backed away, she gave them hot looks again. That really got them confused. You could keep men dangling for ever. Oh, she was a big tease, and she knew it.

She had known about men for ages and ages, from the time she was small. Sleeping in the same room as her mother and father, naturally she heard everything, and saw too: Sunday mornings with the light coming through the curtains, while pretending to be asleep still. Her mother saying, ''Shhh! Shhh! You'll wake the child, she'll hear,'' but her father didn't care. ''She's got to know sometime,'' she heard him say. And he didn't even bother to cover himself properly.

When Mama was ill with the fever, she slept in the small bed by herself, and Franzi slept in the big bed with her father. He'd rock her to sleep in his arms, and sing her songs.

There were times her father didn't wear any pyjamas when he was rocking her to sleep and squeezing her and she felt his big thing brush against her, and once she woke up and found there was a wet sticky patch on her nightdress.

There were rows all the time between him and her mother, and he came home less and less. But when he did come home he brought her presents, made a fuss of her, told her they were going to be rich soon, because of a certain horse that was going to win an important race.

And oh! what a heartbreaker she was going to be! He always said that to her. She was going to drive men mad, he said, bouncing her on his knees.

Then one day when she was eight or nine, her mother told her the reason her Papa hadn't been home for so long was because he was in prison.

He was in for two years, that time. For thieving and forgery.

The surprising thing was she didn't hate her father, even though he was a thief and forger and did things with her that she knew were bad. No — she loved him and missed him dreadfully when he was in prison, and was never happier than when he came back, and happiest of all when Mama was ill and Franzi had to sleep next to him in the big bed.

When she was very little she used to pray she could always be in her father's bed, next to him, and then one day he would marry her, when her mother was dead, and they'd be husband and wife.

The one person she couldn't get to take any notice of her was Kurt Springer, no matter how many times she cycled up and down in front of his garage, giving him hot looks. He treated her as a child. It was true he had once given her a ride on his motorbike, and she'd held on and held on, her heart in her mouth as they roared through the city streets towards the river: between the statues of the kaisers on their horses — whiskered and helmeted and stern — and under the arch of the towered abutments. It was like entering a medieval castle. Kurt was going at 100 kilometres an hour at least, and ahead stretched the long girder bridge, leaping the river in great iron strides, and the sun flashed through the lattice-work of struts and trusses, flashed in her eyes, her hair streamed out, and she hung on to Kurt tightly, put her head against his back. Looking the other way, she saw the barges going along the river, the cargo boats, the pleasure steamers with musicians playing on the decks. It was one of the most wonderful moments of her life. But afterwards all Kurt said to her was, "You shouldn't be wearing lipstick at your age. And those stupid earrings! The way you dress you make yourself look like a little streetwalker."

"I'm not a child," she shouted at him angrily. "You're about the only one who hasn't noticed."

"Oh, I've noticed," he said scoffingly. "I've noticed the way you dress and behave. Nobody can help noticing that." He'd laughed at her.

The way he acted, you'd think he wasn't a bit interested in her in that way, though when she was clinging to him on the motorbike and let her hand drop to his thigh, sort of by accident, she'd felt the way his whole body stiffened — oh, everywhere — and once when she went by her window without any clothes on she'd seen him look up. Of course, straight away he'd looked down again.

It was the training course he was doing, to be a youth leader, that made him talk the way he did, about self-sacrifice and self-overcoming in order to build a New Front. Well, she

106

didn't want to overcome herself, she wanted to *be* herself and have a nice time. It really was a pity about Kurt going straight. She'd really fancied him before, when he was getting up to all those villainies with Rolf and Otto, lifting stuff off the back of lorries. The things he said now just didn't sound like him. She couldn't believe it was the same person. Going on about some young people finding more meaning in their life than just having fun. Saying that these young people were ready to sacrifice themselves for Germany — meaning she should be, too. But she didn't want to sacrifice herself for anyone. It didn't interest her. She couldn't understand all these young girls suddenly being so eager to sacrifice themselves. What for? Still, it was a pity about Kurt having got caught up in it, because he was ever so handsome, like cut out of marble he was, with his beautiful strong features and strong arms and thighs — he could have posed for those statues of "The Young Heroes" in the Adolf Hitler Sports Palast. It was really a waste!

Though once or twice — especially after he'd had a few beers — she had seen his eyes on her, and from the expression in them she couldn't believe that he really believed that stuff about sacrificing yourself for Germany, and the rest of it — about Jews. She was sure he just said it because he had to. She tried giving him encouraging looks. But the moment she did that he shied off, as if he was scared of what might happen. She couldn't see what there was to be scared about. She wouldn't tell anyone. Anyway, she wasn't a child. *She* knew that she wasn't, whatever the date on her birth certificate.

Franzi noticed that her mother was worse since Rolf had gone away. Now she sat at her window all the time, not only during daylight but often into the night as well, waiting for him to come home — she was expecting him anytime, and so she kept leaning out and looking for him.

"When is that boy coming home, it's late," she kept saying. "Look, it's almost dark and he's not yet home. Where's he got to?"

"Mama, you know he's at the hostel. Come on. Go to bed, Mama."

But she wouldn't. "I've got to get this scarf finished. He'll be back and the scarf won't be finished. Even if I've got to keep knitting all night long, I'm going to finish it. He needs a nice warm scarf."

"But, Mama, he's got dozens of scarves. And it's going to be summer soon. Go to bed. Please, please, Mama."

"A scarf's got to be nice and long, to keep the neck warm. You've got to be able to wind it round your neck several times," she explained, knitting feverishly.

Next day Franzi was amazed to see her mother fully dressed, in her green overcoat with the synthetic fur collar and her galoshes, umbrella in hand.

"I'm going out," she announced.

"Where to, Mama?"

"I'm going for a walk. I have to see some people."

"I'll take you and bring you back."

"No, you've got to go to school. I can go by myself. I'm not an invalid. I can walk."

"But Mama . . ."

"Stop arguing with me. I'm your mother!"

When Franzi came back from school she found her mother in bed, sleeping deeply. The doctor had come and given her an injection to sedate her. Some neighbours had brought her back after she'd fainted in the street, just on the corner, where she had gone to harangue the passers-by. She had shouted at them that they were evil men, and God saw and would punish them, and a great wind and fire would sweep across the city of the plains and burn everything to cinders, and nothing would be left except ruin and rubble. Then she'd fainted.

Next day a new doctor came to see her. Dr. Leventhal had given up his practice and left, and this young man was replacing him: he was about twenty-six and looked cross. The woman on the bed did not occupy him for more than a minute, during which he briefly shone a thin torch-light in her eyes and held her pulse; after that his remarks were all addressed to Franzi, as if her mother were not there, or couldn't hear.

"We shall have to do something about her," young Dr. Laurentius informed Franzi. He looked around. The sheets on the bed had not been changed for weeks; there was dirty laundry scattered about the room, on the floor, in corners; the mouldering remains of meals had been left on trays pushed under the wardrobe; the dressing table top was densely cluttered with pastes and creams and lotions and medicines of every kind, soiled pieces of cotton wool, combs thickly entangled with white hair.

"She's deteriorating rapidly," Dr. Laurentius informed Franzi. "That's only to be expected in these cases. These sorts of conditions rarely improve. . . ."

"What's the matter with her, Herr Doktor?"

"My dear girl, she's *non compos mentis*. Mad."

"Sometimes she's perfectly all right," Franzi insisted. "She's very good at knitting. Look, Herr Doktor . . ."

"Knitting is neither here nor there," young Dr. Laurentius muttered, impatiently glancing around. "Look at this place. Look at the state of it. It's not — hygienic. She can't take care of herself, that's the fact of the matter." He drew a curtain aside to let in more light, and there on the floor was a pile of dried-up excrement.

Dr. Laurentius took Franzi by the arm and firmly ushered her outside.

"She's a health hazard — to you, to the neighbourhood," he declared.

"I'll see her room's kept clean," Franzi promised. "She doesn't do any harm, honestly. I can take care of her, Herr Doktor."

"I don't know about that," he said. "We shall have to look into it. It's a public health matter."

Worried and not knowing what to do, Franzi, after school, went to see her mother's brother Fred, who lived down the road from her. He was shaving as she arrived; being a night worker he had only just got up—he worked at a factory in Nippes that made metal tops for beer bottles.

"Weak nerves," he said, running the safety razor upwards through the thick lather under his chin, and flicking excess soap into the sink. "Always had weak nerves, Greta. Nerves are the fusing system of the human body. You put too high current into the system and *puff!*—all the fuses blow. That's what's happened to poor old Greta. All the troubles she's had with your father, and with that little good-for-nothing brother of yours. Gives a lot of worries, that. And I hear you give her a lot of worries too, going out with men at your age." He gave her a sidelong glance, looking her over.

"What we going to do about Mama?"

Uncle Fred cut broad, swift swaths through the foaming lather.

"You ask my opinion," he said, "she ought to be in a home. One of those rest homes. She needs a good, long rest, free of worry. You know? Where they look after those who can't look after themselves. I know they're not very nice places, some of them. But she'd get treatment. They do those electrical treatments nowadays for the nerves. They stimulate the nervous system, that's what they do. It's like I used to have electrical treatment for my flat feet. Same principle."

"You've still got flat feet, Uncle Fred."

"That's because I didn't continue the treatment." He wiped the remaining lather from his face with a face towel, and looked at Franzi. "Don't worry, I'll keep my eye on you while your mother's gone. I'm only down the road. Got a bit of free time now. If you get in any trouble, come to your Uncle Fred," he said, giving her a wink and a little slap on the behind.

The following day Herr Gast paid a call.

"I've had a report from your doctor, Dr. Laurentius," he

110

said. "He thinks your mother needs special treatment. He thinks she should be sent to a place where she could be looked after properly."

"I can look after her."

"Are you a doctor, Franzi? Are you medically qualified?"

"Oh, she's all right."

"She goes wandering off in the streets by herself and fainting. She could have an accident. Anything could happen while you're at school. People like her are a danger to themselves. She could set fire to herself. She could fall out of the window."

"No — she's not that bad."

"It's not fair on you," Gast said. "You shouldn't have to be tied down with her." He paused, considering. "Leave it to me," he said, "and I'll do my best for you. I know you can't afford private sanatoriums. I'll look into it."

"I don't want her to be sent away," Franzi called after him as he was halfway down the stairs.

"Don't worry," he called up. "I'll do what's best for her, and you."

On a Monday morning in the last week of May, two men arrived at the door wearing white coats and said they had come to fetch Frau Greta Hacker. Franzi said there must be some mistake, she hadn't called for an ambulance: her mother was much better now. No, they said, no mistake: they had the papers right there, all signed and witnessed.

"But I didn't ask for anybody," she said.

That didn't make any difference, they said.

Franzi didn't want to let them in; she said she was going to go and talk to her uncle about this, but they just pushed past her and went into her mother's bedroom.

"Now come along, Greta. Be a good girl. Put your teeth in, *liebling.* And let's get cracking! Haven't got all day, you know . . . There's others that need us too."

When Greta Hacker saw that these men had come to take

111

her away whether she liked it or not, she shouted at them, "'And it shall come to pass, that I shall send an Angel of Death down from heaven to lay waste the lands of Egypt, and I shall visit plagues upon them . . .'" She kicked and scratched and struggled. The two brawny men had a job holding her; they exchanged looks, and while one held her with her arms pinned to her sides, the other got something out of his medical bag, rolled up in a bundle. At a nod from the first man the second one undid the bundle and held up the garment, with its armholes towards Franzi's mother. Then with the smoothness of an oft-practised manoeuvre, the two men came together, the woman between them, and in swift succession pushed first one then the other of her arms through the armholes, and the man behind her quickly pulled her arms back and tied them tightly into her body by means of the sturdy tapes all down the length of the jacket, until she was trussed up from neck to thigh in a tight sheath of canvas. Her legs were not tied, and she kicked wildly at her nurses, and when they started dragging her away she became possessed of a maniac's strength, succeeded in breaking free, and was able to stumble a few steps to the open window and to stick her head outside and yell at the top of her voice:

"Murderers! Murderers! Murderers are taking me!"

They had to gag her to stop her screams, and then they carried her choking and heaving to the wagon with the barred windows that was waiting by the entrance to the flats.

So that she wouldn't be put in care, Franzi got her Uncle Fred to sign a paper saying she was living under his roof, and he was responsible for her. It meant that her public assistance entitlement was paid to him; he doled it out to her on a day-to-day basis and soon forgot it was hers, acted as if he was taking it out of his own pocket. Some days he said he didn't have any money to give her — she spent it like water.

"How'm I going to eat, Uncle Fred?"

"Stop painting your fingernails," was the answer.

112

If she buttered him up, and he wasn't in too bad a mood, he relented, eventually, and grumblingly gave her a few coins. But she hated having to beg him, and the way he made her hang around.

It was strange being in the flat all by herself. She couldn't be bothered to cook and lived largely on sandwiches, and hardly ever made her bed. When her mother and Rolf were living there, she'd cooked and done all the housework, but now, just for herself, she didn't see the point.

The place was getting to look squalid. She paid attention to her own appearance, spending long periods in front of the mirror, but neglected the cleaning, and if she didn't feel like going round to butter up Uncle Fred, she just didn't eat.

She was feeling very strange. She found she was talking to herself, and once catching sight of her face in a mirror, said out loud: "I look like Mama," and it gave her the shivers.

Even Uncle Fred noticed that she wasn't well.

"What's the matter with you — you not eating properly?"

"You don't give me any money."

"The shameless ingratitude!" Uncle Fred complained, peeved. "I'm giving you money all the time — you squander it!"

But it wasn't just the lack of food that was causing her to deteriorate: it was the emptiness of the flat — not having her mother there, not having Rolf. Sometimes she lay on her bed and cried and cried for hours. Tear-stained and dishevelled at the end of such a weeping fit, she went to the mirror and pulled faces and pretended to be mad.

"It goes in the family, doesn't it?" she said to the deranged face.

At school she put on a big act so nobody would know what had happened. She didn't want them to find out that her mother had been put in a lunatic asylum, and her thieving brother sent to a State hostel. For the same reason, she didn't spend much time with any of her friends after class. What would she say to them?

The only person who came to see her was Herr Gast, the street leader. At first she was very cross with him, because it was he who had got her mother put in the asylum, but he explained that it was best for her, and best for Franzi.

"When can I see her?" Franzi asked him. He promised to arrange it. And also to arrange for her to go and visit her brother at the hostel.

"You'll see," he said, "it's not as bad as you think. He's got his friends there. Otto and Theo and Benno. They were all in need of care. It'll do them good. Make men of them."

Anyway — Herr Gast seemed to be the only one who gave a damn if she was dead or alive.

At first he came every two or three days, and then every day. Just for a minute. To see if she was all right. As street leader he told her she came under his aegis.

She always said she was fine, talking to him at the door, without letting him come in. She couldn't let anyone see the state of the flat. That would have been too humiliating.

Herr Gast said he was talking to the authorities about her visiting her mother, and also her brother. That was what he came to tell her every day. About how all that was going. Even though he only stayed for a minute or so, outside the door, it was a person to talk to, and it cheered her up that *somebody* was concerned about her. She thought he was quite handsome for an older man; not like Kurt, of course. But Herr Gast did get things done — everybody said that. He had influence and contacts, and he was working on getting permission for her to visit the lunatic asylum. While he was talking to her, a couple of his Storm Troopers waited in the street below and she felt his powerfulness, and it was gratifying (and flattering) that he was using a little bit of this powerfulness on her behalf, arranging a visit to her mother. Whereas as far as Kurt was concerned, she might have been dead, for all the interest he took.

When you were in trouble, you found out who your real friends were.

114

Then, one day, Herr Gast came in the early evening, after she'd returned from school, and standing outside the door said, "You know, Franzi, one of my jobs, Franzi, is to bring people news that isn't always good news." She felt a shiver of dread go through her. Grave-faced, he continued, "*That's* what being leader entails. I have these duties to perform, and they can be hard, like now. You can't push these duties onto somebody else. You have to bear them. That's why I'm leader and the other person isn't." He made it sound hard and noble, being a leader. A führer. Like *the* Führer. Only on a smaller scale. She thought: he's a strong man, and a hard man, and he can do hard things. He's not squeamish. About anything. She thought he was not like those men who when she gave them hot looks got scared because she was under-age. He wouldn't get scared.

He was holding a big jar in his hands, and she remembered that people sometimes called him "the bird of death," because he came around with these jars that contained the ashes of a dear one. The way he was looking at her intently, peering deeply into her eyes, not saying anything, you'd think he was trying to seduce her, but what he was telling her was that her father was dead.

She started to cry and couldn't stop. It was all the misery of the past two weeks welling up in her, and now her father's death on top of it! She was letting everything pour out of her, at last.

He went to the kitchen, got her a glass of water, and held it to her mouth while she drank. He stroked her hair a little bit, then, to comfort her. It *was* comforting. Taking out a handkerchief, he wiped away her tears and dabbed her chin and neck and the front of her dress, because with her jaw trembling so much she had spilt water over herself. She was biting on her fist hard, and he drew it away from her mouth and made her open her tightly clenched fingers; she had to take her hand away from her heaving breast to make him take *his* hand away.

115

She said, "I'm not feeling well. I feel faint."

"You better lie down."

He helped her to her bed, and when she was lying down, he said to breathe in deep, and she did as he told her, because she thought she was going to pass out. She felt him unbutton the front of her dress: something about tight clothing. He was dipping his handkerchief in the glass of water and dabbing her forehead, and then her neck, and lower, where her bodice was open, dabbing cold water on her plump little immature breasts and making her gasp. Next he told her to lift her knees, and to pull up her dress a little, and he dipped the handkerchief in the water again and pressed it as a cold compress behind one knee and then the other, explaining, "A man in my position has got to know a bit about first aid. You have to be quite a doctor." The cold sensation behind her knees seemed to revive her, and she no longer felt she was going to faint.

"Obviously," Gast said, "I can't leave you like this, by yourself. You better come with me."

He took her outside and they walked. She had no idea where he was taking her, he was not saying anything as she trailed after him. He didn't even look around to see if she was following.

In the backyard of a restaurant she saw a shiny new car standing among the dustbins and vegetable peels and empty bottles. When he opened the door for her to get in she could smell the new leather. The car started with a quiet purr, and seemed to just drift off, and she with it.

They drove to different places. She was crying some of the time, while he went off to attend to his business.

After a good deal of driving around, they finally stopped at a block of flats in a smart neighbourhood, near the Aachenerstrasse. He opened the glass and wrought-iron entrance door with his key and they crossed a hall to the lift and went up to the third floor, where he opened the door of a small flat: *de luxe,* she saw at once.

116

He had things to do and told her to go and lie down until she felt better. She went into the bedroom and lay on the bed. She didn't dare open it, but also she was nervous of lying on the expensive blue silk coverlet, in case she crumpled it or dirtied it. She told herself: he said to lie down, and so she did, kicking her shoes off first. She could hear him talking on the phone in the room next door—a steady, soothing sound. Soothed, she closed her eyes and dropped off. When she opened them he was standing over her. "Drink this," he said. "It'll make you feel better." She drank and it burned her throat. It was alcohol. Probably cognac. The taste of cognac, she knew; she had drunk it once before. "Go on," he said, urging her to drink up, "it's medicinal." It was true that it made her feel better; it drew a protective cover over her head and made the feeling of rawness in her chest less painful. For an hour she slept deeply. Waking, she still had a hazy sensation in her head from the cognac. I must go home, she thought, getting up. He was on the phone; she could hear him talking expansively while she tidied herself, and washed and made up. There was an Eau de Cologne spray on a shelf and she sprayed herself with it and put some on her fingers and sniffed it to revive herself. A bad wave came and she was on the point of breaking down again: to snap out of it she made herself go in the room where he was on the phone. He took no notice of her and she wasn't sure if she was supposed to have come in without asking. Looking around, she saw it was the sort of flat people had in films. There was a cocktail cabinet with differently coloured drinks—liqueurs and cocktails, she wouldn't be surprised. The sofa was satiny soft. There were beautiful mirrors on the walls. And paintings. Everything was softly illuminated. All the places she'd ever been in were lit by hard light that gave you a pasty white appearance, as if someone was shining an electric torch straight in your face. It was either that kind of brightness or dingy darkness. The dark of smelly back alleys. But here the light was neither glaring nor dingy. It was lovely. As Herr

117

Gast was still talking on the phone she started to look at the paintings. Naked women. They were mostly of naked women. In daring poses. She knew it was different if it was a painting, but still! At last he put down the phone.

"You're better?"

Being asked made her sob again, and he gave her another cognac quickly.

"Go on," he said. "Drink!"

"No, I better not. My head's still turning from the last one you gave me."

"It's like medicine. Drink up," he said severely, and she did what she was told, and it made her feel better.

"I've got to go home. I've got school tomorrow."

"I'll let you have a note for your teacher."

The way he said it gave her the impression that he was going to help her get away with something. "You may not be able to go to school for days," he said, and now there was no doubting that he was in league with her, and proposing something wicked. She had seen this change of expression coming over men, and she knew what it meant.

Now he was being severe again, looking at her crumpled dress. "If you want to change," he said, "there are clothes in the cupboard in the bedroom. See if anything fits you." He was already dialling, dismissing her, and she went back to the bedroom.

"Anything that fits you, you can have," he called.

There was a long built-in closet and it was full of clothes: dresses, skirts, blouses, costumes, trouser suits; of silk and of satin, of lamé and wispy light cotton and rich, thick wool angora and camel hair. She took out one silk dress, silvery and long, the kind that women wore in nightclubs, draped it against herself, and looked in the mirror. The dress transformed her, made her no longer a little girl but a woman. She tried other dresses against herself excitedly. Did he really mean that she could have anything that fitted her? Any-

118

thing? He couldn't mean *any* of these beautiful dresses. Opening a drawer, she let her hands rummage amid lacy underwear and fine-quality stockings. How delicate and fine! Perhaps his wife had died and he was giving all this away. He was obviously a rich man, with a new car and a *de luxe* flat.

In an impulsive movement she pulled off the crumpled old dress she was wearing, and stepped out of her drawers. And off with the woollen knee-socks kept up by elastic bands! The stockings were a little long for her, she discovered, laying them along her leg and thigh: the tops came right to the line of her groin. She giggled, flouncing about in front of the mirror, as audacious as the nudes in the pictures on the walls, and as pretty, with her neat bush of blond hair and her plump little breasts. She was aware that the bedroom door was not firmly shut—which just added to the excitement. Presently she realized that the door had opened further; she started putting on one stocking, pretending she hadn't noticed that Herr Gast was standing watching her; there came a point, after a while, when she couldn't pretend anymore, and she bit her lip in a formal token of shame. Now it was too late to cover her nakedness, and she didn't bother.

"They fit you?"

"Almost. . . ."

"They're too big for you," he said, coming right up to her and seeing where the stocking came to. He stooped and continued smoothing it on her leg, over knee and thigh, and then higher up, until it was fully smoothed out and reached to the little blond bush. He smoothed the stocking quite roughly, so that she thought he might tear it.

"And the other one?" he said.

This time he knelt and started smoothing the stocking at the ankle, with both hands, and then over her calf and knee and thigh. When he got to the top he said, "Bend your knees," and she did so, and he told her, "More," and she did it more, until she was half squatting, and then he put his fingers inside her and made her shake all over.

Later, he made her go and lie on the bed, and put great big soft feather pillows under her buttocks to raise her there: arranged her just the way he wanted. He was a man who had to have everything just the way he wanted.

SIX

Rolf had been in the hostel about four weeks when he received a letter from Franzi, the first time he'd heard from her since he'd left home. He knew she wasn't much good at writing, any more than he was, and hadn't expected any letters from her, so this one came as a surprise.

He opened it as soon as he had a recreation period, and seeing the letter was quite long, took it to the lav to read, that being the only place where you could have any privacy in the hostel.

DEAR ROLFIE (HE READ),

How you getting on at the hostel not to mizrable I hope and not doing two many stupid things like you do sometime. Im talking about villainees. One thing you should be getting is plenty of fresh air WITCH IS GOOD FOR YOU. YOUR TO PALE!!! Is the dissyplinn very bad? I no you dont like it but youve got to try and do your best. One bad thing witch happened is that Mama was taken away, I cried a lot as you can imagine. I think the place theyve taken her is a Home (asylum). Uncle Fred sayed he thinks shell get elektrik treatment. He had elektrik treatment for his feat and it dosnt hurt at all only tingles a bit. Mama wasnt right in her head and couldnt look after herself and was a DANGER to herself and others. Thats what they sayed. The other thing I've got to tell you Rolfie and I dont no how thats why I only came to it now is that our father is dead. YES its true. Im sorry to tell you this Rolfie my darling little brother because I know it will grief you as it did me and I cried a lot. Remember he had a bad coff. It was all the smoking gave him the coff. It all happened one thing after the other you going away to the hostel and them taking Mama away to the Home and after that Papa. I thought I was going MAD!!! And there was NOBODY. But Herr Gast the street loader was nice to me (he brot the news about our father) and looked after me when I was sad and comforted me ever so much and became my friend. I mean my man friend witch your two young to understand but hes been good to me and takes me to restrants and has even given me money and treats me like a Queen. He has got a very nice flat (LUXURY!!!) and lets me wear some of the cloths that somebody left in the flat who was very rich. She has got lots of silk and things witch Im allowed to wear. Ive left school now cos I wasnt getting on there very well (like you!) and also it woodnt look right for Herr Gast if I was going to school. We have to say Im over 16 or he could get into trouble cos of my age. He says one day when Im old enuff well get married. Hes going to be rich when this person dies whos left him a lot of money in his Will. Dearest Rolfie my sweet angel little brother I love you very much and were alone now and all weve got left in the world is each other and I will always look after you Rolfie and not let bad things happen to you if I can help it. Lots and lots of love and XXXXXXs from your loving sister Franzi.

P.S. Most of the time Im living at Herr Gasts flat now becos he prefers it so thats where I am but I cant give you the address we have got to keep it secret about me becos of my age. You can leave a message with Uncle Fred. I had to move out of OUR flat cos I didnt have any money for the rent and Uncle Fred woodnt give it. He said Herr Gast shood witch wasnt fair.

Sitting in the lav at the hostel, reading his sister's letter, Rolf wanted to cry when he heard about his mother having been put in an asylum and his father being dead, but the tears wouldn't come. They sort of stuck in his throat. He could hardly remember his father. It was about five years since he'd last seen him. Practically all he could remember was that he had sunken cheeks and nicotine-stained fingers and coughed all the time, especially coming up the stairs, and at night. Rolf tried to recall other things. The *nicest* memory he had was of a photograph: his father playing the accordion in his green costume jacket with the horn buttons. That wasn't much to remember about somebody's whole life, but his father had been away a lot.

Next he thought about his mother being in a home. He had to think about one thing at a time to be able to grasp it (though his *feelings* were all mixed up together and consisted of wanting to cry and to smash everything to bits and to run away and to hide, and he wanted to go to the lavatory, he had such a stomach ache, but when he tried he couldn't); the thought that surfaced out of all the cross-currents was: *Mutti shouldn't be in an asylum, she's not MAD,* just a bit strange in the head. The idea of his mother being locked up in some place with lunatics made him feel sick, and he blamed Franzi for having let it happen. He wouldn't have let it happen if he'd been there. He'd have killed them all before he let them take his mother to such a place. He was raging now, raging at Franzi. She was nothing but a little prostitute, going with a man like Herr Gast. Taking money from him. God, was he ashamed of her! His own sister. It was what Kurt had said would happen to her if she carried on the way she was doing, giving men hot looks, and showing herself to them at the window. Standing there naked for everybody to see. And that time under the stairs with the soldier. Now she was living in the same flat as Herr Gast, which made her a *Naziwhore.* The anger boiled up in him and he banged his fists repeatedly — rhythmically — against the lavatory door, making the sort of clatter that prisoners made in jails (he'd seen it in films) when one of them was going to be executed.

During P.T. he managed to get next to Theo—they'd all been sent to the hostel, as being in need of care, Theo, Benno, and Otto—and said to him in an urgent undertone:

"I've got to run away. I've got to see my sister. She's become a *Naziwhore*."

"We're all going to run away," Theo the Brains promised. "I'm working on it."

"You better hurry up," Rolf said. "I haven't got a lot of time."

"These things've got to be *planned*," Theo said in a strong whisper while doing knee-bends. "In any case, Benno isn't out of hospital yet."

"When's he coming out?"

"Any day."

Benno—stupid Benno—had got his ear shot off by another boy. They'd been practising with live ammo as part of the military training programme, and Benno had forgotten the password. Naturally, he would have. He was always getting lost on route marches, falling into anti-tank ditches, triggering booby traps. His navigation stank, and his knots came undone. On this important military exercise, the objective of which was for one side to cut the other side's life thread, he'd been returning to base camp on his own (having as usual fallen behind and got lost), and on being challenged by the lookout hadn't known that day's password. Just said, "It's Benno," which the guard couldn't accept and so had fired a warning shot over his head. The guard was small and the rifle heavy and it dropped as he fired, and the bullet took off the top of Benno's ear. There was a lot of blood, but he wasn't dead, as they'd at first thought.

As they stood in line for jumping over the vaulting horse, Rolf whispered to Theo, "Pass it on to Otto that we're running away as soon as Benno's out of the hospital."

They had a conference about it, the three of them, during

124

their after-supper recreation period. If you could call it supper. A few lettuce leaves and some disgusting tinned fish in a tomato sauce.

They hated everything about the hostel, and were in complete accord with Rolf's plan to escape. They hated the food, the cleanliness inspections, the P.T., the route marches, the army discipline, the lack of privacy. The ceremonials they had to take part in made them want to be sick. Rolf refused to sing Nazi songs. Said he couldn't sing, was tone-deaf. Or his voice had gone. Never would they get him to sing one note of those songs. Everybody had to sit around bonfires while people made "fire speeches," and then they had to chant in unison, "We were born to die for Germany!" "Not me, I wasn't," Rolf added under his breath.

At their secret meeting to plan the escape, Theo said it'd have to be at night because during the day there were too many roll-calls and their absence would be discovered before they'd got very far. They'd have to have provisions; a compass, flashlights, sturdy walking boots, groundsheets for sleeping in the open, plenty of matches, good knives, iodine, tin openers, water canteens, and several days' supply of food, and of course rucksacks in which to carry these things. So they couldn't just run away like that. First they would have to get their provisions, and he proposed they set about doing this straight away.

Before anything else, they had to find a safe hiding place where they could keep their stuff until they were ready to leave. All of them should keep their eyes open.

Returning from the three-kilometre early-morning cross-country run next day, Theo told them he'd seen a broken culvert on the edge of the hostel grounds, probably part of the former water drainage system: he'd taken a quick look and formed the impression that it was not in service.

Their evening recreation period was used to explore the culvert, and when they put their hands inside it they found it was dry. They could put their stuff in bags, or haversacks, and

125

hide them deep in the culvert, out of reach of anybody who didn't know they were there. A long stick with a bent nail at the end would suffice for getting everything out, when they were ready.

The following day they started to lay in provisions. While on kitchen duty Rolf managed to fill his pockets with potatoes in the morning, and with tins of sardines in the afternoon. That night, after lights-out, Otto climbed from his first-floor dormitory by way of a lavatory soil pipe, and made his way to the stores. The locks on the doors were no great problem to a robber of his standing. He stole four haversacks, and stuffed them with tarpaulin groundsheets, water canteens, matches, flashlights, rope, candles, lavatory paper, and strong boots of the kind they were given for route marches. Then he took all this stuff to the edge of the hostel grounds and pushed it deep into the culvert, after which he covered over the broken opening with twigs and ferns, and returned to his dormitory, clambering up the soil pipe by which he had left.

The wardens of course discovered the robbery and instituted a search, but the culvert was not discovered. Bit by bit, the boys added to their essential supplies.

At the end of the week Benno was discharged from hospital, the side of his head still heavily bandaged. He had to go to the hostel infirmary to have his dressings changed every day, and they coached him to steal iodine, lint, bandages, surgical scissors, and pills against diarrhoea. They were terrified that, being Benno, he would get caught, but to their amazement and delight he obtained all of these things without being discovered.

They were adding to their food supplies on a day-by-day basis, picking up what they could when they could; in early June, a run-through of everything so far amassed revealed that all they now lacked were maps, a compass, and sharp meat knives.

As soon as they had got hold of these items they could run away.

Just then, when almost ready to go, they were thrown by the arrival of Kurt Springer, acting as a summer replacement for a junior youth leader on holiday.

They saw him at the evening "fire speech."

Banners stretched out between high poles proclaimed: "Be Fighters!"

A stage had been constructed in the open air, with a black backdrop on which the hostel workshop had painted a giant swastika at the centre of an enormous sun whose golden beams radiated into the surrounding darkness. The sun, having been painted with luminous paint, shone day and night, and its glittering symmetrical rays lit the upturned faces of the massed boys.

The atmosphere was worshipful and solemn as choristers filed onto the platform to give a recitation, and there was Kurt, leading them. They couldn't believe it. Old Kurt — with whom they used to steal cigarettes off lorries, now looking like an overgrown choirboy, in short trousers, white knee-socks, uniform shirt. Face aglow. Their chortling disrespect earned them formal black marks from the hostel youth police in their row, which was the front row.

The choristers ranged in tiers behind him, Kurt stepped to the microphone and announced:

"A poem by the Reich Youth Leader Baldur von Schirach, entitled 'Hitler.'"

A gong was struck three times, and handsome boys leapt hand in hand through the flames of the bonfire.

A deep hush settled over the cross-legged audience seated on the ground, and the choristers began:

> *You are many thousands behind me*
> *And you are I and I am you.*
> *I have received no tribute*
> *Save the prayer from your heart.*

127

Kurt was the apex of a human triangle — a solitary, noble figure.

Rolf was seated immediately below the platform, only a metre away, staring straight up.

> *And as I form words, I know none,*
> *That is not of your Will . . .*

Kurt recited. His solemn handsome face seemed carved out of marble, ready for the pedestal. And then, unmistakably, the marble face winked at Rolf.

Afterwards, in defence of Kurt, Rolf told the others about that wink.

"What d'you want to bet he doesn't believe all that bilge. He's one of us, Kurt. I swear. He couldn't be one of *them*. He's just . . . sort of keeping in with them. To get on. Kurt wants to get on — he's just doing it for that."

But Theo wasn't so sure.

"People change," Theo said. "Society corrupts them. It's the system that does it to them. You couldn't say what Kurt wouldn't do for his own self-advancement, if that's how he is. That's what capitalist society breeds in people."

"I thought Nazis were Socialists," Benno said.

"*National* Socialists, idiot!" Theo rebuked him. "National Socialists aren't *Socialists*, they're State capitalists. It's only Communists who've got the true interests of workers at heart."

"What do we do then about running away?" Rolf asked, stifling a yawn. Politics bored him.

Theo considered carefully, and then spoke.

"Our plans being made, we've got to act. We can't cancel now. What we'll have to do, after we've got away, is lie low for a bit, because Kurt knows all our hangouts if we went home, and he could give us away to the cops."

"He wouldn't do that. Kurt'd never do that," Rolf protested.

"We can't take any risks," Theo said. "We'll just wander around until they've stopped looking for us."

It was Kurt who led them on the early morning run through the woods next day. The grass underfoot was wet with dew, mist covered the trees.

As was his custom, Rolf stayed among the last of the runners. No point killing yourself to run faster than everybody else. He was saving his energy for other things. After being with the boys in the lead at the beginning, Kurt gradually let himself fall behind until he was level with Rolf.

"Last as usual, Louse Boy."

"Didn't somebody say those that are last will be first?"

"If only you were as fast as your tongue."

They ran side by side in silence, under the dripping trees. Casually, Kurt asked, "You ever hear from your sister?"

"Why?"

"I just wondered."

"I had a letter from her, matter of fact."

"Yes? Where's she living now?"

"What d'you mean, Kurt?"

"She's not living where she used to. Didn't you know?"

"No."

"She's gone — I think she couldn't pay the rent. I expect she was sent to a hostel as well. Don't you know?"

"I expect you're right."

"Where was the letter from?"

"I didn't notice."

"She's not around in the street anymore, where she always used to be. And she's not at her old school. She disappeared after your mother was taken away."

For a while they ran on in silence, and then Rolf couldn't hold it back anymore, it was bursting in him, and he had to tell somebody.

"She's taken up with somebody, that's what's happened. Some man who's a lot older and gives her money and takes

129

her to restaurants. She lives in his flat.'' He looked at Kurt sideways. ''Makes you want to be sick, doesn't it?''

''Who's the man?''

''Don't tell anyone. Because it's supposed to be secret, and she could get into trouble, being under-age. It's Herr Gast.''

Kurt seemed to be gasping from the exertion of running so early in the morning in this damp air. He was having difficulty catching his breath.

He didn't speak for some time, and then he said with bitterness and scorn, ''Gast's street leader. That impresses immature little girls like her, they think he's a big man, because he's got thugs at his beck and call and can throw his weight around. He's a big fish, doesn't matter how little the pond, so they're impressed.''

''I expect you're right, Kurt. I expect that's what it is.'' He hesitated. ''If I see her, you want me to give her a message?''

''You expecting to see her?''

''Who knows?'' They exchanged conspiratorial looks, and Kurt smiled secretively; it was the old Kurt smile that he'd had when they used to steal from lorries and tear around on his motorbike.

''No message,'' Kurt said. ''I'll tell her myself.''

''You do that, Kurt,'' Rolf encouraged him. ''I know she likes you a lot.''

''I will — when I'm ready to,'' Kurt said.

The escape was planned for the following night: a Saturday. It was when the wardens had guests in, sometimes lady friends, and got drunk. They never prowled the corridors on a Saturday night listening for suggestive *creak-creaks*, having better things to do, and so it was a good time to escape.

Otto spent the afternoon obtaining the last essential items on their list, and fully equipped now, they synchronized their watches and decided to make their break at quarter to midnight. By then the wardens would be good and drunk or fast asleep or otherwise occupied, and the dormitories should be quiet.

In their separate dormitories, at the appointed time, they got out of bed, arranged their pillows under the blankets, to give the impression of a sleeping boy with bedding pulled over his head (which was how a lot of them did sleep), and then, with their boots tied around their necks, made their way in stockinged feet to the toilet, the window of which gave onto the rear courtyard where the rubbish bins were. The ground was higher at the back, and they only had to shin down two metres of soil pipe. They managed it almost without mishap. In dropping down the last bit, Benno knocked the lid off one of the dustbins; it made a horrible clatter on the cobbles and they stood not moving, fearing that the entire hostel would have woken up. But nothing stirred inside. Daring to breathe again, they put on their boots and ran by the vegetable beds, past the toolshed, through a field of rough prairie grass to the culvert. They scraped away the mud and leaves and twigs and got out their painstakingly accumulated provisions, and each boy slung his full rucksack on his back. Theo's eyes shone in the dark night.

"Come on," he said.

In a short while, they entered the sudden deeper darkness of the woods, and they all felt on the threshold of the great mystery of growing up, which nobody before them had ever solved.

As they trampled over bracken, the ground became spongy, damp, and thick with fungi and wild plants: elated by their escape, they aimed kicks at giant toadstools that sprouted at the base of massive trees, and crushed woodruff underfoot. They were powerful, rough men making their way in the cruel world, and they felt how sweet it was to be free. The trees became of increasing height as the woods deepened. Through the dome of high foliage, summer moonlight shone down in fitful flashes.

Theo was taking them into the densest bracken, so as to make the task of their pursuers more difficult. Thorns tore their flesh and nettles stung their legs and knees. Insects bit them. For the first couple of hours they didn't mind the hardships too much, but then they began to get hungry and tired and to feel all the pricks and bites more. Why was Theo taking them by such a difficult route? Readings from the stars! they mocked. Some navigator, he was. Couldn't navigate shit out of his own arse. Why not take an existing path? Why did they have to be sodding path*finders?*

Unswerving Theo was not put out by such comments: he kept on leading the way, face scratched and bleeding, arms scarred by undergrowth, guiding them. Nobody else had the slightest idea of where they were, and so they had to follow him and trust him. He was the Brains, and even if they complained bitterly about the course he was taking, they had no practical alternative.

When they got to a shallow river, he made them take off their boots and walk along the riverbed for half a kilometre. This was to throw hunter dogs off their tracks, he told them.

It was 5 A.M., by which time they were all exhausted and starving, before Theo permitted a halt. They'd got almost as far as planned by then and he was ready to let them have a break. Slashes of colour were appearing in the sky as they found a clearing where they could rest and have breakfast.

They all gathered pine cones and dry twigs to start a fire, and then Otto found a piece of a tree trunk which was solid enough and thick enough to be used as a griddle on which they could put their potatoes to roast. It was fairly flat on one side and therefore suitable.

The fire was built up around it, and with pointed sticks they speared their potatoes and placed them on the flat part of the trunk. They were excited and hungry as huntsmen, and Benno was imagining that he had killed a wild pig with his pointed stick. Stuck it through the throat! Having first pursued it through the thick undergrowth. Kill the beastie! Kill the beastie! He was far away in a dream of the hunt as he lowered another potato onto the ledge. Right through the pig's fat neck — and now it was difficult to get his potato off the stick, and in trying to do so with another stick, he did something clumsy and knocked all the potatoes in the fire. They tried to save them, furiously poking in the flames with their sticks but without much success, and by the time somebody thought of putting out the fire, most of their potatoes were so badly burnt as to be uneatable.

They shared out what there was and ate glumly.

Otto having eaten his piece, and seeing Benno still eating, accused Theo:

"You gave Benno more'n me."

"No, I didn't."

"Yes, you did."

"I shouldn't get *any*," Benno offered, "as I was the one got them burnt."

"Shut up — you stupid little potato-burner," Rolf told him.

"The one who's responsible should be made to pay," Otto said.

"It wasn't his fault," Theo said. "It was an accident."

"Benno's always having accidents," Otto pointed out.

"He can't help it," Theo said, "can he? He doesn't do it deliberate."

"He should pay," Otto said.

"I think I should, I think Otto's right," Benno said.

"You shut up," Theo told him.

"We ought to have a proper leader," Otto said sulkily, "or else we'll always be arguing, and burning potatoes because of some stupid accident *somebody* is always having."

"I thought we didn't want to have anybody telling us what to do," Rolf said.

"I know, but if people keep having stupid accidents they ought to be punished. Serve them right," Otto said, hungry and resentful.

"Who you want to be leader?" Rolf asked. "You?"

"No—though I'm the strongest, and could be if I wanted. No—let Theo be leader, if he likes."

"What's the point of my being leader if you're the strongest and can beat us all?" Theo asked.

"You're the Brains," Otto said with a sly grin. "So you lead."

"We don't want to follow any leader," Benno said.

"You shut up, you stupid little potato-burner," Otto said.

Rolf said, "I agree with Benno, we don't want a leader. We all decide together. In any case, it's no use having a leader that Otto could beat, and we don't want Otto as leader because he hasn't got the brains, so I say—no leader."

"I agree," Theo said, and that settled it for the time being.

They returned to the road and after walking for an hour came to a village.

"Let's eat some of our sardines," Benno said.

"Shut up, *you!*" Otto told him.

"I'm hungry."

"Shame we don't have any bread," Rolf said, "we could make a sardine sandwich."

The village was quiet. They went to the fountain in the little square and had a drink of water and sat on the ground. It was early still. The shops weren't open yet. They heard the *clink-clink* of the milkman making deliveries, and their ears pricked up. Rolf and Otto exchanged looks.

"You said you wanted a sardine sandwich," Otto said, motioning them all to stay where they were and ignore the milk cart. They didn't move. Otto was the robber. They left it to him.

After ten minutes a baker's horse and cart arrived in the square, and they followed it with their eyes. The baker's boy was setting down panniers of bread on doorsteps. They waited until he got to the Gasthaus Wagner and heard him give a tradesman's *"ooooh-ooooh!"* call, whereupon Otto gave the others a nod to get going and leave this to him.

The village was stirring awake now; shopkeepers were rolling up their shutters; the tobacconist was turning his CLOSED sign around to read OPEN; and at the Gasthaus Wagner a blind was raised and yawny old Wagner looked out and saw that his bread was there. Otto began strolling towards the entrance; the stroll became a fast walk, a run, a sudden sprint. Old Wagner was drawing the bolts of his door and unlocking as Otto swooped down like a bird out of the sky, grabbed the bread pannier from under the sleepy inn-keeper's nose, and vanished around a corner to rejoin his friends.

Buoyed by the thought of their coming meal, they had a lively step as they took a rising road out of the village. Soon green hills opened ahead of them, extending distance on all sides, and they were no longer hemmed in by houses or woods or anything else, had all the space in the world to themselves. There was nothing that stood between them and the horizon. They climbed higher and higher, with happy faces and watering mouths as they thought of their breakfast. The sun mounted with them. Soon they were so hot from walking that they took their shirts off and carried their ruck-sacks on bare backs. An occasional breeze cooled their sweaty thighs.

They could have stopped anywhere here and devoured their fresh bread, but there was an unspoken wish to keep on, to go still higher. Plum trees and pear trees grew by the roadside, and the hedgerows were thick with raspberries, blackberries, black currant, wild strawberries. They picked berries and ate them as they walked, their mouths and faces becoming stained, and since this fruit was so plentiful they put the berries that they couldn't eat in oilskin hoods that they had brought.

As they climbed higher, they could see streams gush clear as glass out of wooded slopes, then fall steeply to feed a hilltop lake. It did not seem too far away, and they thought that if they could get to it they would be able to have a refreshing bathe after their long climb. But after walking another hour, by which time it was almost eleven, they were still no nearer, it seemed, to the lake, and now their hunger overruled all other thoughts and it was decided to stop. They'd eat and then go on. The tops of the sardine tins were rolled back, the big, freshly baked loaves broken open and filled with the oily silver fishes, and the remainder of the oil in the tins poured over them — the soft, white pulp of the bread sopped it all up — and then the long sandwiches were closed and held like flutes before their eager faces. Grins of expectancy were exchanged. Benno rubbed his stomach and rolled his eyes, and then his mouth opened in an enormous bite, and his teeth closed on the crunchy bread. The others followed suit, ferociously devouring their flutes.

Benno was the first to finish. He belched noisily and everybody laughed. Then with a grunt of contented fullness, Otto opened the top button of his shorts and settled back on the ground, giving himself up to the hot weight of the sun.

Benno wanted to do something.

"Let's paint ourselves," he proposed.

"Paint?" Rolf asked.

"Like Red Indians."

"There's no paint," Otto said.

"There is," Benno said. He pointed to the oilskin hoods full of berries.

"Nawww," Rolf said. "What for?" He raised himself a little on his elbows. In him, too, a restless impulse was at work, a desire to do something. But he didn't know what, any more than Benno did, just felt the need to celebrate their escape from the hostel.

"We need to have some laws," Theo said. The restlessness to do something had got into him too. "You know — *rules.*"

"What for?" Rolf demanded harshly. His voice took on a stubborn note. "I thought we were against laws. Aren't we?"

"Well," Theo began in a conciliatory fashion, "I don't mean laws *like that*. I mean . . . We can make any laws we like." He gestured like a politician appealing to the crowd's better instinct. "We can make a law saying we won't have laws. That any of us don't want to keep, see?"

"Don't see the point of laws you don't have to keep," Benno said, and returned to his original idea. "I think we should paint ourselves."

He was very drawn by the hoods full of berries, stuck a finger in, drew it out, and gave a lick. Liking the taste, he licked to the knuckle, and then stuck his hand in the berries up to the wrist and, after looking from left to right slyly, licked the whole of it clean. When he took his hand away, his face was covered with bluish-red stain.

"Messy little pig," Theo said. He turned to the others. "What I mean by laws is . . ." He searched for the right word to express what he meant. "It's more like a . . . a . . . credo."

"What's a credo?" Rolf asked.

"What we're for, what we're against. What we believe in."

"That's easy," Rolf said. "We don't need laws for that. What we're against is the cops, grown-ups, specially teachers, hostel wardens, youth leaders, Nazis, and *Blockleiters* like Fat Schlammer. And street leaders like Herr Gast — everybody who orders you about."

Theo said, "Law number one: no ordering anybody about."

"No leaders," Benno proposed, entering the spirit of this lawmaking.

"That's right. No sodding führers," Rolf said.

"No sodding little group leaders either," Benno added.

"We want to be free," Rolf declared. "That's what."

"That's right: we want to be ourselves," Benno said.

"No lights-out," Otto sniggered.

"Nobody telling us how short our hair's got to be," Benno said.

"Or how long," Theo said.

"Or how long," they all agreed.

137

"Nobody to tell us, 'eat your greens,'" Benno said, and added, "*Uhgg.*"

"Or wash behind the ears," Rolf said.

"Or wash our arses," Otto said.

"No parades," Theo said.

"No P.T.," Otto said.

"No route marches," Rolf said.

"No war games," Theo said.

"We *won't* do what we're told," Rolf joyfully declared, as a matter of principle.

"Not if we don't want to," Benno agreed. "Kill the Nazi beastie! Kill the Nazi beastie!" he declaimed enthusiastically.

In his excitement, he delved into the berries and stirred and crushed them into a pulpy, thick dye. Pulling out his dripping hand, he smeared it laughingly all over his neck and chest, staining himself a dark bluish-red colour.

Joining in the spirit of this, Theo used berry juice to paint a sign on Benno's bare belly: an upright stalk, terminating in a round centre with several projecting points.

"What's that supposed to be?" Benno asked, giggling.

"It's an edelweiss," Theo said.

"What's that?"

"It's a flower, you idiot. Don't you know anything? It's a mountain flower."

"I don't want a flower on my belly," Benno said, trying to rub it off.

"You're an Edelweiss Pirate," Theo told him.

"A pirate?" Benno said, more interested now. "What sort of pirate is that?"

"It's a fighter for freedom," Theo said.

"I've heard of Edelweiss Pirates," Rolf said. "They're Communists."

Benno didn't seem to care what they were, had entered into the piratical spirit of things and dropped his shorts and underpants to sit himself down, right in the mess of crushed-up berries. He looked funny with his blue-red bum, and carried away by an inexplicable impulse, Rolf and Otto joined in the antic, stripping, and daubing themselves and each other wildly. Otto rubbed berry stain around his loins, making himself all purple and blue there, with red trickles running down thighs and legs, and Theo solemnly smeared his buttocks with red stain, and Rolf painted his face with streaks and blobs, turning himself into a Red Indian brave, and that inspired Benno to go a bit too far and submerge his whole face and neck in the berries and emerge a dripping, naked savage, grinning from ear to ear, and he and Otto did a war dance together.

It reached a certain point of madness, and then, abruptly, the mood fizzled out, and all of them feeling a bit silly, they calmed down, wiped themselves clean with leaves and water from their canteens, and got dressed.

Now they began to live off the fat of the land. They stole milk from doorsteps, bread from delivery vans, potatoes and carrots out of the earth. They raided chicken coops for fresh eggs, and on a hot midsummer's night, after lying in wait crafty as foxes, got away with a chicken, which they carried off to the woods, where they killed it, plucked it, and roasted it on a spit — for which purpose they used a piece of iron they'd found on a rubbish dump. They soon became expert in cooking on an open fire and had no more accidents. They slept in barns, in the waiting rooms of railway stations, and in woods and fields, in boathouses, on bandstands in village squares, under bridges, on park benches.

All the time they continued to head in a southerly direction through the Rhine valley, following the course of the river, which was now in full summer flood from the melted glaciers. The countryside consisted of vineyards and woods and vinegrowers' villages and the changing aspects of the river basin, sometimes gorge-like with escarpments of harsh rock, sometimes open to the sun and densely planted with vines.

There seemed to be plenty of others like themselves, wan-

dering about, idlers and drifters, with nowhere particular
to go, some their age, some older. One bunch they encountered and liked a lot all wore white silk scarves, and it made
them want to have white silk scarves too, and so Otto stole
some from a department store. They also — because they
liked the look — took to wearing white knee-socks, rolled
down over the boot tops. Encountering other kids who also
wore their socks in this way, they felt an immediate kinship
with them. They were from all over, these fellow wanderers:
from Berlin, Hamburg, Hannover, Dresden, Munich. To his
amazement Rolf discovered that they knew a lot of the same
songs that he knew. And they also hated HJs, cops, particularly the black pigs, and all those other old arseholes sometimes laughingly referred to as their elders and betters. Having this natural kinship, they warned each other of places to
avoid — where the cops were particularly hard on those like
themselves. And they told of good places, too, friendly villages and towns, areas that afforded easy pickings, where
there were unprotected chicken coops, apple orchards far
from any house, open barns, Alpine shelters, good railway
station waiting rooms, friendly farmers' wives. . . .

Sometimes they'd have sing-songs together around a
campfire before going their separate ways. Rolf was amazed
how catchwords like "Swing Heil" and "Heil Benny Goodman" and "Howdewitza" and others had got around. If a
youth came up to you and said, "Ship Ahoi," you knew it was
a friend, not a lousy HJ or anyone like that. Also, if somebody
wore a white silk scarf he was all right, or white shirt with
short trousers . . . or white socks rolled down over the tops
of the boots. If somebody gave the sign, you could trust him.

"I ought to go back and find Franzi," Rolf said one hot
night while they were roasting a rabbit they'd trapped. With
all the fun they were having running about free in the moun-
tains, he'd almost forgotten the reason why he'd run away in
the first place — his duty towards Franzi, now that his father
was dead and Rolf was the man of the house.

"She's not going to listen to you, is she?" Theo pointed out. "A little titch of ten."

"Ten-and-a-half—soon be eleven," Rolf said. "She might listen to me. She's been a good sister to me, and she loves me."

"I know what she loves," Otto said with a guffaw.

"Shut up, Robber. You're filthy."

With one thing and another, the plan to return to Cologne and put Franzi straight kept being postponed.

They thought of themselves as outlaws, hunted, everybody looking for them, and so they kept to the hills, and avoided towns and big villages, steered clear of any kind of official person. They lost track of the date, knew only that it was high summer and that the days were long and hot.

From time to time formations of aeroplanes cast their many-winged shadows over the hillsides, darkening the landscape. Making eye shields of their hands, they stood looking up at these planes and following their passage across the bright sky, and their shadows moving from one range of hills to the next. On one occasion they recognized the Stuka dive-bombers from their gull-shaped wings—they had a little dip in them—and their undercarriages like a hawk's talons.

The sight of these planes made them silent and broody for a while, and a few days later, as they walked along a high mountain path, some of the long twisting curls of mist in the valley drifted aside to show them convoys of motorized vehicles, escorted by motorcycle outriders, heading eastwards.

The nights were getting chilly now, up where they were: the height of summer was past and the air had a warning bite to it at times, even during the day.

When they began to get hoarfrost on the ground in the mornings, they decided to go lower, and at the first village that they came to, learned that the war had started and that the victorious German armies had reached Warsaw.

Now they could no longer sleep in the open; there were

141

black pigs everywhere, checking railway station waiting rooms and bus shelters, rounding up vagrants and putting them to work in the munitions factories.

To get out of the rain they sometimes slept in abandoned vehicles on municipal rubbish dumps or stowed away on trains of coal barges plying the Rhine. It might be several days before the tug's pilot found them. Food was proving much harder to come by now that they couldn't sleep out in fields and raid a chicken coop in the dead of night.

Then winter started to set in, and their boots were worn out and they had no overcoats (they'd been going around with their blankets draped around themselves). One morning, waiting shivering in an open barn and seeing snow everywhere, Theo said what they had all been thinking for some days: that their wandering would have to be brought to a stop and they'd have to go home.

PART TWO
Cologne
Autumn–Winter
1944–5

THE RUBBLE HEAP

SEVEN

Rolf had kicked his stone all the way along the Komöd-ienstrasse, stopping periodically to search for it in a pile of rubble. You'd have thought that there was something special about this stone, instead of its being just one of millions and millions. The whole city was a pile of stones. "Come on!" Otto kept saying, pulling his filthy white silk scarf up over his mouth and nose as Rolf stirred up the acrid dust searching for his stone again.

Rolf had grown — he was almost sixteen — but was still a lot smaller than Otto, who had shot up and broadened out, and developed a long slouching stride, a lolling tongue, and a leering eye. Now, his hands, as usual, were stuck deep in trouser pockets and his shoulders hunched forward inside a tattered blue blazer, made in England, whose one remaining gilt anchor button hung by a thread. On his head, at the angle of a sinking ship going down bow first, sat a Hungarian diplomat hat, dusty and battered. A fag end was stuck in a

145

corner of his mouth, sending curls of smoke up his face. Rolf, too, was in English attire: in his case, a checkered golfing jacket, much too big for him, hanging halfway down his thighs, filthy, his elbows sticking through the sleeves. He also had a white silk scarf, which he wore knotted, not like a tie but at the breastbone. He wore short trousers and white socks rolled down over the boot tops. His boots were good quality, army, laced up with string. And he had his guitar with the elaborate inlaying around the sound hole and the ebony fingerboard with inlaid pearl position dots.

His dark and dirty hair spilled in uncut profusion over his face, requiring frequent combing-back movements of his fingers to restore to him some limited degree of vision. Behind this tumbledown mass of impenetrable seaweed, his eyes were as alert and searching as a bandit's peering through the slits in his mask.

Both he and Otto were on the lookout for food: all they'd eaten last night were potato peels, and since then nothing.

To take his mind off his stomach, Rolf unslung his guitar and began to sing in a jaunty voice:

> *When the buffalo races over the prairie,*
> *And the cowboy throws his lasso,*
> *Never a girl said No.*
> *When Johnny sings his love song.*

Otto took off his hat and turned it upside down to hold out to passers-by. Nobody put anything in it. One person spat. Rolf's song wasn't appreciated. Dreamily he remembered how he and Otto used to go stealing milk bottles from people's doorsteps — it was easy then. Nowadays people didn't even have doorsteps, with everything blown to bits the way it was.

Rolf carried on singing. You could never know: sometimes you struck lucky and your singing was liked and rewarded.

They were ambling towards the cathedral square. A small section of sky had cleared and a pale sun shone through the drifting smoke. People had come out of the *Dom-bunker* and were standing against the shrapnel-pitted concrete to catch a few precious rays, eyes closed, faces turned up. Some of the women lay on the narrow strips of grass verge between the steel doors of the bunker, as if they were in a park or something, and let their children play in the debris. There didn't seem to be any danger for the moment, though they hadn't heard the all-clear. Often the all-clear didn't sound, for one reason or another; and just as often the alarm sounded for no reason.

The unexpected sunshine was bringing more and more women out of the bunker; they stood all in a row like wallflowers at a dance. Old men sat on stone steps holding leatherette briefcases, filled with potatoes, tightly to their chests. People were eating. A mother was carefully dividing a bar of chocolate and handing out squares to her three children. One of the wallflowers bit into a jam roll. A thin, wheezy old man, without his false teeth, crushed orange segments between his lips and pressed out the juice. Rolf and Otto exchanged glances at the sight of such brazen eating; with an ingratiating air they ambled up to the mothers, and Rolf plucked his guitar and sang:

> *When the sirens are sounding in Hamburg,*
> *A sailor's got to return to ship.*

The mothers didn't look up, they carried on sunning themselves, or munching, or giving chocolate to their children, quite immune to such blandishments from louse boys.

> *In the den a little girl is sitting,*

Rolf sang with a jaunty swing beat,

> *Dreaming of the great big world.*
> *Rio de Janeiro, ahoi caballero.*
> *Hamburger girls are faithful.*

147

Otto was shuffling around, his Hungarian diplomat hat out. Only the children responded at all to these strangely dressed youths, with their long hair. The mothers shook their heads disapprovingly as Rolf crossed his eyes and wiggled his ears.

Rio de Janeiro, ahoi caballero!
Schlaf!! Krabom!!! Krakatakataaa!!!!

The children were delighted.

"We haven't ate in two days, we're war orphans," Rolf said in his most appealing manner.

The mothers remained untouched: they had husbands and sons at the front, fighting — dying — for their country and thereby earning their dependants the right to eat. They knew all about these work-shy idlers, ruffians, good-for-nothings. Why weren't they at the Westwall digging trenches, if they wanted to eat?

"I got a bad leg," Rolf said, making his leg go lame, "and my friend's got a disease. Tuberculosis." Otto went into a convulsive fit of coughing. The mothers remained stony-faced throughout these histrionics, the old men glum; the children giggled.

"Come on," Rolf snarled, tugging Otto's blazer sleeve: the snarl lay just inside his appealing smile. They skipped off up to the Domplatz. The vast stone-flagged square was littered with the dismembered carcases of abandoned motor vehicles stripped to the bare rusting metal of their chassis-frames, everything removable having been scavenged long ago. The debris had been shovelled into neat heaps, leaving the access to the cathedral clear. There were sand piles every few metres, and receptacles containing grappling hooks for handling incendiary bombs, and stirrup pumps by the side of water tanks.

Sunlight, lightly laced with wisps of drifting smoke from across the Rhine, struck the massive expanse of clerestory stained glass; the cathedral blazed briefly; then the flame was

148

extinguished by a passage of clouds, and the twin Gothic spires loomed, intact, over the surrounding devastation. The *Dom* had suffered only light damage — a pillar of the north-west tower had been brought down and a hole ten metres high torn out of the wall. This hole had been bricked up and the damage was hardly apparent from outside.

"Could I eat a great big fat piece of meat — could I eat a horse!" Rolf said, gnawing the palm of his hand.

"What you got to say that for? Have you got to remind me?"

A group of *Hitlerjugend* were approaching: they had the officious, self-important strut of a *Strafendienst* patrol. Rolf and Otto exchanged looks. When the HJs were about ten metres away they stopped and conferred among themselves, seemingly somewhat hesitant about coming any nearer.

"Got your papers?" the leader of the patrol called across the safe distance that he was wisely keeping.

"Kiss my arse, arse-licker!" Rolf replied smartly.

"Don't you know," the patrol leader said sternly, "that everybody over fifteen has to register for war work? Even girls," he added sneeringly.

"Why don't you come nearer, if you want to see our papers," Otto invited.

"Come into my parlour, said the spider to the fly," Rolf boldly enticed. The *Hitlerjugend* stood stubbornly still, jaw stuck out.

"He's waiting for reinforcements," Otto taunted.

Rolf examined the HJ closely and said, as a formal declaration of war:" If my arse looked like your face, I'd be ashamed to shit."

The HJ replied, "What makes you think everybody looks like you, shit-face?"

After this ritual exchange, honour had to be satisfied, and commanding his men to follow, the leader advanced.

"Papers," he blurted out. "Let's see your papers."

Rolf and Otto, not having papers, produced their knives

instead: they flashed in the sun. The HJ patrol leader stopped, considered his options, and decided against tackling these ruffians. HJs had been known to be stabbed in such encounters. Opting for the cautious approach, he unbuttoned the pleated flap pocket of his shirt, took out a small notebook with attached pencil, and made an official note.

"It's all been noted down," he told them. "Everything. It'll all be in my report."

"Want our names?" Rolf demanded. There was something familiar about the patrol leader.

"I know who you are. You're Rolf—I *know*. You're Rolf Hacker, the Louse Boy. And your friend's Otto. Otto the Robber. Still up to no good, I see."

"It's Addi," Rolf cried. "It's old prick-face Addi."

"Heil Hitler!" Addi said.

"Heil Benny Goodman!" Rolf replied.

"Swing Heil!" Otto said.

When the *Strafendienst* patrol had beaten their retreat, Rolf remarked, "Imagine! *Addi*. Goody-goody Addi still at it. *Could I eat a horse!*"

"You already said that," Otto objected. "You're just making me hungrier saying it all the time."

"Let's give the station a try," Rolf countered.

The cobbled forecourt area of the main railway station was packed with would-be travellers, who sat on the ground, or on their suitcases, surrounded by bundles, children, and grannies. The great dome showed its bare iron ribs; the mullioned lights above the arched entranceway had become a black void; the big bow windows were bricked up, reducing them to narrow slits. The imperial crown sat askew on top of a corbelled tower, whose rose window had become a huge, sightless eye; the national emblem—the Nazi eagle—was missing one of its wings; and the station clock had stopped, its hands at five past noon.

Ordnugspolizei and red-capped railway officials guarded the station to keep unauthorized travellers at bay.

What interested Rolf and Otto was the fact that many of the waiting people were eating — it was, approximately speaking, lunchtime. Wandering between brown paper parcels, bundles, and bags, the two boys kept a sharp lookout for half-eaten sandwiches that might have been left lying around, or for any unwatched Thermos flasks or bread tins.

Now, Rolf and Otto joined a group of women arguing with a railway official. The women were waving pieces of paper in the air, and the official was shaking his head exasperatedly — couldn't they understand that their pieces of paper were no use? What good were pieces of paper if there were no trains, and there *were* no trains, except for troop trains. In response to their cries of protest, the official advised road travel. Ah yes, petrol was a problem. He quite agreed: unobtainable. As unobtainable as a seat on a train. He didn't doubt it at all. Bicycles? he wondered. Might they be the solution? Or a horse and cart? No, no, of course, horses had to be fed . . . A bicycle, then. That was the solution. He wished to wash his hands of these clamorous women, but they said that they didn't have bicycles, bicycles were hard to find — impossible to find. That left walking, the official suggested. The weather was good . . . Yes, but what about babies and grannies, the aged and the sick? Yes, yes, he agreed, the aged and the sick were a problem, but what could he do? There were no trains. He could not *make* trains out of thin air, could he? He was only an official. Still the women around him refused to leave. They knew all about such officials. He might suddenly discover that he did have a few seats after all — seats that had become unexpectedly free — and then would allocate these to anyone prepared to make it worth his while. So the women waited outside the station. In any case, they had nowhere else to go. In the evening if they had not found a place on a train they would have to return to the air-raid shelters.

While the railway official and the *Ordnugspolizei* were fully occupied with these women, Rolf and Otto slipped under a chain barrier and into the station. In the vast, high-ceilinged ticket hall every window had a CLOSED blind pulled down, with the exception of one which had a stand in front of it on which was written: SPECIAL TRAVEL AUTHORIZATIONS (BLUE) ONLY. A long queue extended from it, past all the closed windows, almost as far as the left-luggage hall.

"Black pigs," Rolf hissed, ducking down and pulling Otto. The boys made their way to the end of the queue, keeping low, and then to the central arrivals and departures area, where they wound their way through groups of soldiers waiting in the long echoing halls. Shattered Belle Epoch windows let in cross-currents of draughts sweeping litter back and forth along the platform where a troop train stood under the curved skydome. Of the dome's thousands of panes of glass, not one remained intact. Then back along the platform, as another draught predominated, came the dust-laden wave of litter, washing up railway tickets, peanut shells, cigarette ends, balls of silver paper, old magazines at the feet of the soldiers. Some, exhausted, had lain down on the ground and taken off their heavy pack harnesses, unslung their rifles, loosened belts and straps, and unclipped their more bulky equipment. It was piled all around — ribbed metal gas-mask cannisters, entrenchment tools, Schmeisser pouches, the folded *Zeltbahnen* (waterproof capes that became one-man tents), machine-gun barrels in long leather carrying cases. Rolf and Otto were looking for mess tins. Usually soldiers carried them clipped to the back of their belts but had to unclip them to lie down.

Keeping their eyes peeled, the two boys moved among the soldiers, and Rolf unslung his guitar and sang:

> *When the buffalo races over the prairie,*
> *And the cowboy throws his lasso,*
> *Never a girl said No.*
> *When Johnny sings his love song.*

Meanwhile, Otto importuned the soldiers:

"Got any old bits of chocolate you don't want? . . . American chewing gum? . . . You still want that stale old bun? . . . You going to eat that, or you going to throw it away?"

None of the soldiers responded to Otto's requests. Some of them were asleep or half-asleep on the ground, using their rolled-up greatcoats as pillows. They were grey and dusty men in grey and dusty uniforms made of wool waste and rayon and shoddy. The material did not hang well; it crumpled easily. It had a coarse and unpleasant feel to the skin. Their field caps, with battered, shapeless brims, sat lopsidedly on slumped heads, or had been placed over the eyes of men trying to get a few winks of sleep. There was opportunity here. As he went from man to man, Otto made a point of knocking over mess tins, and in righting them established if they were empty or not.

The welcome that they were getting from the soldiers was no warmer than from the mothers. Rolf's singing wasn't appreciated. Perhaps these troops preferred more sentimental songs. Perhaps they didn't like the way Rolf and Otto were dressed, their long dishevelled hair, the glass collar stud that Rolf wore in his lapel as if it was a decoration. Perhaps these soldiers didn't think that such a work-shy youth merited a decoration.

Otto was giving Rolf eye signals. They had it all worked out. Had done this lots of times before. After they'd grabbed something, they hared off in opposite directions and then met at the steamboat arrivals quay.

There were notices up all over the station, addressing warnings to the soldiers:

BEWARE THIEVES AND PICKPOCKETS!

and,

WATCH YOUR TONGUE — THE ENEMY IS LISTENING

Loose talk of a demoralizing nature must be avoided; it was a grave offence to spread panic and dismay.

Other posters spoke of other dangers:

SOLDATEN! BE PROTECTED ALSO WHEN YOU GO
INTO ACTION ON THE HOME FRONT — WEAR YOUR
"COMBAT SOCKS." PROTECT YOURSELVES AGAINST
VENEREAL DISEASES.

Otto was getting ready to pounce. He'd found a mess tin by a sleeping soldier, and it appeared to be full. His mouth was drooling at the thought of what it might contain — liver paste? bread? ham sausage? He was signalling Rolf to be ready. But now the sleeping soldier suddenly opened his eyes, yawned, stretched. Was he going back to sleep again? Rolf was carrying on singing, meanwhile; he caught sight of a new poster, its message rather too close to home for his liking.

BEWARE THE ROBBER-CHILDREN!

In this time of trial for the German people . . .

he read with a sour expression,

. . . a new pest has arisen in our hard-hit cities: dispossessed itinerant children, belonging nowhere and to no one, who prey on weary and careless soldiers, robbing them of their possessions, money, equipment, and food rations. Some of these robbers are very young, as young as ten or twelve. Mostly they are youths between fourteen and eighteen. Attention! The robber-children have appealing ways, winning smiles, they masquerade as minstrels and entertainers, offer little services, tell touching stories. They may seem pathetic and lost. BUT BEWARE! REMEMBER THE WOLF-BOY HAS BEEN NURTURED BY THE WOLF AND BEFORE YOU KNOW IT HIS TEETH ARE IN YOUR THROAT.

BEWARE THE WOLF CHILDREN!

154

Rolf exchanged looks with Otto. Otto shrugged: these propaganda posters were everywhere. Nobody gave them more than a passing glance, or so he hoped. But the soldier who had just woken up was looking suspicious, his face covered in sweat; his skin and eyes were yellow, his breathing strained.

"There!" he suddenly cried, pointing at Otto. "That's one of them. That's one of the Wolf Children — they take the food out of our mouths."

It was obvious that the soldier was sick with fever, and seeing things. All the same, now that Otto had been pointed out, other eyes went to him, and to the notice, and seeing these two strangely attired youths, one with a guitar singing *Hottmusik,* the other skulking around up to no good, the soldiers told them: "Piss off, scum!"

Rolf decided to take the hint and went, and Otto followed him. A quick look round to see if they were being observed and then they both ducked under a ticket barrier and ran along the platform where the troop train was drawn up.

Walking the length of the train, they called up to soldiers at the windows:

"Want your boots cleaned?"

"Got any chocolate?"

"Give us a bit of your bread."

"Want some addresses of girls? Very clean, very good."

But they were making no more headway with their new approach than with Rolf's guitar-playing and singing. They reached the last carriage, which had all its blinds pulled down, and walked the length of it slowly, trying to look in. A sleeping car for officers.

"I got to take a piss," Rolf said.

"Me too."

Rolf unbuttoned himself and directed a stream of urine with considerable accuracy into the oiling valve of the wheel axle. "Get it in there," he urged Otto, who was wasting his piss on the rail tracks.

"What for?"

"Acid!" Rolf explained. "Rusts up the lubrication joints. Gets the wheel axles rusted up." He grinned broadly. "Grinds the trains to a halt."

"So how many troop trains you ground to a halt with your piss, Louse Boy?" Otto scoffed.

"Hundreds of them," Rolf boasted.

"Oh yes?"

"I've got burning piss," Rolf said powerfully.

It was worth trying, Otto decided. No point wasting it. So he redirected the last trickle towards the wheel axle: to burn it up.

As they were buttoning their flies they realized they were being observed. A blind in one of the sleeping compartments had been raised and a man with a plump and rosy face was looking down.

"Well, now, what have we here? Lads of the street. Wild youth. Pissing on the Reich's railway carriages! Such exciting criminality!" He turned his head slightly to speak to somebody behind him. "But they're a couple of filthy street brats," he said to this person. "Wolfgang! you're incorrigible."

Upon reflection, he nonetheless acceded to his companion's suggestion.

"Boys! I'm sure you must be hungry. Two big lads like you. Must have a ravenous appetite, and what chance to satisfy it in such terrible times as these. Would you care for something to eat?"

"Yes, we would," Rolf said.

"Step up, my lads, step up. We'll see what we can manage, I cannot promise you cordon bleu . . . hah-hah! But — chicken sandwiches? Would that suit?" His cheeks were becoming rosier and rosier.

Neither Rolf nor Otto had ever been inside a sleeping car and were astonished that so much luxuriousness could be compressed into such a small space. The walls were of gleaming wood with borders of marquetry inlay; the seats were

156

deeply upholstered in red plush; white antimacassars protected the headrests and armrests. Below the window, a half-oval folding table had been opened out and was covered with a tablecloth. On it stood a bottle of Remy Martin cognac and small white plates with the leftovers of the cheese course. It was evident that the rosy-cheeked man was an officer, an *Oberleutnant,* perhaps, perhaps even a *Hauptmann.* There was no encrusted mud on his riding boots: they were polished to a high brilliance and the tops tightly strapped to the calf; his uniform was not made of shoddy and waste wool like the uniforms of the ordinary soldiers — his was of an excellent cloth, it fitted, and did not crease unduly. There were emblems on his shoulder straps, two gilt pips on light-blue braiding, and two bars on his stiff collar, which cut a little into the flesh of his chin. The other man in the train compartment was slimmer and younger and had fair hair and only one pip on his shoulder strap and one bar at the collar, which did not cut into his chin. His riding boots were just as impeccable as the higher officer's, and his smile as furtive, as the two boys were bidden to enter and to make themselves at ease in the red plush seats, which they had reason to believe could rapidly become beds.

"Wolfgang," the rosy-cheeked one commanded the other, "go and see what we can find for these boys to eat. The stewards are so long, always. Chicken? That would suit you?" he asked the two boys with exquisite politeness. "And beers, I think, Wolfgang. Beers. Beers will suit you young gentlemen? Or shall it be something stronger?" He indicated the bottle of cognac. "And, Wolfgang, bring towels. The boys may wish to wash their hands. Hmm?"

In the course of squeezing past them in the tight space, Wolfgang gave each boy an encouraging shoulder squeeze. The rosy-cheeked officer sat down by the window and patted the place next to him. Otto sat there and Rolf opposite. They were offered cigarettes from a silver cigarette case. The officer consulted his wristwatch at some length, pursing his lips and working out a complicated timetable. The outcome was satisfactory and he beamed. After a minute or so he drummed his fingers on the upholstery. Impatiently he drummed Otto's thigh next, and then lowered the window blind.

"It's best that nobody sees you boys eating. This train is reserved for military personnel. People might get jealous." With the blind down, the officer's nature underwent an abrupt unbending: he became highly relaxed in his posture, virtually sprawled; he stretched his legs and smiled intimately at the boys.

"One more day of freedom," he said, taking them into his confidence, "and then tomorrow it's back to respectability." He rubbed his face wearily at that dull and dismal prospect. "Of course," he added slyly, "for boys like you that presents no problem, eh? — respectability. Lucky you! Hmm?"

By way of emphasis, he gave a pat to Otto's thigh, and then absentmindedly left his hand there. He carried on talking as if this errant hand had nothing to do with him. "I have always envied youths such as yourselves. With nothing to lose — no *position* to lose. Nothing expected of you. How delightful! The life of the primitive savage. Instead of . . ." His free hand went around, taking in the polished wood and the red plush. ". . . instead of all these useless appurtenances of position." He let them into a secret. "I detest my position, let me tell you. How I envy you boys of the streets; you are free, beholden to no one. Wonderful, wonderful! Ah, there you are, Wolfgang!"

Wolfgang had returned with chicken sandwiches cut into triangular halves, and with beer. The plates and glasses were put on the table, and at once the two boys fell upon the food, stuffing their mouths full.

"What appetites," observed the rosy Hauptmann, "what wonderful appetites." He moved the hand that had been casually resting on Otto's thigh up to his crotch, only for a moment, as if from a further access of absentmindedness.

Otto stopped eating and looked at Rolf. Then both boys ate faster. Wolfgang had seated himself next to Rolf, and in leaning across him towards the half-oval window table to give him a beer, placed an arm lightly around his shoulder, in a comradely fashion. Rolf ate faster still. The rosy Hauptmann was off again on his absentminded wanderings, and Otto looked as if he wasn't enjoying his chicken sandwich. Wolfgang's comradely hand was playing with the long, tousled hair over Rolf's ears while Rolf tried to get a stack of three chicken sandwiches into his mouth — he had managed one bite when Wolfgang's abrupt change of tactics (commencing to unbutton Rolf's flies) brought Rolf to his feet. He took a quick gulp of beer to wash down a mouthful of chicken and bread, and said:

"Sir, we've got to leave now."

"Yes, that's right," Otto said, also getting to his feet; to do so he had to violently disengage the hand clamped on his genitals. The rosy Hauptmann's cheeks now were a deep red.

"Sit down!" he commanded. "You have not been given permission to leave the table. Eat!"

"We're not hungry," Otto said unconvincingly.

"We'll eat later, thanks ever so much," Rolf said, trying to fill his pockets with chicken sandwiches.

"No, you won't," the Hauptmann declared, reaching across and knocking the sandwiches on the floor. Rolf at once got on his knees to pick them up, only to find the sole of a highly shined boot pressed against his face. A hard push and he went sprawling.

"Get out of here, riffraff," the Hauptmann ordered. "Diseases of your mothers' bellies. Out! Out!"

"Herr Hauptmann, we're going, Herr Hauptmann. Straight away. If you wouldn't mind unchaining the door, Herr Hauptmann?"

Wolfgang, as pale as his superior was red, unchained the door, and becoming even paler, sped on each boy with a kick

159

in the behind, sending them tumbling down the steps of the train.

Smoke from the fires on the right bank was drifting slowly across the river, creeping under the Rhine bridges. Falling wet ash produced a sudden rainbow. Then it was gone. The boys felt the ash on their faces, in their hair. The air was alternately bright and vibrant and then dim and acrid as gusts of wind toppled the high smoke and blew it towards them.

The whole riverside area was a wasteland, and the river itself a turgidly flowing scum that washed up on the upended hulls of sunken ships. The cargo vessels and barges still plying their routes had to run an obstacle course of drifting hulks. The pleasure steamers *Beethoven* and *Overstolz* had been sunk more than three years ago, and now there were many newer wrecks, rusting and covered in slime and river filth, to make this stretch of the Rhine a graveyard of ships and boats of all kinds. The battered quaysides added to the general picture of desolation and decay; a few hundred metres from the embankment, in the Altermarkt, the tall, gabled houses with their steeply pitched roofs and differently coloured façades had mostly been destroyed or rendered unhabitable. The ancient Town Hall lay in ruins, the flames had reached as far as the old "firewatcher's room" in the Gothic spire of the high tower; the Spanischer Bau was no more than a heap of stones. Rolf and Otto kicked around in this rubble in a desultory fashion. There was always a chance of finding something that could be sold or bartered for food. But their random excavations were yielding no results today, and they made their way to the Hohe Strasse, where, here and there, a few shops remained open: behind their half-lowered iron shutters business, of one sort or another, still went on. Some of the great old firms continued to deal, if on a much reduced scale, in jewels and furs and gold and objets d'art, and hanging around here Rolf and Otto had sometimes earned themselves twenty pfennigs cleaning shoes. There was a stand in a

160

side street further along where for twenty pfennigs you could get a piece of bread soaked in beetroot juice. If they were lucky they might even pick up a couple of marks conducting officers to one of several cafés where whisky or cognac was served in coffee cups, or something called "Hollyvoot cocktail," a sickly mixture of grenadine syrup and rum, and where young girls of a better type than the railway station whores were to be found.

Slouching around on the lookout for customers (either for a shoeshine or a girl), they suddenly caught sight of Kriminalassistent Nold ducking under one of the half-lowered shutters behind which expensive pleasures were available. Well, well, well, they said to themselves. Who could be treating the Herr Kriminalassistent today? A Kriminalassistent's pay for a month was hardly enough to buy one of these expensive girls and the obligatory "champagne" or "whisky" in coffee cups. Rolf ducked his head under the shutter to take a look-see; at once he was grabbed by the scruff of the neck by the establishment's bouncer.

"What d'you want, Louse Boy?"

"Just taking a look what you got. Might have a customer for you."

Held by the neck, he was permitted a look lasting about one second and then kicked out. But it was long enough for him to have seen in the candlelit bar two girls, Herr Gast, and Kriminalassistent Nold. Nold was known to be in Gast's pocket; the thin, tense detective had a weakness for girls, and Gast was a past master at catering to those who might be useful to him someday. Detective Nold was no one very important, but he *was* in the Gestapo, and even if his rank was lowly he must be quite useful to have in your pocket, they supposed.

They continued to prowl around the area of the Hohe Strasse, looking for a meal. There were restaurants here. They could smell waffle-baking. They could smell rich sauces made with butter. With money, you could eat — eat well, even these days: game, fish, poultry, such luxury items were

161

off-ration. But they had no money, and no food cards with which to get ordinary rations, and the bites of chicken sandwich had made them even hungrier than they were before.

As night fell they had still eaten nothing else and were ravenous as wolves. Now they were no longer looking for a shoeshine to buy them bread soaked in beetroot juice. Their hunger had got beyond that stage. There was an emptiness in their bellies, a taste of ash in their mouths, and a chill on their hearts that made them ready for anything, honed them down to bare essentials: robber eyes and thieving fingers.

They were standing in a doorway, smoking their cigarette stubs down to the last drag, when both of them saw the rosy-cheeked Hauptmann of the highly shined riding boots. He was on the prowl too, but not for food.

He turned into a side street to explore, and automatically, without as much as a look passing between them, they followed him. He was putting his head under half-lowered shutters, pushing open curtained doors, and peering into dim interiors. Well, they knew what he was looking for. They followed his glittering riding boots through the dark night from one joint to another. Sometimes he went into a place, if it seemed to hold out some promise for him; but he was soon out again, unaccompanied. To find what he was seeking required a certain knowledge of the lowlife of these streets, which he lacked. But he seemed willing to explore. The night was young for him, and tomorrow it was the return to respectability. The prospect of that gave him energy and incentive for his *louche* trek: his shiny boots crunched through the debris as he ventured further afield, trying here, trying there. He trudged across bomb sites, glass shattering and tinkling; he splashed through puddles of stagnant water from burst water mains, and his boots were beginning to lose their glitter. From time to time he got out his cigarette lighter — must be the gold lighter, they told themselves — lit it, and moved the long thin flame this way and that, to try and make out objects in the dark. He peered ahead — there was some con-

162

gress of shadows that lured him, and he stumbled over the rough ground, his boots getting muddier and muddier now. Once or twice he almost fell. But that simply made him walk faster, sure that something was going on further in the dark. Following the light of his cigarette lighter, they realised that he was making towards the old marketplace with the fountain, and the gutted church on the far side. It seemed to be towards the church that he was heading. It was roofless, but its thick main walls had resisted the fire. Matches were being struck, cigarette lighters lit, battery torches switched on and off—winks of light that evidently had an unmistakable meaning to him, for he was hurrying towards them eagerly. They increased their pace to catch up with him, and then called, "Herr Hauptmann . . . Herr Hauptmann . . ." He stopped and turned and struck his cigarette lighter and held it up to see their faces. He recognized the wild youths from the railway station who had dealt his aroused expectations such a cruel disappointment earlier that day. So! They were regretting now that they had not been more accommodating. Had evidently changed their minds and were accosting him. He could not resist a little smile of triumph. His cheeks burned with the scarlet fever. Having rejected his earlier offer, they were now coming crawling to him — how exciting! He would be severe with them; not needing to play the seducer, he would be the master. What delights he had in store! And since Wolfgang was not with him, he would have them both to himself. A double delight before the return to respectability on the morrow. He waited for them with masterful ease in a patch of high weeds. The desolateness of the setting added to his arousal. No warning bells sounded in his head, or if they did, they were thrillingly blended with his excitement, heightening his expectancy.

His eyes became filmy as he saw them produce their knives; he did not try to run. The rosiness emptied out of his cheeks, leaving only pinpoints of red; he was in a half-faint of voluptuous terror. Rolf pressed the point of his knife into the

Hauptmann's double chin, above the stiff uniform collar, while Otto slashed open the tunic with rapid strokes and emptied out pockets — the silver cigarette case he stuffed in his jacket, and the gold lighter; the army papers and food card he took as well. But where was his money? Otto inserted the point of his knife into the fine-quality trouser material just below the crotch and cut upwards through the pocket and heard a few coins fall out; he scrabbled around for these in the dark but they did not amount to much. He repeated the same action on the other side and was rewarded with a further tinkling of coins and gathered these too — a pittance! Keys . . . Where was the money? He jabbed his hand into the slashed pockets, searching around the soft belly for a money belt, and felt some blood on his fingers: the Hauptmann's thigh had been lightly scored by the knife point.

Otto grumbled, "He's got no money."

"He must have." Pressing the point of his knife into the double chin, Rolf demanded: "Where d'you keep your money?" but the Hauptmann had fainted. Matches were being struck a dozen metres away, a cigarette lighter was lit. A voice demanded if anyone had a torch. They saw a soldier draw a pistol.

"He must have a secret pocket," Rolf said.

They turned over the prostrate body and used their knives to slash open flap pockets, tunic lining, and their hands went everywhere, searching.

"Get his watch," Rolf said, and Otto quickly unstrapped it from the Hauptmann's wrist.

Meanwhile, Rolf was tearing open the shirt and searching the armpits for some kind of body purse strapped there. Nothing. Nothing.

"He can't have come out without money," Otto said, enraged. Rolf thought Otto might kill the Hauptmann out of frustration.

"Come on," Rolf said.

164

Matches were being struck close by and voices were calling out, demanding to know what was going on here. The tattered Hauptmann was stirring on the ground, groaning, whimpering—he could be heard.

They had no choice but to run. In seconds the ruins had swallowed them as the cry "Wolf Children" went up.

By roundabout routes they made their way to the Breite Strasse and from there across the Hohenzollernring to the tramway stop in Friesen Platz. They were in luck, a tram was coming—a rare sight: overfull, of course, with passengers clinging to the footplates, and there was a crowd at the stop desperate to get on, fighting and pushing. Rolf and Otto ignored the undignified scramble and stayed back until the tram started to move off again, spilling excess passengers in all directions. The two boys ran alongside while it gathered speed, and as the first carriage passed them, leapt up onto the coupling. Rolf balanced himself on the narrow, shaking iron plate.

"I know where he kept his money," he said, suddenly wanting to be sick. "In his boots. In his lousy, pissy, shining boots, that's where. We should have took his boots off."

In his fury Otto kicked the tram carriage hard enough to make a dent.

They rode on the coupling plate as far as the Ehrenfeldgürtel, where they jumped off, Otto saying he knew a Herr Ruffentauer who would give them a good price for the gold cigarette lighter, gold wristwatch, and silver cigarette case. But when they got to his premises in the Subbelratherstrasse they found them closed, the roller shutters down and plastered with proclamations and propaganda posters.

"What do we do now?" Rolf demanded. Otto was the robber; he was supposed to know about getting rid of stolen goods.

"We'll find somebody else to take the stuff," Otto said airily. "Tomorrow. It's going to have to be tomorrow. See, everything's closed now, isn't it?"

Disconsolately, hands in pockets, shoulders hunched, they ambled on, feeling their failure in their empty stomachs.

They turned into their own street, and it was like going down a coal hole, it was so black. Half the stray dogs of the neighbourhood scurried under their feet, howling for food. Otto kicked them away, threw stones at them, but they continued to trail after the two boys. Wouldn't go away.

And then suddenly they all went howling off to the other side of the street, the whole mangy, rabid pack of them, and were snarling and pawing at something on the ground, and barking excitedly.

"They've got a rat," Otto said.

Rolf peered into the dark, thinking that whatever it was, it was a lot bigger than a rat — there were dogs pulling and tearing at it from all sides.

"A dead cat, what d'you want to bet," Rolf said.

"No, it's bigger'n a cat."

Crossing the road to see what the dogs had got hold of, Rolf saw them tearing at a pair of worn-out boots, the uppers separated from the soles, only held together by puttee bindings, which avid canine teeth were pulling undone. The man in the boots did not resist, or move even. He looked dead. The dogs, having got the puttee bindings partially unwound, moved up the still form. They tore ravenously at the army greatcoat and approached the throat. Rolf tried to shoo them away with shouts and by throwing stones, but they took no notice, and it was only when Otto started kicking them, and slashing at them with his knife, that they began to back away, showing their teeth, snarling and growling.

"He isn't dead," Rolf said.

The form on the ground was moving. They heard laboured breathing interspersed with groans.

Taking him under the armpits, they began to drag him to his feet; at first he was a dead weight, but he seemed to become aware of being helped and contributed what little strength he had to the business of getting up. He was breathing gaspingly, and they could smell vomit on him, and the stench of feverish perspiration, and piss and excrement.

"He's sick," Rolf said.

"Maybe he's got the typhus," Otto said, letting go of the tottering man all of a sudden and causing him to sway about violently, since Rolf couldn't support him alone.

"Let him go," Otto said. "I tell you he's got typhus. You want to catch it?"

"Give me a light," Rolf demanded, struggling to keep the tottering man standing.

Otto approached warily and struck a match and held it up to the man's face, and then another and another. Sickness and exhaustion and hunger had wasted him, hollowed out his cheeks, stretched his flesh thinly over jagged bones, and made it as yellow as old parchment.

"Come closer," Rolf insisted. "What you scared of? Come on, hold the match up."

Otto approached gingerly and held the match higher, almost to the level of the man's eyes, which stared fixedly at a distant point, not reacting to the light; the eyes seemed unaware of the two boys helping him, but the body, acting of its own accord, availed itself of the help, and he flung an arm around Rolf's shoulder and transferred some of his weight to him.

"Come on, Robber," Rolf called. "I can't hold him myself. Help me."

"Leave him go, leave the bugger go," Otto said.

"You seen who it is?"

"What?"

"I said — you seen who it is?"

Otto struck another match and brought it close to the face of the slumped man, to his staring, unreacting eyes. He moved the match all around, up and down, doubtingly, not quite ready to believe what he was seeing.

"It's Kurt," he said finally. "That's who it is."

"Come on, give me a hand, Robber."

167

"What for? He's half-dead, might as well let him . . ."

"Help me, Robber," Rolf insisted.

"What he ever do for you?" Otto objected, and then added sarcastically, " 'Course he was sweet on your sister, I know that."

"We can't just leave him here, with all these dogs," Rolf said matter-of-factly. "They'd tear him to bits."

Churlishly, Otto took Kurt's other arm and draped it around himself to give support and take some of the weight off Rolf.

"What we helping him for?" Otto demanded as together they half dragged, half carried the collapsed form down the road. "He's no friend of ours."

"We know him," Rolf said. "We can't just leave him, can we?"

"Why not?" Otto demanded surlily. "You think he'd do anything for us?"

"He's a deserter, isn't he?" Rolf said. "Must be. Stands to reason. Look at him. Look at the state he's in. Look at his feet. God Almighty! *Look!* He's a deserter, all right. They'll shoot him if they catch him."

"No skin off my nose," Otto said.

Struggling under the weight, Rolf said a touch peevishly, "We can't leave him. Don't you remember how he used to give us rides on his motorbike?"

EIGHT

They managed to get Kurt the hundred-or-so metres to a crumbling house with its windows all boarded up and its top floor open to the sky. They propped him against the front door, which was kept in one piece by two planks nailed across it in the form of an X, and while Otto held him, Rolf rapped on a board with the handle of his knife. Two knocks, a pause, then three knocks, a pause, then one knock.

Nervously they looked this way and that. It was dark in the street, but any moment a police patrol might come by, and how were they going to explain Kurt — a deserter? It was hard enough explaining themselves.

Eventually, they saw a crumpled ball of newspaper being removed from one of the gaps between boards, and an eye appeared; there followed the sound of unoiled bolts being drawn and of a piece of heavy furniture being pushed. It was only pushed so far as to enable the door to be opened wide enough to let one person at a time squeeze through. As soon as they were all in, they pushed the wardrobe back across the gap and shot home thick iron bolts at floor, middle, and top.

In the dark, a woman's voice said suspiciously, "Three? Three of you?"

"He's sick, we found him lying in the street," Rolf said.

"Who?" Franzi asked.

"The dogs would have tore him to bits."

"So! Another mouth to feed."

Franzi struck a match and held it to the face of the man being supported on Rolf's and Otto's shoulders. She pulled in her breath and the match went out.

For several seconds they stood in the dark, saying nothing. Then Franzi said, "How we going to get him down the ladder?"

"Otto goes down first," Rolf said, "and we lower him."

All in darkness, the trapdoor was lifted, and Otto went halfway down the ladder, and then Kurt was dragged to the hatch, his legs were pushed into the space, and while Rolf and Franzi held him under the arms, Otto got a hold on him from below, and rung by rung the descent was made.

Rolf and Franzi followed.

Down below they listened for the sound of the trapdoor being put back in place, and the bolts shot home, and only then did someone light a candle — a memorial candle in a glass, of the "everlasting" type. It gave such a small, pale flame it was not possible for Theo and Benno to make out the face of the sick man who had been brought into the cellar.

"Who is it?" Theo asked.

"It's Kurt," Franzi said matter-of-factly. "Kurt Springer. They found him in the street."

"We don't have enough grub for ourselves," Benno pointed out.

"We couldn't leave him," Rolf said sheepishly.

"The Louse Boy couldn't," Otto corrected.

"Well, he's here now, and that's that," Franzi said. "We'll just have to share between six instead of five. A little bit less for each of us. Can't be helped. It's done now."

Kurt was tottering. They took hold of him and laid him down on a pile of old ragged overcoats in a corner of the cellar. He was conscious but unfocused and seemed not to have registered where he was or with whom, and then his eyes rolled upwards and he seemed to pass out.

"Crikey! He's *sick*," Benno said.

"I think he's got the typhus," Otto said.

"You brought somebody here who may have typhus," Theo accused.

"We don't know that he's got typhus," Rolf excused himself, "do we?"

"Can't be helped," Franzi said again. "It can't be helped now. It's done, so there it is."

She lit another candle, one that gave more light, and went with it to where Kurt was slumped on the ground. She touched his brow with the back of her hand.

"He's burning up," she said. She looked carefully at his eyes, pulling the lids up with her fingers. She examined the sores and scabs around his mouth and on his cheek. She took his pulse, and opening his coat and shirt, placed her ear against his chest to listen to his heart.

"Bring a glass of water," she said.

Benno brought it to her.

She propped Kurt up, raising his head to an upright position, and pressed the glass to his mouth and tried to make him drink. Much of the water spilled down his chin and neck, but a small amount was taken in. The body seemed to know its need and drank, even though the mind was absent.

"More water," Franzi said when the glass was empty. "It's dehydration. From the dysentery." A sip at a time, she managed to get him to drink, and his eyes seemed to take on a better focus, even though he did not see.

171

"What d'you think he's got?" Rolf asked.

"I don't know. He's quite sick, I think." She shook her head. "Either he'll get better, or he'll die." It was as simple as that. "Maybe he's just starving like the rest of us, only more so."

She got up from the floor. She was twenty-one and the flirty little girl was no more; she was a proper woman now.

"Well," she said to Rolf and Otto, "did you get anything?"

"We got a silver cigarette case, and a watch and a gold lighter and . . ."

"Try eating a gold lighter," she said. "No food? No money?" She went to the paraffin stove, wound up the wick and lit it, and then lowered the flame carefully to reduce the smoking as much as possible, and closed the stove.

"Otto thinks he can sell the stuff," Rolf said. "He knows a fence."

"Well, we'll see, won't we?"

Now she occupied herself with the cooking; she took a large iron pot from the floor and placed it on the paraffin stove, and out of a piece of newspaper she unwrapped some bits of pork fat, cut them up very small, and threw them in the pot; from another tiny bundle she took a small shrivelled onion and carefully cut away the black parts, and what was left she sliced up and put in the hot fat and stirred; next, she reached in a paper bag and got out a fistful of potato peels, and added them to the pot. Stirring all the time, she threw in another fistful and another — making a mushy stew — until the smell and the smoke of frying had become almost unbearable in the cellar ventilated only by cracks and gaps in the ceiling.

"Better open the 'breakthrough,' " she told Rolf.

He went to do what she said, running his hands over the rough wall behind the stove until he had found the place where the bricks were loose; he extricated one or two at a time, piling them on the floor, until a hole the size of a man's

172

head and shoulders had been made. An updraft tugged at the cooking fumes, carrying them into the adjoining cellar and up through big holes in the floor and out into the rubble above.

Benno stared disgustedly at the brownish mess in the cooking pot and made a face.

"Good for you!" Franzi said, stirring hard to keep the stew from sticking. "Potato peels contain vitamins. Don't you know that? Plates! Come on, everyone. It's ready."

Otto pushed his plate forward and Franzi gave him a big dollop of the fried potato peels. Measuring each portion in relation to what was left in the pot, she served the others and herself and also filled a plate for Kurt. Seating herself next to him on the floor, she began to feed the semi-comatose man and he let himself be fed, opening his mouth and swallowing like a baby.

The meal was consumed in a couple of minutes, and to forget how hungry they still were, they at once lay down under overcoats and tattered old blankets and tried to sleep. Franzi occupied herself with Kurt, making her bed next to him, and arranging a coat for him as a pillow.

She watched him as he tossed and turned, groaning, gasping, teeth chattering, slipping off into moments of fraught sleep from which he awoke abruptly, eyes staring, face bathed in sweat, mumbling deliriously. The others eventually fell asleep, but she remained awake. From time to time she bent over him with a wet handkerchief and wiped the foaming saliva from his lips, and dabbed his forehead. To touch him was like touching a hot radiator. There was nothing more that she could do, having no medicines, not even an aspirin. If the fever got any higher, he would certainly die.

Towards 2 A.M. she dropped off and a few minutes later woke up to the sound of falling bombs and the steady, low thunder of aeroplanes. The planes were still some distance away, but coming nearer. From the comparative infrequency of explosions in relation to the noise of engines, she concluded that it was probably a firebomb raid. There were going to be hundreds of new fires by morning.

The others in the cellar were sleeping on, their internal alarm systems not yet activated by this level of sound. But the bombers had roused Kurt from his shallow fever sleep; his eyes were open and he was listening intently, with a kind of self-satisfied smirk on his face, as if in some way pleased that bombs were falling.

His eyes darted about with each distant thud. He seemed to be counting the explosions.

The high fever was making his body shake and his teeth rattle in sudden violent spasms. The explosions excited him, made him want to speak: words welled up in his mouth, forcing their way through the barrier of chattering teeth.

". . . Hecht said to him, 'Your trees will be growing better soon . . .'" The rattling teeth locked the rest of the sentence inside his mouth, until words were again forced through. ". . . Old men drew the shit carts . . . not enough horses . . . the old men were the beasts of burden . . . and children. Children . . . Child'd been dead five weeks under the floorboards . . . For the bread coupons, they said. That was what . . . He was a wedding entertainer, the father. Played the violin, told jokes. Did recitations . . . The bread ration'd been reduced again . . . It was the stench that finally . . ." Rattle, rattle, shiver, shiver! He shook all over. ". . . Beards weren't permitted . . . they did it for a joke . . . 'Here, Jew! Here!' . . . With their bayonets. They shaved him with their bayonets . . . He was terrified, naturally. Didn't know if they were going to cut his beard or his throat . . ."

Another bout of violent shivering and shaking reduced his words to an incomprehensible babble.

She urged him, "Don't tire yourself out."

Exhausted, he sank back onto the folded coat that served as a pillow.

174

He was mumbling. "It was true, the trees did grow better, as Hecht said they would," and then his eyes rolled up into his skull and he fell into a fever-coma.

They all woke at 5 A.M., except Kurt, who was still in a state of delirious slumber.

Franzi touched his hot, glistening face and shook her head. "He needs medicines."

She climbed the ladder to the ground floor and went to peer out through the boarded-up windows. The sky was red and smoky, the street empty. With the others who had joined her, she made an assessment of where the smoke was coming from. It wasn't far away, they decided.

"Come on, then," Franzi said, and the others, by saying nothing, consented. "Benno'd better stay here. In case . . ."

Theo nodded and Benno went back down the ladder, lowering the trapdoor behind him.

Otto, Rolf, Franzi, and Theo left one at a time at thirty-second intervals, wending their way through the rubble-littered streets, clambering across bomb sites, picking their way between piles of debris; they walked along shaky planks spanning craters, skirted open sections of sewer, waded through darkly gleaming lakes formed by burst water mains, slithered down glaciers of hardened margarine oil, the boiling torrent of a week ago now a yellow-green slime. Up to their ankles in broken glass, they stamped through sunken floors; under archways supporting nothing, past tottering walls, sliding and slithering and tramping, following their noses (and Theo's sense of direction) to the fire. As they got nearer to it, they heard the crackling of the flames, and a little further on began to see dense showers of burning embers against the morning dusk. As the air thickened with smoke and fumes, they dipped their scarves in a puddle and tied them around their faces, covering noses and mouths. They were getting right into it now; a heavy rain of ash and cinders and airborne debris fell on them as they went past the charred outer walls of houses that no longer had any interiors. The ground was hot and sometimes burning underfoot, and the soles of their feet were scorched. They crept into gutted houses with blackened rafters, where whole sections of floor had been gobbled up by the blaze. There were finds to be made, and they moved about quickly and expertly, systematic scavengers in the ashes. They found charred stamp albums and photo albums; packages of lavender letters scorched at the edges; a singed silver fox in a cupboard; hats burnt to a frazzle. A black mud lay over everything. They poked about in closets and cupboards, under stairs, in vaults and larders and wardrobes and chests. Sifting through the cinders, they slipped stealthy hands into dressing-table drawers and into metal trunks under beds, felt beneath mattresses, levered up floorboards.

Others were searching too. A white-haired man was calling, "Helene! Helene! Where are you? It's Uli. Helene, it's Uli. *Uli.* ULI!!! You don't hear me, Helene? Why don't you answer?" He was in pyjamas and barefoot. He had lost his glasses and could not see. Sometimes he stumbled and fell and picked himself up with difficulty, peering frowningly. "Where are my glasses?" he mumbled to himself. "Where could I have put them? Helene, where did I put my glasses? I can't see a thing." He shook his head crossly. "Damned glasses!" Stumbling here and there, he nearly bumped into a woman in her nightdress, crawling about on her hands and knees, calling, "Pussy-pussy-pussy." Pinned under an oak wardrobe, dying, an old man was calling to his dog Putzi.

Theo was digging for his cat Siegfried. That was what he would say if challenged by anyone. It was vital to have a story ready. You could be shot for looting.

Rolf and Franzi were digging for their mother and father, using a little perforated-brass coal-fire shovel.

Otto had found a dead body, only shallowly buried, whitened by ceiling plaster. A man. He was holding a dachshund in his arms. The dog was dead too. Whatever the man had

176

been wearing had been burnt off him, and he was naked in the white dust. Otto, seeing that the man had nothing worth stealing, re-covered him and dug elsewhere.

Going into a ground-floor kitchen, Franzi discovered a zinc cold box; inside there was a jar of gherkins, mustard, half a packet of cocoa, an egg, a small amount of lard. She quickly stuffed these items into the voluminous pockets of her long army greatcoat, the train of which was trailing through the rubble.

Otto had found another dead body, a young woman's this time, also naked. Not badly burnt. Must have died of asphyxia. There was a gold cross and chain around her neck, and he unfastened the chain carefully so as not to break it. Examining her hands, he found she was wearing an engagement ring: a simple gold band with three small diamonds. He had some difficulty getting it off her finger, eventually succeeding by using his spit for lubrication. He examined her earlobes — pierced, bare. Where were the earrings? He felt around on the ground but didn't find them. He saw she was wearing good leather shoes and stuffed them inside his belt.

A woman with her head in a turban, wearing a dressing gown and flashing a torch about in the air, was making whistling sounds for her parrot, who had evidently flown from his cage. The light beam fell on Otto, and her brow darkened, seeing him with the girl's shoes in his belt.

"Who are you? What are you doing here?" she demanded.

"Just having a look around for something I lost," Otto said.

In her dazed condition it took her a few seconds to react, and then she began to shout: "Fire thieves! Fire thieves! Polizei! Polizei!"

Franzi, Rolf, Theo, and Otto exchanged quick signals and ran.

It was light now, as light as it ever got these days with the smoke of hundreds of fires casting a permanent shadow over the city.

177

They'd eaten nothing since the potato peels last night and were ravenous as they ran through empty streets to get away from the shouts of "fire thieves!" In some of these streets only one or two houses remained standing — in weird isolation — with everything laid waste all around. They knew their way through the ruins, and the widespread destruction enabled them to go as the crow flies. They were making towards the upper end of Subbelratherstrasse, to the junction with Lessingstrasse, where the local Party office was situated, hopeful of some pickings from the dustbins of the restaurants patronised by Gast and his henchmen. Places frequented by them were in a favoured position when it came to getting food in short supply. Benno had once found a whole chicken breast, hardly even nibbled on, in the dustbin of the Ristorante Roma. The dustbins of the Acropolis, two doors along, sometimes contained chunky pieces of shishkebab meat, quite edible when the burnt part was cut away. These restaurants enjoying the patronage of Party officials were unusually extravagant in discarding the outer leaves of lettuces, cauliflowers, and cabbages. They threw away milk that had gone sour and cheese that had hardened. The potato peels in these dustbins were among the best to be found, since the staff used knives, not peelers, and in their hurry peeled thickly. On some days Rolf had found chicken necks, chicken feet, duck entrails, goose fat, bacon rind, the discarded fat of pork chops, meat bones containing marrow, sometimes with bits of meat still attached, fish heads and tails, coffee grains that had not been brewed more than once and still could yield one or two acceptable cups, tea leaves that could be restewed.

But today they were unlucky. The dogs had been there before them and devoured everything edible. They'd had a feast, judging from the refuse strewn all around. Rolf and Otto dug in the kitchen sweepings, the dog shit, and the rat droppings, finding a blackened potato here, a shrivelled carrot there, a maggoty piece of cheese somewhere else. Much time spent on rubbish dumps had inured them to the fetid stench, the filth, the contamination of the putrid, paltry dregs in which they scrabbled. But after five minutes, having found nothing, they gave up and rejoined their friends.

"I saw you find something before," Rolf said to Franzi. She took the gherkins and mustard out of her pocket and from her other pocket brought out the egg.

Rolf took it thoughtfully, pondering on the problem of dividing one raw egg between four. Finally he hit upon the solution, took out his pocket knife, extracted a narrow blade, and with the point of it carefully made a small incision in the shell.

"One suck each," he said. "Franzi first, since she found it."

They stood watching intently as Franzi pressed the egg to her lips and sucked out a little of its goodness.

"Shake it up," Rolf advised, "or you won't get any yellow, which is the best."

She did so, took a little more, and then licked her glistening lips.

"She's had enough," Otto said, putting out his hand.

"No, the Robber goes last," Rolf ruled. "He'll take it all, the greedy guts." Theo came next, and after him Rolf took his turn, shaking the egg to determine how much of it remained, and on this basis judged his fair share and left the rest for Otto, who drank his at a gulp and then broke open the shell and licked it dry in his palm.

The taste of food had made Rolf wild for anything that might fill his stomach a little, and he asked Franzi for the jar of gherkins. He got one out of the brine and ate it. Shuddering at the sour taste, he fished out another and this time dipped it in the mustard.

"It's all got nourishment," he explained, his mouth burning and his scalp prickling, so that he had to scratch himself everywhere.

Otto followed Rolf's example and ate one or two gherkins in mustard, but Franzi and Theo didn't want any.

Along the broad main street, shops were opening and

street vendors were setting up their pavement stalls and laying out their wares: secondhand clothing, shirt collars, collar studs, buttons, women's stockings and underwear, hats. Signs said:

NO —

CANDLES
SEWING THREAD
TOILET PAPER
SOAP

Rolf nudged Otto and made a questioning expression, tapping his pocket, which contained the rosy Hauptmann's cigarette case, gold lighter, gold watch.

"Naaawww!" Otto indicated.

"Where's this fence of yours?" Rolf demanded with scorn. "Call yourself a robber!"

Continuing along the street, they saw that the Agrippa music hall had closed its doors. This must have happened quite recently, as a result of the newest orders closing such places, as well as theatres, cabarets, concert halls, circuses, horse racing tracks. . . . Already the chained and padlocked doors had been plastered over with posters and notices. A group of women were gathered around, reading them. Rolf sidled up, tapping coat pockets and bags to see if they contained anything worth stealing. Pushing to the front, he read a notice saying that the bread ration was to be reduced by two hundred grammes a week and "German coffee" by eighty-five grammes. Another notice said that the telephone service for private subscribers was suspended, and those requiring a telephone for essential war work must apply for special dispensation to retain their lines.

All holidays were suspended forthwith.

There was to be no further horse racing.

All concerts were cancelled as of next month.

Cabarets and nightclubs were required to close down.

Next to these notices there were posters and proclamations in bold type:

WORK FOR VICTORY!
TOTAL WAR REQUIRES TOTAL FANATICISM
BEWARE THE WOLF CHILDREN!

This last poster showed a pointed child's face, adorned by the artist with wolf ears and wolf teeth.

The boldly printed text below declared that, despite their often innocent and even becoming appearance, the Wolf Children were the enemy of the people. They were the spanner in the works. They had big ears and heard everything that was said. And they listened above all for stories that would spread demoralisation and panic. They spread such stories with relish because Wolf Children were creatures that fouled their own nest, wished to see their country defeated by the enemy, admired everything American and British. Despondent words, careless complaints, laments to God in Heaven above were all grist to the mill of the Wolf Children, who throve on the misery of others and would exaggerate and spread tales of woe. They were the germ carriers of despair, a plague of the spirit. And they stole the milk from their mothers' breasts, the food out of their brothers' mouths.

The poster went on to describe the appearance of Wolf Children, saying that they frequently left their hair long, and dressed in English sports jackets, tweeds or herringbone, wore white silk scarves, and sported Hungarian diplomat hats decorated with badges and insignia.

Rolf was wearing a shabby tweed jacket, and his hair was long and unkempt, and he had a white silk scarf; the women, becoming aware of him in their midst, exchanged warning glances. *"It's one of them,"* they muttered to each other. They held their bags more tightly, kept their hands over their pockets, and edged away, talking rapidly among themselves. It was quite true, they said, children were becoming uncon-

181

trollable; they lacked any respect. It was a contamination that the Wolf Children had spread, and now even normal children, of decent parents, disparaged their own mothers and fathers, spat on them, decried their valour and self-sacrifice, mocked the war effort in the cause of which others laid down their lives. These "swing" youths wouldn't work on the Westwall, wouldn't dig trenches, wouldn't fight: all they wanted to do was laze around and be free.

Rolf, seeing the way he was being regarded, decided it was time to leave.

At the next corner there was a church, its entrance set back a little way from the street at the end of a short drive. A showcase contained the week's quotation from the Bible. They gathered around with an air of piety, and having made sure nobody was coming, Theo fished out some chalk from his trouser pocket and scrawled on the wall:

WORKERS AND SOLDIERS!
NOT ONE MORE HOUR FOR HITLER'S WAR!
REFUSE TO FIGHT!!
DESERT!!!
FIGHT WITH US FOR FREEDOM!
LONG LIVE STALIN!

Rolf was getting impatient. Somebody might come any minute.

"Hurry up!" he complained.

Theo was still writing; once he got going it was difficult to stop him. Looked like he wanted to cover the whole sodding wall.

"Black pigs!" Rolf hissed in a tone of alarm, and in mid-sentence Theo dropped his chalk and they all ran for it.

"Liar! Where?"

Rolf sometimes cried wolf, just for a joke, to give them all a scare.

"There."

It wasn't a false alarm this time: an SS motorcycle-and-sidecar combination was coming up Subbelratherstrasse at a walking pace. The reason for the slow progress was that people were following on foot, first four civilians with their hands tied behind their backs and then half a dozen slovenly black pigs carrying rifles. The SS on the motorcycle kept glancing over their shoulders to see how the others were keeping up and making impatient hand gestures to them to move faster.

The dismal group was followed by a straggly procession of onlookers.

Through the smoke pall a steady drizzle fell, a thin, grey rain that scarcely wetted the heads and faces of the prisoners and their escort, merely made them damp and steamy at the neck.

"What's happening?" Rolf asked. He didn't get any reply. He repeated the question, and people looked angrily at him. He could see that Franzi had gone white. She was making head signs for them not to hang around here. But Rolf wanted to see what was happening.

Of the four with their hands tied behind their backs, one was a middle-aged man in a suit and hat; behind him came a man in his twenties, wearing workman's overalls, and then a small grey-haired woman, and lastly a younger woman, in her late thirties, who was looking round all the time.

The procession was drawing more and more onlookers, pale, nervous people who kept well back and did not form groups, each person remaining as far as possible by himself, talking to no one and looking at no one.

The men on the motorcycle seemed to be searching for somewhere to stop and finally found a place and dismounted, bulkily, from their vehicle. They had goggles up on their caps, above the peak, like huge extra eyes, and were completely swathed from neck to boot in rubberized waterproofs that buttoned up at the legs. They strode to the edge of the bomb site and looked around, weighing up the suitability of the foundations of a destroyed house with a short section of wall still standing. It appeared that this would do, and they made commanding hand movements to the prisoners to descend. The prisoners did not want to move and had to be prodded and pushed at rifle point before they would start across the rough, unlevel ground; they were slithering and stumbling and falling — the older woman fell several times and with her hands tied behind her back could not get back on her feet unaided and had to be pulled up by a young guard. The middle-aged man in the suit and Homburg was turning round, seeking to talk to the motorcyclists: arguing, explaining. He was trying to be reasonable, and when reason did not work he offered money, but the motorcyclists seemed not to be interested. The woman in her late thirties, with hair and face in disarray, was sobbing and begging for mercy, pleading, "I'm still young, I'm pretty." She turned imploringly from one man to another. "Please, *please*. Won't you spare me? I'll do anything. Help me! *Help me!* Ask anything of me. I'm pretty — *look!*" She wanted to show them, but they were sullen, lumpish young men and they didn't even glance at her; one of them took out a hip flask and passed it around, and they ignored the still-young woman when she fell on her knees at their feet. She wouldn't budge another inch, and so they pulled her up roughly and pushed her, and since she nevertheless refused to go, they had to carry her kicking and struggling to the wall where the others were being lined up. The reasonable individual's hat had fallen off and he was breathing gaspingly while trying to bargain: talking the whole time. The older woman and the workman in overalls were silent and reconciled to their fate.

Having got all four prisoners in a row, the members of the firing squad moved back five paces, which took them about halfway up the slight slope descending to the foundations.

From where they stood, their marksmanship was not going to be put to the test. They raised their rifles, aiming slightly downwards. The still-young woman was attempting to escape by scrambling sideways on her bleeding knees through the debris, and they shot her first. A bullet went through her neck and severed the carotid artery, causing a fountain of blood to spurt out of her. There was a look of disbelief on her face.

The reasonable man was all the time arguing as the firing squad discharged their weapons in a ragged volley.

The executions had taken no more than a few minutes, and now the motorcyclists, their rubberized waterproofs glistening in the drizzle, went back to their vehicle, leaving the firing squad to pour chlorinated lime over the bodies and give them a hasty burial in the foundations, by shovelling debris over them.

Before leaving they posted an official notice.

Rolf read that the still-young woman, Helga Giese, had helped her eighteen-year-old son to fake a bladder complaint in order to avoid his being sent to the front line; that the older woman, Marlene Langen, had looted pillowcases, sheets, and blankets from a destroyed air-raid shelter; that the workman, exempted from military service because of his job in munitions production, had subverted fellow workers by spreading defeatism, saying that the war was lost; and that the argumentative man had engaged in the selling of butter on the black market.

As they came down Subbelratherstrasse, word of what had happened already had gone ahead; shopkeepers in their aprons and overalls stood talking in the street, spreading rumours and fear and high nervous excitement. The executions had temporarily made Rolf forget how hungry he was — but now he remembered once more and stared wantonly into the windows of *Lebensmittel* stores. Long lines were already forming. Outside Bombacher's, a slate by the door said:

TODAY
EGGS
PORK SAUSAGES
BUTTER
OIL
LIVER SAUSAGE
VINEGAR
SUGAR

Rolf studied the list cynically. Grocers were all a bunch of crooks — and Bombacher was one of the crookedest. They lured you inside with their fancy lists — pork sausages! eggs! butter! — and then when you'd queued for an hour they said, no more pork sausages, no more eggs, no more butter, but you could have plum jam, white beans, dried lentils. It was enough to make you sick. Though at this moment Rolf would have been happy to get plum jam, white beans . . . anything.

Clenching and unclenching his fists inside his jacket pockets, he was hotly gripping the Hauptmann's cigarette case, and all of a sudden he decided to risk it and started pushing his way through the queue. Franzi, fearful of what he was going to do, came after him.

"Excuse, excuse me," Rolf said to the people he pushed past, and when they started turning nasty he said mournfully, "Family. Yes. We're relatives . . . Terrible, terrible . . ." The terrible news he bore upon his young shoulders made them stand out of his way, and he pushed into the shop, making the doorbell on its metal spring jump and jangle. There was just one person inside. Bombacher only let customers in singly.

Under the dangling rolls of flypaper, heavy with several days' catches, the glass counter shelves were bare except for dummy hams and sausages marked FOR DISPLAY ONLY. The shopkeeper was engaged in some activity in the back. He reemerged carrying various wrapped items, which he placed directly in the customer's basket. The customer, a frail old woman, seemed pleased enough.

"How much do I owe you, Herr Bombacher?"

He calculated in his head and said a sum, which she paid unquestioningly, at the same time handing over her ration book, from which the grocer snipped several coupons and tossed them into a metal bin.

He called, "Next," and saw Rolf and Franzi standing there. "Are you in the queue?"

"This is business, Herr Bombacher," Rolf said in a low voice.

"Get off with you! I don't want your kind of business. I know your kind. What are you — Wolf Children?"

"No, we're war orphans."

Stepping quickly forward, Rolf got the cigarette case out and held it inside his jacket to show Bombacher.

"Very reasonable," he said. "It's silver. I'll trade . . ."

Bombacher examined the cigarette case, weighed it in his hand, and gave a snort. He was a large, round man, with white hair and white apron, and carried his prominent belly before him like a valuable possession.

"Go on, get out! You want to get me put up against a wall, dealing with riffraff like you. Go on, *out!* I wasn't born yesterday, lad." Then he took in Franzi standing just behind Rolf; he peered at her over his glasses. "You're little Franzi — no? My, you've grown! Grown up into a young woman."

She smiled at the shopkeeper in her most appealing way. "Couldn't you help us, Herr Bombacher? We're hungry."

"What d'you expect if you live 'black'? Sign up for work and you'll get food coupons and wages like everybody else." She remained silent, looking straight at him. Her eyes didn't waver, and she didn't blink. He stared back and slapped his belly thoughtfully. Shaking his head at such foolish generosity on his part, he reached under the counter and produced a couple of seeded rolls, which he pushed across to her.

"Our friends," Franzi said, "they're hungry as well."

187

"I can't help that," Herr Bombacher said. "That's the best I can do, for now." He looked from her to Rolf and then back to her again. "I've got a shop to run, I have to serve my customers. Right now, I'm busy."

Theo tried next. But nobody wanted the cigarette case, or the lighter, or the watch. They'd be asked where they'd got such expensive things. And what would they say? That they'd bought them off some young roughneck? Dealing in looted property was a capital offence.

He returned to his friends and reported, "No luck."

"We better split up," Franzi proposed. "Let's all try on our own — that way we've got more chances. Maybe one of us'll strike it lucky."

Franzi hung about until lunchtime, until Bombacher had pulled down the roller blind saying CLOSED, and then tapped lightly on the glass and waited. No response. She tapped again and again and presently heard puffing and blowing and muttering from inside and a shuffle of feet. The roller blind was pulled to one side and she found herself staring into a disgruntled, suspicious eye, to which she gave her sweetest smile. There came a sound of unlocking; Bombacher opened the door a fraction and said sternly, "I'm closed. What d'you want?"

She looked down. "You said to come back when you weren't so busy."

"I said that?"

"You said you might be able to help us."

"I think there must be something wrong with your hearing, Franzi."

"I'm sorry," she said, and hung her head.

He took her chin in his fingers, raised her head, and asked, "You're hungry?"

She nodded.

"Come inside, Franzi." When he had re-locked the door, three times, he remarked, "You know, to give aid to people

188

like you — 'social undesirables' — it's an offence. You know what a risk I'm running!"

She nodded and said, "I'm ever so grateful to you."

He walked to the back of the shop, and she followed him into a curtained-off rear section where there were shelves up to the ceiling, a cold store, and crates of empties. He used one crate to sit on and another, covered in greaseproof paper, as his table. On it were sausage meats, pickled cucumbers, beer, bread, butter, a knife.

"Go on!" he said. "Make yourself an open sandwich. I treat you."

Eagerly she cut herself a thick piece of bread, heaped slices of smoked sausage on it, and took an enormous bite.

Bombacher laughed. "A girl with a good appetite. I like that — I like to see a young, pretty girl eat well. Points to a sensual nature." He pinched her cheek.

"We've been living on potato peels and dustbin refuse," Franzi said with her mouth full to bursting point.

"Eat slow," he cautioned, "eat slow. You'll choke." He shook his head in amazement and disapproval. "Lovely young girl like you shouldn't have to eat from dustbins. Plenty of men would be only too glad . . ."

"I have a fiancé," she said quickly.

"Oh! You have? In the army? He must be a long way away." He gave her a wink. "What the ear doesn't hear, the heart doesn't grieve? Eh?"

He continued to watch her, not eating himself but drinking beer. He drank one glass after the other while she stuffed herself with as much food as she could put away. When she could swallow down no more, she wiped her mouth with the back of her hand and stood up.

"Could I take something for my little brother and my friends?" she asked boldly.

"You're not shy to ask," he remarked, and added a little breathlessly, "I expect you're not too shy in other respects either — eh?"

"Could I?" she asked.

"What's it you want?"

She stood up and from a deep pocket of the army greatcoat took out a canvas holdall, unfolded it, went to the shelves, and started to calmly fill her bag. A packet of rice. Noodles. Sugar. Cocoa. Powdered milk. Powdered eggs. Flour. Oil. Half a dozen tins of Portuguese sardines in olive oil. Beans. Sauerkraut. She tried to reach an upper shelf but was not quite tall enough.

"These are expensive items you're taking, Franzi. Can you pay for them? D'you have food coupons?"

She shook her head, but did not turn around, was still trying to reach the high shelf.

"Well, how d'you expect to pay for these things, then?"

"I don't know."

"What are you trying to get from that shelf, Franzi?"

"Matches . . ."

"You need matches? Let me. Let me, Franzi."

He stood behind her on tiptoes, got the matches, and tossed them into her zipper bag.

"Anything else you need, while I'm on this top shelf?"

She stayed absolutely still as his bulk swung against her.

"Aspirins," she said.

He searched around on the top shelf for aspirins, breathing hard, his belly rolling over her like a steamroller. The edges of the shelves cut into her. His body smelled of smoked sausage and pickled cucumber and his breath of beer and pumpernickel bread.

"What about some tinned fruit while I'm on this shelf?" he asked, his breathlessness increasing. "Peaches in syrup? Or you prefer apricots? Have both." He handed the tins down to her.

"Herr Bombacher, you're crushing me."

He stood behind her, breathing hard — it was like the sound of bellows being pumped. Then his body began to move against hers in a regular way.

190

"You mustn't do that, Herr Bombacher. You mustn't be bad," she scolded. "No, please, I've got to go . . ." She reached down for the bag and he kicked it away from her.

"Please, Herr Bombacher . . . Let me go."

"I'll let you go in a minute," he promised. "Just stand still. Just stand still."

She rested her chin on a shelf, and remained still. The sound of bellows pumping: faster, harder. He was bundling her long greatcoat to one side and pulling up her dress at the back.

"No, not that."

"Just a little, Franzile. The coat's rough. . . ."

"I don't want to run any risks. . . ."

"No risks, Franzile. No risks. I won't . . ."

She kept completely still while he went about his low business, his fingers on her face touching her lips, lightly at first, and then more roughly, then hurtingly squeezing her mouth into a high oval and pushing his thick fingers into it, in and out, in and out. He began to puff and pant as he belaboured her from in front and from behind. He had dropped his trousers and hoisted his apron, and as she looked over her shoulder his massive swinging belly made her think of an iron ball with which demolition workers broke down walls.

She closed her eyes and hoped it wouldn't last long, this demolition work. To counteract how she was feeling, which was bad, very bad she told herself that it didn't really count as long as the man didn't put it inside you, and at least they'd all eat for a few days.

Rolf and Otto were the first to return to the cellar. Rolf had found half a loaf of stale bread in a dustbin, and Otto the Robber had succeeded in stealing a plate of cat food from under a cat's nose, in doing so receiving scratches that were now festering.

Benno opened the door, and his big hungry eyes fixed on them.

191

"We didn't get anything. Well, nothing much. Some cat food."

Benno swallowed and said, "I didn't eat all day."

"Neither have we," Rolf said, and then looked a bit sheepish, remembering the shared raw egg and the gherkins dipped in mustard. "But we saw four people get executed," he added keenly, for lack of more encouraging news to impart. "For looting and things."

"Gosh!" Benno said. "You saw it?"

"Ten metres away," Otto boasted.

"Weren't you scared?"

"No, not me," Otto said.

"I was, *a bit*, but I didn't let on," Rolf said with a dare-devil grin. "How's old Kurt then? Still in the land of the living?"

"He's better," Benno told them in a low voice. "Any rate, he's woke up. Been asking for food."

"Food? What's that? Never heard of it," Rolf said.

They lifted the trapdoor and went down into the cellar. Kurt was lying under a pile of old coats, covered up to the neck, shivering convulsively every so often and looking like death, but his eyes had a more definite focus today: he saw them and knew who they were.

"Well," he said weakly, a lopsided smile on his face. "If it isn't the Louse Boy all grown up."

"Still don't see any profit in it. Don't know why I bothered."

"And the Robber?" Kurt asked without having much breath left.

"That's it," Otto admitted. "You're right there."

"Hope you robbed us some food." Kurt spoke hopefully with the last of his strength.

"All the Robber managed to rob today was a cat — so there isn't too much to eat. But you shouldn't complain. You ate yesterday."

"I ate?"

192

"Franzi spoon-fed you like you were a babe in arms," Rolf said.

"Franzi . . . ?" There was a light in his face, but his voice was not strong enough to enable him to go on.

"You don't remember us finding you in the street and bringing you here?"

"No."

"You were pretty much gone. We thought you were as good as dead."

"So did I, "Kurt said, trying to grin, and succeeding only in making a ghastly grimace.

He attempted to raise himself into a sitting-up position; the effort made him gasp for breath and he sank back.

"Where is Franzi?"

"Looking for food." Rolf saw Kurt's boots sticking out from under the coats, the uppers attached to the soles only by the swath of bindings. "What you do? Walk all the way from Russia, did you?"

"Almost," Kurt said.

"You desert?"

Kurt gave a faint nod.

"Good for you!" Rolf grinned. "We don't hold with armies, never did. We think armies are stupid. What they good for, except getting people killed? We don't blame anybody not wanting to get killed."

Theo was next to return. He'd got hold of a three-kilo bag of buckwheat poultry food.

"If only we were cats and chickens we'd be all right," Rolf said with glum humour.

Kurt slept fitfully; he was woken by Franzi's voice, telling about her amazing stroke of luck — this grocer, this kind man who'd known her mother, and remembered Franzi from when she was small.

She had unzipped the canvas holdall and spread out before their disbelieving eyes the fruits of her day's foraging: coffee powder, cocoa, flour, rice, noodles, sugar, powdered eggs, powdered milk. And tins of sardines! And pork sausages! — chains of them, which she pulled out of the sleeves of her greatcoat like a conjurer. There was still more to come. Soap. Matches. Beer. Plum jam. Biscuits. Aspirins.

Kurt's starved face lit up, making his skin almost transparent and his skullbone stand out.

"Our angel," he said, "our angel of mercy . . ."

Before cooking their meal, Franzi took some water in a tin bowl and washed Kurt. With the new piece of soap that she had obtained, she washed away the grime of months of sickness and fever and dysentery. He was deeply ashamed of his condition — his thin body, his sores, his foul-smelling underclothes. Across the corner where he lay, she stretched a clothes-line and hung old overcoats over it to make a hanging screen, behind which she occupied herself with him.

"I hate that you see me like this, that you should have to do this," he told her.

"I still think you're a handsome man, I always did," she told him. "Think of me as a nurse, and don't be embarrassed. You're suffering from starvation and exhaustion, and lack of vitamins. Once you eat proper you'll get better."

For the start of the meal she gave them all a sardine on a dry biscuit; and this was followed by a portion of boiled rice and one pork sausage each. They shared two bottles of beer between them. Then Franzi mixed together a little ersatz coffee, sugar, a teaspoonful of flour, added a cup of water, and let the paste simmer on the paraffin stove while they all watched spellbound, intoxicated by the unbelievable sweet odour. When the paste was smooth, she took it off the fire and let it cool and then beat it with a fork. Now, she mixed egg powder with water, added sugar and flour, and in this batter she dipped little balls of rice, and fried these in some of the lard that she had found that morning in the burnt-down building. Each person received two rice balls and over them she poured the sweet dark-brown cream sauce that she had made.

"There," she said, "rice pancakes in mocha cream!"

"Not only an angel of mercy, but a cook as well," Kurt marvelled, his mind reeling from so much rich and unexpected nourishment.

Next day, since they had food, they did not go out scavenging in the ruins, just lazed about, as if it were some kind of holiday.

Periodically somebody climbed the ladder to look through the cracks in the boarded-up windows. There wasn't much to see: the same drifts of white masonry dust; occasionally a troop train or a munitions train rattling by on the railway viaduct; bombed-outs wandering about dazed, clutching a few cooking pots and bundles, looking for shelter; from time to time an SS motorcycle patrol. The sky glowed a dull red. The new smoke pillars spread out after a certain height and merged into the general dark pall.

Kurt was improving. Now he was able to sit up and feed himself. The food gave him strength and the aspirin reduced his fever.

This improvement continued during the next few days, while their food lasted. Each day he got a little stronger. Within a week he was able to stand up by himself and to walk about for some minutes unaided, though he was not yet sufficiently recovered to attempt the ladder. In any case, he would not be able to go outside during daylight.

Franzi looked after him. When he had an attack of the shakes and shivers, she gave him aspirins and covered him with coats until the convulsions had subsided and he felt better again. She could see the terror, or whatever it was, come over him. Since he hated for the others to observe him in this state, she hung coats over the clothes-line during an attack, and behind this screen he held on to her.

When the fit had passed, he called her his saviour and his angel of mercy.

Gradually he got better.

Though he was desperately thin, his skin no longer hung

on his face like crumpled linen: it had smoothed out, and the sores on his body were healing, his eyes looked clearer, and he had a better smell, and his bowel movements had become more solid.

"You're not going to die," she told him.

"What happens when the food runs out?" he asked.

"We get some more."

By the beginning of his second week in the cellar, Kurt had become strong enough to make a trial sortie, and Rolf said he'd go with him down the road as soon as it was dark.

They walked first to the cul-de-sac, Kurt still shaky but gathering strength. At the railway arches they turned around and went back, past the cellar, as far as the corner bomb site at the end of their street, where bombed-outs had built themselves lean-tos in the ruins of a poorhouse. Some of those who now occupied the weird shacks, made of whatever had been found lying around—floorboards, doors, window frames, roof tiles, tarpaper, mattresses—previously had lived right there in the poorhouse, but others had become homeless more recently. The little community included derelicts and hobos, old women from State institutions, young girls with their fatherless babies, war-orphaned small children under the care of a neighbour, a Gypsy beggarwoman, a badly burnt man, the victim of a fire raid, sick men exempt from military service because of their grave maladies. They were the poorest of the poor, those with nowhere else to go, no family or friends in better circumstances to shelter them. They lived under such dire conditions, emptying their slops and their latrines into an open cesspit to one side of their hovels, that the police patrols, fearful of contamination, gave the site a wide berth. Nobody wanted to come near these people, and so it was safe for Rolf to take Kurt there.

As they arrived, tiny tots were rolling about in the dirt and rubble, getting themselves soaked in puddles of filthy stagnant water, sucking their grimy fingers which had been dipped in earth and masonry dust. Their young mothers, children themselves, sat about dazed and bewildered, doing nothing. There was nothing to be done, except wait for the mobile field kitchen that sometimes came by, sent by a church welfare organisation. The authorities appeared to have given up on these derelicts. They were not on any register, and so there was nothing that could be done for them officially.

The moment Rolf and Kurt were spotted they were surrounded by small children with their hands held out, begging for food.

"Are you from the Committee?"

The speaker was the man who had been so badly burnt. He had no hair, no eyebrows, no eyelashes. His eyes seemed indecently exposed within their bare sockets, which were like unduly large slits in a mask. His face was red and mauve and pink and shiny, seamed with scarlet ridges, a stitched-together patchwork, and totally blank. A stretching around the gash of a mouth occurred when he spoke — it was the only facial movement of which he was capable. But the voice was friendly, eager, passionate.

"You're from the Committee?"

"What Committee?" Kurt asked.

The voice sounded disappointed, became unsure, cautious, but it was impossible to tell, without the benefit of facial expressions, the nature of this man's concern.

"Somebody came . . . from some Committee or other. . . . They promised us food," he explained.

"No, I'm sorry."

The burnt man spread his hands, indicating his miserable hovel, and the iron cooking pot that gave off an aroma of horse stables. He stirred a wooden spoon in the pot, and said in his expressionless way, "Soup! Want some? Help yourselves, if you're hungry. I know it's the colour of dog shit. But it contains *some* nourishment. Proteins, no. That would be asking too much. Sugar, none. Fat, none. But there are some

197

peas. A few. Traces of groats, I believe . . ." He was searching in the gruel with the wooden spoon.

The naked eyes lifted to stare at them fixedly.

"You're sure you are not from the Committee?"

Rolf tugged at Kurt's sleeve, indicating they should go.

During the night Kurt had another fit of the shivering and shaking. Franzi, lying next to him on the cellar floor, could see it was the terrors again, that he felt "out of his body," and she gave him her hand to hold.

"I feel I'm slipping away," he said, his teeth rattling like a scarecrow of old tin cans. She moved closer to him under the pile of coats and put her body against his, which had no feeling in these states. She thought he might at least sense her closeness and be comforted.

Shaking, he said, "I can feel you."

"That's good," she said. "How do I feel?"

"Good," he said.

They lay together, with him shaking in her arms, both covered in several layers of clothing.

He pleaded, "Kiss me."

She said, with a little laugh: "I think you're feverish enough, as it is."

He insisted. It seemed to be a matter of life and death. She kissed him on the lips, simply, in the same way as she had fed him and washed him, when he needed to be fed and washed. He stayed with his mouth on hers, drawing life from her.

When he demanded, "Let me touch your breasts," she, without fuss, undid the buttons of the army greatcoat, and of the coat she wore underneath, drew aside various layers of materials, and pressed his hands to her soft rounded flesh, and he seemed to get better. After a while he stopped shaking, and then fell asleep clinging to her.

The first night that they lay together under the pile of coats no more than this happened. Next morning he asked her, "Did I say anything when I was out of my head?"

"I can't remember."

"Try to remember."

"You were rambling — you had a big fever. You didn't say anything that made sense. About some Jew that they shaved with their bayonets."

"Yes? What did I say about that?"

"Nothing — *that's all,* Kurt. That's all I remember. And there was something about trees growing better afterwards . . ."

"After what?"

"I don't know."

During the night he got the terrors again and asked to touch her sex. She took his hand and placed it there. When he kissed her it became obvious that she was aroused.

"You can't say you don't feel your body now," she said to him teasingly, looking into his eyes, and a moment later: "Even if you can't, I can."

Whether he could feel it or not, his body had risen to her, and it was as simple as an embrace. He lay still inside her, holding on tight, making no movement, for the moment, and she talked to him softly. "I always loved you, Kurt. All my life. From the time I was little. I used to cycle up and down in front of you when you were working on your motorbikes, to make you notice me. But you never did."

"Oh, didn't I!"

"You never showed it."

"You were a child."

"I wasn't, Kurt."

"Yes, I found that out." Even after all this time, his voice was bitter.

"Oh, Kurt! Oh, Kurt! In my heart it was you, that's the truth. I swear to God. It was always you. Always." She giggled. "I used to pretend to myself you were my fiancé. I was so proud."

"But you went with that pig Gast."

"I know." She hung her head in shame, against his neck. "You didn't take any notice of me, and I was all alone after

199

Rolf'd been sent to the hostel, and they took away Mama, and then on top of that Papa died . . .'' She mumbled into Kurt's neck. "I was completely alone, and I thought he was a big man, the street leader. . . .''

He stabbed upwards into her, harsh rapid blows, and she began to shake and shiver as if he was passing on his terrors to her. Their nerves were tightly drawn and the first strong flow came as a quick release. Her shaking had barely finished before he began again: the brutal stabbing movements.

"Making up for lost time, are we?'' she teased.

But he was in no mood for banter.

Now they had to go out looking for food again, since their store was almost exhausted. All they had left was one tin of sardines, the bag of poultry feed, and about a tablespoonful each of plum jam.

They followed the trails of new fires, creeping right into the burning ruins.

Kurt, recovering but still weak, stayed in the cellar, to protect it against squatters and to look after their property: the mattresses, the stove, the cooking pots, the latrine bucket, the water pail, the enamel washing bowl, and other valuables such as matches, candles, soap, paraffin, and their food—what they had left. *And* their cigarette ends. They collected these all the time, picking them up off the street, from the floors of railway station waiting rooms, from ashtrays in telephone kiosks, from trams, from public lavatories —from which they also, whenever they could find any, stole wads of the folded brown toilet paper, a rare commodity, much too precious for wiping your arse (for that newspaper would do). They used the hard brown lavatory paper to make cigarettes, and Theo used it to write manifestos, when he had time.

Wrapped in old newspaper there was a mound of cigarette stubs and a small pair of scissors, with a length of metal chain still attached to the finger grip (the scissors had previously been attached to a grocer's counter for cutting out food coupons, until Benno had detached them). These scissors were now used to snip open cigarette butts. The tobacco was then carefully sorted, burnt particles removed, and what remained arranged in a row of equal piles. Next the lavatory paper was cut up into cigarette-length strips of the right width to give a good overlap, for they had nothing to stick the cigarette paper with except spit, and had to make sure the paper held.

This was what occupied Kurt while everybody else was out scavenging. His cigarettes were not as neat or round as Ostas from Croatia or Ballerinas or the pre-war Schwarz und Weiss (rarely to be found now); in fact, they were rather flat and soggy-looking, but smokable all the same, and in street trading, farm workers would give one egg for three (instead of the standard price of one for one, which applied in the case of factory-made brand-name cigarettes).

Before leaving with the others to look for food, Theo had told Kurt about the breakthroughs. Behind the paraffin stove there was a section of loosened brickwork that was removable, enabling them to get into the next cellar. The bricks could be slid out and then put back again, and anyone who didn't know wouldn't be able to tell that the opening was there. In the next cellar there was another section of loosened brickwork that was also removable. Altogether there were six cellars linked in this way under the ruins. If you knew where the breakthroughs were, you could get from cellar to cellar and come out by way of an opening in the rubble blocked up by a large piece of masonry. If you lifted it off like a manhole cover, you emerged in the middle of the rubbish dump at the end of the road, by the spot where the bombed-outs had dug a cesspit to empty their latrines. It was a filthy, pestilential spot, swarming with flies and rats. The stench was unbelievable. Nobody would go nosing around in such a disgusting area, and so it was a good place to hide. There were lots of derelict cars there, stripped of their seats, their mirrors, their motors, their wheels — nothing but metal skeletons. He'd hide in one of those, Theo said, if he had to. If he was surrounded by black pigs, for instance.

That night they all returned empty-handed. The whole district was crawling with black pigs. Because of the wide-spread looting that now went on everywhere, there were Secret Police, in civilian clothes, with the fire fighters, ready to pounce on anyone who looked suspicious. They could shoot you on the spot if they caught you looting.

The stray dogs were another danger. Hunger made them ready to tear you to pieces.

It was really bad, they all reported, coming back with nothing.

They ate the last of their food, and next day set off to try once more, their minds made up that they would have to venture further into the fires, where the danger was highest and the Secret Police were unlikely to risk their necks.

Again they were unlucky. In the centre of the blazes everything was burnt to a cinder and there was nothing edible to be found. The following day they were obliged to set off with empty stomachs.

This time Kurt insisted on going too. He would go by himself, and if caught would admit to being a deserter, and say that he was alone. They would probably shoot him without asking too many questions.

He fared no better than the rest. There simply was no food to be found in the streets.

"We're starving to death," Otto said, "that's what we are."

"God, are you intelligent!" Rolf remarked as they all sat slumped in gloom.

Though Kurt had not succeeded in finding any food in the course of his lone scavenging, he'd found something else, it seemed, and extending his closed fist to Franzi, he asked her to guess what.

"Valuable?" she asked.

"Yes."

"Matches?"

"No."

"A piece of candle?"

"No."

"Soap."

"No."

Whatever it was, it had to be small, since it was contained within his fist.

"I give up," she declared.

"Close your eyes," he instructed.

He took her hand in his and opened his fist and pushed the thin gold band onto her finger.

"With this ring we are wed," he said, smiling but solemn.

"Don't I even get asked?" Franzi demanded.

"I'm asking."

"Then I say yes."

Because it was sort of his sister's wedding night, and they had no other way of celebrating the occasion, Rolf sang them a song.

> *In Junker's tavern with wine and pipe,*
> *We were sitting together.*
> *A good drop of malt and hop,*
> *The devil's leading us.*
> *Hey! where the men are singing,*
> *And the guitars are sounding.*
> *And the girls join in.*
> *What has the Hitler life to bring?*
> *We want to be free.*
> *We want to be free.*
> *Hey! where the knives are flashing,*
> *And the Hitlerjugend running.*
> *Ahoi caballero.*
> *Hello, Rio de Janeiro.*
> *Rhinelander girls are true.*

"Are they?" Kurt asked.

"Oh, ever so," Franzi said.

During the night firebombs fell close by, in their own neighbourhood and in adjoining Nippes, and around 2 A.M., they set off while the blazes were at their height, very determined after twenty-four hours without food.

Rolf returned first. He'd found some chocolate and a small bottle of schnapps on the body of a dead air-raid warden. Otto came back soon afterwards, with nothing. Then came Theo. He also seemed to have got nothing, but opening his coat he showed them that he had a dead cat. He proposed that they skin it and cook it. It would keep them alive.

The others hesitated.

"Let's see if Kurt or Franzi got anything," Benno suggested.

Kurt came back with nothing, having come close to being caught several times. He was extremely low. Said he didn't care if he was caught. They were all going to die, anyway. A bullet was quicker than starving.

"Looks like it's going to be the cat," Benno said, trying to be cheerful. "Bet it tastes just like chicken."

They were about to start skinning it when taps on the boarded window signalled that Franzi had come back, and Benno went to let her in. He had a big grin on his face as he scrambled back down the ladder like a fireman.

"You can forget about the cat," he said, proud to announce such news. "Franzi's got food!"

"Good old Franzile!" they all cried joyously.

She was quiet as she came down into the cellar, said she was tired, and she looked it as she emptied her pockets and her zipper bag. It was another feast she was spreading before them, but she wasn't even smiling: potatoes, big potatoes; a dozen fresh eggs; bread — a whole loaf of bread; a chain of knackwursts, chunky fat sausages full of meat and goodness; margarine; cheese; biscuits; plum jam.

At first they just stood and stared, saying nothing, and then big grins spread across their faces.

Only Kurt wasn't grinning. He was staring at Franzi, and she was avoiding his eyes. She started to peel the potatoes, very carefully, so as to leave as little as possible under the skins.

"Our saviour," Kurt said, "our lady of the potatoes and plum jam! What would we do without her! Knackwurst — imagine! We should kiss her feet, that's what. Bless her! Bless her! The holy mother — feeder of the lost little children. The bountiful-breasted Franzile . . ."

"Shut up," Franzi told him.

"How do you do it?" Kurt demanded. "You're the only one who ever brings anything eatable back. How? *How?*"

Franzi ignored him and asked, "Is somebody going to help me peel the potatoes?"

"I will," Kurt said. "When you've let us into the secret of how you do it."

"I found a purse on a bomb site," Franzi said. "There was a bit of money in it. Enough to buy these things. . . ."

"Without a food card?" Kurt asked in a tone of mild surprise.

"He was a kind man," Franzi said. "I said I'd lost my food card and that my mother was sick."

"He gave you food without a food card, this kind man?" Kurt said in a less mild tone.

"Peel the potatoes, if you're going to," Franzi said.

"This kind man — he didn't ask for any payment *in kind?* Was that the sort of kind man he was?" Kurt demanded accusingly.

She didn't answer.

"Imagine!" Kurt said, taking her silence as an admission. "She does it for us. To feed the starving children. Sacrifices herself for us. Or isn't it such a sacrifice? Perhaps she enjoys it, our Franzile. Making the kind men be kind to her. Hmm?"

"Shut up, Kurt."

"Yes, shut up," Rolf said. "Leave her be. She's got food for us, you should be grateful to her."

"Who asked you to speak, Louse Boy?"

"I don't ask your permission, see."

Kurt glared, fury rising in him like a liquid that is going to overflow. He controlled it, but only just, and said:

"You peel the potatoes, Louse Boy. I wouldn't want to contaminate my hands." He turned his back on them, pulling one of the coats over his shoulders.

"I bet he won't mind contaminating his stomach eating them," Rolf said, starting to peel. Kurt ignored the remark, and it was as Rolf said: when the meal was ready, Kurt ate and became more reasonable. At the end, he said:

"What we need is a gun."

Otto was interested. "Yes — *yes*. A gun. You're right."

"With a gun," Kurt said, "you can get things. You're not dependent on the kindness of kind shopkeepers."

"How'd we get a gun?" Rolf asked.

"Oh, we could get one," Kurt said. "Franzi could get one for us, I'm sure. She's good at getting things. If she can get knackwurst and plum jam, it should not be impossible for Franzile to get a gun."

"How?" she asked suspiciously.

"The same way you get other things. By using your charm."

"I didn't use 'my charm' to get the food. I told you — I paid."

"You'd have to use your charm to get us a gun."

"What d'you want her to do, Kurt?" Rolf demanded, protecting his sister.

"Nothing bad, Louse Boy. Nothing really *bad*. She'd just have to get a soldier to dance with her."

They all looked at each other.

"It's taking a risk," Rolf said.

"What risk?" Kurt scoffed. "Dancing with a soldier? Franzi has danced with soldiers before now, and I'm sure one or two took their gun belts off. At some point. Out of politeness?"

"It's risky," Rolf said. "Stealing guns from soldiers is taking a big risk."

"We'd take the risk with her," Kurt said. "We wouldn't ask her to do it all alone."

"It's not worth the risk," Rolf said.

"Risk!" Kurt scoffed. "Tonight we've eaten. In two or three days we'll be starving again. What's riskier than starving?"

"We got to think about it," Benno said.

"Of course the question is, would Franzi do it?" Kurt said. "Would you?"

She thought for a moment and said: "I'll do it. If you want me to."

NINE

The blind accordion player, his round black-lens glasses halfway down his nose, had his blank eyes fixed in an upward stare as he played. He was sitting on a wooden bench, a filthy old felt hat beside him to receive coins.

The soldier dancing with the prostitute belonged to the noisy group of gunners by the bar. They were all putting away large quantities of beer, especially the one who was dancing. He held the beer mug behind the woman's back as he staggered about, and periodically lifted it over her head and drank copiously. It looked as if he was engaged in some bet. The prostitute had stiff orange-dyed hair and was old enough to be his mother and none too appealing.

Kurt and Rolf and Franzi were in the dimmest part of the bar, close by the door. Otto, Theo, and Benno were posted outside as lookouts.

"Him," Kurt said to Franzi, indicating the drunken dancer.

It was the fourth beerhall they'd been to and the only one where anyone was dancing. The soldier was wearing the standard gun belt, with pistol holster, its flap held closed by a short strap secured by a belt buckle.

"It'll have to be him. He's the best so far. You'll have to get him to take his gun belt off," Kurt said.

Franzi stared at the soldier and said nothing.

"Go on, you've got to do it," Kurt said. "Go on. Go on." He was practically pushing her. She was looking at him, shaking her head slightly, but finally she started to walk towards the bar. Her long army greatcoat was unbuttoned, and underneath she wore a cotton dress that showed off her figure. The neckline was sufficiently low cut to afford a glimpse of shapely breasts. Attention was drawn to them by the gold cross and chain, taken off the dead girl, that Otto had loaned her for the evening. Her lips were crimson, their bow shape strongly outlined, her eyelashes thickened with mascara, and she wore perfume looted from a cabaret dancer's apartment. As she passed under electric light bulbs her hair shimmered. The gunners were all eyeing her and calling out pleasantries and inviting her for a drink. She said, no thanks, she was with her brothers. But they wouldn't take no for an answer. They were very young men: eighteen-year-olds, twenty-year-olds, in the new field-blouse uniforms that didn't keep their shape. They'd been spilling beer and cigarette ash over themselves, and their faces were pale and blotchy and unhealthy-looking. They thought Franzi was the cat's whiskers. As she waited in the crush to be served, she glanced towards the soldier dancing with the prostitute. He was a brawny fellow, twenty at most, with a coarse face, the rough hands of a farm worker, and big feet in heavy boots. He was practically falling over his own feet — an oaf, a drunken oaf.

When the accordionist stopped playing and went round with his hat, not having heard many coins tinkling into it, the gunners hit upon the idea of getting the drunken oaf to ask

Franzi for a dance. It would take him down a peg or two when she refused. Now they were encouraging him, winking and nudging, and making signs that he was onto a good thing. Looking Franzi over, he accepted that he was. So he lumbered up to her and asked her to dance. To the astonishment of his comrades, she accepted. It was for a joke, obviously, they told each other. She was doing it to make fun of him.

The accordionist resumed playing and started to sing a sentimental German love song about a soldier on leave and his sweetheart. Franzi danced with the oaf. At first she kept him at a distance, but when he — emboldened by beer and the dares of his friends — pulled her close, she didn't push him away. Oh, he was onto a good thing, *definitely!* The other gunners couldn't believe it, the way she was letting him hold her. Some hot number she must be.

"Ow! That hurts! Your holster's pressing into me and it hurts," Franzi complained.

"That's not all that's pressing into you," the bold gunner boasted in a whisper, and she gave him a flirty scolding look for his boldness.

He continued to hold her close in oafish ecstasy.

"No, *really!*" she said. "Can't you take that thing off? It's hurting me. It hurts me when you press up against me," and she pushed him away from her.

"It's not allowed," the gunner said.

"What's not allowed?"

"Not allowed for a member of the armed forces to take his gun belt off."

"Never?" she teased.

"*Well* . . ."

She pushed him away from her, and when the music stopped broke free, saying she had to go back to her brothers. He was clearly disappointed; but his comrades, for the fun of it, urged him to keep trying.

210

By the entrance Franzi said to Kurt, "He won't take his belt off."

"Get him to."

"He won't," she said. "I tried."

"Try harder," Kurt told her. "Don't tell me you don't know how!"

Franzi searched Kurt's eyes for a clue to his true wishes. But they were difficult to know: he went about things in roundabout ways. Did he want her to refuse? To say, "I can't, I'd rather starve"? Or . . . ?

Franzi returned to the bar and the soldier.

"Dance?"

She shrugged and didn't refuse. The oaf pulled her close and winked at his friends. Swaying about to the music of the accordion, he was holding her under her army greatcoat, and his hands slipped lower down.

"Oh, you're so big," she whispered. "I can feel." Again she complained, "Your belt's hurting me. It really is."

She had an audacious idea, her eyes bright and wicked. "Let's go in there," she said. She was indicating with her head the dusty curtains hanging across the entrance to the closed dining area of the beerhall. Breathless with anticipation, the soldier followed the insistent tug of her hand as she drew him along after her. Blunderingly, he knocked over a chair, and she scolded him teasingly: "Clumsy big thing." She was leading him to the furthest corner, weaving between tables on which chairs were stacked upside down. She finally let him crush her against a wall, and kissed him with her tongue while he was getting her dress up.

"No," she said. "Not here."

"Nobody can see us."

She appeared to weigh this, and coming round to the same point of view, insisted: "But you've got to take your belt off—it's hurting me."

Now he couldn't take it off fast enough. He searched for

211

somewhere to hang it up, feeling along the wall with his hands.

"Just throw it anywhere," she urged impatiently.

He'd found a moose-head coatrack. Feathered Tyrolean hats came tumbling down as he hooked the gun belt over a branched antler. He was wild to have her, but she wasn't comfortable, it seemed, and was edging along the wall to find a better position for herself. He was trying to hold her still — what was the matter now? He'd taken the gun belt off, hadn't he? What was she doing?

Rolf had crept in. She was aware of him feeling around in the dark and prayed he wouldn't knock over the chairs on the tables. While fending off the soldier as best she could, without actually discouraging him, she was making signs behind his back to Rolf. There! *There!* He couldn't see where she was pointing. He was bumping into things, and only just managed to catch a tumbling chair in time. The soldier was too preoccupied to notice, she would have to keep him that way. To take his mind off peculiar noises in the dark, she whispered in his ear. Rolf was blindly sweeping the walls with his hands. Unbuttoning feverishly, the soldier heard nothing except his own triumphant heartbeat. Oh, this girl was hot for him! Rolf's sweeping hands had at last found the spreading antlers of the moose head, just as the soldier succeeded in divesting himself of trousers and underpants. She had asked him in her own honeyed little voice. But then it all got to be too much. He crossed his legs, trying to hold back, but it was too late. He groaned — with dismay and relief. His groans were noisy and so he didn't hear the jangle of his gun belt being pulled off the antlers as he stood with his inferior-quality army trousers about his knees. It was a good minute before he had recovered himself; then, looking for the girl, he became aware that she was no longer where she had been just before. He felt for her in the dark, thinking she was perhaps playing games with him still, but all he succeeded in embrac-

212

ing were chairs turned upside down on tables. Tiring of this, he lifted a corner of the curtain to have more light. That was when he had to recognize that she had definitely gone, and when he looked towards the moose head he saw that his gun belt had gone too.

Kurt was tremendously excited with the pistol. It was a Walther P38 with double-action trigger mechanism and a six-round magazine. An excellent pistol. Kurt handled it lovingly. He wanted to make use of it straight away — why waste time? — and they went skulking around the dark streets looking for a place to hold up, but nothing was open this time of night except beerhalls and small restaurants, and being full of people, these presented too much risk.

The blackout afforded them protection. Directing the beams of their torches on the pavement ahead, a group of women were leaving a Winter Relief whist drive. The organiser of the drive, an elderly man, was locking up the hall. When all the little discs of light had disappeared around a corner, Kurt stuck his gun into the man's neck and told him to unlock again.

There was not a great deal in the church hall that was worth taking: cast-off winter clothing donated for the troops, gloves, long underwear, scarves, socks. They took the best stuff, left the rest. In a cupboard they found a packet of biscuits, milk powder, coffee powder, sugar, several jam tartlets, some slices of plum cake. Anything that was edible they took; and they broke open a metal cash-box and pocketed the small amount of money in it.

There was nothing else, and leaving the old man to lock up, they ran home, elated at having brought off their first armed robbery.

Back in the cellar they shared out the food, drank coffee, and counted the money from the cash-box: seven marks. All in all, not bad. Kurt was very pleased with the success of his plan, but said nothing to Franzi — not a word of praise to her for having got them the gun. It was as if he had done it all himself.

In the course of the next few days they raided several small food shops. Kurt went in with the gun, accompanied by Otto or Rolf, while the others kept watch outside. The method was to dash in and out. They grabbed what they could, stuffed their pockets, and ran. In this way they were able to feed themselves quite adequately on a day-by-day basis. But they never got away with very much, being always in too great a hurry. And since they were dependent on running away fast, they couldn't load themselves down. After one such raid, they were nearly caught when two patrolling policemen asked them to empty their suspiciously bulging pockets. They really had to run then.

That night in the cellar Kurt said that they were taking too many risks for such meagre returns. What they needed was a getaway vehicle, and then they could go in for bigger robberies.

"Like bank robbers," Benno chimed in excitedly.

"That's right," Kurt said. "We've got to do robberies that are worthwhile. It's stupid risking our necks for a few tins of sardines."

"I could eat a great big piece of beef. Or pork," Rolf said.

"Me too," Benno said. "Yum-yum."

They all looked at Otto the Robber for his expert opinion.

"I say we've got to find some food depot to rob. Then we'll be able to lay back and take it easy."

"How about a butcher's shop?" Rolf said.

"Got to find one that's got some meat," Otto pointed out.

"That's our objective, then," Kurt said. "Everybody agreed?"

They all nodded eagerly.

Rolf and Benno, casing the area between Liebigstrasse and Lukasstrasse, passed Rolf's old school, burnt down in a raid

214

during the last days of September. It had been a big raid, putting an end to the notion, inspired by the summer lull, that the city was henceforth going to be spared. High-explosive bombs had fallen in great numbers, as well as a small quantity of firebombs. Some of the latter had gutted the school that Rolf had once attended. He looked now through the iron railings, across the concrete playground with the single pollarded plane tree, its branches black and leafless, past the long line of iron bicycle racks to the shell of the building where he had spent so many boring hours, and which he had always fervently wanted to burn to the ground.

Now it was burnt down he didn't even care. You could never get to enjoy anything. That was life.

A muddy rain had been falling for days, disgorged by clouds swollen with smoke and heat. The rain had a sulphurous taste and smell; it turned the cratered streets into a thick mire that clung to boots and shoes, giving everybody enormous feet. Rolf and Benno picked their way through the rubble, towards the municipal slaughterhouse. It was like being inside a milk bottle, everything a smoke-white blur as they clambered over piles of debris and dragged their feet through the scarred earth. They were coughing and spitting all the time to clear their throats of the acrid filth in the air.

The recent raids had started hundreds of new blazes, and the many pillars of smoke were joining together to form a darkness over the city, a porous black dome that reduced daylight to permanent dusk. From time to time a sudden strong wind blew through this murk, suddenly exposing to the eye a skeletal vision of free-standing walls, of scaffolds of steel girders holding up nothing. The bare bones of rooftops stuck out, doorways entered nowhere, windows looked out of nowhere.

The municipal slaughterhouse, though badly damaged by high-explosive bombs, was still functioning, if on a reduced scale, and as Rolf and Benno approached the place they heard the bellowing of animals being driven off the cattle trucks

215

from the Netherlands and forced into pens and lairages. The boys exchanged looks: so there was meat to be had. They hung around outside the tripe shop and watched the butchers' vans draw up, the men in white aprons going into the cold store and coming out with beef and pork carcases on their shoulders.

Keeping going through the rain, the boys crossed the Ehrenfeldgürtel and entered the crescent of sports fields and lakes and green open spaces — now largely mudflats — forming the periphery of the old town and separating it from its outer suburbs. Rolf suddenly remembered that there was an SS barracks around here, between the Gereon main goods depot and the Hornstrasse slave labour camp. It was from here that the black pigs on their motorcycle-and-sidecar combinations set off to hunt down deserters, looters, shirkers, defeatists, escaped *Ostarbeiters*, wall-daubers, Wolf Children. Excitedly, Rolf pressed on through thin, vaporous curtains of rain that hung down from the bare trees. It was here somewhere, the SS barracks, he was sure.

"Where we going?" Benno wanted to know.

"I bet the black pigs get good meat to eat. All we got to do is find out where they get it from, and that's the place we raid."

"That's brilliant."

Benno was always saying things were brilliant. He admired people like his brother Theo — the Brains — whereas Rolf didn't admire anyone too much, because if you did, you were bound to be disappointed. He'd discovered that.

Ahead, a darker grey in the grey of the ash-rain, he saw low buildings, a water tower, stables, vehicles, and they both heard the kick-start of a motorcycle.

"This is it."

A feeble light spilled out of a low, long hut and was instantly extinguished. Smoke puffed steadily from clusters of metal chimney-flues. The black pigs were keeping close to their stoves. There wasn't much danger of them coming snooping around outside on a filthy day like this — apart from those going on patrols.

Soaked to the skin but happy, the two boys picked their way carefully across the compound and took shelter under the big tank of the water tower. It provided some cover from the rain while they waited and watched. They saw patrols setting out, others returning. They saw the cook carrying a sack of potatoes from a storeroom to the kitchen, but otherwise nothing much happened, and after having hung around for a couple of hours they were about to leave, when they observed a man arriving at the storeroom pushing a tarpaulin-covered barrow. The cook came out of his kitchen, the tarpaulin was drawn back, and a carcase of meat was lifted out and carried inside.

Rolf and Benno exchanged looks.

When the man with the barrow left, they followed him to the premises, two or three streets away, of H. H. Keller, Butchers & Sausage Makers. A queue had formed despite the lowered shutters and the sign saying NO MEAT. Rolf and Benno watched the man pull the bell of the wooden double gates of a rear yard, and when they were opened, slip in quick.

The smoke had not dispersed. It was fixed in the sky in an unbudging mass that grew denser each day as more and more of the city went up in flames. It was still raining and, away from the great heat of the burning buildings, cold. Benno, outside the municipal slaughterhouse, was stamping his feet. It was the fourth day he'd been hanging around here, begging for bits of offal. He could do with a nice piece of meat. Meat kept the cold out. Not like tinned sardines. In any case, there weren't any more of those either.

Just before noon he spotted the van he and the others had been waiting for these past three days: H. H. Keller, Butchers & Sausage Makers. At once Benno gave the prearranged signal to Theo on the next corner, who alerted Franzi one street further on, and she signalled to Rolf, who signalled to Otto and Kurt.

Benno watched a big, red-faced man with a striped oilcloth apron over his overcoat get out of the van and go across to the cold store; he had the years and the weight to be the butcher H. H. Keller in person. After some minutes, he came out carrying a carcase of meat on his shoulder. He opened the rear doors of his van, hung the meat on a rail, closed the doors and locked them, and went back into the building; two minutes later he was out again, carrying another carcase. Once more he hung the meat and locked the doors of the van; then he went to the window of a small office, counting out notes from a thick wad. The butchers' boys were having a smoke at the entrance and he slipped each of them something and they raised their fingers to their foreheads respectfully. He was looking for someone else, and they directed him. Finding this individual, who wore a suit and an overcoat, Keller stood talking to him under a glass canopy, and at the end of their chat passed him an envelope. After that, Keller got into his van and started the motor and the windscreen wipers.

While he was waiting for his engine to warm up and the wipers to clear the mud and rain, a signal went from Benno to Theo; Theo signalled Franzi, and so the word was passed on down the line to Otto and Kurt, waiting in a small street that had become a dead end with the collapse of a corner building.

The butcher was moving off slowly, peering through the rain and drifting smoke that reduced visibility to one or two metres. He had to brake abruptly to avoid running into the first DIVERSION sign; he opened the door of the van, looked out, muttered under his breath, and then reversing so as to have enough space to turn, took the new direction indicated. Less than an hour ago when he had come this way the street had been open: a damaged building must have collapsed, blocking the road. It happened all the time. The city was becoming a maze of ruins that only rats and Wolf Children could find their way around in. He was looking for the next DIVERSION sign and was relieved when he spotted it, though he felt a certain unease about the direction it showed him to take.

Didn't seem right somehow, but he followed the arrow.

In front of him the road swung to the left: the wipers were not clearing his windscreen fast enough in this downpour, and to add to his difficulties the de-mister wasn't working and he was having to use the palm of his hand to make clear circles to see through. It was in one of these circles that he suddenly saw a man holding a gun, and braked at once. He was not one to defy armed force. As he came to a halt, the door of his van was wrenched open and Kurt jumped in beside him, pressing a pistol into the butcher's side. Otto got in the other door and Keller was ordered to reverse out — there wasn't room to turn around. In the highly nervous state that he was in, the butcher nearly reversed into the basement of a burnt-out house, and Kurt had to grab the wheel from him and straighten the van, which had tilted over precariously, with one wheel off the ground.

Once out of the dead end, the van went back to pick up the others, and with them hiding behind the swinging meat carcases, jolted and rolled and rattled through side streets until it was back on the main road. The tramway line here had been torn up and was a tangle of twisted metal. Severed power cables dangled down uselessly. A tram carriage lay overturned on the pavement. Deep pot-holes had filled up with rain-water and bubbled and steamed like hot springs. Weighed down with parcels, suitcases, zipper bags, bags of potatoes, sacks of coal, a few people were dragging themselves through the mud and the rain as the lurching van continued on its bone-shaking journey. Benno felt as if his stomach was coming out of his mouth and prayed he wouldn't be sick.

They reached the butcher's street half an hour later. Muddy rain-water was streaming along it and making a cascade on the steps going down to an air-raid shelter. The shutters of H. H. Keller's were rolled three-quarters down and there was again a sign on the door saying NO MEAT. Despite this, a queue had formed, pressed against the wall under the narrow shelter of a first-floor cornice. The approach of the butcher's van was registered with sullen hopefulness.

Outside the gates of the rear yard, Kurt pressed the pistol into the butcher's thick neck and told him:

"Give them the signal to open up — and no tricks!"

"No tricks, of course. Of course — understood completely," the butcher immediately agreed. He hooted his horn once, paused, then hooted twice, and presently the wooden gates were opened. The van drove into a muddy rear yard, deeply furrowed by the comings and goings of vans, barrows, motorcycles, horse carts.

The butcher's boy, having closed the gates, was about to refix the padlock when Otto leapt on him, wrapped one arm across his neck, and put a knee in his back, ready to break him in two.

"We're loading today, not unloading," he told him.

The sulphurous rain that dissolved the earth had turned the backyard into a bog: ankle-deep in muck, they all crossed to the rear entrance and got into the shop by way of the delivery hatch, the butcher sliding in first, like a pink pork belly, and Kurt after him, gun in hand.

"Who's on the premises?"

"Just the boy."

"Nobody else? Don't make any mistakes."

"My wife and daughter."

"Call them."

"Mutti!" Keller called from the bottom of narrow wooden stairs. "Mutti, come down. Bring Mathilde with you."

On the white-tiled walls there were posters of sheep and cows and different cuts of meat, but nothing hung from the meat hooks, and the faience plates beneath the glass counter were empty; the chopping block was scrubbed clean, and in its rack, the choppers, saws, and knives were spotless. The weighing machine was unsullied white.

"Get the knives," Kurt told Franzi. To Keller he said, "Where's all the meat?"

The butcher indicated the door of a cold-storage chamber, and Kurt waved him towards it with the gun. Otto, Theo, Rolf, and Benno went in and started to unhook the hams and the feathered poultry suspended from the ceiling rails, and to carry everything out to the van.

"*Move,*" Kurt urged, seeing Benno mesmerized by the sight of so much to eat.

In response to her husband's earlier calls, the butcher's wife was coming down the stairs with her daughter. "What's the matter now?" she asked grumpily, and then saw the youths emptying the meat safe, her husband held up at gunpoint, Franzi with her arms full of knives.

"Keep an eye on them," Kurt told Franzi.

Frau Keller had one leg shorter than the other and wore a surgical boot to compensate for this. She walked tilting to one side, supporting herself with a cane. Her hair was white, square-cut and short, coming no further than the nape of the neck. Her face had the texture of dry leaves. She seemed unafraid of Franzi with the meat axe, regarded her bitterly, contemptuous of her bow lips, the golden shimmer in her hair, her young body.

"Move!" Franzi told her.

"You addressing me?" the woman asked, nodding her head bitterly.

Franzi made a threatening gesture with the meat axe, and the Frau Butcher moved as required, becoming white, more from the indignity of being subjected to such intimidation by this slip of a girl than out of fear.

The daughter was about thirteen or fourteen, dark, with opaque eyes and abnormally pale skin. The sight of the meat axe being brandished and robbers emptying her father's shop had brought a little colour to her cheeks and a faint glimmer to her dull eyes.

The Frau Butcher spat and said, "I know who you are. You're Wolf Children. I am right? You are the lowest of the low," she added.

"That's right, mother. That's who we are," Franzi said. "Wolf Children, and we eat up old witches like you."

The woman shook her head in grim disbelief at such disrespect, such impertinence.

"Aren't you ashamed of yourself?" she demanded. "Aren't you? Robbing innocent people, attacking the disabled and old. . . ."

"We haven't attacked you yet, mother."

"Murdering . . ."

"Who've we murdered?"

"I know about your sort." She shot a look at her silent daughter, who had a sullen smile on her face, as if far away and mulling over secrets known only to herself.

"You bring children into the world," the butcher's wife said. "With pain. With pain. And this is what happens. They turn against you. Your own children."

Franzi looked at the daughter, Mathilde. There was definitely some colour in her cheeks now, a faint tinge of red, as in someone coming out of a faint.

"I advise you to keep your mouth shut, mother," Franzi told her. "You're getting on people's nerves. Everybody's a bit jumpy. We wouldn't want any accidents . . ."

The daughter's half-smile became full, harsh and hateful. The butcher, passing by, called to his wife, "Mutti, don't provoke them. I beg you. Don't say anything. Let me deal with it." He was being made to strip his shop bare, carrying out platters of game pie and hare with blood-stained white fur.

Benno suddenly was feeling sick. He'd known he was going to have an "accident" and spoil everything. It was

222

the smell of blood and raw meat. He pressed his nose and mouth to the grille of a ventilator to draw in fresh air. Peering through the rain, he saw that a motorcycle-and-sidecar combination had drawn up at the end of the street. The men on it were clad from head to foot in waterproof capes, with leggings going down to their overboots. Black pigs! One with a loudhailer addressed the people in the queue outside the butcher's shop and anyone else within hearing: *"Attention! Attention!* Criminal gangs of looters and robbers are active in this area. Many of them are youths of between fourteen and eighteen. These Wolf Children are dangerous. Anyone possessing information that may lead to the arrest and punishment of such saboteurs and traitors must report it instantly to the police. Persons withholding information in their possession will be considered accomplices of the Wolf Children and dealt with accordingly."

The two SS men had dismounted from their motorcycle and were walking along the length of the queue, asking questions. They were coming nearer. In a couple of minutes they would enter the shop to question the butcher.

The Keller woman had a gloating look of satisfaction on her face; her husband looked terrified.

"Get back in the van! Quick," Kurt yelled.

"What about them?" Otto demanded, indicating the butcher and his wife and daughter. "They'll give us away."

Kurt said, "Go on — in the van, I'll cover them."

"Kill them," Otto said. "I say kill them. They'll give us away."

"I swear," Keller began, and choked on his words. The daughter's cheeks were glowing, her eyes alight. The woman was derisive, unafraid.

Theo said quickly, "We can't shoot them, it'd be heard — black pigs'd be in here in a minute. Have to do it with those." He indicated the knives and meat axes.

"We'll scream," the Keller woman said, "they'll hear and you'll be done for. They'll hang you all."

"In the van—quick. *Quick!*" Kurt urged, and they all scrambled out while Kurt pushed the butcher, the boy, the woman, and the daughter into the cold-storage chamber and locked it. Then he ran to join the others in the van.

While Kurt revved the engine, Rolf, keeping flat against the wall, crept to the end of the yard and looked out to see where the SS men were now. He saw them, bulky forms in their mud-spattered waterproofs, lumbering along the queue, throwing out questions. The sudden jangle of a doorbell told him they had gone into the butcher's shop, and he gave a hand signal to Kurt, who pressed down hard on the accelerator, making the van's wheels spin and churn in the mud, and then the van careered towards where Rolf was in the act of throwing open the gates. They hauled him in without stopping and lurched out into the streaming road, bumping aside the motorcycle combination and turning sharply to disappear into the black rain.

As their thudding heartbeats quietened down, big grins appeared on their faces. Benno began to giggle uncontrollably, and it spread to the others, and soon they were all laughing, not able to contain themselves.

"Our first 'b-b-bank' robbery," Benno said, chortling.

Otto said, "We ought to celebrate," and made a knocking-back motion of his hand. A smirk on his face, he said to Kurt: "Give me the gun, I'll get us some booze." Kurt didn't respond. "Don't you trust me, don't you trust me with the gun?" Otto taunted.

"I trust you," Kurt said. "But take Rolf and Theo with you. All right?"

"Yah," Otto agreed, eager for the gun.

"Hold on, hold on," Kurt cautioned. He was slowing down by *Lebensmittel* shops that might have booze under the counter, looking into dimly lit interiors: it was a matter of following your hunch, picking the right one.

"How about him?" he said, seeing a shopkeeper standing

in his doorway with an air of being there to lure customers in. "He looks as though he might have something tucked away. We could try him."

"Give me the gun," Otto said.

"Let me handle it," Kurt countered, "you can come along."

"You don't trust me, do you?" Otto said. "You think I can't do it alone."

"I'll watch over the Robber," Rolf promised. "Me and Theo will. We won't let him shoot anybody unless he has to. Will we, Brains?"

Kurt pulled up round the corner from the chosen *Lebensmittel* shop and handed the gun to Otto. He smiled warily.

"Since you're doing the shopping, we also need pepper, salt—"

"Cooking fat," Franzi said.

"And mustard," Kurt added.

"I like mustard with my meat," Benno said. "Don't forget —get the hot one."

"I'll get everything," Otto said.

Kurt gave him the gun.

"Now take it easy—hmm? And don't be long. In and out—" He snapped his fingers.

"Yah."

The three of them got out of the van and slunk around the corner in the continuing rain. When they were no longer in sight, Kurt started nervously hitting his fists together.

"I hope that wasn't a mistake," he said to Franzi. "They're kids, and Otto's pretty wild. If anything goes wrong . . ."

He had kept the motor running, and clenched and unclenched his hands on the steering wheel. Three minutes went by. Four. He looked at his watch, obsessively, every few seconds.

"They've been ages," he suddenly said. "Something's wrong." He started to reverse the van around the corner, and

225

adjusted his side mirror to have the shop entrance in view. No movement. No sign of anyone. The van crawled back along the kerb. A few steps from the shop, he stopped.

"I'm going in to see," he said, and just as he was about to go after them, he spotted Rolf in the side mirror, coming out, pulling his white scarf down from his face, followed by Otto holding a bulging paper bag clutched to his chest, the gun in the other hand, and then Theo, who also had a paper bag. As they ran there was the sound of clinking bottles.

They handed their "shopping" up to Franzi and Benno, and threw themselves in as the van started to move off.

"What kept you?" Kurt snapped.

"The old arsehole couldn't find the hot mustard. He only had the mild, and Benno wanted the hot. We made him have a good look. And we got it," Otto said with satisfaction. "We got everything. Schnapps. Plenty of schnapps." He was already opening one of the bottles and taking a celebratory gulp before passing it on. They all drank and felt good.

"The gun," Kurt said.

"We should take it in turn to have it," Otto proposed.

Kurt looked at the others. "No," he said. "I'll keep it."

"Why always you?" Otto complained. "You're not our leader. We don't believe in leaders, do we?"

"That's right," Kurt said, "but all the same, I keep the gun." He drove with one hand and held out his other one. Otto made no move, and Kurt put his foot down on the accelerator, making the van skid around corners in the wet. He kept his hand out for the gun as the van went faster and faster.

"Go on, give him the gun, Robber," Rolf said, and finally, sulkily, Otto handed it over.

TEN

They lazed around and drank schnapps and ate *Bratwurst* and *Zigeunerwurst*. Oh, this was the life — being robbers!

"How we going to eat all this?" Benno asked, surveying their over-abundant haul. "It's enough to feed an army."

"That's what we'll do — feed the poor blighters down the road," Kurt said.

"We going to give away our meat?" Otto said, angry. "That's stupid."

"We can't eat it all," Theo pointed out. "And it'll go bad. Besides, we need somewhere to cook it. We couldn't cook it down here — not enough ventilation. We'd get smoked out."

"We risked our lives to get this meat," Otto protested. "It's ours. Even if it goes rotten."

"I say we share it," Benno said. "Those people are starving like we were."

Rolf said, "Once or twice when the soup kitchen passed, they let me have some of their soup. I say we share with them. We can't eat it all ourselves."

Franzi agreed with Rolf.

Theo said, "I say we share," and quoted: " 'From each according to his means, to each according to his needs.' That's fair."

"Lousy little Bolshy," Otto grumbled under his breath, but he was outvoted and had to accept the majority decision.

A carcase of beef was selected, suspended from a broomstick, hoisted up the ladder, and then carried by Kurt and Theo, as if they were huntsmen carrying shot game on a pole along the street, the others following.

The bombed-outs sitting by their lean-tos saw the procession approaching and got to their feet disbelievingly. Who were these youths bringing meat? Was it a dream? The tiny tots started to jump about excitedly, the old men pinched themselves. Word was spreading, and one by one people were coming out of their hovels and standing there staring.

"Comrades and friends," Kurt said, addressing them all, "there is food for everyone." He beckoned to them to come closer, not to be afraid. It was not a trap.

But they were hanging back. The authorities had been known to lure people to some central location with bait of one kind or another, and then arrest them and cart them off to an unknown destination. Perhaps the purpose of this meat was to make people come out of hiding, reveal their illegal status, that they were not on any register and officially did not exist.

Kurt could see their doubts vying with their hunger. He produced bottles of schnapps, held them up.

"Comrades, don't be afraid—we're the same as you. We're also 'illegals.' There's nothing to fear from us. We're friends." He looked around and saw the suspicion in their eyes. The legend END THE WAR — BRING OUR BOYS HOME!

was scrawled on an iron drum by the cess-pit. "We also want the war to end," he told them. "Believe me."

A man came forward. He had the mottled red nose of a chronic boozer, and was licking dry, trembling lips. He reached out for the schnapps and Kurt gave it to him, and let him drink. After he'd taken several long gulps, Kurt had to retrieve the bottle, or it would have been drained.

People laughed, knowing the boozer for what he was. It had served to break the ice.

A young woman with white hair said suddenly, "They're Wolf Children." She turned to the others, awe in her voice. "Wolf Children are holy thieves. God blesses their thefts. They rob for the good of others."

Somebody else whispered, "Edelweiss Pirates. . . ."

The burnt man brought them a rusty old window grille: it would serve as a gridiron for roasting the meat. Rolf and Benno went around looking for firewood in the debris, picking out suitable bits of floorboard, wall battens, and roof rafters, and chopped them up with their meat choppers, and then laid the pieces in a pile on top of rags which they soaked with the fuel from their cigarette lighters. They lit the fire and placed the window grille over it, and Franzi and the white-haired young woman prepared the meat, salting and peppering it, rubbing it with cooking fat while waiting for the flames to diminish, and when the wood was burning steadily, the meat was placed in position by Kurt and Otto.

The entire encampment, by the look of it, was now around the fire. As the smell of roasting beef began to spice the air, and the running fat sputtered into sudden blue flashes of flame, broad smiles broke out all around in the circle of faces, and some eyes had tears in them.

After a while, Kurt took one of the long, sharp butcher's knives and sliced off a piece of the roasting meat: it looked raw still and he said they'd have to wait. Everybody was getting impatient now. They wanted to eat the meat half-raw as it was, fearful that with every minute that passed, the chance grew of something intervening to deprive them of the promised feast. But Kurt told them to wait and not worry, that they would all eat their fill. He vowed it.

Finally the meat was cooked and he began to carve, slashing off thick, fat chunks of the beef. But he was not able to serve fast enough, and some among those who were waiting began to tear at the carcase with their bare hands, clawing off pieces and stuffing them into their mouths and into the mouths of the hungry children. To help, Kurt handed out all the butcher's knives that they had and told these people to take as much meat as they wanted.

He had been on top of the fire too long and, needing to get away from the heat, handed over his knife to someone else and withdrew to the water barrel. He was wetting his face to cool off when he saw a young girl staring at him. Her face was shiny with grease, as were her fingers. She wiped them on her rough shift several times.

"Wolf Children mean holy children?" she asked in a foreign voice. "Excuse my speak, I do not much speak." She seemed confused and distressed, and unable to find the words for what she wished to say to him, she pulled him urgently by his sleeve, imploring him to come with her.

He said to her in Polish, "What's it you want?" and she replied in a rush of unintelligible words, pointing to one of the lean-tos. It seemed she wanted him to go with her to this flimsy hovel made of tin cans, mattresses, salvaged doors, rags, and bits and pieces of other junk. A blanket hung down over the entrance, and she drew it aside and asked him in. He followed uncertainly.

It was like a bat's cave in there, filthy and poisonous and thick, and he recoiled and wanted to leave at once but the imploring childish eyes held on to him and wouldn't let him go. He could hear breathing which was not the girl's; it sounded like an antiquated pump straining to draw air where there was none. As Kurt's eyes became accustomed to the

230

murk, he saw that the agonized breathing came from the malodorous heap on the ground, which moved and was suddenly convulsed by a fit of coughing, making the atmosphere even more poisonous. The girl had lit a candle and she brought it closer to the wasted form: Kurt saw a cadaverous man, an army greatcoat up to his chin. The coat was very stained. Dipping a handkerchief in a bowl of water, the girl wiped the lips oozing blood and phlegm. When she had wiped away the worst, she rinsed the handkerchief and made a wet compress which she placed on the man's forehead. His face was hollowed out to the bone, the thin flesh eroding fast. He appeared to be burning up before their eyes, his skull growing to awesome prominence.

"Who are you?" Kurt asked him.

The man replied in German, "One who has 'escaped.'"

"Is she your daughter?"

"She's my wife."

"She is — Polish?"

"Yes."

The girl spoke excitedly in her own language.

"What's she saying?" Kurt asked.

"She is very young and doesn't understand. She thinks I can be saved with medicines. She thinks you are a 'holy thief,' that you can get anything, even medicines." Another bout of coughing convulsed him, and the girl wiped away blood. He shook his head. "My lungs are all gone. Full of holes as a pair of old socks."

Kurt reached in his pocket, took out the schnapps bottle, and passed it to the man on the ground, who drank eagerly, greedily.

"That's good medicine," he said. "The best."

The alcohol had reanimated him and was burning in his eyes as a flame of pure energy.

"I can perhaps get aspirin," Kurt said.

"That will help. But schnapps is best. Best of all . . ." He tugged at Kurt's sleeve, pulling him close enough to speak into his ear secretly. ". . . best of all would be a — pistol. You wouldn't have such a thing to lend a fellow soldier? Would you, my friend?"

The hand on Kurt's arm was surprisingly strong, determined: it would not let go. Another spasm of coughing racked the sick man, making him twist and roll about. In the course of his violent movements, the much-stained army greatcoat was partially dislodged and Kurt saw the black uniform underneath. He pulled back, placing himself beyond the reach of the demanding hands.

The man had seen and understood Kurt's reaction.

"Now you're not so willing to help me?" He tapped his chest. "You can still lend me your gun," he said in a sly little whisper.

Kurt spoke coldly, "I have no gun."

"Don't be so quick to judge me, my friend. *'Let him who is without guilt cast the first stone.'* Ask *her* about me. Go on, ask her. She is a Jew. I saved her."

"A pretty little Jew-girl to keep your bed warm," Kurt said harshly.

"Before the Almighty we are man and wife. I love her."

"Yes, that helps," Kurt agreed. "Can make you feel almost human."

"Then you know," the SS man said. "You were there yourself?

Kurt said nothing, and the man on the ground continued in a rush, fast burning up the flame of energy in his eyes. "I was in the army, too. Like you? I fell asleep on guard duty. That never happened to you? I did some other things that were not approved of. They said to me, you can go into a police troop on the Eastern Front, an SS *Einsatzgruppe* — yes, one of those. Or you can take the consequences. You do anything to save your skin, don't you? So I went. I had no choice. Then they put you there, and they put a bottle of schnapps in your hand and a rifle in the other, and they say, 'Go on. Do it. It's got to

232

be done. It's a nasty business, nobody wants to do it, but it's got to be done.' You have a good drink of schnapps and you do it. You're not there to ask questions, you're a soldier, and soldiers have to do what they're ordered to do. Or take the consequences. You look at me with contempt, my friend. What were *you* doing there? You know what the army did while we did the dirty work? Sent their men into the forests to gather firewood. So their morale wouldn't suffer. Perhaps you know about that. Perhaps you gathered firewood yourself." Suddenly his eyes overflowed with gross tears. He spoke in a low thick voice. "You think it was easy to do? It was hard, my friend. A lot of us cracked under the strain. The hardest on us was . . . the small children. Seeing their fathers trying to comfort them just before . . . seeing them stroke their heads and point up at the sky. That was the hardest. . . ." He was shaking and weeping. Kurt turned away disgusted. These grotesque tears were for himself. Oh, how he pitied himself having had to do such hard things!

Kurt was pulling aside the filthy tattered blanket to get out, to get out of there before he threw up.

"Whatever you think of me . . ." The SS man had calmed himself sufficiently to plead for the last time. "It doesn't matter . . . does it? You can still lend me your gun. What is it to you? One bullet. Even they . . . even in our outfit, they permit a man that. To redeem himself. So he can be considered to have fallen honourably in battle." He gave a hard, mocking laugh. "Honourably — yes."

"I have no gun," Kurt said without turning round, pushing his way out, gasping.

Outside the sky was lit by magnesium flares. Everything appeared bright as day — brighter, since there had been no bright days for some time now. He saw Franzi and the others and ran towards them. The marker bombs were falling, encircling the encampment in a smoky red mist. As the high-pitched whistle turned to a piercing scream, they all threw

233

themselves to the ground, their hands over their heads. Theo heard his brother pray and was disgusted. "Long Live the Revolution, Long Live Stalin!" he cried softly and waited to be transformed into nothingness, into the material of the universe, for God was just another trick of the bourgeoisie for exploiting the masses.

Air and earth quaked as the blast wave cut through the encampment, and then came the widespread pitter-patter of firebombs falling out of the sky.

Kurt scrambled to his feet. They were alive! On this razed ground, the blast had passed over them as if through an open door. Here and there, some of the lean-tos had been knocked down and reduced again to the bits of junk of which they had been constructed. But others still stood. Further away, he saw flames rising and a red glow encompassing the sky, and there was a dark joy in his heart. Yes: it must all burn. It was the Great Fire that had made the earth clean again after the Black Death.

He went back to the hut where the SS deserter lay on the ground coughing up his lungs, choking on his own being.

Seeing Kurt, his dull, exhausted eyes, from which the alcohol energy had completely gone, glistened feebly.

"You've brought me something for the pain?" he demanded eagerly.

Kurt nodded.

The SS man reached out and knocked over the pail by his side, spilling the water onto the ground. He apologised to the girl, profusely. For putting her to so much trouble. He was contrite. Begged her to forgive him. She seemed to be saying in Polish that it was nothing, that she would go and get more water, and she was puzzled by the way he kissed her hands so gratefully. Finally, he let go of her and she left.

Kurt hesitated.

"You will do it?" the SS man asked.

"No; it's for you to do."

"Then give it to me, quickly. She will be back in a minute."

Kurt took the pistol out of his pocket and gave it to him and went outside.

The next lean-to had had its tin roof blown off and he helped the old people refix it and weigh it down with stones. While he was doing this he saw the girl come back with the pail, water slopping onto the ground as she hauled herself through the rubble. She was not very strong and had to stop once or twice to transfer the pail from one hand to the other. When she was only a few metres from her lean-to, a muffled sound came from inside that she did not distinguish from the other noises of the night, and she would have gone in unthinkingly had not Kurt stopped her.

"Niezyje!" he said, remembering the Polish word meaning that a death has occurred.

Her expression became distraught, and he wondered if she knew what this man had done, and if she had loved him nonetheless, or if he had somehow concealed it from her. Kurt spoke to her in German. "There was no hope for him — he was done for, one way or the other." And she nodded that she understood, and calmed down.

"Tak jest najlepiej," she said. It was a phrase he had heard used: it meant that it was for the best — God's will.

Kurt went in first.

The black-uniformed body lay in a state of wide-thighed self-abandonment, the army greatcoat wrapped around the head. Kurt had to unwind the blood-soaked garment in order to retrieve his gun. He told the girl not to look but she did not understand, or did not wish to heed him, and looked with dulled eyes at the shattered skull. She began to weep, and Kurt stared at her, amazed by her grief.

As he was leaving the encampment, the burnt man caught up with him.

"The man from the Committee came today," he said.

"Yes?"

"He said — for anyone who might be interested, he would be by the Südbrücke tomorrow, between eleven and noon."

The twin spires of the *Dom*, with their great height, could be seen from far beyond the periphery of the old town. Sometimes shrouded in thick smoke, at other times in stark silhouette, they were a point of orientation in the midst of chaos. Even now, the cathedral windows presented to the eye an amazing — a miraculous — mass of radiant glass, and to the faithful this was a sign of an ultimate order, yes, a divine purpose, notwithstanding the time of terror and disorder in which they lived.

Rolf, however, had no such illusions, no such faith. The reason the cathedral had not been destroyed was because it was the most prominent landmark in the city. It could be seen clearly from the air. He knew that at night the pathfinders dropped their flares above it and then the bombers knew exactly where they were. So he didn't believe all that eyewash about God giving signs. If God was so powerful and could do anything and wanted to give you signs, why didn't He give clearer signs? Since God was supposed to be Almighty, couldn't He give signs that everybody understood? Why'd He have to be so mysterious about it?

Kurt drove the butcher's van in his usual manner, which was like a maniac, tearing around corners on two wheels, bouncing and rattling across bomb sites. With all the smoke, and buildings no longer there from one day to the next, you didn't know where you were half the time, and then suddenly there were the spires looming up, one the shadow of the other, or side by side, depending on where you were coming from. The river was ahead of them now, and black smoke (with a bright-orange inner lining) was rushing upwards from the Deutzer docks on the opposite bank. The van pulled up on the embankment. It looked like a deserted battlefield. They sat watching the blaze and Kurt's eyes were bright. He seemed well-satisfied. The Südbrücke was wreathed in

236

smoke from end to end, they could see nothing moving on it. To the north, the Mullheimerbrücke was little more than two projecting stumps. But the three great steel arches of the cathedral bridge — the Hohenzollern — were intact: a steady stream of fire engines and relief vehicles was crossing the river to Deutz.

"What we come here for?" Rolf asked.

"I have to see somebody."

Rolf looked around on all sides: there was nobody in this burnt wasteland.

"Who's it you got to see?"

"The man from the Committee."

"What Committee?"

Kurt didn't answer. It was after eleven and there was no sign of anybody: he began to get restless, turned on the van's ignition, and kept the motor running. "We might have to leave in a hurry," he told Rolf.

"Look!" Rolf was indicating with his head.

Somebody was approaching from the direction of the Süd- brücke, coming out of the smoke, a handkerchief held across his nose and mouth. He was a stout man, rather red-faced and panting: he carried a walking stick to help him negotiate the rough, unlevel ground.

"Is that him?" Rolf asked.

Kurt looked around. There was nobody else to be seen. He got out of the van and said to Rolf, "Keep the engine run- ning," and then walked rapidly towards the approaching man.

Drawing level with him, Kurt stopped and asked for a light, which the man provided. They stood talking as if they were on a boulevard, from time to time looking around to see if anyone was coming, but there was no one else. It was the red-faced man who was talking mostly. Rolf could see that he was very vehement; he gesticulated forcefully, and Kurt lis- tened attentively, nodding his head a good deal.

Rolf watched the thick smoke from the Deutzer docks coming down and across the river. It was like a trapdoor closing. The little daylight that came through the narrowing crack was bringing into sharp silhouette the long northern skyline with its numerous travelling cranes, its coal-tippers, huge oil-storage tanks, grain silos, warehouses, great shining copper globes, acres of twisting and curving metal tubes, purple-flaming chimneys. The fire was fanning out from the Deutzer docks, spreading northwards.

He remembered how the arteries in his mother's neck had stood out, you could see them pulsing. Her hair was dirty white and dishevelled. She had no time to look after herself, was too busy warning people of the fire and flame that would consume everything. She smelled terrible. Had no time to wash. She'd lain on the ground and he had felt her wildly beating pulses. You couldn't count the beats they were so fast.

The Rhine was slimy and putrid, its surface shimmering with oil spills and floating bottles and tin cans; the strong current swept along a wide range of drifting flotsam: a beer barrel, a woman's hat, a wooden file cabinet, a trail of office papers, a cardboard suitcase, clothing, underwear, a shop sign, a dead dog.

A smouldering burnt-out tramp steamer was sinking slowly in the Rheinauhafen, joining previously sunken ships, their rusty and slime-encrusted hulls lapped by the filthy water.

It was just as his mother had predicted. She wasn't so mad!

Funny, but since she'd died, all those years ago, he'd thought about her more than when she was alive.

The sky was almost completely dark now, the trapdoor had virtually closed, leaving only a faint straight line of light on the horizon.

Rolf saw the red-faced man had finished speaking and was looking around, waiting for Kurt to respond. Kurt seemed to be asking questions, and the man was replying to them briefly. He felt inside his overcoat and produced a piece of paper, which he gave to Kurt. Kurt glanced at it. The man seemed to be saying to read it later, that he had to go now. Kurt nodded and they shook hands with the air of men who have agreed upon something.

Checking once more that there was nobody else waiting to see him, the red-faced man turned around and picked his way, with the help of his walking stick, through the littered, torn-up embankment, back towards the smoking Südbrücke.

In the van, before driving off, Kurt removed his left shoe and sock and concealed the piece of paper he had just been given under his heel.

"Was he the man?" Rolf asked, since he was not being told anything.

Kurt had started the van.

"Yes."

"What did he want?"

"I'll tell you later. I want to tell you all together. It concerns all of us."

After they'd eaten and were smoking their home-made cigarettes, Kurt said, "Everybody listen. I've got something to say. Today I met a man from the Free Germany Committee."

"Who're they?" Otto asked suspiciously.

"They're people like us. From around here. Who believe this war must be brought to an end, the slaughter stopped. They're organizing resistance groups."

"Politicals, are they?" Otto asked.

"They stand for our interests," Kurt said.

"Oh yes? What they want *us* to do?" Rolf demanded, knowing there was always a catch.

"They want us to blow up the EL-DE-Haus," Kurt said. "That's one of the things they want us to do."

"That's all?" Rolf said. "That's all they want? That's nothing, is it? That's easy as piss in the air, isn't it?" He paused. "Why us? Why we been given the honour? Why can't we leave it to *them?*" He jerked his head upwards, meaning the bombers. "They're blowing up everything else."

"The Committee believe Germans must act to free themselves or we'll never be able to raise our heads."

Rolf laughed. "Is that so?" He nodded. "Can be dangerous raising your head, you're liable to get it shot off." He thought for a moment. "How we supposed to blow up the EL-DE-Haus? What with? *Farts?*"

"Dynamite," Kurt said.

"How we supposed to get dynamite?"

"Buy it."

"Yes? With what?"

"With money."

"And how do we get money, genius?"

"Butter. We steal butter. I've been told where we can lay our hands on one hundred kilos. Butter sells for six hundred marks a kilo on the black market. If we only get three hundred, that's thirty thousand marks. We can get dynamite for that, and guns, too."

"I think 'genius' here wants to get us all killed," Rolf said.

"Why're you so keen on living, Louse Boy? I thought you didn't see the advantage of it."

"I don't see the advantage of getting killed."

"Nobody lives forever," Kurt said. "At least you could say you'd done something."

"Suppose I don't want to say I've done something?"

"What are you?"

"What d'you mean, what am I?"

"I mean—what are you, on this earth?"

"Me? I'm Rolf the Louse Boy. I'm a thief. And I'm the son of a thief. That's what I am."

"You don't have to be. You can be anything you like."

"Me? You joking?"

"No, I'm not joking. A man can be what he wants to be. He can decide."

"Who's been putting that stuff in your head? The Committee? The fat man with the red face? I bet they're a bunch of Bolshies."

"I want you to listen to something," Kurt said. "I'm going to read something to you, and I want you to listen."

He took off his left shoe and his sock, and from under his heel produced a piece of folded paper, taped with transparent sticky tape along its folds, like a precious document. Carefully, he unfolded it and read in a matter-of-fact voice:

" 'Each word that comes out of Hitler's mouth is a lie. When he says peace he means war, and when he sacrilegiously mentions the name of the Almighty he means the power of the wicked, the fallen angel Satan. His mouth is the stinking jaw of hell, and his might is rotten at the foundations. It is true that the fight against the National Socialist state of terror must be led with rational means; he who still doubts, however, the real existence of the demonic powers has not understood by far the metaphysical background of this war. Behind all practical logical considerations stands the irrational. . . . Our fight is against the demon, the messenger of the anti-Christ.' "

Kurt paused, looking around at their faces, and then spoke the next sentence with quiet emphasis. " 'The German name will be disgraced forever if German youth fails to rise, to take revenge, to atone — and to build a new and spiritual Europe.' "

"Sounds to me like one of those religious loonies," Rolf said when Kurt had finished. "All that about God and demons." He shook his head. "God and me," he said, "are sort of like fire and water, we don't mix too well. Who said all that, anyway?"

"A saint," Kurt said.

"A saint? Is that a fact? What kind of a saint? A loony saint?"

"Her name was Sophie."

"Saint Sophie?" Rolf sneered.

"Sophie Scholl—she was nineteen years old. A beautiful young girl."

"What happened to her?" Benno asked, rapt.

"They caught her, her and her brother. Caught them handing out this leaflet I've just read to you."

"Stupid to get caught," Rolf pointed out.

"What happened to her?" Benno asked again, insistently.

"They were both . . . executed. Beheaded."

Rolf made a *"phfuttt!"* sound and brought the side of his hand down sharply on his palm. He rubbed the back of his neck.

"Ouch!" he said. "Getting your head cut off hurts."

"It was reported," Kurt said, "that they were very calm climbing the steps to the guillotine, and that they looked straight into the sun."

"Nobody can do that," Rolf said, "not without getting blinded."

"I'm with Kurt," Theo announced. "I'm for blowing up the EL-DE-Haus."

"And getting your head cut off?" Rolf asked. "Not me."

"Take a vote," Kurt said.

He and Theo were for, Benno wasn't sure, Rolf and Otto were against, and Franzi said she'd go along with whatever the majority decided. Stalemate.

"You vote *for*," Theo told his brother.

"I make up my own mind," Benno protested. "I've got a vote like everybody else."

"But no brain. Therefore I decide for you. Benno votes *for*."

"We don't accept that," Rolf said. "That's intimidation. That's not a proper vote. He's got to decide for himself."

"We'll decide tomorrow," Kurt said, anxious to avoid a showdown there and then. "We'll all mull it over, and then we'll make up our minds."

Rolf didn't want to mull it over. Thinking wasn't his strong

242

point — as he used to answer-back in school when told, "Think, Hacker! Use your brain."

It wasn't that he had a cabbage for a brain, as his teachers sometimes said, but that he couldn't think things through logically, step-by-step. He wasn't logical. Things came to him all in a rush, and then he *knew,* without having thought it out. So he didn't really think about blowing up the EL-DE-Haus, but waking during the night he went to where Kurt was sleeping and gave him a dig in the back.

"I'm just asking, see. For the sake of argument. If we did want to get this dynamite, where'd we get it? And the guns?"

"In the black market."

"Do we know somebody in the black market?"

"Willi Gast."

"Gast! *Herr* Gast?"

"Yes. He's one of the biggest crooks in this whole neighbourhood. He's got his fat fingers in every pie. He can get us arms. And he'd take the butter. He sells butter for six hundred marks a kilo."

"How d'you know this, Kurt?"

"The Committee — they know about him."

"If we go to Gast, he could give us away. He's the ward leader. He'd get us arrested."

"He won't do that, if it's good business for him not to. Franzi can go and see him, in the first place. He won't give Franzi away. He's still got a soft spot for Franzi, I wouldn't be surprised."

"You think Franzi'd do it?"

"We can only ask her, Rolf. We can ask her in the morning, and see what she says."

"Yes," Rolf said, and went back to sleep under his pile of coats.

ELEVEN

As the war had gone on and things had got worse and worse, Gast's fortunes had improved and his domain had grown. In his own area he was undisputed king of the rubble heap — and even beyond. For with so many streets reduced to debris and dust, who was to say where one satrap's fiefdom ended and another's commenced? When local Party bigwigs — the "Golden Pheasants" — fled, leaving their streets rulerless, their spies with no one to report back to, Gast stepped in smartly, taking over their areas. With no electricity or gas, and food supplies down to iron rations for the general population, with tens of thousands homeless and without shelter, medical supplies practically nonexistent, the fire-fighting services overwhelmed — and even the burial of the dead getting beyond the resources of the authorities — Gast throve. Whilst the ordinary person could not find potatoes or bread, for his special clients Gast succeeded in obtaining goose, carp, Italian salamis, Swiss cheeses, Dutch veal,

244

Polish beef, fresh eggs, French wines and cognacs—champagne. The German armies in retreat, carrying in their kit bags the spoils of abandoned territories and driving before them the cattle herds of Holland, Poland, and other countries, required customers for their plundered goods and Gast was a good customer. Rounds of Dutch cheeses found their way to his requisitioned storehouses, Bries from Maux, geese from Périgord, perfumes from Grasse, American nylons and chewing gum, aspirin. For those seeking a more definite solution, he had potassium-cyanide capsules, instantly acting, efficacious, guaranteed.

It was all expensive. But what else was there to spend money on? One of his best lines was graves. Things being as they were, people without connections were liable to see their nearest and dearest, if buried at all, put in a mass grave, thrown naked into the earth, men and women piled promiscuously one on top of the other, nameless beings. Knowing Gast could make all the difference. He could still provide private graves in cemeteries, a privileged resting place among the very best families, a funeral ceremony conducted by an ordained cleric, proper coffins and headstones, *in memoriam* candles.

Such fancy final rites only the richest could afford. But even those of lesser means could at least ensure burial for their dead—in a communal grave—if they came to Gast, and without Gast, who could say how long their nearest and dearest might have to rot unburied? And meanwhile there was the indignity of quicklime or the risk of typhus. Gast had a supply of slave labour from a factory in Venloerstrasse to draw on and could get mass graves dug quickly. For this public service he levied a special local "tax." The burying of the dead was not merely serving the relatives of the deceased: it was not only from one's nearest and dearest that one could get typhus, and therefore when anyone was pulled out of the debris and buried, the entire neighbourhood was made to pay the burial tax. He sent his Storm Troopers out to collect it, and those who had no money were able to discharge their public indebtedness with family treasures, or failing those, by digging alongside the slave labourers in a burial detail. That made them look under their mattresses!

So when Franzi arrived at local Party headquarters she found him very busy. Gast's kingdom now extended as far as the West Cemetery and the city gasworks to the west, Ossendorf to the north, Blücher Park to the east, and the Aachenerstrasse to the south, and within this expanded territory sixty people had, on the basis of a first rough count, met their death in last night's air attacks and would have to be either buried or disposed of in airtight sacks. Those who were anxious to avoid the airtight sacks for their dear departed would have to purchase private burial rights. In the cemeteries in his district there were plots of earth reserved as "Gast's graves," where those who could afford it might be laid to rest decently. The premium was high, though variable according to means: those with the greatest means had to pay most, naturally; those of lesser means were made a price. It was always, therefore, a matter of ticklish negotiation, and Gast was presently occupied in this way with some of the most recently bereaved, while at the same time arranging for deliveries of meat, poultry, and cheeses to other clients. He was also on the track of a large quantity of butter that he had heard about. Then there was a secret report on his desk about some sacks of Brazilian coffee — real coffee — stored at the Sprinzer warehouse in Deutzer docks. Coffee was black gold. Coffee he could sell for 1,600 marks a kilo. For one kilo of coffee he could get more than a senior public servant earned in a month!

This was the moment when Franzi walked into his life again. If she had come to see him, she must want something, and when people wanted something from Gast he was in his element, for beggars couldn't be choosers! Glancing up from his overflowing desk (pickled cucumbers and smoked ham on bread left on top of chits and special authorizations and

246

passes issued by his authority), he tried to guess what Franzi might want from him. A grave? Had she come to beg a grave for her lover?

How he wished it was that!

But perhaps it was not for a grave that she had come, perhaps it was for food. She looked thin and drawn and worn out, a creature of the rubble like the rest, but for all that: desirable. With her golden-ringed irises — the smoking rings of Saturn! As enticing as ever, even though now, five years later, he could no longer think of her as his "child bride." She must be over twenty. Still, she was the only one for him, she was "high quality," no question, and if he could have her, oh! he would take her like a shot: she would be the ultimate proof of his self-advancement and self-overcoming, and the justification of everything he had had to do in these terrible but financially rewarding years.

Franzi waited in the crowded, shabby little room, like everybody else. She was aware that he was aware of her, even while he continued dealing with others, and she could tell he still wanted her. You could always tell. It was in the grip of the eyes.

He had become very important, she could see. Though it was a mountain of rubble that he ruled over, he was king. He ordered his minions around. He dealt roughly with those who had come to wheedle a grave or a goose out of him. Though well paid for his services, he had the air of a monarch dispensing favours. It wasn't strictly business, not *just* business: it was also largesse, reward and punishment. Despite the way his eyes gripped hers whenever he looked up, she could not tell at this point if she might not be punished for having left him. Before being readmitted to his favours, she might have to pay some forfeit. She wasn't sure. He wasn't sure either — to what extent he would make her pay. It depended on what she wanted from him, how dire her need was. He prayed it was very dire so that she would be utterly at his mercy. How he would enjoy that! When his hands were

247

around somebody's throat he was at his best: generous to a fault.

He let her wait twenty minutes and then found a moment to talk to her.

"You can see," he said, "I'm up to my neck. But for you I make time. Come."

He left the room full of people — let them all wait — and took her outside into the street.

"So," he said, "you've come to see me, after all these years." Before she could speak, he put in quickly, "I want you to know, I don't hold anything against you. The way you left me. I understand perfectly. I understand. You were a young girl. You were not yet mature. It was understandable." It made him feel good to forgive her like this. "Did you ever think about me?" he asked.

"Yes," she said noncommittally.

He gave her an intimate look. "Say what you like, in certain respects, which I don't need to mention, we got on like a house on fire."

Though it made her shudder inside to remember, what he said was true and she gave him a secret little smile. He was gratified, since his way with women was one of his proudest boasts. Oh yes, Herr Gast knew how to handle women. Women didn't put on airs with him! He went straight to the heart of the matter and at heart all women were whores, as he was fond of saying. And no worse for it! At the same time, it was gratifying if sometimes they were not *actually* whores. To find in a little girl on the threshold of womanhood all the passionate ways of a fully experienced woman — ah! He had brought that out in her. He prided himself that he had awakened her sexually — Herr Gast, the magician — from the sleep of childhood. If he was not the first, he was the one who had taught her what it meant to have a real man. He had given her satisfaction. He had taught her bodily pleasure. Had practically formed her in her womanliness. Before him, from

248

what she'd told him, it was just fumbling in the dark: nothing to speak of. And afterwards?

"You are happy?" he asked.

She nodded, suggesting happiness in moderation, but leaving a door open to him. He saw the open door and almost rushed in with some wild declaration, but restrained himself at the last: careful, Herr Gast! Go easy, Herr Gast! he told himself. All in good time. No hurry. See what she wants. Play her in nicely.

"You need something from me?" he asked. "I'm a busy man, I come to the point. Say what it is. For you, Franzi, I would do more than for almost anybody. For you . . ."

"Machine guns," she said, "can you supply machine guns to us? Hand grenades? Dynamite, with fuses?"

He looked astonished, but recovered quickly. Nothing astonished Gast for long.

"Ah!" He spread his hands. "Nothing's impossible. Herr Gast can get anything. While there's not so much demand for machine guns and hand grenades, and therefore no *market*, I'm sure these items can be obtained. But such goods come expensive. How can you pay for them?"

"We can pay," she said. "We can pay in other goods. We can supply you with butter, coffee . . ."

"Butter? Coffee!" He was astonished, and lowered his voice. "You are coming to me with a business proposition?"

"Yes."

"How much butter?"

"I don't know. Quite a lot."

He shook his head. "Why should I get mixed up in arms dealings?" He gave a contemptuous shrug. "You'll get yourself killed, Franzi."

"You can get yourself killed in any case."

"Hand grenades? Dynamite?" He shook his head.

"With fuses."

"Naturally with fuses. Otherwise . . . What are you

going to blow up?'' She remained silent. ''It's a secret? Then don't tell me.'' He spread his hands around. ''Does it matter what else is blown up?''

''Yes.''

''It can all be got,'' he said. ''It is all very feasible. But I'd have to discuss the terms, the details. We'd have to negotiate a price, delivery dates. All sorts of things. This is a complicated matter, Franzi.''

He had seen immediately that the complications were to his advantage. If there were to be protracted dealings, with Franzi as the go-between, it gave him a fresh chance with her. He did not know if he was going to get involved in anything as dangerous as the supplying of arms, but what did it cost him to say yes? He could string her along. It meant he would get a chance to see her again. Some opportunity might present itself — you never knew. He was a believer in opportunity, in waiting for it, in seizing it. In creating it. It was all to his possible advantage, the complicated dealings that would have to ensue. Like all such dealings they would drag on and on. Yes, *yes*.

''You'll have to talk to Kurt about that,'' she said.

''Kurt? Kurt Springer? You know he's a deserter. If I'm seen with him, the Gestapo'll know in two minutes. We'll all be finished. He'll have to make his propositions through you.''

''He wants to see you.''

Gast thought. ''All right. I will see him — you and him together. You have to come as well. Come tomorrow to eleven o'clock mass at the *Dom*. I will see you both there. Don't approach me. I'll find you and approach you when it's safe. Now I've got to go. People are waiting inside.''

To Franzi a cathedral was an alien place, and especially this cathedral, with its soaring twin spires and its multitude of turrets and pinnacles. Disbelievers by nature, she and Rolf were never much for churchgoing.

250

The Domplatz on this murky October day was lashed by violent winds that buffeted the people going to morning mass; heads down, collars up, hanging on to their hats, they picked their way around the torn-up flagging stones, the sand dumps, the rust-eaten water reservoirs, stepped gingerly over the fire hoses that snaked across the square, sought to avoid the puddles of stagnant water. Airborne litter was strewn all around. Drifting black smoke from across the river clung to the cathedral's walls, provoking the fanciful notion of something rising out of the mist of ages. Against its charred and blackened towers leaned enormously high firemen's ladders, and its upper structure was hung with ropes and pulleys and builders' hoists. Scaffolds piled with sandbags protected the illustrious expanses of glass, cutting out most of the daylight, turning the nave below into a dark and gloomy pit. It was packed this morning. Franzi could find nowhere to sit. Then she saw a smallish space at the end of a choir-stall and made the others move up so that she could squeeze in. It was the last row of the nave.

Shortly afterwards, a man on crutches, in his early twenties, came in at the back of the cathedral and began to push his way through the people jammed around the door. Though shabbily dressed in civilian clothes, it was assumed that his condition must be due to war injuries, and room was made for him. Somebody offered him his seat, but he refused this and took his place behind the last choir-stall, where the young blonde girl had just sat down.

Franzi hated the church smell: a kind of holy mustiness. She thought of it as the smell of souls. Must be a lot of them floating about under the high vaulting. They made the air stuffy with their solemn presence, despite the soaring spaciousness of the cathedral. Yes, yes, it was all those souls who took up the room and made the air stuffy. Her eye was drawn upwards by the clusters of slender pillars: she supposed that was a way of getting you to look heavenward. She was never very good at that. More of an earthbound creature. The figures of the Apostles in the chancel pillars and the saintly forms that darkly looked down from the dim stained glass made Franzi uneasy. She glanced around for Gast: it was going to be hard finding someone in this crowd. In any case, he had said not to approach him, that he would approach them when it was safe. Behind her, Kurt, on crutches, whispered: "No sign of him."

A priest was censing the congregation. The little puffs of smoking incense were a long way away: a remote and strange rite. He moved the ciborium in the form of a cross.

" 'I believe in God the Father Almighty, Maker of heaven and earth: And in Jesus Christ his only Son our Lord: Who was conceived by the Holy Ghost, Born of the Virgin Mary . . .' "

The white robe, the long black cassock, the silver vessel, the grey curling smoke, the solemn hush, the devoutness of the worshippers in this dark place — none of it meant anything to her: she was a nonbeliever. It was all superstition and ignorance, this great edifice and all its jewels and gold and glass and marble. What she believed in was what she could see, what she could touch and taste and feel in her heart and body. And she believed that when you were dead, you were dead once and for all, there was no resurrection, no afterlife to hope for. Nothing at the other end. It was all now or never. Instead of staring with the fixed gaze of worship towards the High Altar and shrine, she kept looking around for Gast, her low-life former lover, a man of scant ceremonies and no reserve whatsoever, a most improper man, and an awful man.

Breathing the thin, close, slightly smelly spirituality in the cathedral, she thought she must be a wicked person, a sinner, and this was why churches revolted her, and why she had allowed herself to be seduced by Gast, had fallen into his hands all those years ago. She had freed herself from him forever, she'd thought, but now it seemed it was not so. She was not quite free of him yet. The monotonous sing-song of

252

the priest's voice: "'. . . He descended into hell; The third day he rose again from the dead: He ascended into heaven, And sitteth on the right hand of God the Father Almighty: From thence he shall come to judge the quick and the dead.'"

She had seen how Gast looked at her. Oh, he wanted her, and he was the sort of man who when he wanted something went after it and usually got it. What am I going to do? she thought. What am I getting into? Willi Gast in full and bulbous erection was a most indecent sight, why did it spring into her mind now, here? Was it a way of confessing and asking forgiveness? Or was it, on the contrary, defiance, flaunting the indecency?

Another cleric, in scarlet with scarlet hat, clearly more important than the one who had swung the censer and chanted the Lord's Prayer, was climbing the steps to the pulpit. He was far away, and it was difficult for Franzi to make out his face in any detail: but she had an impression of severity and nobility and luminous energy, so that he constituted the brightest single spot in the general gloom; also, the arrangement of the sandbags allowed a little light to filter down just here and fall on the pulpit for dramatic effect. He seemed preoccupied with "higher things" up on his high pedestal and oblivious of the tense congregation waiting for him to speak. An electric current passed from him, through the massed souls who made the air stuffy, and then his voice cracked like a whip over the heads of those below him in the choir-stalls, below him actually but also below him in standing and status, the princely voice implied. He began:

"'Beware of false prophets which come to you in sheep's clothing, but inwardly they are ravening wolves.' Matthew seven: fifteen." He paused for effect, and then continued: "That mistakes are sometimes made in the conduct of human affairs, that great nations suffer defeats as well as victories, is evident from the whole course of human history. But great nations can righten their mistakes and reverse their defeats, whilst they retain the unity of nationhood. It is much harder to fight the insidious enemy within, the ravening wolf in sheep's clothing. I speak to you today to warn of a pestilence that overruns our society: the Wolf Children. The countenance of a child is a dear thing to us, is it not? And we are loath to think ill of those of tender years, so close to innocence. But beware the ravening wolf, said the Apostle Matthew. And I say to you: beware the Wolf Children! These children and youths who infest the ruins of our city have become worse than a nuisance, worse than just hooligans and petty criminals: they contain within them — and spread, and *spread!* — the seed of unruliness, of disobedience, of anarchy. *They know better than their elders and betters!* Therein lies the arrogance and sinfulness of their position. Whether they be pickpockets, or small-time gangsters, or robbers of the dead, or street-corner thugs who prey on old ladies, whether they call themselves Edelweiss Pirates, or Street Mobsters, or Navajos, or Swing Youths, they have in common a total disrespect for those forces and institutions that the rest of us cherish and honour. They are therefore in the deepest and profoundest sense *outlaws. They wish to be outside our laws,* to be ruled only by their desires and impulses, and the dark forces of their turbulent natures. Everyone admires high spirits in youth, and a degree of rejection of the values and practices of their parents is normal. But such rejection, to be normal, must be contained within a broad framework of accepted standards. These Wolf Children have no standards, no higher authority to which they bend their knee, no lawfulness. There is embodied within their natures the malefic spirit that wishes to bite the hand that has fed it, to destroy the very breast at which it was suckled, to spit out the mother's milk in disgust and blasphemy. I raise my voice in warning against these unruly spirits today, because there are those among you, in this time of terrible trial, who may only see the faces of lost little children, the human wreckage of war. Cast any such sentimental notion out of your minds. These children are evil. They are the seed of disorder, and as such must be stamped out.''

The passion of the prophets could be seen in Cardinal Leupold's luminous features: he was a man given an insight into the profoundest, darkest truths. His noble visage was torn by anguish, by a terrible duty. His voice resounded within the cathedral walls. ''The Apostle Matthew said: 'But the children of the kingdom shall be cast out into outer darkness: there shall be weeping and gnashing of teeth.' ''

Throughout the sermon Franzi was looking around for Gast: no sign of him. Perhaps he had changed his mind. He was apt to do that. Now she was hanging back in the general press of people going out. Slowly she was carried towards the doors. A voice spoke in her ear in the crush: ''A good sermon, you agree? An excellent sermon.'' She looked round at Gast and nodded nervously. He followed her out. In the wind-blown Domplatz he put on his Homburg hat, turned up his coat collar. His glittering eyes sized her up and then he approached her and raised his hat.

''May I . . . accompany you, fräulein? Streets aren't safe. These Wolf Children . . . !'' In an undertone he told her, ''Walk away from me, I'll follow you.''

She did as he instructed; it appeared as if she was turning away from an unwelcome approach. Gast followed and caught her up, evidently a man experienced in accosting women in the street, and successful! For he was not being sent on his way, he was being listened to. As he made his approach, he was turning to avoid the stinging debris dust that the wind was whipping up off the ground, one moment facing the girl, and the next facing the man on crutches, the beggar holding out his hat.

''I need dynamite,'' Kurt was saying. ''With fuses. And guns. Machine guns. Automatic rifles. Pistols. Hand grenades. A bazooka.''

''Ah,'' Gast said, turning around in the wind.

"Well?"

Gast searched in his pockets for small change. "In principle it can be done," he said. "In principle there's nothing can't be done. But it'll be expensive. Such commodities come expensive." He appeared unable to find a suitable coin to give the beggar. He sorted through those in his palm. "I've got to cover myself," he explained. "Cover my risk."

"How much would cover your risk?"

"It's going to be in the region . . . in the region of twenty, thirty thousand marks minimum. For just the most basic of these items."

"I can get butter," Kurt said.

"How much?"

"How much will you pay me?"

"For a smaller quantity, or a larger amount?"

"A larger amount."

"Two hundred marks a kilo."

"You sell for six hundred."

"I have my expenses. You understand. . . ." He spun in the wind, this way and that, like a weather vane. He appeared to be questioning the beggar about his affliction, and using this conversation to hold the young girl's interest. "If I hadn't got a lot of sympathy for your struggle, I wouldn't even consider such a proposition," he told them. "A risky business! I don't need it, thank you very much. Frankly, as a business proposition, it isn't worth it to me to take the risk. If I do it, it's because I sympathize with . . . the cause. You understand? I hope you'll remember that. If ever wild charges are flung about. People can be so vengeful! When they want to settle old scores they'll take any excuse. I want it remembered, when the war is over, what my role has been in all this."

"It'll be remembered," Kurt promised.

Gast was able to turn to face Franzi as the wind dropped.

"I make you a proposition, as follows," he told her in his most gallant manner. "I propose an initial exchange on a small scale. As a test. A certain amount of butter for a certain amount of arms. To establish a working relationship, mutual trust. For when can you get the butter?"

Kurt said, "I can have a consignment for you the day after tomorrow. Can you have some arms for me by then? If we start with ten kilos. At your price, that's two thousand marks."

"*Fifteen* kilos. I can get you some rifles and some hand grenades for that."

"Dynamite?"

"That I can't promise to put my hands on so quick, but in due course . . . I'm sure."

"Where shall we meet?"

"You and I can't meet," Gast said, smiling seductively at Franzi. "Impossible. This, now, is dangerous enough. We mustn't be seen together again. You're a deserter. I can't have dealings with deserters. That's self-evident."

"Then how?"

"Through Franzi," Gast proposed, glittering. "It's the only way. An affair of the heart. Herr Gast has become heart-stricken. . . . We meet in a little hotel that I have used before for such purposes. She has a suitcase, I have a suitcase. Our overnight things. In the privacy of our room, we make the exchange. Butter for guns. She leaves with her suitcase, I with mine." He slapped his hands diagonally against each other to indicate the cleanness of the operation.

Kurt weighed the proposition with distaste. A dubious arrangement.

"It's not what I'd expected."

"Make up your mind," Gast said roughly. The edgy charm that he could put on like a hat was coming off like a pair of muddied boots. "I can't stand here talking all day. It begins to look very suspicious."

Kurt glanced questioningly at Franzi. Her expression told him nothing.

"We'll have to give you our answer—"

"You have to give me your answer *now*," Gast quietly raged. "I'm not taking the risk of further meetings while you make up your minds. Yes or no. Take it or leave it."

Franzi said, "Kurt would have to bring me to the meetings, and take me back."

Gast frowned at such bargaining.

"He will have to wait downstairs, in the lobby. He can't come up. He mustn't be seen coming to see me. You have to come up alone."

Franzi looked at Kurt, and he thought: she wants to do it; she likes these ambiguous situations, these shady dangerous dealings, as long as they are about her.

"No," Kurt said, "that will not work."

"In that case —" Gast raised his hat to the lady, gave a cold smile, and started to walk away.

Kurt and Franzi exchanged quick, urgent looks. She made a questioning gesture of her hand — Well? "Wait!" she called after Gast, and he stopped, keeping his back to them while Kurt and Franzi exchanged further deep, searching looks. "Don't you think you can trust me?" she said softly.

"I don't know."

"You'll be downstairs," she said, "with a gun. What would he try?"

Gast was starting to walk away again.

Kurt nodded to Franzi and she ran after the retreating figure and told him, "We agree."

"The day after tomorrow," Gast said. "The Golden Lamb Hotel in the Komödienstrasse. Six P.M. I will have the guns. You must have the butter. Fifteen kilos."

He raised his hat to her, bowed with charm, and to anyone watching it must have appeared that Herr Gast had made another conquest.

Situated not far from the cathedral and the railway station, the Golden Lamb was a high, narrow little hotel, with a tiny courtyard that could be reached from the street of the "fat

258

dealers," where lively trading went on in doorways, in basements, on the derelict ground floors of bombed buildings, and, on a more important scale, in hotel rooms and rented accommodation.

Everything that the heart desired and the law forbade was bought and sold. Whatever was normally unobtainable could be obtained here. Straight off the troop trains from the West came soldiers with their pockets full of "war souvenirs": silver crucifixes ripped from the bodies of Belgian convent girls, real leather shoes taken from the feet of those who would not be walking anymore, cherries in liqueur, Swiss chocolate truffles, Brazilian cigars. Jeweller's glass in eye, the dealers examined brooches and pearls and the carat markings in gold wedding rings. The currency exchangers held up foreign money to the grey light. The cloth dealers felt materials between their fingers and pronounced on what they were made of. Those who dealt in foodstuffs sniffed and pressed and tasted on their fingers to make sure that caviar was fresh, butter not rancid, French cognac really French, and not some Yugoslav concoction with a fake label. When they were satisfied, a price was mentioned, at which point the soldier experienced in such dealings walked away, and the dealer, after letting him go a few steps, went after him and tugged at his sleeve and improved slightly on his first offer. Once the bargain was concluded, wads of notes were taken out of trouser pockets, fingers were licked and sums counted off, and the soldier became the target of the girls waiting in doorways.

The Golden Lamb was one of the better places along here. Its ogee windows and leaded glass lent it a Venetian air, and there was a Moorish feeling about the lattice-work entrance. Beyond it sat a stern woman at a wooden counter, sternly handing out keys to clients. Girls of the better type came here, the sort who would prefer to give an all-night rate to a single customer rather than drag themselves up and down stairs a dozen times. It was also a place where men met their "little friends" for some hours in the afternoon or early evening. Rooms could be rented on an hourly basis, which was convenient not only for these men but also for dealers whose transactions were too important or delicate to be conducted in doorways or on open bomb sites. People like Gast found it safer not to have any fixed place of trade but to move about from one to another.

Going in, there was a dark little bar on the left where, by the light of memorial candles in glasses, a few people sat around speaking in whispers and drinking.

It was here that Kurt sat down and waited while Franzi went up with her battered cardboard suitcase to meet Gast. Men were waiting for a room to become available — like everything else, such rooms were in short supply — or for a "little friend" to turn up. In this shifty-eyed ambience, nobody looked too closely at anyone else, and Kurt managed not to draw attention to himself.

Gast was on the fourth floor. Breathless from going up so many stairs carrying fifteen kilos of butter, Franzi paused for a moment outside Room 42; he must have been listening for her, because he opened the door before she could knock. He was wearing a scarlet satin dressing gown embossed with golden and blue birds of paradise, confiscated from a Jewish pederast he had sent to Dachau. There was champagne on the table, open — and he was already drinking.

Seeing that she was a little taken aback by the unbusiness-like atmosphere, he said quickly: "For the benefit of anyone who comes in. So it looks like we're genuine lovers. Can't be too careful."

Now that the champagne was open, for the sake of appearances they might as well drink it. It would be a pity to waste such good stuff. She saw no reason not to drink one glass — just one. No harm in that. He proposed a toast:

"To us," he said, adding, as her face indicated some unwillingness to drink to this, ". . . to our business together."

She drank to that and it made her feel pleasantly light and eased her nervousness.

He seemed in no hurry to see the contents of her suitcase; when she had finished the first glass of champagne, he poured a second, and then a third.

"We mustn't rush this," he said, "or it won't appear convincing. Somebody may smell a rat. Take your time, take your time."

Uncomfortably aware, however, of Kurt waiting for her downstairs in the bar and counting the minutes, she asked to see the contents of the case he had brought. He opened it and she saw wrapped up in filmy black lingerie — for camouflage — several hand grenades and the metal parts of unassembled submachine guns, and pistols.

"Don't you want to see what's in my case?" she asked.

"No. I trust you," he said.

But she insisted on checking her goods. The submachine gun parts she could not assess, and she said: "Kurt will have to check this stuff."

"Check! *Check!*" Gast raged. "Don't you trust me? My business is based on trust. There's got to be trust on both sides. Why would I trick you? It's not in my interest."

It was almost an hour before Franzi came down: Kurt noting the slight sway of her step, the bright vagueness of the eyes, accused her of being drunk.

"I had to have a drink with him," she said, "to make it convincing that . . . *you know*. He said — "

"You fall for every cheap tawdry line."

Outside in the street, everybody was dragging suitcases along or carrying heavy parcels and bundles on their shoulders. The smoke pall that had hung over the city for days was sinking like an enormous, holed zeppelin drifting down to earth and leaking noxious gases, pouring out black filth. The destruction all around had a random pattern to it: here, a great fist had punched a deep hole through row after

261

row of buildings, leaving those on either side standing; there, a different kind of devastation had occurred, following the twisting, haphazard course of a runaway destroying angel, some drunk with the flaming sword. There was no rhyme or reason to it: why this coffeehouse stood, why that one had been flattened.

As they made their way back to where Kurt had left the butcher's van, he was all the time seething with impatience to open the suitcase.

"Did you get dynamite?"

"No, he hasn't been able to get any yet."

"He's tricking us."

"He said we had to trust him."

"Trust him? Trust *him!*" Kurt said derisively.

In the van they were able to open the case, and Kurt saw the black lacy underwear in which the submachine gun parts and the hand grenades were wrapped; his face became dark, but he said nothing.

The submachine guns, he saw at once, were Stens: the crude, rough metal work, the skeletal frames—not the most reliable weapons in the world, and given away in the tens of thousands by the British to partisans and Resistance forces. Gast probably had paid next to nothing for them. They had the advantage, however, of being easily taken apart, and the parts could be concealed. He assembled one weapon, clipping the tubular steel barrel onto the stock, and then screwing on the perforated sleeve to hold the barrel in place. Once the butt had been clipped on as well, the weapon was ready to use. He assembled a second Sten. This one was fitted with a Maxim-patterned silencer—a type of gun used in Commando raids — and he was pleased. But there were no magazines.

"He's given us guns without any ammunition—a lot of use they are!" He threw up his hands in fury and disgust. "We've been bamboozled. Couldn't you have examined them more carefully, or did you have other things on your mind?"

"He said next time."

"What?"

"He said we'll get the rest next time."

"When is that?"

"Monday."

"*Monday!* He can't keep away from you, can he?"

At her next meeting with Gast she demanded a sample of the dynamite they had been promised, but he said he had not yet succeeded in laying his hands on any. Ammunition for the Stens? That, too, was difficult to get. However, as a sign of good faith he had brought a whole suitcase full of hand grenades, the British pineapple type and the German stick type. As before, the champagne was already open and must not be wasted. He also had a silk negligée for her, and wanted her to wear it, wanted the hotel maid to see her in it. You couldn't be too careful; it was necessary, if they were to meet frequently, and it looked as though they might have to, with the slowness of everything, that there should be no shadow of suspicion of their relationship being anything but amorous, otherwise the Gestapo might get to hear. Surely after all that had passed between them she was not embarrassed about him seeing her in a negligée, a perfectly decent negligée that had belonged to a respectable woman: a Jewish ladies' hairdresser with premises in the best part of the Ehrenfeldgürtel. He would ring for the maid, and Franzi could undress while the maid was on her way up — and as soon as the maid had seen her in the negligée she could dress again. All perfectly above-board. She remembered how he had seduced her, when she was a child, with the stockings, and this, now, seemed a somewhat stale repetition of the same trick; but when he insisted that it was a safety measure, she thought there might be something in what he said. He was not going to rape her, considering they had business dealings. Besides, he knew that Kurt was downstairs in the bar, armed. So she decided to do what he asked, and when he had rung the bell for the maid, she undressed in a matter-of-fact fashion. He held out the negligée for her.

263

"Put it on the bed," she said.

It might be better, he explained, if she were to be completely naked under the negligée, it would be more convincing for the chambermaid.

As she changed, she felt the heat of his looks (he was not the type of man not to look) and she saw that the situation was rapidly becoming overcharged, business dealings or not, especially as the maid wasn't coming. Perhaps there was no maid. In a hotel of this kind, who could say? Perhaps rooms were not cleaned and beds not made at times such as these. Or else the bell didn't work. No electricity — *of course!* And she had fallen for his latest cheap trick.

Angrily, she dressed.

"You see the effect you have on me still. I'm a man, Franzi."

"You're a pig, Willi. A pig. The Pig-Willi, they call you, and they're right."

He didn't seem to mind her insults, his self-esteem unshakable.

"You're my favourite girl still," he told her.

He threw himself down on the bed, and stretched out his arms to her to join him, impervious to slights and refusals: he was like a clumsy stage conjurer who having bungled one trick went straight on to the next.

"The sheets need to be more crumpled," he said, "or nobody is going to believe that passion took place, leaving no trace. Those chambermaids, they know if there's been a woman in a bed or not. They've got a nose for that. And they all get their retainers from the Gestapo. So we can't be too careful."

"*What* chambermaid?" she threw back at him, pointedly. She said she had to go. He was now methodically bouncing about on the bed, crumpling it as best he could without her help, making the bedsprings squeak wildly and grinning at the memories that brought back. She frowned.

"You can't go yet," he told her. "It's not even half an hour.

Herr Gast is not given to *ejaculatio praecox*. It'll be suspicious if you leave so soon. You come with a big suitcase and you leave with a big suitcase after half an hour! They'll ask themselves: what's wrong with Herr Gast all of a sudden? They'll smell a rat and we'll all be done for, just because you're so eager to rush out of here."

Half convinced by this argument, she sat down again, some distance from bouncing Gast on the squeaking bed.

"Drink some champagne while you're waiting."

"When will you get us the dynamite and the fuses?"

"I'll get it for you. All in good time. Didn't I get you hand grenades? And the British Stens?"

"But no ammo."

"All in good time."

From the window of the room — they were on the fourth floor, and an area between where they were and the river had been flattened by bombing — the turbid water of the Rhine showed up brilliant white in the surrounding darkness. Nothing was what it seemed to be: she had learned that. She saw the "red candles" coming down all around the cathedral: marker flares.

"I better go," she said.

"If there's a raid, you're better off here. They spare the cathedral. Stay — it won't be convincing otherwise."

"And Kurt?"

"Kurt'll be safer, too. There's a cellar here. If the raid is close, the girls and their clients go to the cellar. The girls scream when the bombs fall. Kurt'll have a lovely time comforting them."

"And you expect to have a lovely time comforting me?"

"Ah — you know all my little tricks, what can I do?"

A shimmering cascade of target indicators was falling in mid-river. The effect was of a waterfall. The first firebombs were spilling out of the sky, and the industrial installations on the east bank were lighting, one after the other, like matches being struck. The glow of the spreading fires illumined the dark side of the Rhine. This was the worst month so far. A raid practically every other day. Firebombs falling endlessly in a random pattern of destruction. The enemy no longer cared what they set fire to. It seemed the whole city was to burn.

"I never got over you, Franzile. You know that? Never. With all the things I achieved, my regret was always that I didn't have you at my side. Or it would have been perfect."

"Perfect?" she said sarcastically.

"Well, who was to know it'd all come crashing down?" There was no bitterness in his voice. Nothing amazed Gast. One minute things were like this, the next they were like that. "Of course, they're all finished now," he said. "Any fool can see that Hitler and the Nazis are finished. And about time . . . I'll be glad to see the back of that lot."

She stared at him in stupefaction.

"You say that!"

"You really think I was one of them? Never in my heart of hearts. I swear to you! I was an unpaid functionary. It's an honorary position. Not even paid. My main responsibility was and is measures for the protection of the civilian population. Of course I had to participate in ceremonial functions. It's expected, I had to attend parades, sports festivals. Franzi, what I am is a businessman pure and simple. Politics never interested me. I was interested in making something of myself, that's all. Don't go blaming me for the rest. I don't run the country, do I?" He added craftily, "Don't think I didn't see it coming, this — now. I'm no fool, Franzi. I made provisions. . . ." He got up from the bed and approached her at the window. The fire path appeared to be going at a tangent to where they were, striking out towards Lindenthal, Sulz, Klettenberg. "D'you know how many Jews I *saved?*" he suddenly demanded. "Many, many. Half a dozen or more. *Of which I have written proof.* Whilst my official — honorary — function might seem to contradict this, Franzile, I've been an opponent of Nazism for a long time. Why d'you imagine I

266

supply hand grenades and Sten guns to the Resistance? There are easier ways of making money, less dangerous. I risk my neck. No, no; you can't judge a man by the company he keeps, that's well known. A man has got to be judged by what's inside him.''

"When can you have the rest of the arms for us?'' she asked.

"As soon as possible. That's a promise. Trust me, I'll do my best. Come again on Thursday. I'll see what I can get for you by then.''

"Dynamite,'' she reminded him.

"Yes, dynamite. I know, I know.''

Despite the fact that nothing had happened between herself and Gast (beyond her putting on the negligée at his insistence), she felt guilty when she rejoined Kurt. Her past relationship with Gast condemned her over and over again — in Kurt's eyes and in her own. How could she be trusted now, having once been the Pig-Willi's fancy woman. She couldn't be trusted. Couldn't trust herself. She was too easygoing where men were concerned, and always had been. Lacked moral fibre. But she was loyal to Kurt now, and it hurt that he didn't trust her because of what she had been like when she was fifteen and didn't know better, didn't know what tricksters men could be.

She felt Kurt's eyes boring into her every time she came down from Gast's room: he seemed to be peering into her very heart and soul, and it made her feel much more naked than when she'd been putting on the negligée. Naturally, she didn't tell Kurt about that. He would have gone mad. He'd sensed something from the way she avoided his eyes and straight away launched into explanations, excuses: no dynamite yet, but next time, so Gast had promised, she said.

She had succeeded in getting Gast not to use underwear to wrap the hand grenades in this time, saying it was too provocative.

Instead, dresses and skirts had been placed over the arms.

Even so, Kurt was provoked; he suspected he was the victim of trickery and deception. Franzi had to prove it was not so, that it was him she loved and nobody else.

He scrutinized her face. Was there a flicker of absentness in her expression? Was she less responsive to him? He would be able to tell what had been going on; she must not imagine she could keep anything from him. He would know.

"Did he try to touch you?"

"No."

"I don't believe you. He's the sort who always tries—"

"Well, *jokingly*. . . . He *says* things."

"How *jokingly*? Does he try, for a joke, to put his hands on you?"

"No."

"Not even for a joke?" Kurt said with sarcasm.

"No."

"You're tired, my love. My beloved one. Love of my life. *Why are you tired?* Has he tired you out, Herr Gast? With his business deals? With his jokes?"

"Shut up, Kurt."

"I love you, Franzi."

"I love you."

"Do you?"

"Yes."

"How much? More than your life?"

"Yes. . . ."

"Careful, careful. I may hold you to that, my love."

"Hold me to what?"

"I love you more than your life, too."

"I don't know what you mean by that."

"Don't you?"

TWELVE

Theo's grey eyes, which were all the time getting greyer, peered at them over the gold-rimmed half-lenses, which being much too large for him had slid down almost to the end of his nose. He had found the glasses on the body of a dead Post Office official and appropriated them for his own use. They seemed to improve his eyesight when reading, and he did a lot of reading now, mostly political and historical works, books banned by the authorities, that had been saved from the public burnings, long ago, and passed from hand to hand ever since. Theo pored over them for hours, and in the bad light by which he was often obliged to read, these glasses were of some help. But even with them, he was inclined to screw up his eyes and furrow his brow, and the resultant expression was becoming permanently stamped upon his features, and with the too-large half-lenses sliding down his nose, he was beginning to look more and more like a junior Russian commissar.

It was ages since anyone had seen him smile.

Now he looked at them over his glasses, greyly, and said in his driest manner: "We should draw up a death list."

"A death list?" Otto asked interestedly.

Theo tapped a pencil against the side of his hand in a regular rhythm. This was one of his mannerisms. Lately, he was developing little traits like that. Another one was pursing his lips, narrowing his eyes, and not speaking. It gave the impression he was thinking about something so complicated and deep nobody else could even understand it, therefore what was the point of talking about it?

"Who'd you have in mind?" Rolf asked.

"What kind of death list?" Benno wanted to know.

"Those we'd execute when we're victorious. Traitors to the people."

"Like who?" Rolf asked.

"That's what we've got to decide." He looked from one to the other, tapping his pencil vigorously. "Any suggestions?"

There was silence.

"In that case, I'll begin." He cleared his throat. "I move that the Gestapo chief for Cologne, Stieff, is put at the top of our list. He's the pig's arsehole mainly responsible for the repression of liberty here, and for torture and murder on a massive scale, and I move he deserves to die."

They all agreed that Stieff undoubtedly deserved to die, and Theo wrote his name on a sheet of paper headed:

CONDEMNED TO DEATH BY THE PEOPLE

"If we condemn Stieff," Theo continued logically, "it follows that his principal underlings have got to be condemned. Those that with their own hands committed the crimes. Beat prisoners, tortured them, and executed them by hanging, shooting, and beheading by guillotine or axe. *Therefore:* I move we put on the list Kriminal-Kommissar Horst of the Horst Kommando. As chief of section "B" Youthful Opposition, Unrest and Resistance, it's self-evident he's guilty. Agreed?"

They carried Horst's condemnation on the nod, and listened attentively as Theo, tapping his pencil, went on.

"Next come J. Müller, W. Freisler, J. Wagner, O. W. Schlammer."

All four, according to Theo, were guilty.

"O. W. Schlammer?" Rolf asked. "Is that the same one as Fat Schlammer? The one that was the lavatory attendant in the Giesingerstrasse?"

"One and the same fat arsehole," Theo said.

"If it's Fat Schlammer, he deserves to die," Rolf said. "He practically pulled my ear off, once. He's a torturer, all right."

It was agreed that Fat Schlammer and the other Secret Police men were condemned to death.

Theo wrote each of their names on his list.

"Next," he announced with a certain expeditious briskness, "next comes the public prosecutor, Dr. Leupold." The tapping pencil stayed momentarily poised in mid-air, directed accusingly. The eyes above the half-lenses had a relentless glaze. Tiny white flecks surged up in the grey like the white tops of waves about to descend.

"Why him?" Theo rhetorically asked. "Because he with his name and position gives legitimacy to all the crimes done by the others. He's a real old arsehole, what's more, and the Leupolds, which includes his brother, the sodding Cardinal, have run this city for centuries, exploiting the people and puffing themselves up in self-importance. If, when all this is over, we're going to start new, we've got to get rid of the deadwood, which means all the old arseholes like the Leupolds who've been grinding the workers in the dirt since the Romans."

This was a bit obscure to them, but Theo was probably right, he was the Brains, and so they condemned the public prosecutor to death as well, to get it over with. They were beginning to get bored with condemning people to death. It was getting repetitious now.

"I say we put Gast on the list," Kurt said.

Up till now they'd been condemning people in absentia, and the chances of being able to carry out the sentences were somewhat remote. When were any of them going to get near the Gestapo chief, or the public prosecutor? But Gast was someone they were dealing with, they knew him personally. Kurt had seen him and arranged the arms transaction. Franzi was meeting him again in just a couple of days' time. This wasn't in the same category as the other condemnations. This was real.

"State the case against Gast," Theo demanded formally.

"He's a real pig," Rolf said.

"We can't execute him just because he's a pig," Theo drily observed.

It fell to Kurt, having proposed the name, to justify Gast's being put on the list.

"He's a petty little tyrant. He's exploited people for his own corrupt ends. He's milked them dry. He's used his position to line his pockets. He'd sell his grandmother."

Theo pondered. "All that's true. On the other hand, we're dealing with him. He's supplying us with arms, isn't he? We need him."

"If he's guilty, he should be sentenced like the rest," Benno said uncompromisingly.

Theo said: "If he's helping us, if he's now on the side of the people, that'd be in his defence, wouldn't it?"

"He's a rat leaving a sinking ship," Kurt said.

"But a useful rat," Theo replied. "Sometimes you've got to deal with rats, when you've got no choice. Like the Soviet Union had to deal with Hitler to gain time. We know Gast's a crook and a bastard, but what's he actually *done* to deserve the death penalty?"

"You want evidence?" Kurt asked.

"That's what we *should* have," Theo said, *"ideally."*

272

"The Committee's been amassing evidence against war criminals," Kurt said. "I've seen what they've got on Gast, and it's overwhelming."

"What sort of things?" Theo pressed.

"About his crooked activities, the way he exploited people, bled them white, and then betrayed them to the Gestapo."

"You have some cases you can cite?" Theo asked.

"There's the case of the Hirsches." He looked around. "The button dealer with the five daughters." They nodded. "We saw them being taken away. We were all there that day. We saw that Gast did nothing, didn't lift a finger. In return for so-called 'protection,' Gast had taken over Hirsch's flat and Hirsch's woman. His business. And then he betrayed him! There's documentary evidence. The Hirsches were put on a transport along with lots of other Jews from Cologne and sent to the Lodz ghetto in Poland. At first they were put to work in a garment workshop, producing articles of clothing for the armed forces. This is all documented. There are eye-witness accounts. . . ."

"Go on, Kurt," Theo urged, since Kurt appeared to be holding something back. "You have to tell us everything."

"The Hirsches were among those taken to the Kazimierz Forest," Kurt said, and stopped, and took a deep breath. "There were three thousand designated for resettlement. Men, women, and children. Transportation was by army lorries, with an army escort. SS police troops carried out the action. . . ." Again Kurt stopped, like a heavily burdened man who must stop every so often to draw enough breath and strength to go on. "In the forest they were all made to strip naked and to dig pits. When the pits were deep enough, the executions started with those who were digging. They died in the graves they had dug for themselves. There was one ancient Maxim machine gun, which jammed early on, and otherwise carbines. The executioners were drunk—they had all been given plenty of schnapps—and their aim was erratic. Many of those buried in the pits were not yet dead.

Their bodies twitched and stirred under the earth. Children, pregnant women. . . ." He stopped, breathing hard for several seconds before he could continue. "In the end, it looked as though there wasn't going to be enough ammunition, the aim of the drunken executioners had been so wild. The officer in charge told his men to finish off the job with bayonets. Some didn't have bayonets, and used knives instead. Rusty, blunt knives they had used for cutting firewood. They did not cut well. . . ." Again Kurt stopped, this time for an even longer period than before. His jaw trembled when he spoke next, producing the effect of a faint stutter. "According to the eyewitness account . . . the two youngest Hirsch girls, Ruth and . . . The two youngest . . . screamed the whole time their throats were being cut, and the men being drunk and unsteady it was long. . . . Hirsch fell on his knees before the SS officer and begged for his other daughters and himself the 'golden death' of shooting, but the officer refused, saying there could be no special privileges. There was not enough ammunition to go round—and so the other daughters and finally Hirsch . . ." Kurt came to a stop, unable to finish. He was trembling and shaking, the breath fluttering in his chest.

For a time nobody said anything and then finally Theo spoke:

"Your case is that Gast was responsible for this atrocity, even if he didn't do it with his own hands? Because he stood by and saw the Hirsches being taken away and didn't act to prevent it?"

"Yes."

They all weighed up the evidence, and Theo was first to pronounce his verdict.

"In my opinion, he was responsible. I say he deserves to die. I say put him on the list. Benno?"

"He's the Beast—he should be killed."

"Rolf?"

"He should die."

274

"Otto?"

"I'm in favour."

"Of what?" Theo meticulously insisted.

"Of him being . . . done in," Otto said. "He's got it due to him, no question. What's more," he added with a cunning expression, "we can take over his 'connections'—no need to let them go to waste. Is there?" He looked around at their blank faces. "Now I ask you: what's the point of letting it all go to waste? The rackets he built up. They must be worth a fortune. If we rub him out, *somebody's* going to take them over. Why shouldn't it be us? We'll all get pissing rich."

Kurt said, "We're condemning Gast *for* his crimes, not to take them over."

"The Robber doesn't mean it," Rolf said. "It's because he's a robber. Breaks his heart to miss a trick."

"In my opinion," Theo said, "we shouldn't totally reject Otto's plan. In a robber society you've sometimes got to use robber means. As means to an end, see? Anyways, his *reason* doesn't matter. He's voted *for*. That leaves Kurt and Franzi. Kurt?"

"Need you ask?"

"It's a formal vote, Kurt."

"I vote he dies," Kurt said.

"And you, Franzi?"

They all looked at her, and as she remained silent Rolf said quickly, coming to her help: "You can't ask Franzi. She's a girl and—"

"Everybody's got to vote," Theo said.

They waited for her to give her verdict, and finally she said: "Put him on your list. If that's what you all want."

Seeing that what they wanted most of all was dynamite—dynamite to blow up the EL-DE-Haus—Gast gave them everything but that: he gave them a machine gun to string them along, ammo for the Stens, pistols, rifles (Mauser bolt-action rifles made by the Osterreichische Waffenfabrik of Steyr for the Luftwaffe), and small anti-personnel mines that would go off if trodden on. Finally, when Franzi threatened to cease coming, he brought some dynamite. Not a great deal, not enough to blow up the EL-DE-Haus, but enough to whet their appetite for more. He didn't give them any fuses, however. He said he was working on the fuses. Fast-burning ones of the type Kurt had specified were not easy to come by. But he had been told where he might be able to get some, and he was looking into it.

In this way he lured Franzi to come again and again to the Golden Lamb Hotel, in the hope that one of these days she would not be able to resist him. He had asked her to come away with him. Soon it would be too late to get out. Once the last bridge across the Rhine had been destroyed, there would be no way of getting to the east bank. But if she came with him now, they could escape together — he had the means and the connections to obtain transport.

They would head southwards, through Austria to Italy: that was the escape route. He had some contacts in the Vatican: he hinted, with a wink, that one or two priests were in his pocket, and through them it was possible to get to South America — start a new life.

"Believe me, Franzi, I'm a changed man. I'm leaving all this behind and starting afresh."

She could quite believe that he had that intention: he was not a man to cling to any position once it had become un-tenable.

The thick yellow-brown smoke had remained in the sky for days; it didn't disperse, and what little daylight penetrated the pall came out a sulphurous colour.

From the fourth floor of the Golden Lamb Hotel it was possible to see the ragged patches of fire all over the city. There were hundreds of them, and they were joining to-gether to make great conflagrations. Open squares were swept by burning winds. Showers of red-hot embers, big as five-mark pieces, fell as a red hail. The plane trees of the

276

Stadtgarten looked from a distance like rows upon rows of burnt-out matches. The overhead power cables of the tramways were hung with charred and tattered items of clothing; accordion files dangled down like Chinese lanterns; sheets flapped in the turbulent air; and the sedimentary ash-dust produced, when stirred up, stamp collections, family snapshots, bank statements, visiting cards, doctors' prescriptions, dog licences, love letters, registrations forms, application forms. . . . On parts of the river the oil spills were on fire, suggesting to the perfervid mind that the water itself was burning.

"Don't you want to get out of this hell and *live*?" Gast asked her.

This time—his great trickiness—he had brought fuses, but the wrong sort, it turned out: the slow-burning instead of the fast-burning. How was he to know! Was he an expert on fuses? He was quite willing to change them. But it might take a few days.

It was a way of getting Franzi to come back once more. He was trying everything.

"You're loyal, are you?" he sneered. "Loyal to your Kurt. You'll see, you'll see. In a few days, a couple of weeks, he'll be another decomposing pile under a rubber sheet. That's what he'll be. With his brains spilling out—"

"Don't talk like that."

"You love him! Hoh! Romantic twaddle. What use is he to you? Love is use and be used, mutual benefits accruing—that's the only kind of love that *works;* the rest is not worth the price of sending the sheets to the laundry."

Pacing up and down before the window, trying to think of some way of holding her (for next time he would have to bring the right fuses or it would all be over, he realized that, and if he *did* bring the right fuses it would all be over as well, and therefore he was bound to lose whichever way . . .), he suddenly saw police wagons drawing up at both ends of the street of the "fat dealers" and plainclothes police pouring out of their vehicles.

"It's a police raid," he said. "They're rounding people up. We've got to get out. Come on, Franzi!"

Grabbing their suitcases, they rushed out. The landings and stairs were packed with other dealers making their escape, but Gast, pushing and elbowing, was faster than most, and one of the first to reach the hotel lobby. Here he put down his suitcase and told Franzi to do the same so that they would have nothing incriminating in their possession, and then he ran across the little courtyard and looked up and down the street. The arrests were taking place at the top and at the bottom; in the middle, where they were, dealers were disappearing smartly into the rubble. These police raids could only catch a few. They could not round up everyone. It was not practical. It was not even politic. The authorities made examples of a handful . . . the rest got away. Still watching the street, Gast signalled to Franzi to come, and to bring the suitcases. There was no point leaving valuable *materiel* behind. A quick dash through the foundations of the bombed houses across the road and they would be out of this. The race was to the swift — oh yes — and Gast prided himself on being one of the swiftest. With Franzi in tow, he made the dash, slithering down wrecked cellar steps and then stumbling over piles of debris. A little further along, there were the remains of a wall behind which prostitutes took their short-time clients. Gast was going to be out of there quicker than button-your-flies.

He was around the wall and on his way when he felt himself grabbed and saw the cops crouched low. What a low trick! An ambush! Franzi had been grabbed too. It was so unexpected, there wasn't even time to dump their suitcases. With all that valuable *materiel*. Enough to get them both shot.

THIRTEEN

At the back of the EL-DE-Haus, they were all made to get out and pushed and prodded across a sunken yard, and along by a wall; Franzi tried not to look at this wall, which was in poor condition, with its plaster holed in many places and crumbling. It was a yard on the level of the underground garage and did not look out on anything: enclosed and pit-like.

They entered the building directly to the cellars, by a narrow iron door and then along a dim, low gangway with large central-heating pipes running along the ceiling. There was the smell of a pungent disinfectant, of latrines, and of thin cabbage soup. The smell turned Franzi's stomach, filled her with a sense of despair.

An iron grating was unlocked by a man with a bunch of very large square keys, and the prisoners were herded further along the gangway, past heavy wooden doors with long iron stays coming from their hinges and bulky external locks.

In this dim, smelly corridor they were made to stand with hands raised above their heads, palms to the wall until, one at a time, they were called around the corner.

Shooting a sideways glance to left and right, Franzi could see no further than the person next to her and received a kick in the behind for looking where she wasn't supposed to.

"Eyes front!"

She had not seen Gast coming across the yard or now in the gangway — perhaps he had been taken somewhere else. She felt lost and helpless and confused, and this confusion grew as she stood waiting for her turn to be seen by the person in charge. It seemed as if the weight of her raised arms was slowly breaking her shoulders. When, exhausted, she let fall her hands, she was kicked and had to raise them again. Her mind spun, her eyes blurred and dimmed, and she thought: it's the end, they're going to finish me off here. I'm dead and done for.

Finally she was called around the corner, and she staggered and almost fell in the course of the few steps needed to reach the jailer in his cubicle. It was a cell, the door of which had been removed and replaced by a counter flap. In the small space behind the flap stood a round-jawed, puffy-faced young man with very little hair and damp eyes.

He had called "Next" quite indifferently and now indifferently demanded, "Name?"

"Hacker. Franzi."

"Date of birth."

"February eleventh, nineteen twenty-four."

"Address."

"None. Bombed out, sir."

"Next of kin."

"None. All dead, sir!"

He wrote this information into a thick, vertically lined ledger with marbled covers, frequently dipping the metal-nib pen into a small inkwell. The pen squeaked on the smooth paper.

Her suitcase was open on the counter flap, and in the same indifferent voice he continued: "Yours? Well, you had it in your hand when arrested. So you can't deny possession."

Franzi said nothing.

It was apparent that interrogation was not his forte: he was a clerk, recording facts, that was all.

He read out loud as he wrote in the ledger:

"Two stick-type hand grenades. German manufacture. Unassembled parts of Sten Mark Two (S) submachine gun. With integral silencer. British manufacture. Ammunition. Nine thirty-two – round boxes. Two Walther automatic pistols with twelve eight-round detachable box magazines. Woman's blouse, pink. Cloth skirt, blue . . . Dynamite. Fuses."

A uniformed guard stood next to her, a big, coarse-faced fellow in SS black, with dirty boots.

"Empty pockets," said the puffy-faced jailer. "Put everything on top."

She emptied her pockets as instructed, laying on the counter flap her cigarettes and matches, a few coins, three aspirins wrapped in a scrap of paper, hairclips.

"And the ring?" the jailer said, as if she was trying to get away with something. "You're married?"

She nodded, shook her head contradicting the nod, then stood staring down in confusion.

"Don't you know if you're married?"

She couldn't get the ring off, it was too tight. But the guard with the coarse face succeeded, scraping away some of her skin with it, and making her cry out. The pain of having the ring torn from her finger with such brute force and the accumulated fear and tension of the past hours caused her to burst into tears.

The counter flap was lifted and she was brusquely told, "Inside."

She couldn't imagine where they wanted her to go, there was hardly room for one person in there, but now she saw that at the back there was a small door open, and inside, shelves crammed with articles to which luggage labels were tied, and bundles and one or two shabby suitcases on the floor. They wanted her to go into this tiny room. The guard who had ripped the ring from her finger pushed her forward and she stumbled through the space behind the counter and into the "luggage room."

The man who had made the entries in the ledger fixed his damp eyes on her, trying to contain their dampness.

"Face the wall," he told her. He seemed to be out of breath all of a sudden.

The other one, the brute, said, "Hands against the wall."

"Undress," the first, breathless one instructed.

She did not obey instantly and the brutal one brought his knee up into her back, and so she pulled her dress over her head and dropped it onto the floor, which was filthy and littered with cigarette stubs.

"And the rest — everything. Everything," the jailer said.

High up on the wall, there was a narrow slit window, just above ground level, covered with wire mesh. It let in a limited amount of grey daylight which fell on her thin white naked body suffused by an eruption of goose-pimples. It was cold in the underground room — the two men were in over-coats.

"Please," she said, between sobs, "oh, please . . . oh, please don't . . ."

"Hands against wall, legs apart," the one who had written in the book ordered.

She moved her legs apart as she had been told to do.

"Further," the other one said.

Since she was not spreading herself as widely as required, the guard kicked her ankles further apart, and her bare feet slid over cold, smooth stone until she was stretched as taut as the guy ropes of a tent.

Damp fingers that must have belonged to the one with the

282

damp welling-over eyes spread her from behind: she felt she was being split open, and then the thick fingers penetrated her. The fingers crawled about in her like worms — she felt she was being eaten by worms — and then these worms wriggled together into a fist that punched.

She was sobbing and begging them. "Oh, please don't, oh, don't, oh, please!" She heard their strong exhalations. Then she couldn't hold it back and was being sick against the wall.

Abruptly, it ended, the worms crawled out of her and she was told to get dressed.

The jailer went back behind his counter, to his ledger, the guard to his position on the other side of the flap. She could hear the painstakingly slow *squeak-squeak* of the steel-nib pen.

"Body search negative," the jailer read out slowly as he wrote. He examined a cells chart, took a large key from a key board on the wall, and told the guard, "Number two."

She was taken back along the gangway, past the others with their faces to the wall waiting to be booked. The door of cell two was unlocked, opened just wide enough, and she was forcefully shoved in, squashing those already inside even more tightly together.

It was a windowless, fetid black hole she had been thrown into, and at first she could see nothing. Gradually, the smelly, clammy organism around her adapted itself to her presence, digesting her bit by bit, passing her through its maw, moving her along.

A woman's voice next to her said, "Try to be calm, my dear. Try to be calm."

"I don't feel well," Franzi sobbed. "I feel faint. . . ."

"Don't faint," the same woman advised. "There's no room. There isn't any room to *faint*. Or for anything else. . . ." She gave a little laugh and moved her position slightly, and Franzi became aware of a bosom having been offered to her for resting on. She put her head there gratefully, trying to still her wild gasping for air.

"Oh, God," she cried, "oh, God, I feel so bad, I feel so bad. Oh, I have to lie down, I have to . . . I . . ."

The woman patted her head. "Wouldn't we all like to lie down."

"Where do we sleep?"

"As best we can, standing up."

"How long? How long do they keep you here?"

"I've been here four days, I *think*. But some of the others have been here for a long time. Weeks . . . longer."

"Here, like this?"

"Yes, my dear."

"It's better to be dead."

"I know, I know." She gave a long sigh. "I felt just the same. At first. But I talked myself out of it. While there's life, there's hope, Dora, I told myself. Frau Holbrecht, I told myself, you've got to keep your chin up. You want to drown? You can talk yourself out of anything, I've discovered that. It's really true. Don't let it get you down, my dear. You're young. I can tell. You're a young girl still. You've got your whole life in front of you."

"Don't talk like that, makes it worse," Franzi said bitterly.

"Talk yourself out of it," her new friend Dora advised.

"Shut up! Shut up, you stupid old bag!" Franzi screamed, her nerves snapping.

"Never mind, my dear. Never mind."

The others in the cell took no notice of them. Most of them didn't seem to speak German. Franzi heard them blabber to each other in strange Eastern European languages.

She laid her head on the woman's bosom and sobbed.

"Shhhhh! Shhhhh!"

"I'm so . . . so exhausted," Franzi gasped. "There's no air in here. I can't breathe. How can I stand up all night long and the next night when I'm dropping now, I've no strength. . . ."

"I know, I know," Dora said soothingly. "I know what it feels like. You think you can't stay on your feet another

284

minute. . . . But I'll tell you: when I was your age I was on my feet all night long. Night after night. At balls! *Bals masqué*. Costume balls. Carnival balls. That was in Vienna. I was born in Vienna. I came to Cologne when I married my late husband, God rest his soul. In my youth all the trades and professions used to have their own annual ball. You could go from one to the other and never sleep. . . . Ah — that was a beautiful time, I can tell you. The turn of the century, a new age. It's forty years since I've been to a ball, but I say to myself: think you're at a ball, Dora. *Think* the music in your head. Think all the young men are after you. Those wicked young men, and not-so-young men.''

''You're mad,'' Franzi said, aghast, pulling away from the comforting bosom.

''Only a little,'' Dora said.

Gast, though arrested together with Franzi, had been put in another police wagon, because the first one was full, and hadn't arrived at the EL-DE-Haus until she was already in her cell. Like her and all the others, he had been made to wait in the corridor, hands on the wall, even though he protested strongly and told them he had connections in high places.

''Course you have,'' they agreed, winking. Some claimed they were personal friends of the Gauleiter, or of some other fat arsehole. What had they got to lose making wild claims?

Once you'd fallen as low as the EL-DE-Haus cellars, your high connections didn't cut a lot of ice.

So Gast had to wait with hands up against the wall, until he was brought before the jailer with the damp eyes.

''You know who I am?'' he told him. ''I'm Ortsgruppenleiter Gast.''

''You're booked for black marketeering,'' the jailer told him, unimpressed. ''For selling arms.''

''Get a message to Kriminalassistent Nold on the third floor,'' Gast said, ''and you won't regret it. I promise.''

''Nold?'' The jailer had heard about Nold being on the take. Girls were what he took, mostly, lucky sod. He envied the policeman's mobility, his exposure to men of means in a position to express their appreciation.

"I'll tell Nold when I see him," he promised, vaguely. If the little blonde they'd body-searched was anything to go by, this Gast might have access to some not-bad stuff.

"Number seven," he told the guard, and Gast was led away.

In the night there was an air raid. Franzi assumed it was night, though there was no way of being sure of this in the windowless cell. It just had a feeling of being night.

She was lying against the bosom of her friend Dora, sleeping fitfully. And dreaming. The dream enveloped her in its own world, and was completely convincing while it lasted, and then she was awoken by a long drawn out *wish-wooooosh* rising to a high, whistling scream that pierced the eardrums. Even in her dazed state, half in the dream still, she knew what it was at once: probably a five-hundred-pounder. A big one, anyway. The higher the whistle, the closer the bomb was coming down. This was high. *I don't want to die,* she said. *Please, God. Please.*

She tried to get to the cell door but was stuck in the stinking human bog and couldn't move. They were all trying to get out. Those by the door were banging on it with all their might. There was the same noise coming from the other cells. It was general panic. Why weren't they being let out? They were going to be buried alive.

The explosion seemed to be right inside her head. Instinctively, she and others pressed on their skulls to hold them together, prevent them bursting open. Their brains felt as though they were going to be spilled out. Women screamed. Women fainted standing up. Franzi thought she must have been one of them.

The banging on the cell doors had become a terrible tumult; everybody was crying to be let out as more bombs fell.

"Why don't they let us out? Why don't they let us out?" Franzi screamed. The darkness made the panic worse. Perhaps they were already buried alive, with the entire EL-DE-Haus on top of them.

"It's no use banging," the woman Dora said to Franzi. "There's nobody there."

"The guards—"

"They're not there. They go to the bunker in the Elisenstrasse when there's a raid. There's nobody. Nobody in the whole building, except us."

At 5:45 A.M. the cell was opened by two guards carrying storm lanterns that shone a yellow light on those packed inside like pressed meat in a can.

One of the men had a list.

"The following outside," he announced.

There was weeping as the names were read out, and hasty, desperate leave-taking. Women who knew each other only from this dark cell embraced for the last time, like sisters, like mothers and daughters.

Franzi was biting into her chin, listening for her own name.

"Holbrecht, D," the guard read out, coming to the end of his list and folding it away.

"That's me, my dear," the woman Dora said. "They've called me."

"No, can't be," Franzi protested. "Must be a mistake. Don't go. Refuse to go—"

"If you don't go of your own free will, they drag you out and beat you," Dora explained. "Don't worry about me, dear. I've had a good life. I've had enough. Mustn't be greedy. I'm in my sixties. It's worse for those who're young, like some of the others. Who haven't had anything. I'm only giving up a few years, not that much. . . ."

"God bless you, Dora!" Franzi called after her, brokenly.

The older woman looked back and gave a little sigh.

"And you, my dear. And you. . . ."

When the guards came to Gast's cell and read out their list, his name was on it.

"There's been a mistake," he protested at once. "You're making a big mistake."

In the corridor he was separated from the others.

"He's got to go up to the third floor," the jailer said. In an undertone he added, "Now don't you go forgetting. I talked to Nold for you. You got me to thank."

"I'll see to it you're thanked," Gast promised.

Fat Schlammer sat in his buttoned coat in the overheated room, by a glassless window. Though still enormous, he was not as fat as before. He had been shedding kilos and his shiny grey suit hung loosely on his diminishing frame. His face was as grey as his suit, his nose a maze of broken capillaries, and a breeze of alcohol fumes came from his breath.

He was gloating at the sight of the great Gast brought before him in such dire circumstances. Caught red-handed in a nest of black marketeers, with the girl — proof of their crime in their hands: one suitcase full of butter, the other packed with arms.

Schlammer had his former mentor now, had him in the palm of his hand; it was a great joy to him to be able to revenge himself on somebody who had once helped him. To pay him back with interest!

"What is this?" Gast snarled. "Why didn't you tell them who I am? I've been kept a whole night in one of your filthy, stinking cells — somebody'll pay for this."

Schlammer's big head rocked on his body. He exchanged a smug secret look with his underling Nold, standing by the door.

Gast followed the look.

"I warn you, I hold you responsible," he exploded in his best bullying manner. He had been browbeating people too long to be intimidated by this fat slug, this former lavatory attendant, for whom he had obtained the position of *Block-leiter* and thus set him upon the first rung of the ladder into the Secret Police department.

Schlammer, since those days, had also learned how to browbeat; indeed, how to beat into a pulp, with fists, bars of iron, or lengths of roof timber, anyone who ran foul of him. From the safety of his power bastion on the third floor of the EL-DE-Haus he could afford to disregard Gast's threats. Gast undoubtedly had connections, and at local Party head-quarters in Ehrenfeld he had a couple of dozen Storm Troopers under his command, more men than Schlammer, but here, for all his power, he was subject to the law. Even Gauleiters had been undone for their crookeries. It would be a pleasure to undo Gast: to have his head.

"D'you mean to say," he demanded, "that you deny the charges against you?"

"Deny! Deny!" Gast stormed. "Am I—*Herr Gast*—required to defend myself? *I*? Schlammer, if you go on with this game I will take it very bad, very bad."

Schlammer was enjoying himself greatly.

"You've been selling arms," he observed. "Selling arms to terror bands. That's grave. The girl is part of a gang of robbers and traitors. They rob stores and steal butter. Which they sell to you for arms." He shook his head. "You sell the butter for six hundred marks a kilo on the black market. Which is more'n I earn in a month."

"Is that my fault, that you're so badly paid?"

"Your little whore," Schlammer cut him short, "is an Edel-weiss Pirate. They're in with Communists and saboteurs. And you have dealings with such people! This isn't the kind of thing can be smoothed over with a little of the usual. Many people are put up against a wall for a lot less."

"You threatening me, you fat arsehole?"

"Watch your language, Gast," Schlammer said, hoisting himself out of his chair and standing on his dignity. "I've got to uphold the law, and the law says—"

"You bag of shit! You intend to get me, do you?"

Schlammer smirked with deep satisfaction.

"You've been growing a bit too big for your boots, 'Herr'

289

Gast. It's time you were took down a peg or two. A bullet through the head'd take you down a nice few pegs."

"Don't imagine you get me so easy. I've got connections."

"The telephone lines are all down," Schlammer complained. "The teletype system hasn't worked for days. I don't even have dispatch riders to send out for instructions. So — have to decide myself. It falls to me, that heavy burden." He guffawed. "By the time your connections start pulling strings, you'll be under the earth."

"And you with me, Schlammer."

"Me? You make me laugh."

"Don't laugh too soon, Schlammer. Don't laugh too soon. You think you're safe? I'll let you into a little secret. Nold here, keeping so quiet, he's a quiet man, but he's got ears and eyes — Nold knows everything about you, because I made it my business he should. And Nold, let me tell you, is *my* man. Not yours. Because *I* pay him, and pay him more'n he's paid here. You said so yourself. Six hundred marks a month! What's that? All right? Understood? You put me up against a wall, and Nold goes up one flight of stairs and swears out a complaint against you for fraudulence in office, for receiving bribes. Including bribes from me, delivered by him. Proof, you see. *Proof!*"

Schlammer's face had gone red with indignation.

"I never had a pfennig from you."

"What about those farm chickens, what about the eggs, the sugar? What about the bottles of schnapps? You think such presents come from Santa Claus? Putting up against a wall the man you've been getting these illicit items from, that looks like saving your skin by means of murder. And that kind of murder they're not so keen on up on the fourth floor."

Schlammer slumped into his chair. He stared at Nold. Gast, unstoppable, continued: "Of course, Nold — if you ask him — won't say it to your face, will he? But you think you can

290

trust him? Nold? Who has been bought and sold more times than you've had hot dinners."

Nold said nothing. It was difficult for him to make up his mind whom he despised more, Gast or Schlammer. Gast paid better. And put girls his way. Nold knew where his interests lay, and he knew when silence was the best policy.

"Look at him," Gast said. "You think he's going to miss the chance to lay evidence against his superior? The man appointed over *his* head. Who's going to miss a chance like that? To bring down Fat Schlammer."

Schlammer thought this over. He was not a quick thinker: his brain turned ponderously. Reasoning wasn't his forte; he acted out of his guts, and his guts were uncomfortable now.

Scratching his unshaven jowl, he gave a thin apologetic laugh.

"Naturally, I was just joking before. It was a little joke of mine, Herr Gast. To see how you'd take it."

"You see how I take it."

"Can't you take a joke?"

"That depends."

"You're free to go," Schlammer told him flatly. "Somebody's made a mistake. You should never have been arrested on such flimsy evidence."

"Well, that's more like it," Gast said. "What about the girl?"

"Ah — the girl." Schlammer snorted phlegm through his nose into his throat and spat out of the paneless window. "That's a different matter. *Somebody's* got to be the owner of the suitcase full of arms. Somebody's got to pay."

"Pick somebody else."

"Impossible. What is she to you?"

"Never mind. Find another owner for the suitcase. Your cells are full. Anyone'll do."

"The girl's part of a terror gang. We're working to stamp

291

out these gangs. She'll have to pay for her crimes." He added slyly: "*She* doesn't have connections."

"She has me," Gast pointed out. "I'm her connection. I want her released with me."

"There you go too far, you ask the impossible. You're asking me to let go an enemy of the people." His voice became shocked. "In her suitcase we found dynamite, fuses, hand grenades, Sten gun parts. . . ."

"It's a mistake," Gast patiently explained. "Those suitcases all look alike. Hers only had personal items — clothing, et cetera. I vouch for that. She's my fiancée, Schlammer. We're engaged to be married. Would the wife of Herr Gast traffic in arms? Be reasonable. Is that possible? Is that logical? Take my word for it."

Schlammer sat silent, cogitating with his gut. His uncomfortable gut.

"Remember," Gast told him, "the time is going to come soon, very soon, when you'll need somebody with the right connections." He lowered his voice for the first time in the course of their present conversation. "I have connections in the Vatican. That's the only reliable escape route, for people in our position. Use your head, Schlammer. I'm the best bet you have. The Americans will be here in a couple of months at the outside. They'll hang you, if you're not careful. Your only chance is keeping in with me, because nobody else has the kind of connections I have." His voice dropped to a whisper. "I have connections with the Americans. On Eisenhower's staff."

Schlammer turned to Nold. He spoke out of his paining belly. "See the girl is released," he instructed brusquely.

The cell door was opened and the guard called in, "Hacker, F." Franzi hung back, trying to hide herself, and they had to come and drag her out.

Only when she was brought to the jailer's booth and given a brown paper bag containing her personal belongings, including the gold wedding ring they had torn from her finger, did it occur to her that perhaps she was not going to be shot.

She was taken back along the corridor and then up steep stone steps and through a door into the entrance hall of the EL-DE-Haus, where they left her. Did this mean that she could leave, that nobody would stop her? She kept looking around uncertainly, thinking it was some trick. They were not beyond giving you hope for the pure pleasure of dashing it. She had heard that they played such games with people in the EL-DE-Haus. But — for the moment — she was not being stopped. She could leave. Hesitantly she made her way out and started down the street. Oh, but it was certainly a trick.

"Franzi! Franzi!"

She stopped, fearing the worst, and was trembling and shaking when Gast caught up with her.

He said, "It's all right, it's all right. They've let us go."

She stared at him with dazed eyes.

"I got us out. I — persuaded them to let us go. We're free. All the same — no point to tempt fate. Let's not hang about."

As they left the Appellhofplatz behind, she saw the newly charred and smouldering buildings and the pillars of smoke interweaving in the sky.

Here and there they passed a pollarded tree burnt down to a stump, with a few blackened branches sticking out against rolling plains of rubble. She could see many new fires raging in different parts of the city. The air was thick, and acrid with smoke, and it was difficult to breathe.

She did not know where Gast was taking her and kept falling behind, striken by paralysing exhaustion. He was urging her on, and she shuffled after him, panting loudly through a half-closed throat. He frowned. Was she sick? Had they abused her physically?

They had to walk — there was no transport. The tramlines lay in tangles and the overhead conductor cables trailed to the ground. A tram carriage, spirited from the road to the pavement, was on its side against a wall.

The streets were deserted, except for one or two people struggling with suitcases, bundles, and — the lucky ones — handcarts. A wagon drawn by a pair of dray horses came clattering by and Gast called out, asking if they could have a lift, but thought better of the request seeing the stiff forms in the back loosely covered by tarpaulin.

Franzi felt her daze deepen with increasing exhaustion and all that dust. The dust was in her eyes and in her hair, in her throat and nose and in her lungs. She swallowed and ate dust and it lay heavily in her stomach, lined her intestines. Her whole body was filled with dust and smoke.

They walked through a landscape of ruins. She had no idea where they were going, but he seemed to know and she left it all to him. Several times she fell from exhaustion and lay weeping on the ground and didn't want to go on, but he made her.

They must have walked for almost two hours, and then she saw that they were in a familiar street — what was left of it. There was the façade of swirling-haired maidens. It was the block of flats in which she had lived with Gast years ago. The building was very badly damaged, some floors were completely open to the street, and the interiors — what was left of a kitchen, a dining room, a bathroom — exposed to view. The stonework was blackened by fire, the windows dark blanks. Behind a screen of barbed wire, a sign said: UNSAFE BOMB-DAMAGED STRUCTURE — KEEP OUT! BY ORDER.

Gast led her through a breach in the wire and made her climb after him into the littered hall with the smashed chandelier scattered all around the black-and-white checkerboard marble floor. The crashed lift was a pile of wreckage at basement level with tons of iron and rubble on top of it. Many of the balusters in the marble balustrades of the stairs and landings had been knocked out, like so many teeth, but the staircase itself appeared solid enough and Gast proceeded to climb it, urging Franzi to follow him.

"It's somewhere to go. We have to go somewhere," he said.

His flat on the second floor was locked up with a heavy cast-iron padlock. He had the key to it (his bunch of keys having been returned to him) and was able to get in.

She looked around. Fire had swept through the apartment in a random fashion, here reducing the sofa to its metal frame and springs, there leaving the cocktail cabinet of mirror glass shattered but standing, with its bottles seemingly undamaged. In their heavy gilt frame the recumbent odalisques in the Turkish seraglio were just badly streaked with burn marks. But the daring Can-Can dancers were burnt to a frazzle. Curtains, carpets, rugs, table coverings, cushions were charred tatters. In the bedroom the external wall was down almost to floor level, the ceiling had fallen, and a twisted steel beam hung over the rubble-piled bed. The passage was less damaged, and just wide enough for someone to lie down in. Gast got bedding from a hall cupboard and spread it out for Franzi on the floor. He told her he had to go out to see to one or two things, and that while he was gone she should try to rest and get her strength back.

She lay down obediently, with no mind of her own to think about anything, and fell into a sleep of total exhaustion; she didn't wake up until Gast returned, bringing candles and matches and food. They ate in the narrow passage. When they'd finished eating he showed her, immediately below, in the courtyard, a high, square vehicle, with red crosses on its doors: an ambulance car.

"I got it for us! Petrol as well! And papers for us both."

"I've got to get back," she said.

"Get back," he scoffed. "Where? To what? Everything's finished now, Franzi."

"I have to get back," she insisted.

"How?" he threw at her. "How will you? *Walk?* You want to walk? You can hardly stand on your feet. You're in no state. Don't be a little fool, Franzi. Your friends, they're finished and done for. As good as dead, believe me. They'll all be rounded up and shot. D'you know how close you came to being shot? Both of us. It was near, but I got us out."

She kept shaking her head and repeating, "I've got to go, I've got to leave. They'll be looking for me. . . ."

He put a hand on her arm. "You know why I saved you, Franzi? You know? I didn't have to. I could have just saved my own skin. But I saved you as well. Because I always loved you, Franzi. I want to marry you."

It was a stroke of inspiration: yes, marry her! Not just carry her off with him as he had at first planned, but actually marry her. A properly documented marriage. It would complete the picture. A man who had saved Jews, protected them against the Nazi laws by putting their businesses in his name, *and* paid them a salary! A man who had done his utmost to prevent them being deported, and had succeeded in several cases in delaying such deportations for months. A man who had supplied arms to Edelweiss Pirates, and was married to a freedom fighter.

Moreover, he had to admit that it wouldn't be any hardship to be married to hot-blooded little Franzi.

And it was true. He loved her. He was becoming convinced of it.

"We'll have money," he promised her. "Herr Gast is no fool."

"I love Kurt," she said staring out, mesmerized by fire.

"What about me?"

She said nothing.

"And *me?*" he persisted.

She shrugged.

"You weren't so indifferent to me, once."

"I didn't know my own mind then. I was only fifteen . . ."

"You think you know your own mind now?" He nodded his head up and down, bitterly, at the sheer ingratitude of women. After all he had done for her — after he'd saved her life! "Beggars can't be choosers," he told her to her face. He was not a man to mince words when angered. "You don't have to do me any favours, Franzi. If you want to go, go! Go!" She nodded that she was going and he was pushing her out of the door when the perilous building began to shake. He grabbed her and pulled her out, along the landing, down the marble staircase, dodging falling masonry. They had just managed to get beyond the barbed-wire screen when the entire structure gave a massive shudder and caved in.

Bombs were beginning to fall now, all around, and Gast broke into a run, dragging Franzi after him.

"Come on! There's a shelter in this road."

A bunch of kids were hanging around outside the entrance, smoking cigarettes, drinking, getting up to no good, boys and girls close together in the dangerous darkness. There were more of them on the concrete stairs going down.

Gast banged on the shelter door again and again and eventually it was opened and they were let in. They looked for somewhere to put themselves. All the seats around the walls under the ventilator shafts were taken: people fought for these places to get the first breath of air from the rusty grilles. Further in, what you got was used air, the waste of other people's lungs.

Gast and Franzi had to sit on the floor, in the middle, next to the water pails.

There was a forced jollity in the shelter, with a lot of chatter and even some snatches of singing, an accordion being played, drinking. It was as noisy as a tavern.

"Well? You thought about what I said?" Gast asked amid the hubbub.

"What?"

"We get out together, Franzi. I can save you."

"I love Kurt," she said.

Kurt — always Kurt! Gast fumed inside himself.

"Love, love," he scoffed. "What good does it do you if he's

dead? I told you, he hasn't got a chance. You stay with him and you're a dead duck too. You have any idea of the situation here?'' He spoke intently into her ear. ''Everything is falling apart. They can't even bury the dead. There are some cases of typhus already. Once it gets a hold it'll spread like wildfire. The river's practically blocked; soon nothing'll be able to move. There'll be no way across, once all the bridges are down. Our backs to the Rhine! There's hardly enough food now to keep the population alive, and things'll get worse. In addition to which, the British and Americans come back day in, day out: they're going to pound us into dust.'' He paused, examining her face to see the effect his words were having on her; her expression had remained unchanged. Nothing seemed to penetrate her dazed, apathetic state.

The bombs were falling closer and the shelter had grown quiet. People were coming to the water pails and wetting scarves or other pieces of material and tying them around their faces, over nose and mouth. Near the ventilators shallow breathing was being practised. The air coming into the shelter was not good. Some women were moaning to themselves in a regular chant-like fashion. Children were crying. There was panicky gasping.

Gast looked around, assessing the situation.

''We better get out of here,'' he said. ''We're better off outside.''

She followed him through the crush of bodies. The shelter leader didn't want to open the iron doors — to do so would let in more of the bad air — and Gast had to force him at pistol point.

The kids were tightly pressed together on the lower part of the stairs. Gast pushed through, dragging Franzi after him. With each step it became hotter. At the top, at street level, the heat scorched their faces. It seemed impossible to venture into this furnace, and Franzi drew back, and had to be forced out by Gast.

In the entrance he picked up one of the water buckets and

emptied it over her and another over himself, and then pulled her into the burning air.

The fire was coming towards them from several directions, with flames snaking along the ground, curling around whatever they encountered and igniting it instantly, and climbing through window and door frames. Gast made Franzi tear off her coat and tie it around her head, and he did the same with his. He was trying to find a way through the fire, the part where the circle was not yet closed.

They had to struggle against a powerful wind that was pulling them back; it drew everything into its centre: blazing chairs and roof timbers and tables and banisters. And they, too, were being sucked into the inferno. Gast dragged Franzi into a doorway, and at once the pull of the wind dropped and the flames swept past them. He broke down the door and they entered the building. The fire was all around outside, but for the moment they were protected by the walls. He ran from room to room, looking out of windows, and saw that the fire had not reached the courtyard yet. The courtyard led to an alley. He shoved Franzi through a rear door and they stepped out into the alley, the end of which was dark. He grabbed Franzi's hand and pulled her towards the gap in the fire. He had to drag her, with considerable force; she was so exhausted she just wanted to lie down, even if it was in the path of the fire. "Just a little bit more, a little bit," he kept urging her.

And then they were through the gap, and out, though not yet beyond the reach of the fast-spreading flames, and so it was necessary to keep going, after a brief pause for breath.

"You see, you're safe. Who do you have to thank for that? That's the second time I saved you. First from the Gestapo, then from the fire. You stay with me, Franzi, and you'll be all right, you'll see."

She did not answer, but followed tamely as he led the way back to where the ambulance car had been left. It took more than an hour and a half to cover the half-mile to the collapsed apartment building. In the courtyard they found the car battered and dented and covered in a mire of debris dust. It looked a complete wreck. Gast at once tried to start it and after five minutes of demonic hand-cranking the engine at last fired.

She got in next to him and said nothing, neither protesting nor assenting, as he drove across the Hohenzollernring and out towards the green belt. The headlamps pierced the murk to light up smouldering rubble and charred, shrunken bodies that resembled burnt logs. The familiar ash-rain was falling, thickening the mire on the ground. The air had a taint of putrefaction to it. In the Richard Wagner Strasse several bodies were stuck in the molten asphalt like flies to flypaper. He was looking for somewhere to pull up, so they could rest, and the green open spaces marking the periphery of the old city seemed safer than anywhere else just then — at least they would be clear of falling buildings or spreading fire.

"We'll rest here till it gets light," he said. "It may surprise you to hear it, but I'm also human, and I also need a rest sometimes." She said nothing to this, being too far in her daze of exhaustion to be able to reply. Doing exactly what he told her, she lay down on the stretcher bed in the rear section of the ambulance.

"I'll stay in front," he said, "and try to get forty winks. You don't have to worry, I'm a light sleeper and I'll wake up if need be."

In the morning no dawn came; the light barely changed. The smoke from the fires blotted out daylight.

Gast drove off without waking Franzi: she lay dead to the world while he negotiated the rubble of the Aachenerstrasse, pulling up a hundred metres from the main entrance to the Melaten cemetery. It had sustained heavy damage during the night, and thick columns of yellow-brown smoke were rising from its eastern and southern sections.

"Why've we stopped at the cemetery?" Franzi asked when she woke.

"You'll see," he promised. "Stay here, wait for me."

He got out of the vehicle. After a couple of steps he turned round and said to her, "Now don't go running away. Where would you go? You're in no condition to walk. Apart from which, you start wandering around by yourself, you'll get picked up by a patrol. Next time I won't be there to save you. So . . ." He spoke with rough forcefulness. "Stay where you are. Keep the doors locked."

She said nothing, being still too weary to talk, and watched him pick his way across the Aachenerstrasse to the cemetery's main gate.

In the state she was in, she had no sense of time having passed, and then Gast was returning, riding towards her on a bicycle: laden, bent low, full rucksack on his back, bundles tied to the rear saddlebag. Overloaded, he wobbled towards her. As he came nearer she saw his face. It was exultant. He leaned the bike against the ambulance, unlocked the door, and got in next to her. With a self-satisfied expression, he offered her a brown paper bag as if it were a bag of sweets to dip her fingers in.

"Go on!" he coaxed, "*go on!*"

Obediently, she put her hand in the bag and brought out a fistful of wedding rings. She stared at them in her open palm, remembering how the wedding ring had been torn from her finger.

"How'd you get these?"

"Never mind. What's it matter?"

Looking inside the gold bands, she saw that some were inscribed with names and dates.

"What's it matter," she agreed flatly.

"They were repayments of debts," he said, "if you want to know. People who couldn't pay their dues."

He took other objects from the rucksack, and unwrapped some to show her: silver candlesticks, silver Passover platters, a heavy ceremonial goblet, a jewelled powder compact, gold chains and crucifixes and Stars of David.

"That's not all," he said. "That's just some of it. Where I got this there's more."

"Where's that?"

"Gast's graves."

"Graves?"

"Yes. They're my bank vaults." He was flushed with dark pride. "That's where I keep my goods. It's all in Gast's graves." He lowered his voice. "It's a little fortune, Franzi. Believe me. A little fortune. You see how I trust you. Nobody else knows. I've told nobody. It's what I've worked for all these years."

He opened the car door to make another trip to the cemetery to gather up his loot, but drew back, seeing a funeral cortège entering by the main gate. They must be burying some Party bigshot, judging from the number of uniformed SS who followed the coffin. It was as well to wait until they were past; this was not a time to be asked questions. He spoke softly, compellingly, to Franzi while watching the procession move along the central avenue between the great mausoleums.

"Come with me, Franzi, I've worked it all out."

From one of his pockets he produced two triangles of yellow cloth and placed them inversely upon each other, making a six-pointed Star of David. "A few stitches," he said, "that's all . . . in case we should run into the Americans. Or if it's . . . the other lot . . ." From another pocket he produced a small metal badge inscribed with a hammer and sickle. He was allowing enough time for the funeral procession to have gone past his graves before returning to his business in the cemetery. "You'll come with me?" he asked.

"I'm Kurt's girl," she said flatly. "I love him."

"Always Kurt, always Kurt." Gast was furious to have his plan frustrated for such paltry, sentimental reasons. "What good is he to you, Franzi? Can he get you out? He can only get you shot. Why's he so much better than me? What can he

302

offer you? What?" A rage of jealousy passed through him. "Ah — your fine Kurt! Did you know he was in the Gestapo?"

Only as he said it and saw the effect it had on her did he fully appreciate what a masterstroke he had intuitively delivered.

"No, that's not true," she said.

"It's true. I swear it. I personally was instrumental in getting him accepted for training. They asked my assessment of him, as his street leader. I said I could thoroughly recommend him. I said he was the right type. Wanted to get on and make something of himself. Ambitious . . ."

"It's a lie," she said. "It's to trick me. You're full of tricks like always."

"No, it's no lie, Franzi. It's the truth. I can show you the letter I wrote to Dr. Isselhorst with my testimonial. I remember the exact date, because it was not long after you and I had got together and were living at the apartment. They took him on as a trainee and he worked at the EL-DE-Haus. He worked in the cellars, and he worked in the guard room and on the third floor as well."

Gast, never slow to seize an advantage when it presented itself, saw that he had managed to shake Franzi in her beliefs, in her whole outlook, and was careful not to overplay his hand. He wished to show that he was a fair and reasonable man who wasn't making himself out better than Kurt — but he was no worse either!

"Remember," he said, being fair and reasonable, "this was nineteen thirty-nine, and what did any of us know? The Gestapo was the place for an ambitious young man who wanted to rise in the world but lacked . . . qualifications. To be accepted for training was a feather in any young man's cap. How did he know? *How did I know?* Turned out he *wasn't* exactly the right material. It turned out that way and they got rid of him. You see, I'm fair, Franzi. I don't tell you these things because I've got an axe to grind. I just tell you what happened. He was called up and sent to Poland. Now I'm going to tell you some other things about your Kurt, because I don't suppose he's told you. As his street leader, I received all the papers and all the reports, so I know. He had a nervous breakdown in Poland. Went out of his head. It was after that business in the Kazimierz Forest. He tell you about that? Obviously not. It was dreadful. Appalling. You remember the Hirsches? The button dealer, with the five daughters? They were sent to Lodz, in Poland. The wife died during the journey. The rest . . . they all died in a most terrible way. They were killed in the Kazimierz Forest, and Kurt saw it all, and that was when he had the breakdown. Guilt, I suppose. Though he was not one of the ones who did it, I'm not saying that he was. It was done by an SS police troop. Bastards. Sheer, inhuman bastards. The army stood by. Made the men gather firewood in the forest, while it was happening. And what did Kurt do? What could he do? Nothing. Any more than I could! I'd done my best for the Hirsches. The day they arrested them I stood in the street arguing with the police. I bargained. I offered them bribes, money, anything. . . . Believe me, I tried everything, because I have a conscience . . . and I had promised. But what could I do? They wouldn't play. I remember now — you were there that day. I offered you a crocodile toiletry case, remember, and you refused. Because of something Kurt said. Very stupid of him. He was being a stickler for the letter of the law, and he got the cops scared. In front of all those people, talking about it being improper, not strictly correct . . . If he hadn't talked like that perhaps I could have still bargained with them and saved the Hirsches. But after what he said I had no chance. You see how it is, Franzi. You see how it is."

The funeral procession was out of sight now, and Gast judged it safe to make another trip to his graves. He considered he had said enough to Franzi. No need to say more. He was confident now. He had made the point that in these terrible times no man was entirely blameless, and, on the other hand, no man could be blamed for things that he had not known about, and not been able to do anything to remedy. Perhaps she wouldn't understand this immediately. That was where forcefulness was called for. Women often did not know their own minds, and then a man had to decide for them. *I won't give her a chance to say no. It will be a fait accompli and she can argue afterwards.* He would take her with him whether she liked it or not, and he did not think she would have the will or the strength to resist, and one day she would thank him.

Gast got out of the car and gave Franzi his gun.

"It's to protect yourself," he said, "in case anyone bothers you while I'm gone. But I won't be long. Keep the car doors locked."

When he had left on his bicycle, she tried on wedding rings — some were much too loose and fell off when she moved her hand, others were too tight and she couldn't remove them once they were on her fingers. Pulling on these rings, she fell into a torpor, staring straight ahead, her brain darkening until it was dark enough for dreams. In her dream, the Hirsches were all naked, the father and the five daughters, and all bearded. Kurt was shaving them with his bayonet and cutting their throats, one after the other. While cutting their throats he drank schnapps. He kept their bodies under the floorboards, perfectly preserved. A neat red slash across their throats, otherwise their beauty was unimpaired. She, Franzi, sat before a mirror, making up her face, painting her lips crimson. She had a crocodile toiletry box that was full of lipsticks of every colour, including black. The toiletry box belonged to one of the Hirsch girls, who was now under the floorboards. The woman Dora chattered the whole time they led her to be shot, talking herself out of it. You could talk yourself out of anything, she insisted. Even being shot. There were worse things in life. Having your throat cut with a rusty, blunt knife. Thank God for the golden death of shooting, said Dora with her capacity for looking on the bright side.

FOURTEEN

aving seen Franzi and Gast bundled roughly into a police wagon, Kurt hadn't waited around. For one thing, he was himself in considerable danger, and what could he do there? By himself, nothing. In any case, his first duty, as he saw it, was to get back to the cellar and warn the others. A new hideout would have to be found, fast. They had always agreed that if one of them was caught, the others could not count on that person keeping silent under intensive questioning.

The air was hot and cold by turn as he ran to where he had left the van. They needed it more than ever now that they'd have to find another hideout. A cold wind cut through the smoky air. He was trying to calm himself, to still the bells tolling "disaster" in his head. A way of springing Franzi would have to be found. Somehow it'd have to be done. They couldn't leave her in the hands of those sodding pigs. Even if it meant blowing up the place with her in it, better than leaving her to *them.*

Atone and revenge! It had to be. What did it matter if they all died, as long as they took some of those sods with them.

Thank God the van was still there. Battered and dented, its bodywork rust-eaten, it looked just like any one of the thousands of other wrecks abandoned in the streets. Whenever he left it anywhere, he disconnected the battery and slipped off the fuel-delivery hose, so that anyone trying to start it up would not be able to without some difficulty. Now, he quickly reconnected the battery and slipped the fuel delivery back on and tightened the metal collar; when he switched on the ignition, the motor spluttered and wheezed, as usual, and then started.

During the whole of the journey back to the cellar his mind was churning about in circles, trying to think of some way of getting Franzi out of the EL-DE-Haus.

It was as he was giving the bad news to the others — telling them how Franzi and Gast had been arrested in a roundup of black marketeers — that the idea came to him. Of course! That was the solution! That was the way to do it!

Excitedly he outlined his plan to them. "They all run shit-scared when there's a big raid. They run to their rat hole. The new *Gestapobunker* in the Elisenstrasse. That's where they go when there's a raid. They lock in the prisoners and run for it. That's when we do it. When there's nobody there. Blast our way in. We can use the dynamite, with a short, slow fuse. With nobody there, we've got time. *That's the way.* We go in through the drive and the yard, in the back way, straight into the cellars. The keys to the cells are left on a board in the jailer's cubicle. We'll get everybody out and we'll blow up the whole place."

They were all looking at him with questioning eyes. How did he know so much about the EL-DE-Haus? Had he been held there himself? And escaped? It was said nobody ever escaped from there. Had he been in the cellar — maybe even

307

in the deep cellar, which was where they tortured people? They might be torturing Franzi right now. It was so deep below ground, seven metres or more, that you could scream as much as you liked, nobody heard you.

Kurt, getting a hold on himself, said more calmly: "Next big raid we'll get Franzi out."

Now they had to think of themselves, however. If Franzi was tortured she might give away where their hideout was, and so they would have to evacuate straight away. They couldn't risk staying. The rule, for anyone who was caught, was to hold out as long as possible so as to give the others a chance to escape. But nobody could say how long "as long as possible" was.

They started straight away loading up the van with their stuff, their arms and ammo, the dynamite, their paraffin stove and latrine bucket, their cooking utensils, their remaining stock of food and water and petrol. When it was all in, Rolf and Otto went back into the cellar and bolted and barricaded the entrance door from inside — you never knew, they might want to come back there some day. If they discovered Franzi *hadn't* talked, for instance. They made it as hard as they could for squatters to get in: filled the big wardrobe behind the door with rubble and wedged a heavy roof beam between it and the opposite wall. Then they crawled from cellar to cellar by way of the breakthroughs (carefully putting the bricks back in place again after they'd gone through) and came out behind the bombed-outs' cess-pit, and from there rejoined the others.

As they set off, all were aware that it wasn't going to be easy finding another hideout. They weren't the only ones looking for a roof over their heads. There were tens of thousands of bombed-outs roaming the streets, seeking shelter.

Two hours of looking around and clambering through the rubble having brought them no nearer to finding anywhere, Kurt said they might have to sleep in the van tonight, with pairs of them taking turns to watch out for patrols.

308

With darkness, they saw the muzzle flashes of the anti-aircraft batteries against the horizon, and from the amount of flak it looked as though this could be a big raid. If it was, then they'd have their chance to spring Franzi.

There were flares being dropped around the *Dom* — they could see its sombre spires brilliantly marked out against the dark sky — and this suggested that the target area was the centre of the *Altstadt*. Which was perfect for them. The rats would be running already, scurrying off to their holes in the *Gestapobunker*.

And so Kurt kept straight on, driving towards the centre, a twisted sort of satisfaction on his face as the bombs fell closer and closer and everybody in the van flinched and shuddered at the explosions.

It was mad, they were going right into it: but it was their only chance to save Franzi.

As they were careering along the Hohenzollernring and about to turn into Friesenstrasse, which would take them to Appellhofplatz, there were bomb bursts all around and the van was sent hurtling across the wide boulevard, out of control; it hit a lamp-post, bending it sideways, and they were all thrown violently forward and hit by flying glass from the shattered windshield. The van was producing a lot of dense smoke and they scrambled out of it as fast as they could, afraid that it might at any moment burst into flames. They were all cut and bruised and badly shaken, but had suffered nothing worse, it seemed, upon first examination, as they felt bones and heads and tried movements. Their vehicle, however, had not fared as well. Its rear axle was broken, they saw, and, in any case, the impact with the lamp-post had crushed the radiator and the engine into a flat concertina of metal parts. The van was a write-off. They took out their Stens and pistols and stuffed their pockets full of sticks of dynamite, and filled rucksacks with food and water, but there was much they had to leave behind: their machine gun, their precious paraffin stove, their buckets and enamel bowls and cooking utensils, all of it hard-earned. They concealed everything as best they could under layers of debris, hoping to come back once they'd found some other form of transport. This was now their most urgent necessity. Without transport they couldn't hope to spring Franzi.

They didn't have a clue what to do next and for a while wandered in a daze through the torn-up streets, not knowing where they were going. Theo stopped their aimless meandering, saying, "What we need is a plan of action." They agreed. They were ready for any kind of desperate action, with rage and fear curdling in their bellies.

"What do we do, Theo?" Benno asked. "You tell us. You're the Brains."

"That's right. You think of something," Otto threw out. "See if you can."

Theo paused to think, and then said, "Let's make for the Gereon goods station. Sometimes there's lorries there, waiting for the freight trains to unload. We could hijack a lorry."

"Yes," they said.

It was the best idea anyone of them had had, and so they went along with it, and trudged all the way to Gereon, only to find the station on fire, and the lorries burnt-out hulks.

"Well, that was a brilliant plan," Otto said.

Rolf told him to shut up. Exhausted and dispirited, they would have collapsed onto the ground where they were, but there was danger from falling wreckage as the fire raged on, and from the fire fighters who might demand who they were and what they were doing there, so they had to move. They were not far from the *Stadtgarten*, and without thinking they wandered in that direction. In the park trees were reduced to charred trunks, and flower beds had been turned into improvised graves. Some of these were marked with crossed sticks tied together, upon which a name had been scratched, others did not even bear the name of the person buried there. The ground was soggy and they sank up to their ankles in mud and in doing so disturbed shallowly dug

310

graves, dislodging human remains. Benno found a skull, and dropped it quickly with a horrified gasp of "Let's get out of here." But as they were making their way to the sports fields and playgrounds that adjoined the park, Benno's grisly find gave him a brainwave.

"I know where we could go and hide," he said. "In the cemetery. In graves. They wouldn't think of looking for anyone there."

"I don't want to get myself buried just yet," Rolf piped up.

"Some of those great big tombs at Melaten, they're as big as houses practically. You could live in them," Benno said.

They were all silent. It was true that some of those mausoleums were substantial places.

"Be a bit gloomy in there," Rolf said, but he was coming round to the idea. "How'd we breathe?"

"They've got doors to go in," Kurt said. "We could leave the doors open a bit."

"Yes," Otto said, "yes, it'd be no trouble breaking into them, I don't suppose they've got burglar-proof locks on them."

Theo said, "I think maybe Benno's got something," and Benno beamed with gratification at such praise from his brainy brother.

In any case, nobody had a better plan, and so they set off, dragging themselves through boggy mudflats that had once been parade grounds, towards Melaten cemetery. They arrived there just as a faint luminescence in the sky indicated that it was dawn, they walked outside the high iron railings, looking in at the mausoleums where generations of city fathers lay buried.

"God! are we going to be grand," Rolf said. "We're going to be living with the Wallrafs and the von Grootes and the Leupolds. We're going to be with the nobs."

"What about that one?" Benno asked excitedly, pointing to a miniature Gothic cathedral, with towers and turrets and spires.

311

"Too much like a church," Rolf said. "Who wants to live in a church?"

"There?" Theo said, indicating a tomb with a high stone obelisk, a gated entrance, a forecourt, a massive bronze door with stone lions either side, and busts of some of its most illustrious dead in a niched gallery.

"You think we can afford the rent?" Rolf quipped.

"We requisition it on behalf of the people," Theo announced. "Bet you it's some banker's tomb. It looks like a bank."

As they were climbing over the railings, they saw a funeral procession making its way along the central avenue, and ducked down to avoid being spotted. Must be somebody important, with all those black pigs following the coffin. It was a slap-up affair, with a priest and everything, a little old man with a puff of white hair and a dirty white wide-sleeved surplice over his mud-streaked cassock. He was going along swinging a smoking censer, and chanting. And the black pigs were doing a funeral march.

In the background, somewhere, behind all the smoke and dust, a bulldozer was clanking and whirring continuously, digging a mass grave for those less-privileged individuals who did not rate private burial these days.

Kurt gestured to them to spread out and keep their heads down until this funeral was over. They didn't want to tangle with black pigs now.

He and Rolf hid together behind a gravestone; the others found places on either side.

"What kind of funeral d'you want when it's your turn?" Rolf asked Kurt in a low voice, with a grisly grin.

"I want to be cremated," Kurt said.

"Me, too," Rolf whispered wildly. "It's less mumbo-jumbo and you don't rot in the earth and you don't get eaten by worms. My mother and father were cremated. . . . Not together. Separate. My father died in prison. He had a bad cough. And my mother, she died in that place they sent her

312

to. Where they put her away. Not the home. It wasn't the place they sent her to first; it was the other place, in Berlin. It was a special place for treating incurables like her. She died the day after she got there."

"Yes," Kurt said.

Rolf looked at him. "You knew about that? Don't you think that was weird? The day after they took her there she died."

"Yes."

"You don't sound too surprised about it. She'd never had any heart trouble. I don't know she was *that* mad either — all that about a wind of fire and the angel of death." He laughed. "If I believed in God I could almost believe He told her."

"Yes," Kurt said again, flatly.

"You don't sound surprised," Rolf persisted. "About my mother dying the way she did. At that place. The day after she got to that place for incurables."

Kurt remained silent.

"You heard something about that place? You know something?" Rolf reflected. "You know a lot about the EL-DE-Haus. About where all the cells are and where they keep the keys, I thought you might know about that place in Berlin."

"Look! Over there," Theo called in an undertone.

Visibility was changing the whole time, and looking in the direction he'd indicated, they saw a high, square vehicle standing in the smoke and dust of the Aachenerstrasse.

"What is it?" Benno asked.

Kurt examined it. "Looks like a small truck, or van. Could be an ambulance."

They exchanged looks.

"Let's go and see," Kurt said.

Watchful for the return of the funeral procession, though for the moment there was no sign of it, they crept behind gravestones and monuments towards the cemetery's main gate, and then out into the street. From a distance of ten

313

metres they were able to make out the Red Cross markings on the doors of the vehicle. Battered and dented and covered in rubble grime though it was, it did not look like an abandoned wreck. It might be functioning — ambulances were among the few types of vehicles to receive a petrol allocation.

They watched out for any movements, but saw nothing. At a sign from Kurt they all got their Stens out from under their coats and made a dash, flattening themselves against the sides of the ambulance when they got to it. Kurt rapped on the window and ordered whoever was inside to come out with hands up. There was no answer. Kurt repeated the order, and when there was still no answer, pressed down on the door handle, and the door flew open. They called out not to move, levelling their guns. Nothing moved. There was nobody inside.

The bonnet of the vehicle was warm, and Kurt told the others to keep him covered while he tried to start the engine with the hand crank. He produced a series of splutterings that died away to nothing. If the driver was anywhere nearby he was bound to hear, and Kurt kept looking around tensely, peering into the shifting smoke haze. Here and there a faint glimmer of daylight thinned the murk, and it was in one such spot that Kurt suddenly saw a girl, who looked just like Franzi, sitting in the gutter next to a dead cat, and pulling agitatedly at her fingers. He dropped the crank and started towards her.

"Franzi? Franzi?" he called to her disbelievingly, as he was approaching. In some respects the girl looked like Franzi, but in other respects she didn't; in other respects she looked like an old madwoman. Then he was close enough and saw that this girl *was* Franzi, and he swept her up into his arms.

"Franzi! Franzi! You're all right. You are all right? You're not hurt?"

She said nothing, and he called the amazing news over his shoulder: "It's Franzi. She's safe. It's her."

314

They approached uncertainly, not knowing what to expect, and she stood there, saying nothing, just pulling at her fingers and staring.

"What's the matter, Franzi? Did they do something to you? Did they . . . ?" Kurt demanded. He took her hands and saw all the wedding rings and frowned. "What happened to you?"

Rolf said in a low voice, "Franzi, you all right? Did they torture you?"

She looked up. She had her dead mother's mad eyes now. Abruptly, she began to weep and sob, all the time frantically pulling at her fingers, trying to tear off the wedding rings. But some of them wouldn't come off.

"Who gave you these?" Kurt demanded harshly. "Was it Gast? Did *he* get you out? Pulled strings, did he?" He looked into her face, forcing her to meet his eyes. "Is that what happened? Is that why they let you go? Well, that was *kind* of him, saving you as well. What a kind man!" Kurt said with bitter sarcasm, shaking her. "And what's your side of the bargain? Did you agree to get out with him — did you?" He also began to pull at the rings, violently tearing them off her fingers and throwing them on the ground.

"Leave her alone!" Rolf protested. "Can't you see she's hurt bad? Can't you see? They must have done something to her, torture or something. Leave her alone!" He pulled at Kurt's arm.

"Where's Gast?" Kurt demanded, shaking Franzi.

She nodded towards the cemetery with her head.

"Dead?"

"Gone to get his fortune," Franzi said in her strange voice. She looked at Kurt with her mother's knowing eyes. "He says you were in the Gestapo. That you worked in the EL-DE-Haus. He says — you and he, you're just the same. . . ."

"We're not. We're not the same," Kurt said, very white, his head trembling as if he was about to get one of his attacks of

315

shivering and shaking that he used to have when they'd first found him.

"But you wcre in the Gestapo," Franzi said.

"I was a trainee, that's all I ever was . . . a trainee. . . . I quit when I saw —"

"When you saw, *when you saw,*" she echoed him exhaustedly. "He says the same, that he didn't know. He says he was trying to *save* the Hirsches that time and you —"

"It's a lie, that's all I can say: a lie. Gast is evil. You see how he tricks you again and again. And you believe him."

Angrily, he turned away from them and started towards the cemetery.

"Where you going, Kurt?" Rolf called after him. "Kurt! Kurt!" When Kurt didn't answer, Rolf said, "We're coming with you."

"Somebody's got to guard the vehicle," Kurt called back. "We need it."

Rolf nodded to Theo and Benno to stay and look after Franzi and the vehicle, and then he and Otto ran to catch up with Kurt.

Making their way along the central avenue between the mausoleums, they came upon a little old priest peeing into the open ground and enjoying a secret smoke. They had crept up on him unheard, and he swung around startled. They could see the clusters of senile warts around his eyes, their thready excrescences like tiny flowers in morbid bloom.

"Who are you? What d'you want here?" he snapped at them. "You have no business here."

"We're visiting our mother's grave," Rolf explained. "She's in one of those big tombs. Wallraf's her name."

"*Rotzbuben!*" the priest cried angrily. "Get out of here before I call the police."

"Funny you should say that, because we were just going, your holiness," Rolf told him, starting to run.

316

They had seen the funeral procession dispersing and black pigs coming along the central avenue, and they could hear the bulldozer churning and clanking, with, in between, the hiss and whine of the claw being lowered and raised on cables. Here and there daylight seeped through the smoke pall. They dodged around gravestones and dashed down side alleys to avoid the SS men, who, having buried their colleague, were now hurriedly leaving.

"What we doing here?" Rolf demanded. "The black pigs may see the ambulance. What do we do then?"

"They're in a hurry," Kurt said. "They'll take it for another wreck."

"Kurt, what we doing here?" Rolf persisted in asking nonetheless.

"We're looking for Gast," Kurt said.

"Why? What do we want with Gast?"

"Didn't you hear what Franzi said, about his fortune?" Otto said.

"That's right," Kurt said. "His fortune."

They stayed out of sight until everyone from the funeral procession had passed, and then they started looking around for Gast. Presently, as they searched for him, an ash-rain began to fall, with engorged black clouds bursting open. In seconds they were drenched and their faces smudged and streaked. Running back to the ambulance, they heard somewhere behind them a regular *slush-slush* sound, and Kurt ran less hard, and finally came to halt and stood listening. *Slush-slush-slush!* It sounded like a bicycle tyre in the wet. *Slush-slush-slush!* Louder. Kurt was wearing his coat draped over his shoulders, the empty sleeves swinging loose, and Rolf, stopping and turning around, saw him shrug off the coat and take something out of his pocket.

Slush-slush-slush! Kurt began to walk slowly towards this sound. He thought of the Rhine maidens in white blouses with their golden hair bound in Gretchen coronets, those betraying Loreleis who sucked a man under. Oh, he knew! He knew! They were all the same. He had splashed their white blouses with mud, with disgust. When you knew the truth it was all disgusting. Life was disgusting. He trusted only Saint Sophie, his holy ghost. Atone and revenge! She was right. It had to be. Or they could not raise their heads again. In his heart he had declared *Nazijagd*. The hunt of the wild boar. With its jagged mane and ferocious — omnivorous — appetite it tore up the earth, destroying everything in its path, all the cultivated lands, snorting through the undergrowth with its greedy snout and its murderous tusks. Sniffing around, it smelled out the delectable black earth-fruits. Tear and lick, tear and lick — a slimy business, life. The wild boar had to be exterminated. It was a menace to the cultivated fields. It tore up the vines. So — had to be destroyed. Kill the Beast! Kill the Beast! It was the only way.

Laden down with loot and pedalling hard, Gast could hardly see anything in this filthy downpour. The ash was getting into his hair and eyes. A big mausoleum loomed up, with an obelisk and marble angels in clusters on the cata-falque. That was where he had to turn right and he'd be in the main avenue. And then, a patch of smoke haze lifting ahead, he saw the giant bulldozer, its steel jaws descending with a whine of cables and a clatter of metal parts as it chewed into the earth deeply. The cables hauled up the greedy, full mouth, a lever opened it, and the soggy soil spilled out. His eye drawn to this vision, Gast had not seen the figure stand-ing in front of him, arms extended, grasping a pistol —

Kurt Springer.

Swerving and braking, and seeing the extended arms move with him, the thought flashed through his mind: what for? For a woman. A piece of cunt! And seeing that he could not avoid the arsehole Springer, he tried to make a conciliatory sign to him, as if to say: can't we talk about this? It's only about a woman.

318

It really wasn't worth it for a woman!

One step away, Kurt aimed for the white of the throat, and fired, and saw the neck open and blood gush thickly.

Stricken Gast, on the bicycle, did not fall immediately: the onward momentum carried him past Kurt, after which the bike began to wobble wildly, the wobbles becoming wider and wider, and then machine and rider fell together, and Gast lay completely still by the spinning rear wheel, spouting blood from the neck like a stuck pig.

Rolf and Otto hearing the shot had turned round and begun to run towards the form on the ground. When Rolf saw who it was, he glared up at Kurt.

"What you want to do that for? That was stupid. You didn't have to do it. Franzi's loyal to you, I'll bet you anything. She loves you."

Kurt was shaking his head as if he didn't hear, and walking right past them.

Otto looked around. There was no sign of anybody coming. The clanking and whining of the bulldozer must have drowned the noise of the shot.

"Quick!" Otto said, already on his knees by the dead man. "Let's get his wallet and stuff!" He knelt in the growing puddle of blood, going through Gast's pockets and stuffing the contents into his own.

"Leave it!" Rolf shouted, starting to move away.

"Don't be stupid!" Otto hissed back. "You heard, he's got a fortune. Help me!"

Gast was lying on his back, his full weight on the rucksack, and Otto was having difficulty getting it out from under him.

Rolf was waiting for Otto, who was now cutting through the shoulder straps.

"Cut them your side!" Otto called out. "Cut the straps."

Getting down on his knees in the blood, Rolf cut the straps on his side and they were able to pull the stuffed rucksack clear of the dead man's weight. Otto picked it up.

319

"Let's get out of here," he said, breaking into a run, Rolf following.

Turning where Gast had been planning to turn, by the mausoleum with the catafalque and the wingless clusters of angels, they ran straight into the black pigs led by the little old priest in the dirty white surplice, who pointed at them, calling out: "That's them! They're the murderers!"

FIFTEEN

Rolf tried to not think about where he was. He'd always hated confined spaces, couldn't stand being shut in. That was why he was usually out in the streets in all kinds of weather. Anything was better than being stuck inside. Now he was crammed into this stinking hole, with not enough air to breathe, no room to move, and no light. All he could do was try not to think about it, because whenever he thought about the plight he was in, he wanted to cry, and that wasn't going to do him any good.

"Hey, Robber, *Robber*, where are you?" he called in the dark when he thought he'd got his voice under control. Otto had become separated from him in the squash but couldn't be far, since the whole sodding cell was about the size of a matchbox.

"Here," Otto said eventually, only about two bodies away in the pressed meatloaf.

Rolf could tell that Otto was also trying to control his voice.

"How long d'you suppose they'll keep us here, like this? How long d'you suppose, Robber?"

"Don't know. How should I know? Anyway, they're bound to take us out before tonight. They got to put us somewhere else to sleep — stands to reason."

"We sleep here," one of the upright bodies remarked.

"Here? Where?" Rolf wanted to know.

"Where you are," this man told him.

"Standing up?"

"That's right. This is the EL-DE-Haus. It isn't famous for its home comforts."

Rolf fought against the waves of panic that swept over him; determinedly he thought of other things. Of open spaces. Of how they'd gone wandering, after running away from the hostel, and up in the hills there was as much air as you could breathe, you could fill your lungs full of it, and nobody to bother you or order you around. He concentrated his mind on a picture of herds of buffaloes thundering across vast prairies — he'd seen that in films.

When the buffalo races across the prairie,
And the cowboy throws his lasso . . .

God! they'd lived off the fat of the land — hadn't they? After the hostel, they really had. That was what he called living. Trapping wild rabbits. Raiding chicken pens in the dead of night and making off with clucking, flapping chickens under their jackets and eggs in their pockets. Jesus Christ! That was the time. Once, they'd descended on a sheep herd and captured a great big sheep, which they'd taken away with them and slaughtered in the hills, and roasted on a spit. They'd found a cave and stored their meat in the cool interior and lived for days without having to budge or lift a finger. When the meat was all gone, they fished in lakes and rivers. There was food to be had everywhere, and it was free. It grew on trees! Was yours for the taking.

322

It was stifling in the cell. Rolf couldn't get enough air. I'm going to suffocate, he thought, and his breathing became fast and panicky.

When they used to roam around the streets, he and Otto had often discussed what was the worst way of dying, and Otto always said drowning, because you couldn't get air. Rolf had argued against that point of view, saying that being crushed to death was worse than drowning, because when you were drowning, if you let yourself go it wasn't so bad. You didn't feel anything once you'd let go. He'd read that somewhere. It was only while you were struggling to breathe that you were in agony. If you gave up breathing, it wasn't even painful. It was like going under the gas at the dentist's, according to this article. Whereas, if you were in a dungeon and the ceiling was descending slowly, centimetre by centimetre, to crush you to death, that *was* bad. He'd challenged Otto to think of anything worse, and Otto said he'd never heard of dungeons with ceilings that came down to crush you, and Rolf said disgustedly that that was because the Robber was so ignorant, he'd never even read a book in his whole life.

Now, remembering his own argument in favour of drowning, Rolf tried to follow the advice and let go: to sink into the waves and not struggle. And, true enough, he did feel a slight easing of the panic. What was the worst that could happen to you? That you died. It's only dying, he told himself. That was all it was.

Hours went by and nobody came to take them out or to give them food and water. Apparently they'd missed the meal-time.

Eventually, from the gurgling in throats and the higgledy-piggledy sprawl of bodies, one propping up the other and not enough space in which to fall, Rolf gathered that people in the cell were asleep, and he, too, dozed off, from time to time, in the clammy embrace of his fellow prisoners.

There wasn't even a chink of light to tell them when it was

323

morning, but it seemed it was, because their cell door had been flung open and some slops were being served for breakfast.

Rolf and Otto didn't have time to get theirs. Their names were called, and a guard pushed them along the corridor to the stairs going down. They knew about the deep cellar. They were supposed to have medieval instruments of torture down there, and it was so deep, seven metres below ground, you could scream as much as you liked, nobody heard you.

The deep cellar had the dank, mouldy smell of a place light and fresh air never reached, and the cell to which they were taken ran with wet.

"You think they going to torture us, Louse Boy?" Otto asked.

" 'Xpect so," Rolf had to say. He didn't see any point in lying. But he kept his voice under control. You had to. He heard Otto sobbing quietly somewhere to the left. To cheer him up, he said, "Maybe they won't torture us, Robber. They don't have the time nowadays. Maybe they'll just shoot us."

That was when the cell door opened and Nold came in, carrying a storm lantern, and after him came the fat one, the one they knew from way back: Fat Schlammer.

Unconsciously, Rolf's hand went to his ear, which had nearly been torn off years and years ago by the man who was now standing before them.

After being questioned, they were taken back to their own cell by Nold.

The iron shutters across the high half-window had been opened, admitting a narrow shaft of dingy grey light. It was enough to reveal to the others the brutal treatment that Rolf had undergone. His face was covered in swellings and abrasions and clotted blood, and he couldn't move his right hand without great pain. His body was shaking the whole time, and regular, unrestrainable sobs came from him. Two men rose from the plank bed against one wall and motioned to

324

him to take their place and lie down. A folded jacket was put under his head, and a lit cigarette passed to him. He was grateful for it.

A man wearing steel-rimmed glasses examined Rolf's bad hand, feeling the finger joints gently, but even so making the boy wince and cry out. The man said that the hand was broken and should be in splints. He looked around for materials: one prisoner offered a pencil, another a tin fork, someone else a handkerchief, and with these things the man in glasses proceeded to bind the hand. It was painful. A prisoner with a medicine bottle uncorked it and offered it to Rolf. It was schnapps — and it burned away the sharp edge of the pain. Rolf drank until the bottle was empty and then fell into a coma-like sleep.

Waking in the dark, in pain, he felt as if he was lying on the rim of the earth and it was slippery and he was slipping off. Could not hold on. Momentarily he couldn't tell up from down, left from right. There were bodies pressed all around him. His hand seemed to be on fire. If he moved it at all, even while keeping the fingers stiff, the fire shot along his arm. The slightest movement cost him dearly in pain, but lying still was painful too: the iron edge of the bunk was driving rivets into his spine.

There was an appalling stench. It came from the corner where the bucket was that served as a latrine. Rolf felt his bowels loosen and his stomach, revolting against these conditions, forcing upwards. Fearful of not being able to hold himself in, he began the difficult journey across the cell; pushing through the crush of bodies without getting his hand knocked was almost impossible, and he cried out several times. He was trying to clear a way for himself with his good hand, pushing people out of the way who were asleep on their feet. They were like drunks holding each other up. Startled awake, they swore and cried out, thinking that they were being taken away to be shot. When they discovered it was just someone trying to get to the bucket, they cursed and groaned and tried to find another prop for themselves so they could sleep again, fitfully. It was like some huge, cumbersome animal rearranging its many limbs. Matches were pressed into Rolf's hand, and he struck one, holding the box in his mouth. The sight of the befouled area around the bucket froze him. But the others were pushing him on, telling him to be done. He added to the mess and the stench and pushed back to the bunk he was sharing with an old man.

He couldn't find a position in which to rest, with his hand hurting so badly he wanted to scream, and scarcely any room for him on the bunk. Still, he realised he was better off there than standing up in the crush of bodies. Trying to find a less painful position for himself, he awkwardly struck match after match, and in the flickering light saw that the wall was densely covered with grafitti and crude drawings. Not of the usual sort. One, scratched with something sharp, consisted of two uprights supporting a horizontal beam, from which hung a matchstick figure. There was an inscription below: "My heart hurts, my head hurts, I will die alone."

The match burnt Rolf's fingers as it went out: he struck another and moved it this way and that. He read names: Helmut Pohl, J. Schumacher, Wuligtroi, Orlando. . . . Another match was needed, and then another. Some of the previous occupants of the cell had been content to simply leave their names inscribed upon the wall, in pencil, or coloured crayon, or charcoal, or chalk, or incised with something sharp; others had made calendars, ticking off the days as they passed, and writing comments against certain days:

> I am here and don't know why
> Food sour, bread withdrawn
> No milk   no bread
> More water than soup
> No bread
> When will we have freedom
> Wednesday 18 August 1944, here 26 days

326

Arseholes
Let them all lick my arse
Freedom
I want to go home

With his last match he read a short, anonymous inscription, undated, formed in large, thick capitals with something sharp, a fragment of glass perhaps:

A MAN IS NOT WHAT HE WAS
A MAN IS WHAT HE DOES

No hope of sleep, under such conditions, with all those names drumming in his head . . . the matchstick figure hanging from the scaffold, the foul atmosphere. He wasn't making good use of the plank bed, so he gave it up to the old man and pushed his way towards the end of the cell; there, making a space for himself with elbows and knees, he sat by the door, his nose pressed to the crack, breathing in the slight draught of air coming from the corridor.

Next morning, before it was light, the cell door was suddenly flung open and the prisoners doused with an icy jet of chlorinated water. Rolf was spared the worst of this, being by the door, right next to the person wielding the garden hose, his thumb over the outlet to widen or narrow the jet, as he chose. It was the damp-eyed jailer who had taken their names on arrival and written them down in his thick book: he was standing well back, his arm extended, so as not to get his boots splashed.

"Well, that's your toilette done," he told the drenched, shivering prisoners, after five minutes of this showering.

Breakfast followed: a piece of stale black bread and some filthy, tepid ersatz coffee. And then Nold came for them again, to take them into the deep cellar for more questioning.

It had turned exceptionally cold in the first week of November, with strong, icy winds blowing through the rubble, creating dense dust storms. Dr. Leupold had need of his fur collar.

Seated in the back of the car that drove him to the *Oberlandesgericht* in the Reichensperger Platz, he wondered how much longer his petrol allocation would be maintained, and what he would do when it was stopped. It was too far to go on foot from his apartment, even though it was in the *Altstadt*. He did not have the strength these days. He would either have to move into a hotel within walking distance of the court building, if such a place could be found, or sleep in the building itself. There was plenty of room there now. The great columned edifice was becoming emptier each day, as more and more of the staff fled while they still could.

His car drew up by the main entrance. Dr. Leupold saw that the curved limestone façade had been daubed with gigantic blood-red legends.

HITLER IS THE MURDERER OF GERMANY,

he read.

Further to the left, on one of the high pillars supporting the massive pediment, someone had written:

YOUTH ARISE — BREAK YOUR CHAINS,

and then in various places by the high gated main door there occurred the words ATONE AND REVENGE! together with the edelweiss symbol. Obviously this was the work of Wolf Children. Nowadays their actions were not confined to writing on walls and pissing in the wheel axles of troop trains: they were going in for shootings and murders as well. Police officials were found hanging from lamp-posts, soldiers with their throats cut and their pockets empty. The latest and most blatant example of this form of gangsterism was the murder of Ortsgruppenleiter Gast in Melaten cemetery. Shot down within sight of a priest! The killers had rifled his pockets as he lay bleeding to death. A nasty piece of goods, by all accounts, this Gast, but his murder under such circumstances was, to

328

Dr. Leupold, a further sign of the times, of the progressive descent into anarchy that was seen on all sides. Goods trains bringing in flour and cereals were held up by masked bandits armed to the teeth. Escaped slave labourers roamed the ruins, raping and pillaging and killing. *Lebensmittel* stores were robbed, their shelves emptied before ordinary citizens could collect their rations. Emergency food stocks were down to two or three weeks' supplies, even on the basis of an ever-declining population. If replenishments did not get through, very soon the population would be starving. And since there was no electricity, no gas, and coal and heating fuels were at very low levels, they would freeze as well with the onset of winter. Very few parts of the city had running water, and water in storage tanks was liable to become contaminated under present conditions. The risk of a typhus epidemic was growing. The civil defence service was not able to cope, fires raged for days, and the remaining hospitals (four more had been destroyed last month) could not deal with all the injured. Some of the dead lay in the streets unburied, the corpses becoming weirdly discoloured, green and purple and blue, giving rise to rumours that the enemy was employing poison gas.

Even in these terrible times Dr. Leupold came every day to his office, and always entered by the main door of the court building, in full view of anyone who was there: with the fabric of society disintegrating around him, he considered it important that the prosecutor should not only continue to exercise his function, but be seen to do so, lest in his presumed absence people took it into their heads that they could flout the law.

Now, in the marble hall under the great dome, Dr. Leupold greeted the porter and then slowly climbed the balustered curving stairs to the fourth floor. In his office, on his desk, there was the usual stack of papers. It was amazing, but even with the city in a state of dissolution the paperwork never seemed to diminish.

It was cold in the room and Dr. Leupold did not remove his overcoat as he sat down.

He did not occupy himself immediately with the papers, but sat staring in front of him, lost in memories. He thought of his dear mother, dead these many a year. Of his dead wife. Of his two sons killed in action. And of his father, a good man, stern and strict, from whom he had first learned of the majesty of the law, its imperatives and its relentlessness. The law was unbending principle. Never would his father compromise any of his deeply held beliefs for the sake of expediency or comfort. A severe taskmaster, but just. To him morality and law were one and the same. The law was simply that which was moral. Morality, coming from the Greek *mores* meaning that which was customary or done, reflected what society as a result of a great deal of trial and error deemed to be correct, and therefore did. And the law was simply the instrument for upholding what society in its correctness had decided to do. Of course, society sometimes was wrong; and then the process of trial and error had to run its course, and rivers of blood might have to be shed before the error was seen. This was the ineluctable process of lawmaking.

On the basis of these principles, inculcated in him from childhood, Dr. Leupold had been bound to submit himself to the law of the New Order, even though he had had the gravest doubts of its correctness. Many of his personal beliefs stood in diametric opposition to the doctrines of Nazism. But Nazism had become the law of the land, and even if the legitimacy of that law was itself now in question, until the question had been resolved the law must stand, and he as an officer of the law must implement it faithfully. The individual could not take the law into his own hands. That way lay disorder — anarchy. Even if the law was tyrannical and unjust it must be observed until it could be amended: it could not simply be discarded and replaced by *lawlessness*. For there lay the greater evil of the Beast from the abyss.

Dr. Leupold's whole moral character had been profoundly

affected by his father's teachings and example, and for this reason it was more than a matter of personal loss when, three years ago, at the age of eighty-five, the elder Leupold had electrocuted himself while in the bath — by removing a light bulb overhead and placing his fingers on the positive and negative. The meaning of this careful and deliberate act was still not clear to Dr. Leupold. Was it an act of despair or, on the contrary, an expression of man's freedom to decide his own destiny?

He was brought out of his cogitations by the entry of Herr Spiedel, his senior law clerk.

"Herr Generalstaatsanwalt, I have Detective Nold outside, with the prisoner Theo Klug — the Bolshevist arrested in connection with the Gast murder. You expressed the wish to question the prisoner personally."

"Yes, yes," Dr. Leupold said. "That's correct. Send him in. There's no need for the policeman, however. Let him wait outside."

He ran his eyes through the youth's file, as he waited for him to be brought in, and removed his monocle in order to refix it even more firmly in place.

"So — you're the wall-writer," he said to Theo when he stood in front of the prosecutor's desk. "Who put you up to it? The Communists?"

"I put myself up to it," Theo replied staunchly.

"But who's behind you? Come, come! It's a grave offence spreading subversive propaganda, not to mention the other things you are accused of. You're very young, and if you've been manipulated by others, by political groups, it is something to be considered in mitigation. I advise you to speak freely and not hold anything back."

"Nobody put me up to it."

"No? It wasn't the Free Germany Committee? Some of your — uh — messages seem to bear their stamp."

Theo said nothing.

"You *are* a Communist — you wouldn't deny that?"

"I consider myself a revolutionary in the workers' movement."

Dr. Leupold nodded understandingly, tolerantly, like a physician faced with a mild case of fever.

"You're too young to have considered these matters very deeply. Under different circumstances, one could have allowed such youthful enthusiasms to spend themselves in the normal course of events. Unfortunately, circumstances are not different. And there is the death list." He shook his head sadly, regarded the list before him. "With a tick against the name of Ortsgruppenleiter Gast. A very incriminating tick. We already have the evidence of your fellow conspirators Rolf and Otto that you were all part of a terror gang, bent on blowing up the EL-DE-Haus and murdering public figures. They have admitted their role in the crime and named Kurt Springer as the killer. You are named as being part of the group, and although you were not actually in the cemetery when Gast was shot down, your complicity in the murder is established by the fact that you escaped in the same vehicle as the murderer."

Dr. Leupold looked directly at Theo.

"I see that I am on your death list as well. May I ask what has earned me that honour, alongside the Gestapo chief and others of his ilk?"

"You've sent plenty of people to their deaths. As public prosecutor."

"I prosecuted them," Dr. Leupold explained. "The courts sentenced them to death."

"You demanded the death penalty."

"When the law required me to. You think I have no charity, no compassion? Believe me, there were occasions when I was deeply grieved to have to make such a demand, knowing as I did that the court was bound to accede. But it was my duty. As it was my sons' duty to fight in this terrible war, and ultimately to give their lives." Theo said nothing. "You see, we have all suffered," Dr. Leupold continued. "But our suf-

332

fering does not relieve us of the burden of duty. And the fact that you, also, have suffered, have lost your parents in shocking circumstances, does not lessen the crimes with which you are charged. Robbery, murder . . . treason. What d'you have to say to that, Theo?"

"Gast deserved to die. That's all I've got to say. He was a little tin-pot tyrant, who tyrannised over people. He exploited everybody, and betrayed everybody. He took people's money and then was instrumental in having them sent to concentration camps."

Dr. Leupold pressed his fingers together in a pyramid of prayer. "Justification," he mused. "That is your plea? In that case you will wish to cite 'natural law,' with its appeal to *supreme* values, overriding the law of the land." He pondered, praying hands intertwined tightly. "It is quite true," Dr. Leupold was continuing, thoughtfully, "that every citizen has the right of self-defence, to defend himself against the robber and intruder. And it could be argued that a man like Gast was such a robber and intruder, yes, *yes*, and that in taking up arms to rid yourself of him you were acting in accordance with your duties as a citizen."

Theo couldn't see what Dr. Leupold was driving at, or why. Was there a signal in his unblinking eye behind the glass? Was the prosecutor a secret sympathizer, a fellow fighter in the cause?

Theo lowered his voice and leaned forward, speaking forcefully, intimately: "Hitler's a black tyrant. It was the bourgeoisie and the pawns of big business that put him in power and kept him in power. It was them that manufactured this war, which is a war against the people for the enrichment of the privileged classes. Only now it's finished them off as well, and they don't want it either. But seeing they're rotted through and through by what they are, which is hypnotized, that's what, hypnotized to obey, the only ones free and able to bring about change are the masses, the workers, by their spontaneous uprising—"

"Let me stop you there, on a point of law," Dr. Leupold interrupted. "*Aliqua spes eventus*. In connection with the employment of resistance, it is always demanded that I have a well-founded hope that I may improve matters by my acts. It is not valid to offer blind resistance to authority. I must have a plan to replace an existing system with something better. As my old theology teacher used to tell me: you can only criticize God if you can think of a better system than His. Furthermore, to be justified in taking action, I must believe that I am serving the general good— the *general* good. My action must not be merely self-serving. I cannot derive personal benefit from it, and of course in your case we have to remember that the car in which you made your escape was full of gold wedding rings and silverware. I must also remind you . . . that the whole moral basis for the slaying of the Tyrant is that 'Brutus is an honourable man', a holder of high office, qualified and entitled to act on behalf of others, as their representative. Whereas in your case, what do we have? Youths of the street. Thieves. Malefactors. Hooligans. In short, Wolf Children."

Theo saw his mistake in having spoken freely. That sort always tricked you. They could twist words, and make you believe they sympathized with you, but they were the tools of their class, they couldn't even help it, the old arseholes.

"For a minute," he said, even whiter-faced than usual, "I thought you were maybe on my side a little bit. I was stupid. Don't know what made me think that. People like you are never on our side. Whatever you pretend. You're all just as bad. Just as bad as Hitler. You put him in power, your lot. Now you see where he's got you and you uhmmm! and ahhh! and arsehole about and say perhaps he's in 'the camp of the robbers' and we the honourable men have the right to remove him. But you don't do it. Do you? You don't do anything. You sit on your fat arses and think about it, and about your sodding honour. When we do something— eliminate a little tyrant like Gast— we're street hooligans and murderers. But at least we didn't pick our clever noses and think about it, we did it. Whilst your lot did nothing. You just hold us back. That's why you've got to be swept away, all of you old arseholes—"

"That's really quite enough," Dr. Leupold said, standing up and pressing his bell to summon his senior law clerk to remove this foul-mouthed youth. Without his being aware of it, the monocle had fallen out and his eye was blinking uncontrollably in a wild tic, water running down his cheek.

When Spiedel came in, Dr. Leupold became aware of his eye being out of control and quickly wedged the eyeglass back in place to prop up the trembling brow.

"I have finished with the prisoner," he said. "Send Nold in to me."

Theo was escorted out, and the policeman came in.

"The Herr Generalstaatsanwalt has finished questioning the prisoner?"

"For the time being."

"Then the police questioning may continue . . . ?"

Dr. Leupold hesitated. "The criminal inquiries must take their course," he said, "but I draw your attention, and the attention of Kriminalsecretär Schlammer, to the regulations concerning the use of force during intensive questioning. The regulations state that blows must be limited to the posteriors, and applied with an authorized cane, and that after twelve blows a medical practitioner must be present."

"Medical practitioners are run off their feet these days, Herr Generalstaatsanwalt," Nold observed.

"I have read the confessions obtained from the prisoners Rolf Hacker and Otto Osche," Dr. Leupold continued. "And I must point out that the phraseology employed is very uncharacteristic of such youths, and the validity of the confessions might be questioned in court."

"Do you really think so, Herr Generalstaatsanwalt? In any case, I don't suppose there'll be time for a court hearing, will there?"

"I represent the court," Dr. Leupold asserted, and suddenly made up his mind. "Inform Kriminalsecretär Schlammer that he is to delay further police questioning as it is my intention to question the two others in the case myself. Arrange it for this afternoon. I will come to the EL-DE-Haus."

After what had been for him a difficult and distressing afternoon questioning the other two accused youths — one of whom, Rolf Hacker, had been very badly beaten, and had a broken hand and many abrasions on his face — Dr. Leupold returned to his office in the *Oberlandesgericht* to find on his desk a copy of a recent communiqué issued by the Reichs-führer-SS, Herr Himmler.

This stated that whilst he, personally, retained supreme authority in the matter of executions, in the event of a breakdown in the chain of command, powers were henceforth given to the district Higher SS and Police Chiefs to order executions on their own sole responsibility, provided that, after the event, when communications were restored, such executions were referred back to him through the chain of command.

So! Dr. Leupold reflected wryly, the role of public prosecutor was being made increasingly irrelevant.

The very next document illustrated this clearly. It was a communication from the Higher SS Chief West, which stated:

"In the interests of safeguarding our national German life, I authorized the open hangings of eleven criminals, and these duly took place. The rest are not to be overlooked, and the same fate awaits them at the final conclusion of present criminal investigations into their acts."

Dr. Leupold had no doubt that "the rest" referred to the murderers of Gast. The authorization for their executions already existing, his own investigation of the case was a pure formality. Still, he noted that the Higher SS Chief West had said "at the final conclusion of present criminal investigations," and so presumably they would at least wait for the prosecutor's report before carrying out sentence.

He was, therefore, not yet completely irrelevant. They were paying lip service, if no more, to the concept of an investigation carried out in accordance with the rule of law, such as it was these days!

The thought that the young boys he had just questioned were already condemned gave him a pang. They were so young! One was not even sixteen — in his case they would have to wait until he had attained his sixteenth birthday before they could hang him. If they paid any attention to the law at all. As for the other two, they were old enough to die on the gallows straight away. Of course, they were ruffians and gangsters, Dr. Leupold did not doubt that. All the same, while not a man to shirk stern measures when they were justified, the thought of these youngsters swinging from the end of a rope perturbed him.

He got up, lit a cigarette, and walked up and down. His disquietude did not pass, and feeling his spirit troubled, he resolved to attend evening mass at the *Dom*, and afterwards have a talk with his brother, the Cardinal. Talking to Ulrich, who had such a profound grasp of moral issues, had often helped to quell the prosecutor's unease.

The line between "obeying God rather than men" and "rendering unto Caesar that which is Caesar's" was a very fine one, but Ulrich had trodden it with exemplary finesse. To anyone with ears to hear such things, there could be no doubt of the Cardinal's profound disapproval of the godless State, and anyone with eyes to see had long ago seen the godless State all around him; therefore, there could be no doubt to the man of God as to where the Cardinal stood.

Herr Spiedel entered with a piece of paper.

"This has just been delivered by dispatch rider. For your attention, Herr Generalstaatsanwalt."

Dr. Leupold ripped open the envelope.

Inside there was a communication from the Higher SS Chief West stating:

"Criminal investigations into the Gast murder now being concluded, and full confessions having been obtained from the three accused, I authorize their executions under the special powers invested in me by the Reichsführer-SS. They are to be executed tomorrow morning together with the other criminals and traitors on whom sentence has already been passed!"

Dr. Leupold reflected that the extreme haste in disposing of the youths was no doubt prompted by his intervention in the case, and his questioning of the prisoners. The Higher SS Chief West was clearly determined to preempt any moves that Dr. Leupold might be contemplating.

Was it God's will that Rolf Hacker, Otto Osche, and Theo Klug should die on the gallows tomorrow? If it was not, it seemed that Dr. Leupold was His sole means of stopping the executions—since the Almighty, omnipotent though He was, chose not to work through miracles but by enlisting the service of the faithful, and had not even intervened in the case of His own Son.

Sorely troubled, Dr. Leupold decided that he must catch his brother before evening mass, to obtain his help in this moment of grave decision.

Downstairs, in the long-unswept hall of the court building, he found his driver and told him they were going at once to the Domplatz. There he alighted, since it was impossible, with all the obstructions that now existed, to drive right up to the cathedral entrance.

It was getting very cold, and there was a stinging wind blowing. By the stopped *Hauptbahnhof* clock the usual clusters of youths, of both sexes, were hanging about, selling black-market goods or services of one sort or another. He saw his brother striding across the square, and caught up with him.

They walked side by side and Dr. Leupold indicated with

his head the sordid transactions being conducted within sight of the untouched house of God.

" 'And no man might buy or sell, save that he had the mark of the name of the Beast, or the number of his name, and without worshipping the Beast, nobody might live,' " he observed.

"We need to put our own house in order," the Cardinal said with that firmness of tone for which he was renowned, but in a voice that was soft and low and confidential, by contrast to his normal declamatory style. "Alas! there is no chance of that while the Beast rules."

"Must he rule?" the prosecutor asked rhetorically.

The Cardinal looked sharply at his brother.

"The fact is he does rule and will continue to do so until he is brought down or removed."

"Exactly," Dr. Leupold said. "Exactly. I sometimes ask myself—"

"Those are dangerous questions to ask oneself," the Cardinal quickly interposed, "and I do not only mean dangerous to life. . . ."

They walked on in silence towards the cathedral.

"You look preoccupied," the Cardinal observed.

"Something is weighing on me," the prosecutor admitted. "Three youths, children virtually—oh, scoundrels, no question—involved in the killing of a Party official. He was the usual type. You know the sort—one hand 'Heil Hitlering,' the other in everyone's pocket. He was murdered a few days ago, and robbed. They did not fire the actual shot, but were involved. To what extent is not quite clear. The point is, nobody'll bother to find out: they're going to hang them. To teach others of their kind a lesson."

"We live in brutal times," the Cardinal observed. "What can any of us do?"

"I could perhaps do something," the prosecutor reflected. "*Unless* I do, they'll execute those three boys tomorrow morning."

339

The Cardinal made the sign of the cross.

"There is no question that they are guilty?" he asked.

"They have confessed. By what means their confessions were obtained . . ."

"There was no trial? You did not prosecute them?"

"No."

"It is not strictly speaking your responsibility then."

"Strictly speaking, I suppose not. The decision was taken under the new emergency powers by the Higher SS Chief West."

"In that case, it's out of your hands."

"The form in which the order for the executions is worded states 'at the final conclusion of criminal investigations.' If I were to inform the Higher SS Chief West — a man of no great consequence, the usual thug — that my investigations are not finally concluded, that I have further questions to put to these boys, I doubt if he would take it upon himself to deny my request. He has plenty of others that he can hang. I think my authority would count for enough to obtain a stay of execution."

"Why do you wish to save them, Josef?"

They had entered the cathedral now, and the Cardinal led the way to the sacristy so that he could start to prepare himself for the evening mass. The prosecutor had been deliberating on his brother's question, and he answered now with a certain degree of formality, almost as if addressing a court of law.

"Why they should be shown mercy?" he asked, and considered the matter deeply. "Well, in the first place, there is their youth to be taken into account. Rolf Hacker was under sixteen at the time the murder was committed. Under wartime emergency laws the death sentence may be imposed on youngsters of sixteen years and over if — I quote — 'their mental and moral development corresponds to that of an adult criminal.' It would normally be for the prosecutor to advise the court of the moral and mental state of the accused,

340

and the court would be bound to accept his advice. I therefore ask myself: is Rolf Hacker, sixteen tomorrow, one whose moral and mental development justifies his being considered an adult? This uneducated, unteachable Louse Boy. This congenital defier of authority, who has all along stubbornly refused to grow up, seeing no advantage in it. His folk hero is the *Kallendresser*, who defecates in the gutters of the rooftops, baring his posterior to the world. Is this an adult responsible for his actions?''

''How can I say? I do not know the boy. But it is well to remember the sin of pride. The pride of defiance. The refusal to bend the knee—''

''Ulrich, we are talking of a crime that will get him hanged tomorrow. I ask myself: to what extent was he influenced by others?'' The prosecutor began to pace up and down, deeply restless. ''Was he led into it by his friend Otto? Who *is* a robber and criminal. Although, in his case too, I have to ask if he is a murderer. He did not fire the actual shot, and there is no evidence that he had planned to kill Gast, except for the death list, which they all agreed on before—true, true. . . . But . . . I will come to that . . . I ask myself: was Otto a conspirator to murder, or an opportunist who, seeing a man dead on the ground, pursues his natural inclination, which is to rob? Then take Theo. The death list is in his handwriting, he drew it up. And he has made a tick against the name of Gast. I admit, that tick condemns him. It proves he was in the conspiracy. Moreover, he does not seek to repudiate what was done, maintains that Gast's death was 'deserved,' although he was not present when the crime was committed, was several hundred metres away, in the ambulance. That he is someone dedicated to the overthrow of the existing order is unquestionable. He is for the elimination of people like Gast — and myself, too, for that matter. He wants a clean sweep, a new beginning. He calls us the 'old arseholes,' and wants to do away with the lot of us. Looking around, can we blame him? The inheritance we have left them is hardly one to be

341

proud of, and even if what he wishes to replace it with is another form of oppression, one can see we have left them little else to turn to."

"They could turn to God."

"God seems to have let them down as much as the 'old arseholes.'"

"Is that the whole of the case for showing them mercy?"

The hour of the mass was drawing near and the Cardinal was beginning to robe, putting on first the scarlet silk cassock and buttoning it carefully.

"The whole of the case?" the prosecutor repeated. "No — not the whole. There is also the question of justification."

"For going against the law?"

"Yes. It all centres on justification. Are these youths conspirators to murder? Or are they resisting the Tyrant? Something we have signally failed to do."

"I have never made any secret of my condemnation of the godless State," the Cardinal said. "I have often preached against the Tyrant."

"Yes, you have preached," the prosecutor agreed, "and I have protested, registered my objections, expressed my deep misgivings, et cetera. But what tangible actions have we taken?"

"What else could we do, without compromising our deepest principles?"

"The right of *resistance* when the State, or king, is the robber — the transgressor — has existed throughout history. Where the king has broken his oath to the people, the people, through the nobles, may remove the king."

The Cardinal was drawing the sleeveless outer vestment over the cassock, draping the ornamental maniple over the wrist of the left arm. Except for his hat he was fully robed: a splendid figure in scarlet, embodying the awesome pomp and power of his calling. He looked at his watch.

"One shall be subject to the authorities (Titus three: one). *But no one may obey orders in which the authority no longer is the minister of God* (Acts four: eighteen to twenty and elsewhere). Oh yes . . . there *is* moral justification for the removal of a tyrant by whatever means are required, provided . . .'' He reached inside his silk robes and drew out a packet of cigarettes and lit one. ''. . . provided, Josef, that those who act to remove him have the authority and the standing in the community to render them, what shall we say: acceptable?''

''If the ones who are acceptable do not act,'' the prosecutor postulated, ''are we entitled to condemn — and hang — those who have acted but were not acceptable?''

The Cardinal puffed thoughtfully at his cigarette.

''If you are so clear in your mind and heart of the innocence of these youths, Josef, or at any rate of their deserving mercy, then you should not agonize any further. You should save them, if you are able.''

The prosecutor sank into a chair and regarded his intertwined hands with grave misgivings, a man at the crossroads: a man who has come to doubt his own vocation.

''That's just it, Ulrich. I am not clear in my mind and heart. Like every lawyer, I am plagued by the form of the debate, the pros and cons, the ability to see the other side. I know that some of my arguments for saving them are simply that: arguments, clever arguments, legal ploys. . . .'' From some unknown reservoir within himself, anger, controlled but powerful, flowed into his voice, disposing of the reasonable air, the dispassionate stance. ''Whatever their varying degrees of guilt in this particular instance, they have pitted themselves in every sense against their elders and betters, committed so many crimes, plundered and looted and stolen, engaged in acts of sedition and rebellion and treason, they could be hanged ten times over. I have twenty-two unsolved murders on my desk. A fire chief bludgeoned to death, a clerk from the *Gauleitung* strung up on a lamp-post. The doings of Wolf Children like them, or of deserters, or slave labourers. It's an army of the ruins, of the dispossessed, and they are all in it. For every crime of which they might be exonerated, a dozen

343

others loom up to condemn them. That is my problem. And this rampage of destruction upon which they are embarked is applauded by the enemy, who seeks to make heroes of them. BBC broadcasts describe them as a new generation, defying and rejecting the system their parents foisted on them. They are represented as wanting 'fresh air,' 'freedom,' 'truth.' The broadcasts speak of the edelweiss symbol as representing the reflowering of freedom in a State where freedom was dead. They say that the young are rising up in armed rebellion to bring down their oppressors. Us! *Us*, Ulrich! The 'old arse-holes.' Are we to be lumped together with the oppressors, the Nazis, the Gestapo, and stand by and see heroes being made of such criminal elements and ruffians? These ignorant gut-tersnipes . . .''

The prosecutor sank back wearily in his chair. The mono-cle had slipped, but unsupported though the eye was, nothing twitched in his grey, exhausted face.

The Cardinal looked at his watch.

''I can see your dilemma, the struggle between compassion on the one hand, and the law's requirement on the other. Do not underestimate that requirement. God is not only the God of mercy, He is also the God of wrath and righteousness. God does not shrink from punishing those who have offended Him. Josef, the theme of my sermon today is the lawless human being who *is* the anti-Christ. He brings about the supreme misfortune: chaos and disorder. We see the godless State passing now into darkness, in agony and blood. But it *will* pass, and we must ensure that what comes after it is not an orgiastic breaking of the chains, a *Walpurgisnacht* of pa-ganism and defiance of law. Or Communism, for that matter. Yes, yes — one's heart breaks for the children, caught be-tween the old and the new, but who would deny that they are outlaws, lawless in their very natures, unable and unwilling to obey and comply? They pervert the powers that are or-dained of God into the animal out of the abyss. A lawless

344

human being acting for himself alone, soars up in his own estimation to become the law of all things."

He paused to place the scarlet cardinal's biretta upon his head, and assessed the effect that his words were having on the prosecutor.

" 'The children shall be cast out into outer darkness and there shall be weeping,' " he said. And went on, "Have the faith of your position, Josef. Is it not the role of the magistrate or prince, when the abyss of lawlessness threatens, to take upon himself the reestablishment of order and justice in the name of an aristocratic democracy? Even if the price is high." Again he paused, and examined himself in a hand mirror to see the effect he made fully robed. He had to twist and pose in order to see all aspects of his splendid appearance. Satisfied, finally, he put down the mirror, and said to his brother:

"Put another way: when the wolf breaks into the village, the farmer may not wait to meet in council with his fellow villagers, but instead must run to slay the beast as an obvious doer of harm. In the words of Goethe: Rather an injustice than disorder."

The prosecutor nodded.

The trial was over.

Tomorrow was Rolf's birthday: he was going to be sixteen years old, time to turn over a new leaf. He always turned over a new leaf on his birthday, and then went straight back to the old one. Couldn't help it. Something got into him. At school he had often made up his mind to pay attention, mend his ways, but when it came to it, he couldn't. The teacher would make some remark, and out would come the insolent answer like a flash. Rolf decided there must be something bad in him that he always wanted to disobey and defy his elders and betters. Louse Boy was the right nickname for him. He just had a rotten character.

Laboriously working with his left hand, he scratched tomorrow's date in the wall plaster, and against it printed:

mY BiRTHdAy   16 years old

He got to thinking about things he didn't normally think
about: why he was a thief, for instance. You just got into
things.

That's how it was: *you got into things*. It was your fate.

If he was given another chance, he really would turn over a
new leaf this time, learn a trade: carpentry or masonry. He
liked to do things with his hands and to be out in the open. He
wouldn't mind being a roofer, climbing up high ladders —
he didn't mind heights — and then walking like a cat across
the rooftops, laying tiles over the rafters. It was a good trade,
being a roofer. (It was what his father had been before he fell
off a ladder one day, dead drunk, and broke his leg.)

People always needed roofs over their heads, didn't they?

It had stuck in his throat, having to sign that confession.
But they made him. They said they were going to break every
bone in his body, one at a time. And he believed them, because hadn't they already broken his right hand? Fat Schlammer had done that with a stool leg. They'd told him that if he
signed the confession he would be sent to prison, but they
wouldn't hang him because of his age, him being under sixteen still. Even the prosecutor had said that.

In the evening they called him out into the corridor to get
his grub, the one meal of the day. It was the usual muck: a
watery mess with bits and pieces of things floating around in
it, *supposedly* potatoes, cabbage, and carrots, and with it they
gave him a chunk of stale black bread.

He was just about to go back into his cell when Nold, who
was standing in the corridor, said to him out of the side of his
mouth to wait a minute. Nold had a peculiar expression on
his face: very green at the gills. He didn't say anything much
at first, just pushed a packet of cigarettes into Rolf's hands.
"Go on, have them." He gave him matches as well. Appar-

346

ently for nothing. All of which was unusual. Rolf had one or two puffs while Nold kept looking around to see if anyone was coming, and Rolf thought he was going to propose some deal or other, how to get moved to a better cell, or get better food . . . Nold was the dealer down there. He was looking completely the other way, making sure nobody was coming, and then, speaking with his lips hardly moving, he said, "They're going to hang you in the morning. You and Otto and Theo and nine others."

At first it was a far-off train coming towards him, a tiny red dot, and then all of a sudden it was big as the sun, and on top of him, having crossed the whole span of his life in a moment. He had always seen it coming, out of the side of his eyes, the red thing, but never big like this, never full-on.

Nold turned to look at him, to see how he was taking it. He seemed to be taking it all right. How else could he take it? Scream? What good would that do him?

"I didn't know if it was better to tell you, or not," Nold said.

"I don't know either."

"I thought you'd want to know, probably. The others won't know until—"

"Isn't there anything you can do, Herr Nold?"

"No, there isn't. There isn't."

So that was that. Rolf couldn't yet believe it completely; if it had been Schlammer who'd said it, it could have been for a joke. Those were the sorts of jokes he enjoyed making: telling people that their mother had died, or their little child, when they hadn't. He liked to see people's expressions when he said it to them. But Nold had been looking the other way, hadn't wanted to see Rolf's expression, and, in any case, he didn't go in for those sorts of jokes. Therefore you had to believe him. But still Rolf couldn't completely. It hadn't hit him yet, he knew. He saw the red thing coming towards him, coming towards him . . .

One of the wardens opened his cell and gave him a shove inside, and that was when it hit him, as the heavy door clanged shut and he was alone in solitary. Now here it comes, he thought, and it did. Tomorrow they were going to put a rope around his neck and choke the life out of him, and after that he wouldn't exist anymore, he'd be in the earth, a cold, dead thing. Since nobody could see him in here, he allowed himself to cry. He cried for about an hour, and then he was too exhausted to cry more and stopped.

There was no point going to sleep. You didn't need your sleep if you were going to be hanged in the morning. It wouldn't make any difference if you were tired or not.

They'd tricked him, those old arseholes! Telling him he wasn't going to be hanged because of his age. Making him sign the confession, saying that he was a criminal and a murderer and no good. That that was what he'd always been and always would be, because he had the badness in him from birth. That he belonged to a gang of criminal traitors, and was ashamed of the crimes he'd committed against his country. Well, he wasn't ashamed! He was proud of having pissed in the wheel axles of troop trains, and he hoped he had ground lots of them to a halt. He was glad to have spat in everybody's face, to have cheeked his elders and betters all his life. He was glad they'd killed the Pig-Willi, the wild boar. And he wished they'd got the fuses so they could have blown up the EL-DE-Haus.

Frantically he searched around on his knees for the piece of glass with which he had scratched his calendar on the wall. He struck match after match. When he'd found the glass fragment, he gripped it in the fingers of his left hand and scratched the words:

LIes LiES

He wanted to write on the wall that the confession he had signed was a lie and that he took it back, and that even if he was a thief and the son of a thief and unruly and lazy and wouldn't work on the Westwall in defence of his country, he wasn't what they said he was and they could all kiss his arse.

But he didn't have anything with which to write such a long tract, and so with the last bit of crumbling glass, his fingers bleeding, he scratched on the wall:

yOU caNt mAke mE if i DoNt wanT To

Then, his writing materials used up, he lay down on the floor and tried to keep warm with only the short, tattered blanket for covering. He was shivering the whole time, thinking of the cold earth he was going to lie in tomorrow when he was dead.

In the morning they threw open his cell door and ordered him to get his breakfast like everybody else: tepid ersatz coffee and stale black bread. But when it was time to go back in their cells, he was told to remain outside, with several others, among them Otto. Otto had an odd sort of smirk on his face, as if he thought they were all going to be released or something. He gave Rolf a wink, and then another. Wild twitching winks, they were.

There was a roll-call. Rolf heard Theo's name called, heard him answer from the end of the corridor. Twelve names altogether. Nold had said they were going to hang twelve prisoners.

"Where we going?" Otto asked.

"Going for a drive," one of the guards said, grinning.

They were told to stand facing the wall and to put their hands behind their backs, and somebody walked along the line putting handcuffs on their wrists.

"Don't you trust us? You think we don't like it here?" Otto joked, and got a punch in the back for his humour. "Where you taking us? Where they taking us?" he asked Rolf. "They're not going to shoot us, are they?"

Rolf stared straight ahead at the wall and kept his lips tight together, holding everything in.

"They're going to shoot us!" one of the twelve said as they were led into the yard. He began to recite, " 'Yea, though I walk through the valley of the shadow of death, I will fear no evil . . .'" But they were not being lined up against the wall, they were being made to climb onto the back of an open lorry that had come out of the underground garage, and the incipient panic was quelled. So they were not going to be shot, after all. They were going to be transferred to another prison: to Brauweiler, or Kingleputz, that was what it was.

Blood returned to ashen faces as the lorry jolted out of the yard and along Elisenstrasse, past the big concrete *Gestapo-bunker,* behind which there was the iron girder structure, with rope ends hanging from meat hooks. They were going right past this scaffold, rattling on down the road, and now the prisoners were almost lighthearted from relief. Obviously, they were being transferred to another prison, where conditions were better than at the EL-DE-Haus, since several of those in the lorry were mere youths. The authorities must have decided that growing boys needed better food than the filthy muck they had been getting.

They called to each other:

"It's Kingleputz."

"No, it's Brauweiler, this is the way to Brauweiler."

With so many streets impassable, there was no means of knowing for certain, from the initial direction taken, where the lorry was headed.

Rolf was pressed against the lorry's side and being thrown against his fellow prisoners with every roll and jolt: having their hands handcuffed behind their backs, they couldn't hold on to anything and fell about and knocked into each other like skittles.

Rolf wondered if he was the only one who knew.

A sudden roll to the left, and he was almost thrown off the lorry. He thought of the time he had been on the train to Düsseldorf, when he was a child, and leaning out of the window (which you were not supposed to do of course, but he'd always done things he wasn't supposed to do), had felt the gritty, hot wind in his face.

350

Always stuck his neck out where he shouldn't, and his nose in. That was his louse-boy nature.

Where were they going? They had gone through the deserted *Altstadt* and were crossing the Hansaring. Anyone would think they were going home. Now they were bumping across a huge bomb site, through broken glass that glittered dully in winter sunlight whenever an opening occurred in the sky. He remembered a rag-and-bone merchant's yard that he had once been in when he was small, a vast place where everything was broken and useless: thrown-away stuff. The rag-and-bone man used to come along their street regularly, calling out his incomprehensible cries, which meant he would take anything: old iron and scrap metal, holed pots and pans, worn-out shoes, moth-eaten clothes, torn mattresses, rusty bedsprings, old cooking stoves. Naughty boys! Everything went to his yard, where it all lay rusting and rotting in mounds and heaps — Rolf's Uncle Fred had taken him there, wearing his brown uniform. It was to teach him a lesson. People were always wanting to teach him a lesson. Uncle Fred wanted to teach him that this was where you ended up if you were disobedient. If you cheeked your teachers. You ended up as discarded rubbish.

Rolf thought: it's all become a rag-and-bone yard, the whole city, and that's where I am being taken, to the rubbish dump, because I was always good for nothing. But against that he remembered the bold writing on the wall:

A MAN IS NOT WHAT HE WAS, A MAN IS WHAT HE DOES.

The jolting of the lorry, the wild beating of his heart, and not having slept put him in a kind of delirium. There were moments when he forgot where he was being taken and for what purpose, as if he was just in a bad dream, from which he could always wake himself before it came to the long fall.

They seemed to be going back to Ehrenfeld. Going home! Perhaps they were going to be released. Perhaps what Nold had told him last night was to give him a scare. He wished he could talk to Theo. Theo, with his brains, would know, but he was too far away.

They crossed open spaces that had formerly been gardens and greens, where the trees were burnt stumps, and in his dazed, drifting state Rolf saw the face of the Chicken-neck Wringer from their building, the woman with the thick arms and thick hands, Frau Bier, who strangled chickens for a few pfennigs, and for a little extra plucked their feathers and ripped their insides out. She had always warned him and Otto they would end up badly, making a wringing motion of her fat hands, and now her prediction was coming true.

They were past the Haupt-Güter-Bahnhof Gereon, and coming up to the silent shuttered city slaughterhouse. And turning left? So they *were* returning to Ehrenfeld.

Elation was building up among the prisoners. They were not being transferred to another prison, they were being released. Now they were sure of it.

"You can let me off here," Otto joked with one of the guards. "I live just round the corner." This made the guards laugh and Otto's face froze: he wasn't used to people laughing at his jokes, and he couldn't see what he'd said that was so funny.

The lorry cut across the Ehrenfeldgürtel, past the burnt-out station, and turned into the street which ran alongside the railway arches. They were being brought right to their own doorsteps!

The others were becoming jubilant: only Rolf understood what this homecoming meant.

They were to be a lesson to others.

The workshops and storerooms and little wholesalers and repair shops under the arches were all closed: shutters down, barred and padlocked like on a public holiday before the war.

The way he was squashed in, he couldn't manage to turn around and look ahead to where they were going: could only look back.

352

The lorry came to a halt, and several of the prisoners fell over in a heap. The guards got them up and started pushing them out, roughly. Rolf couldn't see anything. There were those taller than himself around him. At the back people were pushing forward, and then he felt those in front pressing back with all their weight, and he was in a crush between the two forces.

The backward pressure was not permitted for long: the prisoners were being made to get out by the guards. When it came to Rolf's turn to jump down, he did so without being prodded. What he saw first was a large silver reflector board on a moveable stand, gathering up the grey daylight and directing it towards the men getting off the lorry. It was a poor day for photography, with a pale sun emerging only now and then from behind smoke and cloud, and the official photographer was having to use long exposures on his large plate camera mounted on a revolving tripod. Some of the prisoners were stopped and required to remain still while they were photographed. After that, they were hurried on towards the long wooden gallows that had been erected at right angles to the railway arches. It was a crude structure, consisting of a row of thick wooden uprights, buttressed on either side, carrying the overhead beam, from which at intervals of less than a metre hung twelve ropes, each with a noose at the end. About half a metre above ground, loose wooden planks between the uprights formed a narrow platform, and the prisoners were being pulled up onto it without further ado. As they mounted one by one, they were moved along, until each prisoner had a noose hanging directly above him; it was lengthened or shortened according to his height by an adjustment of the running knot, and then the noose was placed around his neck and a final adjustment made, until the rope was tight but not too tight. When one prisoner dug his heels into the ground and would not mount the platform, he was gagged, his legs and ankles were tied together, and then he was lifted up and the noose was placed around his neck.

The rest, seeing the uselessness of resisting, mostly accepted the hand-up to the platform and walked of their own accord to their places.

Rolf, already mounted, saw Theo mounting. Three other youths followed, and then came Otto, breathing gaspingly, and twisting his head round, as if looking for someone.

To one side, behind a barrier, Rolf saw a crowd come to watch: mostly women carrying shopping bags and holding the hands of their children, and old men. These women had the solemn, respectful expressions of the untaught summoned to a lesson, which they would dutifully learn as they were expected to. Seeing among them a child whose eyes were all over the place, not paying attention, Rolf thought: you're like me, you'll never learn, and felt a shiver of terrible pride that "they" had been able to teach him nothing: the Louse Boy had been impervious to all their lessons.

Behind him the noose, too high because of his small stature, was lowered by an adjustment of the running knot, and then placed around his neck. It was still too high and made him choke, and so they lowered it further, since he must not choke yet, only at the appointed time, which would be any moment now.

What was the delay? The prisoners were all in position, each with a rope around his neck. Some were looking straight ahead, others from side to side in terror and disbelief, gagged and trussed so they could not move or cry out.

The delay was due to the light, which was a soupy grey, making the photographer's task difficult, even though he had reflectors and strobe lamps. He was waiting for the sun, and meanwhile taking shots of the prisoners lined up on the scaffold, and of the crowd beyond, watching. He could not use a slow exposure for the hangings; with all the movement, his pictures would come out a blur. He needed sun.

Not far from the gallows a trestle table had been set up on which stood a bottle of cognac; this was opened and strong measures poured out and handed to the executioners to settle

354

their nerves. The photographer, too, was given a glass, and at the same time told by Fat Schlammer, who was in charge, that they would have to proceed in a minute, sun or no sun. They could not take all day over this. Together they looked up at the sky, assessing the passage of cloud and smoke.

Rolf saw them shake their heads doubtfully. He looked sideways and saw Otto in a state of great agitation; he'd lost his nerve and was sobbing and gasping: "I want my mother, I want my mother. . . ." Further along the line, Theo was very still, ashen but upright, calm, his glasses on crookedly, staring straight ahead, and Rolf thought: Good old Brains, he's going to do it all right, and he told himself, It's only dying, that's all it is. Something to be got through, like life. At the same time as saying this to himself, he was afraid, and unready to give up his young life, which he had not even begun to live yet, properly, and then the sun came out, cold and pale, and he looked straight into it. It was starting: the youth right at the end had been given a push in the back, which sent him swinging off the plank. Rolf heard Theo cry out, *"Stalin lives!"* and then he was swinging too, and someone had kicked away the loosely resting planks from under the prisoners' feet, and they were all swinging in that first section. And then, still staring into the sun, Rolf knew that his turn had come, as it must, and felt the hard push in his back which sent him off the plank in an upward arc, and he was rising as if on a playground swing for an instant before the abrupt fall.

Kurt and Franzi and Benno had to wait until dark to pay their last respects to their comrades. Before then, it would have been too dangerous, the executions having taken place at a busy road intersection.

First Kurt approached the hanging bodies, while Benno and Franzi stayed well back, keeping a lookout, holding their Stens under the overcoats draped about their shoulders.

355

Kurt walked the length of the gallows: twelve bodies, side by side, swinging slightly all the time, heads strangely twisted, out of true, lolling on shoulders: mouths gaped, swollen tongues hung out, eyes bulged. Kurt noted everything. Some were gagged and their legs tied together. In other cases the legs had been left free to kick and dance in the air.

The planks on which the condemned men had stood, and which were knocked away at the moment of the executions, now lay scattered around, as on a building site that has been hastily abandoned by slapdash workmen.

Kurt stopped and looked into the face of each of his friends in turn and appeared to be making a vow.

Then he returned to let Franzi and Benno pay their last respects, while he stood guard.

Benno approached his brother's body slowly, face set. He was carrying a book, one of the thick dusty volumes that Theo, if he hadn't read it from cover to cover, had dipped into from time to time to find resounding phrases to paint on walls. He placed the book at Theo's feet, and took a hand grenade out of his pocket and put it on top of the book. Then, unable to maintain his composure any longer, he broke down and embraced his brother's body, weeping quietly.

Franzi had brought Rolf's guitar. She placed it at his feet.

Kurt put Otto's belt under his gently swaying body, a belt with a fine porcelain buckle and nickel rings to which were clipped an army knife, a water canteen, a necklace of cartridge cases, a marksmanship badge, iron crosses, and other medals. All stolen stuff.

"Come on," Kurt said to Benno, who was still holding on to his brother's legs, not wanting to let go.

Franzi said, "Goodbye, Rolfie."

"Come on," Kurt said again.

Benno looked around, and, taking some chalk out of his

356

pocket, wrote on one of the wooden uprights of the gallows the words ATONE and REVENGE.

* * *

The wind was whipping through the piled-up snow in the Domplatz, creating brief blizzards during which nothing could be seen; the prosecutor several times was obliged to stand still and wait, back to the storm, until the worst was past, and then, sunk inside his fur collar, head down, he could continue.

He was in time to hear his brother's prayer for the city: "*Civitatem istam tu circumda, Domine: et Angeli tui custodiant muros eius* . . . Draw, Lord, a ring around this city: and let your angels defend its walls . . ." Whether God heard the prayer, that was another question. There were moments when Dr. Leupold felt sure that the Lord was punishing them all as He had punished Sodom for its lack of ten righteous men. It was not only the enemy's continuing bombardments, but also the total breakdown of public order that made him believe that they had now finally entered the time of the Beast.

In particular, it was the ubiquitous Wolf Children who made Dr. Leupold despair of the possibility of restoring order. The public executions had achieved nothing; instead of discouraging others, the effect had been to produce an ever-swelling tide of disobedience and revolt. The dissolution had arrived with a vengeance and there were now gangs, a hundred or more strong, fully armed, who lorded over the ruins and made a mockery of the law.

The murderer of Gast, Kurt Springer, was still at large, and according to police reports that arrived on the prosecutor's desk had placed himself at the head of a band of avengers, made up of Wolf Children, slave labourers, and deserters. In these past weeks colourful legends had begun to attach themselves to his name. Some called him "the Pied Piper" because of his ability to whistle up followers, among whom were many youths and children. From the evidence of

357

members of his gang who had been caught and made to talk, he was committed to the extermination of Nazis — the "pig-shoot," he called it. He had become a fanatical hunter of the black pig and would shoot it on sight; his followers claimed that he was dedicated to wiping out all species of the beast, wherever found, in whatever shape or guise, as part of a final reckoning. He was also known as "Mad Kurt" and "Machine-gun Kurt," but perhaps there were several Kurts contributing to the same legend, for the acts attributed to him appeared to be more than any one man could have carried out, although stories of a young girl companion-in-arms, and of a youthful lieutenant known as "One-Ear," said to be the brother of the executed Bolshevist Theo, did point to Kurt Springer.

It was this terror group, according to reports received by the prosecutor, who had been responsible for the killing of the Gestapo chief and one of his underlings, the execrable Fat Schlammer, during the battle of the Grosser Griechenmarkt, which had lasted from 2 P.M. to 2:15 A.M., with machine guns and hand grenades used by both sides. The cellar hideout of the terror gang had been surrounded by crack security forces and a siege mounted. The criminals had refused to surrender, and explosives were used to bring gutted buildings crashing down on them. It was thought that they were all dead under the rubble, but apparently a handful led by Kurt, his girl companion, and his lieutenant One-Ear had utilized the cellar breakthroughs to crawl under the ruins, emerging to the rear of the forces surrounding the hideout, and from there had thrown their hand grenades and fired their Stens, killing the head of the Gestapo and Schlammer.

According to some eyewitnesses, Kurt Springer had been killed in this battle, while others claimed he had escaped with the girl and One-Ear, and that "the Pied Piper" was once more whistling up a new band of followers to join him in the hunt of the black pig.

Dr. Leupold no longer knew what to believe. Ever since his sister's death in an air attack just after Christmas, his existence had become increasingly circumscribed and solitary and unreal: he now lived in a hotel and went every day on foot to the *Oberlandesgericht*, where he continued his paperwork, instituting prosecutions against malefactors, though it was some time since any judicial trials had been held. In the evenings he attended mass at the *Dom*. But he no longer engaged in discussions with his brother — a certain spiritual estrangement had occurred between them. The prosecutor could not help considering his brother's ringing sermons increasingly irrelevant in the face of the reality of the dissolution they were witnessing.

Leaving the cathedral after the service, he made it a practice to walk across the Domplatz in the direction of the *Hauptbahnhof*, where the lawless youths engaged in their desperate transactions. They had come to know who this tall, severe man was, with his monocle firmly wedged in his eye, his brow unbudging, having seen him night after night walking home after mass. The word had spread among them, "It's the public prosecutor, it's that old arsehole Leupold."

With the sound of American artillery getting nearer every day, and the last remaining enforcers of the law fleeing eastward across the one bridge that still stood, the Hohenzollern, the prosecutor felt a greater obligation than ever before to show his face and to assert his official presence, even if only by taking this nightly walk across the square.

The lawless youths would see him and know that unlike the Gestapo and all the rest, *he* had not fled: that he was still on duty, come what may.

On this particular night in late February, there was thick snow on the ground, covering the rubble piles and softening footsteps.

It began to snow anew, and the strong wind blowing into the snow banks created a small blizzard that drastically reduced visibility and made it difficult for Dr. Leupold to see where he was going. He had to stop several times to get his bearings, and in doing so became aware of two youths behind him. Their young eyes would see better than his old ones — the ground was slippery, and with craters and drops everywhere, you could fall and break your neck if you were not careful.

He stopped and called to them that he had lost his bearings and was trying to get to the Komödienstrasse. If they would lead the way, he would make it worth their while, he promised.

They caught him up and began to lead him, and he followed in a gingerly fashion. After a while he had to tell them not to go quite so fast, and they hung back to escort him. One of the youths offered the prosecutor his shoulder, telling him to support himself on it for steadiness, and in doing so Dr. Leupold noticed that this boy had one ear missing and a knife in his hand.

In the remaining moments of life left to the prosecutor, before the knife cut his throat, there flashed into his head the answer to the riddle posed by his father's suicide. And then he was lying on the ground, his lifeblood flowing away into the snow, his monocle dislodged, and his eye twitching wildly for a time before becoming still at last.